Praise for *Coconut*

"What is family—is it shaped through blood, through community, through love? What is the family and parenting we need to feel whole and know ourselves authentically? These are big questions and in *Coconut* John and Elizabeth Clay have written a searching generational novel that tackles it all with originality and surprise. Most importantly I came to love all the characters that wind through this novel. Somehow each of them broke and healed my heart. A powerful debut."

— Victoria Redel, author of *Before Everything*

"*Coconut* makes a deep impression. The story haunts chapter by chapter, following the main characters on a mystery journey. Surging with poetic description, pages sing like Walcott's *Omeros* and Joyce's *Ulysses*. The characters stay real, like people we know or people we would like to be. This is a story that will resonate with readers across generations."

— George Klawitter, CSC, author of *A Little World Made Cunningly*

"*Coconut* is a meticulously crafted, deeply moving novel that exemplifies the complexities of human experience. The rhythm of the lyrical prose is astounding. It is a nuanced, multigenerational family saga that intertwines lives and memories across time periods and locations. Adoption, especially, with all of its intricate ramifications, is deftly explored. *Coconut* will satisfy readers who long for real depth. It sent shivers down my spine."

— Mark Katzman, author of *M7*

A captivating and poignant story that traverses diverse cultures and generations, *Coconut* seamlessly weaves a narrative of heartbreak and hope. I felt deeply connected to each character, like I was right there with them every step of the way.

— Debbie Yee Lan Wong, author of *The Same Sky: A Traveler's Quest for Redemption and Peace*

"I've spent my life out there in the real world, living real-life adventures. *Coconut* is a novel that captures that sense of the real—from childhood dreams to grown-up adversities. And all in beautiful language. If you want to enjoy an engaging well-told story, this is it."

— J. Robert Harris, author of *Way Out There: Adventures of a Wilderness Trekker*

"A piece of art like that archetypical quilt, that jazz combo, that Minnesota style - fast moving and precise, artistic and scientific, chaotic and weaving strings together, intuitive and cultured, brash and optimistic - written with an American sound that's personal, graceful, sophisticated."

— Stephan Peter, author of *Bridging the Gap: Personal Stories of a Trans-Atlantic Civil Society Advocate*

A NOVEL

JOHN & ELIZABETH CLAY

SPACEBOY BOOKS

Denver, Colorado

Published in the United States by:
Spaceboy Books LLC
1627 Vine Street
Denver, CO 80206
www.readspaceboy.com

We gratefully acknowledge Verulam Music for permission to reprint an excerpt from
the lyrics of SHE'S NOT THERE, by Rod Argent. Copyright © 1964 by Verulam Music
Co. Ltd. All USA rights administered by Marquis Songs USA. International Copyright
Secured. All rights reserved. Used by permission.

Cover image by Mary Majka. Copyright 2024 © by Elizabeth Clay. Digital scan by Tim
Kretzmann.

ISBN: 978-1-951393-45-8
First printed July 2025

To our children Ellie, Jack, and River, our parents, Bob and Elaine, and Bob and Winnie, and birth-parents Mary and Larry.

El Caribe, September 2045

Calvert Crossland roused in his seat, stretched his muscled arms toward the seatback before him, his long legs cramped despite First Class, as window shades opened all up and down the airline cabin.

"We'll be touching down in twenty minutes at Maiquetía International Airport... Llegaremos en veinte minutos al Aeropuerto Internacional Maiquetía Simon Bolivar."

He flicked his window shade open, finger-combed the aurora of wild auburn hair from his forehead, eyes squinting into the morning sun. Thirty-two years old. Mom. Da. Mukesh at Telligenz in New York. They all thought he was so damn smart, but he had no fucking idea what he was doing. He just knew his model made sense, it came naturally, intuitively, maybe just something in the way his brain was put together. Analogy, neural networks, but deeper than anyone had gone.

Below whitecap specks grew to white crests patterning the cobalt blue sea, mapping deep wave fields as they coursed toward shore, joining, breaking, rejoining. From the strand of shore rose great green mountains. Foothills of the Andes. Farther distant, peaks rose above peaks in a sea of blossoming clouds. So strangely familiar.

"Sir, your seatback..." He didn't notice her at first, the flight attendant at his side. Her dark eyes reflected light from the window as she gazed at him.

"Do you know that feeling?" he asked as he raised his seat. "When you don't know if you're remembering a place you've been or if it's a place you've only heard of? My parents told me the story, a long time ago. A love story."

"A love story!" She switched off the overhead light, and he thought her cheeks flushed.

"It's never really just a story of two people, is it? It's so many people and places across time, family before you and after." He peered through the window. "It's all one love story."

Let me give to you a gift that can't be seen or held, not material but something of the heart. A gift that may seem meager to some, but to you I hope will be a treasure. A simple but long-awaited realization. — Mary Zadora

Refashion

Sandusky, Ohio 1954

Everything was red, she swung the wooden two-by-four, tall as her, and Ronnie's big six-year-old head whipped back, his whole body followed and thudded onto the driveway, her hands hurt, jarred by it, and Ronnie let out a howl, he was the cry baby now, and he ran for his house.

"Yer gonna get it," Kit said, but his look said *I can't believe it,* and he almost smiled. She dropped the board and stomped inside and then heard Father's voice — "Lil, you should've seen what I saw out the window, what are we going to do with that girl!" — and Mother saying something about penance to do, and quiet and fast Mary ran to her bedroom, the only bedroom on the first floor.

Stupid Ronnie. His words stuck in her head like a record, *She's five, she's too little, let me drive it!* But he was the cry baby, grabbing at her as she held the wheel tight, pushed hard with her feet, toes just touching the pedals, she knew she could keep the shiny sit-in-it car moving. It was Kit's birthday, he was six and always got the niftiest boy presents and she only ever got the girl presents, and Kit said she could drive it. And then Ronnie pulled her out of it, and then, and then...

There was a big loud knock. "Who is it, dear?" She heard Mother's voice from the kitchen, opened the bedroom door a crack, and saw Father at the front door, and there was Mr. Wilson with a stern face, and Ronnie next to him with a big red bump on his forehead. "I want to speak to the child responsible for hitting my boy!"

Father half turned from the door. "Mary!"

As she walked to the door, she saw Mr. Wilson's face change. He was kind of mixed up and shameful and gave a stern face to Ronnie instead and said "Good day!" and dragged Ronnie away. Father gave her a smile like he usually gave Kit.

*

Mary was little, and not just in years. She was petite like a doll with a porcelain face and the darkest brown eyes and a head full of dark hair with curls and curls that shone red in the sunlight. Not tall like Father or short and plump like Mother. Mother called her willful — *Don't interrogate me with those black eyes of yours* — and sometimes she made Father mad, but really, she just knew what she wanted.

She was Wednesday's child, not really the child of Mother and Father, and Kit wasn't either. Mother always said they were delivered by God in answer to her prayer when she learned she and Father couldn't have their own. God must know what's best, Mary was sure.

*

Sandusky, on Lake Erie. She loved the water. How it sparkled, how the big waves splashed the shore, how you could see white caps far far out, how you could see forever. Father called it the little town with big prospects. Playing in the sand at Winnebago Park Beach, Mary watched the lake boats come and go, fishing boats and tugboats and boats full of coal and iron Father said were big enough to sail the seas. Those big boats and the docks and railways and the new factories, they were the big prospects. And the men who knew about the big prospects played golf at Plum Brook Country Club every weekend. Father too.

Still it was a small town, Sandusky, little clapboard houses and little brick shops, not like the sky high buildings in Cleveland. Church with its castle tower was the tallest place anywhere near Monroe Street. Somebody gave the church the sad name *Mother of Sorrows*. Probably God. She wondered if God meant her mother when he named it that. Not her mother, Lillian, of course, who God delivered her to, but her mother. She wondered: from the top of the tower, might she be able to see far enough? Far enough to see where her mother was? How would she recognize her? She didn't even know what she looked like.

She peered into the wind, heavy with the smell of the lake, kind of a fishy smell, kind of a stinky factory smell. The littler boats were on their way out toward Johnson's Island. The fishing boats sailed all summer. Then they sat stored away all winter until the lake ice broke in April or May and the whole parish gathered by the bay for the Mother of Sorrows Blessing of the

Fleet. So many colors flying from sails and ropes, and the colors changed as the clouds passed and the sun broke through. Father Jasinski stood in white robes and a pretty green stole at the wooden podium, and the Knights of Columbus were like real knights, red-white-and-blue sashes over their coats, and white gloves on their hands, their flags held high. God made the boats safe to sail. They still sank sometimes, but Mother got mad when she mentioned that. And it probably would have been even worse without the blessing.

*

On my honor, I will try:
To serve God and my country,
To help people at all times,
And to live by the Brownie Law.

She and Marie always eyed each other at the *I will try* part. It happened, that look, at the first Brownie troop meeting at the beginning of second grade. They weren't even friends then, back in September, but their eyes met and the longer they stared at each other, the harder they tried not to laugh. And every time since, each knew what the other was thinking: *Will you try? Are you trying? You had better try harder than that!*

They played at Marie's house most days after school. Running races from the lilac bush in the front yard to the iron clothesline pole in the back as the leaves crinkled and swooshed under foot and the gray October clouds raced overhead. Hunting for treasures, a fallen leaf, green along the stem and crimson at the tips. A feather. "Marie, from a bluebird!" The blue that wants to be pink. Mary's fingertips traced the edges, opening to her touch and closing again behind. And when the snow blew in across the lake, they drew pictures in Marie's room, Mary's pigtails sprouting feathers she couldn't wear at home, and they talked, sang along with Perry Como and Harry Belafonte, and made a circus of stuffed animals. Marie's mom was so funny, bursting through the door. "You girls will starve your husbands one day if you don't learn to cook! Vai, vai in cucina!" She set them to work cutting and stirring, and delicious smells filled the kitchen, and it wasn't even like work. It was a circus where they were the performers, doing acrobatics as Marie's mom called out the acts. "To the stove...no, no, no, no, no...don't stop stirring! Stir while you pour, while you pour, perfetto!"

"I can feel the smell in my nose!" Mary said.

"Aroma, aroma, little bambolina! And yes, yes, yes. Garlic, oregano, basil, a good cook feels the flavor inside her!"

The life of that home filled Mary's heart like the steaming aromas filled her senses.

*

The lake was so big you couldn't see across. Like the ocean, she imagined, though she'd never been there. Sometimes it was a crazy quilt of waves, and sometimes it was a mirror reflecting the blue sky and puffy white clouds trimmed with gray, a gray that seemed to anchor them in place. She was a good swimmer and every day in summer Mother let her go out back, beyond the yard and across the field and down the steep steps to the beach. The sun shone on her shoulders, the sand coated her wet skin, and day by day a splash of freckles painted her face like Mother's painted-on beauty mark.

Today the beach was filled with bathers tip-toeing across the hot sand, weaving around beach blankets. She stood from her blanket, swimsuit still dripping and dug her feet into the sand, ready to make a dash for the water. But something caught her attention, the feeling of eyes on her. A grownup woman a few blankets away, sandy red curls, red lips, and a pink satin bikini with ruffles on top and pleats on the bottom. Beside her a woman with the same curls, only dark brown. Mary's ears pricked to their words carried by the breeze, and the one with dark curls asked — "What is it?" — and the one with red curls replied — "Nothing, just daydreaming." Mary turned and her feet darted and kicked up sand all the way to the water where the waves broke her body's motion and she fell to her knees, submerged chest high. *What would it be like to be so glamorous, everyone admiring your red curls as you stretch out on your beach blanket?* She stood and looked back, but she couldn't find her, not either of them.

*

Spring 1959

"Mary Lou, the church needs you!" She knew the tone of voice, stern on the outside but self-satisfied on the inside. Her mother smartly removed the green beret and hung the pea coat neatly in the closet. "Father Jasinski is making arrangements for this year's Blessing of the Fleet. He was pleased with the poster you made last year, so he's enlisting you again. He's counting on the Tomczak family!"

Mary leapt in the air. "Yay, yay, yay!" The poster she painted last year went up on bulletin boards and store windows all over town. Her fourth-grade teacher Miss Wallace had even posted it by the chalkboard at the front of the classroom. She was already seeing arced gull wings, the curves of sails. "Yes, Mother, I'll do it, I'll do it!"

Two weeks later, her new poster was up. Mother beamed at Father Jasinski on the church steps after Mass, "The Tomczak family always fulfills our promise."

*

"Did you know my father almost had an accident?" Mary said while she walked arm-in-arm with Marie after school. Warblers flitted among the bare limbs of the beech and basswood whose buds swelled, not quite ready to blossom. "He said a wop wandered into the street and he had to swerve to miss him..."

Marie shook her off. "You shouldn't call us wops. Don't you know it's a mean name for Italians?"

It flashed through Mary's head as she looked into her friend's eyes. Father was always angry when he said wop or Italian. They were on the wrong side of the war, he said, and they should go back where they came from.

"My family is as American as you" — Marie said — "and we're proud of where we came from. I wouldn't be here if Nonno and Nonna didn't make the hard trip and bring mamma and bring the prayers and recipes to keep us strong. Aren't you proud of where you came from?"

She hugged Marie, held on like the flailing swimmer in the cold deep holds onto the lifeguard's shoulders. *The nuns found you abandoned on a doorstep,* Mom had said. *It was God's way of bringing you to us.*

Marie took her hand. "Mary, I'm not cross. Let's skip all the way home!"

Mary's eyes brightened. "Let's! With our arms linked the whole way!"

*

Summer 1962

She would receive the Sacrament of Confirmation in August and begin middle school in September.

God, infinitely perfect and blessed in himself, in a plan of sheer goodness freely created man to make him share in his own blessed life. God draws close to man. He calls together all men, scattered and divided by sin, into the unity of his family, the Church... God sent his Son as Redeemer and Savior. She reread the prologue from the Catechism, pages she had read as a first-grader, and tried to see herself in the words. And there in the pair of upholstered wingback chairs were Father and Kit, his son. Kit the middle school quarterback. Kit the star-hitter on the baseball team. Kit the golf-whiz. Every Saturday on the green, Father shielded his eyes to watch Kit's ball fly while Mary gripped her club, dreading her turn. *Just watch the men,* Mother dutifully admonished, *They'll show you how it's done.*

Mary closed the leather-bound Catechism, fingered the rosary in her sweater pocket, and left her chair.

"Are you going to excuse yourself, young lady?"

"Excuse me, Father." She retreated to her room.

Hail Mary full of Grace, the Lord is with thee. Blessed are thou amongst women and blessed is the fruit of thy womb Jesus. Holy Mary Mother of God, pray for us sinners now and at the hour of our death.

What is it that makes Kit so special to Father and Mother? Is it the sports? Is a son like a savior who can do miracles? Kit was good at sports but he didn't seem miraculous. Holy Mary Mother of God. Daughters become mothers. Boys are special right away and girls have to wait until they're grownup mothers? What would make her special? Her hand pulled the pencil looping and darting across the page as she pondered. She loved the feel of the pencil's drag on the paper's surface, a tiny craft leaving its wake. She thought of the faces and gestures of saints who glowed red, green, blue, and gold in the stained glass windows. An artist made those pictures. Pictures important enough to be part of the church itself.

She rushed to the kitchen. "Mother, I finished this drawing today. Gulls circling the fishing trawler as it comes in, and the clouds are..."

"Mary, it's the middle of summer. The next Blessing of the Fleet is half a year away. Instead of doodling with your pencils, why don't you see to that mountain of laundry in the hamper?"

*

A wind swept the sand and her eyes blinked closed, the sun glowing red through her eyelids, the whitecap of a wave still printed there, a white going black, and she opened her eyes again. What did other people see in the world around them? Did Marie see the shapes that they learned in geometry? And Mother, did she see colors for new upholstery? And what about Father, she couldn't figure out what it was he saw, maybe big greens fields made him think of golf.

Mary saw the lines in everything. The straight lines of a house, how they shift depending on where you stand. The lines of the water on the lake, how they swerve. The gentle curved lines of a face, living lines. Even without a pencil in her hand, her eye traced, and she felt what the pencil would do, press heavier, ease to a wisp, sweep here, stroke sharp there.

In fact there was a pencil in her hand and a sketchbook on her knee, almost always. At the high school cafeteria, in the backseat when Father drove the family to Cleveland, even on the beach. She drew every day but Sunday, and even there in the pew her mind saw the strokes. A boy's square shoulders, the curls beneath a woman's lace veil, the lone hair standing at attention on a bald man's head. What she loved most was faces, the lines that bring out someone's unique look, a long thin nose, a double chin. Sometimes it made her laugh. But the more she drew and the more free her hand became, the more the lines brought out something else. The emotion in someone's eyes. Who they are. Maybe their spirit. Maybe this is what the famous artists do.

*

"The base angle is equal to one hundred eighty degrees, minus the vertex angle..." Mary tried to concentrate on her purple mimeograph worksheet while Marie recited from the textbook. "Mary, are you listening?"

"I'm trying to get this right..."

Marie rolled from her belly to her side. "Mary! You're never going to finish the assignment!" Mary looked up startled until Marie's eyes twinkled

Will you try? Are you even trying? And they burst into fits of giggles as Mary rolled over a pile of pillows, lost her balance, thumped to the floor laughing. "Stop, stop!"

"This isn't just about high school, Mary. It's about college too."

"What are you even talking about?"

"Studying, keeping our grades up. My mom says my sister and I need a college education. It's how to succeed. You and Kit are both going to college right?"

"Kit is. I want to be an artist."

"Then you get a degree in art."

"They really give degrees in art?"

"Don't your parents tell you anything?" Marie focused on the mimeograph papers. "Here's something else someone should tell you: This bird's missing a wing!"

Mary jumped back onto the bed and earnestly examined her homework, the isosceles triangle she had adorned with wing and beak and dangling webbed feet. She announced in her best high school drama voice, "It's because I cannot calculate the correct angle!"

Out of breath from another fit of giggles, in the quiet of exhaustion, Marie's hand cradled hers. "Draw for me. Seagulls, boats, beachgoers, anything you like. Not on your worksheets, on your nice drawing pads. And for every drawing I'll help you, well, I'll do your assignments because let's face it, you're beyond help. Maybe we'll be college roommates together." Marie's smile was so gentle and so dear. Mary wrapped her arms around her best friend, the very best friend anyone could ever have.

*

"Get out of my closet!" Her mother's shaking hand swiped the air just short of her face. "You look like a filthy slut! Don't you ever... My cosmetics!" Mary ran from the closet, the dress and fur stole oversized just enough to hobble her, half-catch on the door handle, her feet swimming in the polished black leather flatties. "Don't you...Mary Lou! Walt, stop her! Walt!"

She dodged to the bathroom and heard Mother hurry down the stairs. Her heart pounded anger and confusion. Didn't Mother know she was thirteen, had to learn how to dress up, had a right to dress up? Her father's heavy feet on the stairs. She dropped the stole in the tub, pulled at the feathers tangled in her hair, grasped for the toilet paper to wipe the lipstick and it unrolled across the floor, a white carpet for her father.

It was raining hard, drops bursting on the asphalt. Tears blurred her vision as she stumbled across the street. He made her undress in the bathtub to her undies, turned on the shower to wash the filth off, threw a towel around her shoulders and thrust his fingers into her hair like her head wasn't attached to her body, wasn't part of somebody. Dragged her by the hair, staggering down the stairs and pushed her through her bedroom doorway. *Dress proper*, was all he said and slammed the door shut.

In a sweater and slacks she was out the bedroom door, out the front door, didn't even look to see if they were there, if they were watching, she didn't care. She was going to tell Marie. She was going to tell Marie's mother. Tell her everything.

Rainwater gushed from the gutter downspout beside her. She pressed the doorbell. Knocked hard. Waited. The sound of water flowing everywhere. She knocked. The windows were dark. And the thing was, this wasn't her home, wasn't her family. She stepped away from the awning and the rain streamed down her eyes. Her home was back across the flooded street.

*

The high school gymnasium was simultaneously cavernous, empty, and filled with possibility. Lights dimmed, no athletes, only thespians beneath the watchful score boards and basketball hoops. Mary gave it everything she had, dashed down the aisle marked with tape along the high-gloss polished gym floor as her words echoed, "I never felt so alone in my whole life. And George over there...!"

"Hold, hold!"

She froze like a statue.

"This blocking is not working." Sister Leticia was a perfectionist. "Mary, you're moving too far too fast..."

"Well, if you love me, help me!" Mary swooned, giggles erupting all around. "All I want is someone to help me with my blocking!" Even Sister Leticia cracked a smile before cracking the whip again. "Enough, enough! I need to work this out. Break for five minutes everyone. Five minutes!"

Mary turned to Wally as he relaxed into a pretend free-throw into the basketball hoop. "All I want is someone to love me," she recited from her lines. Cindy guffawed, "Mary, I can't believe you." Ann struck an ice-frozen pose — "It was the bomb when you stopped cold like that" — and put her arm around Mary.

In the gym with her drama friends and Sister Leticia, she could be anyone she wanted to be. Try on any life like a new skirt, and if it fit, she could make it hers. "Why does it have to be kept inside the gymnasium, inside the little square of the stage? Why can't everywhere be like this?"

"It's a play, Mary." Ann seemed puzzled. "It's great fun, but it's not real life."

*

"Mary, is that you?" Mother's voice trumpeted from the kitchen the very moment she opened the front door, home from Mother of Sorrows High. Her junior year. "Your father wants to have a word with you at dinner tonight."

She ducked into her bedroom. These were the days she wished her bedroom was on the second floor like Kit's. Anywhere but the same floor as Father's living room and Mother's kitchen. These random days of warning, the ever inscrutable warning that Father wanted a word. A tornado warning would be better, seriously. Forget the second floor. She wanted to hide in the basement.

They sat, pulled their chairs in to the table after Father pulled his chair in. They all joined in prayer when Mother began, "Bless us, O Lord, and these, Thy gifts, which we are about to receive from Thy bounty" and Kit, whose voice in prayer was clear and strong, was already eyeing the spare rib at *Thy bounty* and licking his lips at *Amen.*

Mary waited with Mother while Father and Kit piled ribs and boiled pierogi and sauerkraut onto their plates. Could it maybe happen that everyone would be too busy eating to talk? She kept her eyes down while she and Mother filled their own plates and she silently speared a pierogi with her fork and heard Father's voice.

"This city of ours is one of God's miracles, one of America's miracles. I truly believe this. What do you see, Kit, when you look out across the shoreline?"

Kit's eyes peered into an imagined distance. "There are ships. And docks and cranes. Warehouses and factories. There's a lot going on!"

"A lot going on, son. You're starting college next year. And there's opportunity opening along every mile of that shoreline. It's opportunity for you, son, after college. While those idiot commie pinko kids are ranting about Vietnam, you'll be climbing the ladder to your future.

"And it's opportunity for you, Mary, after you finish high school and while you wait for the man you'll marry. Ward Products is hiring smart girls like you as typists."

This was all going too fast. She still had senior year ahead of her. And then the art degree Marie told her about. "Won't I...won't I be going to college?"

Father chuckled. "What would you need college for, young lady?"

Her mind had never run so fast. She didn't even know how she came up with the idea and already it was tumbling out. "All the most eligible young men are at college these days."

Father blinked. Mother opened her mouth as if she had an idea, then closed it and looked to Father. Mary shifted in her chair.

"Pay for college just to meet a man? I don't want to speak uncharitably, young lady, but that's ridiculous." Father sunk his teeth into a rib.

Mary watched Kit smirk and nod. She knew not to say anything more. But she was still thinking as she speared another pierogi.

*

Maybe the Rose Hip lipstick was just subtle enough that Mother wouldn't notice. She pressed her lips together, silky smooth, peered into the mirror and puckered. She looked almost grown up, glamorous.

"Mary Lou!" Mother called from the door. "We're going to be late for Kit's game."

She buried the tube deep within the pocket of her skirt.

At the stadium, she made her escape. "I'm going for a soda, do you want one, Mother?" *No thank you dear,* was the predictable answer. She found Marie at their usual spot at the soda fountain, and they sat together in the stands. "Look there's Davey! Look at those curls. Groovy!" She nudged Marie, "I heard he took Sandra to the passion pit in Cleveland."

Marie rolled her eyes, then gazed wistfully down to the field. "He's always on the make."

"Davey's going to Dayton University in the fall with Kit," Mary said. "I can't wait to bug out of here. I saw a flyer on the bulletin board at school for art scholarships. I'm going to apply."

"Me too! Accounting. Same as always Mary: You take care of the art, I'll take care of the numbers!"

*

She couldn't quite believe it. She bugged out of Sandusky. For Father it was the scholarship. For Mother it was the eligible young men. Kit was flabbergasted, but she knew he didn't really care one way or the other. On the rare occasions when they spied each other across the quad he waved his goofball wave and called out "Don't be late for class, darlin!"

She struggled in freshman math. Let loose in English Lit, soulful poetry and tumultuous essays. Ran splashing into line art and op art. Turned color wheel cartwheels. And the campus — she never could have imagined how huge it was, how many people. She tried to see Marie whenever she could, but they didn't cross paths very often. Her circles were expanding by the day, new people she never could have imagined, young people like her who expected something more of life, something more of the world than another golf tournament or the next blessing of the fleet. Big changes were happening, and everybody was going to be part of it.

We have a Constitutional right to free speech, a human right to free thought, a universal right to say hell no, we won't go to Vietnam to be killing machines on behalf of the corporate state! She felt like she was hearing lines from a play, all the things you can't say in real life, but it was real life. A young man, a student, surrounded by a crowd of young men and women raising their fists, nodding their heads, chanting *Make love, not war!* Her heart raced.

There was a party, somewhere, every night of the week. She wasn't going to bring those stories home to Father and Mother at Christmas. But she did recite her academic successes, everything that proved Graphic Arts was the right choice, a responsible career choice. By sophomore year she had several paintings going in her Lines and Watercolor class and couldn't wait for Painting Studio next year and the Junior Exhibition. Professor Thomas said her work was promising. And she had to tell Father and Mother about the U.D. Players. After designing theater sets last fall, she auditioned for *A*

Funny Thing Happened on the Way to the Forum, got a callback, then found her name on the call-board for a role in the spring production.

After eighteen years holding back, apologizing for living, at Dayton she was living all of life at once — *Restless sighs, soul of wanton ties that want to bend, the will to fly.* Was this really happening? Would it all spin apart, unravel? Was it even possible to knit it all together? What about Father and Mother? Wasn't everything possible now?

Marie, dear Marie, knew her better than anyone. They sat cross legged together on the bed in Marie's dorm room, the radio playing. Marie's gentle smile turned to puzzlement, "What's happening?"

Mary cradled her tummy in a half-dream, a stupor of wonder. "I've been feeling nauseous and haven't had my period for a few months now."

"Oh Mary, who is it?" Marie pulled back, almost tearing up, then took Mary's hand. "Don't tell me you don't know who it is."

She knew Marie was afraid for her. The thing was, Mary wasn't afraid. "He was a very special young man," she said softly. On the radio, The Zombies played.

> But it's too late to say you're sorry
> How would I know, why should I care?
> Please don't bother tryin' to find her
> She's not there
> Well, let me tell you 'bout the way she looked
> The way she'd act and the colour of her hair
> Her voice was soft and cool
> Her eyes were clear and bright
> But she's not there

Prairie Slough

New Ulm, Minnesota, December 1939

"Look at it coming down! Fred and Rick are out there already!" Will's nose pressed the glass of the living room window. Henry ran to stand beside him and watched the big white flakes flying one way just out the window and the other way past the trees and the other way beyond.

Henry was a six-year-old boy, living in the small prairie town in the small wedge of land where the Cottonwood River meets the Minnesota River.

There were important places in that town.

There was Henry's room with the world map on the wall and a few toys under the bed, only a few because mostly he just wanted to play outdoors. And on the map, as on the globe in the living room, the brightly colored countries and blue oceans, and the orange country, Australia, with the black-dot city called Perth.

There was Will's room. He was older, a fourth-grader, and had lots of toys because he thought nothing was more fun than getting a new one. And when Dad said it was a poor use of an allowance, Will would say the other boys at school had more than he did and no wonder when his allowance was only pennies. And that was when Dad would send him outdoors to pick a switch off a bush and learn from a lashing, even though Will never learned.

There was James' room. He was really old, a high school freshman, practically a grownup even though Dad said praying on your knees by the bed was for boys and wouldn't make a man of him. He had lots of books and papers because reading and writing, and maybe praying, made him feel better.

There was Dad's chair in the living room where he relaxed with the top button of his collared white shirt unbuttoned and smoked exactly one cigarette, crunched exactly one dish of pistachios, drank exactly one bottle of Coca-Cola, and played endless games of solitaire on a side table while Mom made dinner. Sometimes he caught little Henry's eye, motioned him to the globe on the corner table, spun it and proclaimed, "From the farm in Arkansas, to John Deere in Iowa, to State Bond and Mortgage in New Ulm, I've journeyed as far as any man."

There was the kitchen that was warm in winter with Mom's homemade bread and fresh in spring with breezes through the window over the sink and was always one of the best places because Mom was there.

And from the kitchen there was the mudroom and the side door and the outdoors and the streets he walked to school and to Dad's office. And the Dump toward the river where Henry played because it wasn't really a dump, it was just sandy and grassy and you felt like you were away from everything. And just across the street, the Orchard where in summer the cherry trees ripened and the shrubs handed you their clumps of currents and long stalks of gooseberries. And when the apples ripened, you knew summer was done. Out there, out under the sky was where he most liked to be.

"Look at it coming down! You can hardly see!" Will shouted and pushed off from the glass and ran for the kitchen, aiming for the mud room.

Henry scrambled after. "Mom! Mom, can I go? Will, wait! Wait!"

She caught Henry's elbow at the mudroom door. "Hold your horses, Henry, you can go, after you put your sweater on...."

"Will's out there..."

"Put your sweater on and then we'll get you bundled up." She held his boots while he stepped in. "I'm sure Will is right across the street at the Orchard, so you'll easily catch up to him." She tugged at his scarf, he buttoned a few buttons, and she buttoned his coat all the way up, looking at his face like each button would keep him safe.

"Can I go now?"

She held out his mittens and he pushed his hands in. And pushed.

"I can't get my thumb in..."

"Here we go, here we go," and she pulled his hat on tight.

"Can I go now?"

"Off you go. Tell Will not to throw those snowballs too hard! Look both ways Henry, both ways when you cross!"

The wind blew and he breathed hard running, boots deep each step, and he couldn't hear anything behind him anymore, just the shouts ahead and the snow swirling and the boys running, arms waving, snowballs flying under the whitening bare branches of the apple trees.

*

April 1940

Henry rushed red-faced into the kitchen where Mom was doing dishes at the sink. "Mom, Mom!" — he panted, his blue eyes desperate — "Will said, he said that one day there was a blizzard, but it was dirt, it wasn't snow, it was dirt. But that can't happen. It can't bliz... It can't be a blizzard... with dirt. But Will said it could..."

Will caught up, ready to make his case — "Mom!" — but she raised her hand like a stop sign. And he stopped.

"Henry, boots off. Look, you tracked mud all the way in. Will, keep your boots on and go outdoors to clean up any stray bits of coal that dropped around the chute."

Will retreated outdoors and his voice trailed behind him, "Was too a dirt blizzard."

Henry looked at her: There, she heard Will say it, she heard him lie, and that meant Will would go to Hell.

But she knelt down and looked straight into his eyes. "We were just back from Sunday Mass. I was carrying you in from the car, you were still a little baby, and a great wind picked up. Your dad opened the door and pointed to a cloud of gray and brown that started so low over the rooftops and crept higher in the sky and darker every moment. All he said was *Get inside, right now.* It was a dust storm, Henry. A black blizzard the newspapers called it."

He flinched because that was what Will called it. "Was it a tornado?"

"No honey, it was dry earth blown up from the ground and gathered into a storm. We had a few in those years, but this was the worst. We shut the door tight and all the windows, and still it blew in through every little crack and I prayed until finally, thank the blessed Virgin, the sky lightened again and it passed on."

He looked at the floor. He was glad Will wasn't going to Hell, but he still wasn't going to play any more with him today.

*

Spring 1941

Henry was seven and looking grown up in his new wire spectacles just like Dad's. He walked briskly up Minnesota Street. The April wind gusted around the three-story brick buildings, swaying the boulevard trees and buffeting the store signs that hung over the sidewalk all along the big street. His short dark hair shook in tufts. He walked everywhere. Dad too — *Gasoline costs money, but your feet are free.* Henry loved the feel of walking under the wide blue sky, walking and thinking.

He could walk really fast, almost as fast as other kids run but without actually running because he was always putting one foot down before lifting the other, so he was actually walking. Sometimes there was something in his way, like that mom with a baby carriage ahead. You could go around by making three sides of a square, like this: left, right, right, left and ahead. So it's four turns. And now he was thinking you could do it in two turns by making a half diamond, but then you might run into the corner of the carriage. He liked the square better. One...two...three...four.... Diamonds and squares and rectangles, even after the carriage he was pondering until the wind gusted and a loud rattle startled him. It was the sign for State Bond swaying on its metal hinges over his head. He almost walked right past it.

He liked to see Dad at work sometimes after school. Dad looked at numbers. They showed him what to do next, who should get a loan and who shouldn't, though it seemed like the numbers said you could only get a loan if you didn't really need one, which didn't quite make sense to Henry even though the numbers did.

At the top of the stairs on the second floor, he opened the office door to the clatter of typewriters and the sight of Mr. Jensen leafing through files in the big wooden cabinet by the window. "Betty have you seen the Hornsdasch Farm files? Mr. Crossland says the boost in demand everybody expected when Europe went to war is finally happening. He wants to take a new look at these loan applications..."

The phone rang and Mrs. Schrupp gave Henry a wink and a nod and raised her finger to Mr. Jensen, like Mom's *hold that thought.* "State Bond, this is Betty."

Henry stood patiently at the edge of her desk, a little nervous. If Dad thought you were wasting time, there could be trouble.

Finally Mrs. Schrupp held her phone receiver out for a moment — "Your father's in the office, go ahead" and "Mr. Jensen did you...?"

"Found it!"

The bustle faded behind him as he stood at the door labeled *Vice President*. He couldn't help a side glance down the hall to the president's office. Dad always said the president was paid way more than everybody else even though the vice presidents kept the company running.

In years to come his dad would have that office down the hall and all talk of who was paid how much would come to an abrupt end. But today Henry knocked on the oak door where he stood and gingerly turned the handle, wanting to see Dad but bracing, just a little as always, to see what words would greet him.

*

Sunday. A hot summer morning. Everybody was moving kind of slowly, especially Will. Mom had a stern face. "Sometimes we don't feel our best, Will. We don't have a cold or flu, Lord bless us, but we just don't feel like getting out of bed and going to Mass. But we do it anyway, don't we? And why do we?"

Will rolled out of bed and whined in surrender. "To keep the third commandment."

"The third commandment," Mom echoed. "Remember to keep holy the Sabbath."

"Mom?"

"Yes, Henry."

"I'm going to Mass today."

"You're my good boy, Henry."

He looked down. "But I was wondering. Since part three, section two, chapter one, article three..." He glanced to Mom, and aside to Will, because they must be seeing how he'd memorized all the numbers, but Will was busy digging in the dresser drawers. "Since it says — *Remember the sabbath day, to keep it holy. Six days you shall labor, but the seventh day is a sabbath to the Lord your God, in it you shall not do any work* — I was wondering if instead of scrubbing up, and dressing, and combing our hair, and all of that..." Mom looked kind of concerned. "I was wondering if it would make more sense to stay in bed."

Mom shook her head smiling but then got serious and patted the bed for Henry to sit beside her. "Henry, the Gospel of Matthew tells us, *The sabbath is the day of the Lord of mercies and a day to honor God.* Rest is not a substitute for Mass!"

Will was eyeing him like he had better shut up, so he did. He quietly nodded.

*

Henry always ran to the globe when Dad talked at breakfast about places on the newspaper's front page, or when he read the New Ulm Review and Minneapolis Tribune himself, which he did now that it was fall and he had started second grade. Not every place got mentioned in the newspapers, not the city of Perth in Australia which he thought must be a curious place to have such a curious name. Mostly the news mentioned Germany and Italy, Poland and Britain and France, and what President Roosevelt in Washington said about them. And by third grade Japan too, and that was when everything would start to change.

He turned the globe in his hands. There was the United States of America. And Minnesota that he lived in. Just colored shapes like the faraway places in the newspapers. Not like New Ulm where he could walk on the streets and see the houses and really be there.

Really be there. He thought about all those places.

*

1942

Henry sat on the grassy ridge where the wind always blew, even when it was just a lazy August breeze like today. It was a place he could think, in the quiet, alone. Except today he wasn't alone. He watched the tall sturdy boy with dark hair from a little ways away, watched him draw in the sandpit and then shake himself clean and walk down the hill away from town. He had seen the boy in the halls at school, at Saint Mary's, and wondered if, like so many classmates, he had a big brother or uncle who was joining up.

It all started last December, on a Sunday after lunch. Henry had come home from Noon Mass with Mom and Will. James was away at Nazareth Hall Preparatory Seminary, his high school in Saint Paul, and Dad, of course, never went to church. *God's not gonna fix it for you, you've got to fix it yourself.*

Dad delivered his own lecture every Sunday at the lunch table — his turn after whatever homily the priest had given. And as Will downed the last slice of ham and Mom cleared away the dishes, there was a loud knock on the side door, "Grace! Grace, open up!"

"For heaven's sake." Mom abandoned the dishes on the kitchen counter.

It was Mrs. Hoffman from next door. "Grace, did you hear? Turn on your radio. Oh it's awful. I'll see you tomorrow at Congregation. I have to get back home."

They stood at the radio in the living room — Dad, Mom, Will, and Henry.

CBS brings you this special announcement. The Japanese have attacked Pearl Harbor in Hawaii from the air. Here again is the report we received from Honolulu: 'Norman Clark, KGMB. The island of Oahu is under attack. Enemy airplanes, they're swarming above the harbor. There was just now a massive explosion...'

Henry lifted up the living room globe. "Dad, it's right here, Oahu..."

"Quiet son."

'.... Smoke is rising from our airfields as well. This is an attack.'

"Holy Mother of God," Mom whispered.

"This was going to happen," Dad said sternly, but not to anyone in particular. "We just didn't know when or where."

That evening after dinner, instead of Lux Radio Theater, it was all news. Monday morning it was the Extra from the Minneapolis Tribune: *Japs Open War on U.S, Bomb Hawaii.* And another Extra: *Jap War on U.S. Spreads, U.S. and British Possessions in Pacific Attacked. Feds Consider Blackout Tonight for Coastal Oregon and Washington.*

"The Great War, our boy, the Crash and the droughts, and now..." Mom said. "We can't go more than a pace without something awful happening."

"That's life on this Earth, Grace." Dad put his arm around her. "It's life on this Earth."

And that's how life was from then on, for everybody. All the kids helped flatten empty tin cans for war recycling — Green Giant Big Tender Peas, Niblets Corn, California Fish Company Tuna. Will stomped on them. Henry used a hammer and got it down to the fewest strokes necessary. Rick Hinz said his dad lined up the cans and rolled his Ford Deluxe right over them, but that might be made up.

And they all learned what to do during the nighttime blackout drills when the Municipal Power Plant steam whistle blew and the police car sirens blared. Stay indoors, shades down so not a sliver of light could escape. Dad made it clear: "Boys, if an Air Raid Warden has to knock on our door, never mind the man in the uniform. It's me you'll be answering to."

But here's what wasn't the same for everybody. In a year Dad would be too old for the draft. And the oldest of the boys, James, was only fifteen and in any case would register as Class IV-D: *Unacceptable for military service, minister of religion or divinity student.* Dad pointed out that Class IV also included persons *Rejected for physical, mental, or moral reasons.* Henry saw why Dad thought it was funny — who would think of priests and moral rejects in the same class? But that was the kind of thing that always came between Mom and Dad. Anyway, the point is that none of the young men and women Henry saw around town in army uniforms, standing at the bus stops with their duffel bags — none of them was his brother or dad or aunt or uncle. And so, in a way, the Crosslands carried on as they always had.

*

November 1942

A heavy gray bank of clouds from the north sailed above Henry's head. The Dump's tall grasses bent under his feet and then sprung up behind him as he tramped downhill toward the sandpit. Every step the swoosh of grass and the smush of snow-dusted fallen leaves. But he heard another set of swooshes and smushes. He paused...nothing. Then again he heard it, swoosh, smush, and he turned — the tall boy with the thick dark hair was reaching out his hand. Henry looked at him, reached for the boy's hand and shook it, like Dad would do. "I'm Henry."

The boy was stunned. "You got me. I'm Victor."

"What do you mean I got you?"

"I snuck all the way up from the slough" — the boy swept his arm, drawing the movements his words described — "circled up and around, and you only heard me at the last, the very last chance, before I could tap your back!"

"Why?"

"Because!"

"Because isn't actually an answer," Henry said. But the way the boy, Victor, was looking at him, kind of surprised and impressed at the same time, he had to smile.

Victor laughed, "I can't believe you got me!"

They stood quiet in the wind that carried the chill of the river.

"Do you play out here sometimes?" Henry asked.

"Sometimes. And I'm always walking here, to and from school."

"I've seen you at school," Henry said.

"Yeah, I think I'm one of the only Goosetown kids there. My mom says the school takes all the Catholics they can get."

"Maybe we can play sometime," Henry said.

"Really?" Victor asked with a smile. A ray of amber broke through the clouds above the town and lit the sand pit and the tall grasses below. "I have to get home to do my chores before my mom is looking for me. I gotta pick up some coal." Victor paused, then repeated, "You know, coal. It'll be the freezing moon soon."

"Don't they deliver it?" Henry asked.

"We get a little at a time. I take my wheelbarrow and pick it up along the railroad tracks."

Henry nodded like he understood.

"We'll play out here sometime," Victor called back as he walked down the hill. "I seen you out here sometimes with those other boys."

"We play Cowboys and Indians."

"I know." Victor kept walking.

*

Mom pulled a pair of trousers from the laundry basket and pushed it down into the sudsy wash tub. Henry liked watching the big bubbles come up.

"Mom?"

"Yes, Henry."

"I was looking at the list of sinful acts under the fifth commandment, You shall not..."

"You shall not kill, yes." She scrubbed the trousers hard against the wash board.

"And I think they included something that doesn't belong there, Extortion."

"It's correct, Henry. Extortion is listed under the fifth commandment."

"But it's described as an act of violence and theft. So it makes more sense to put it under the seventh commandment, You shall not steal."

"Henry Crossland, that's enough! I cannot believe what I am hearing. And from you Henry!"

That night he lay in bed, eyes wide open. Mom acted like he wasn't honoring God when really he was just trying to make the rules better which would actually make them easier to remember. Dad didn't even care about the Catechism! Henry jerked to his side. But if Dad thought Henry wasn't respecting Mom, that would be a problem in itself, and then the backyard and choosing a switch. Why was this even happening? He was only trying to help. He punched the mattress, closed his eyes. Hitting was stupid. He stretched out flat and breathed out a long sigh.

*

December 24, 1943

There's one song everybody wants to hear and tonight more than any night.

As the radio rang out from the living room, Henry set the dinner plates carefully in place and glanced out the dining room window to snow swirling under the streetlight. After dinner they would open presents. And if Henry had the confidence, he would sit down to the living room piano and perform the "Holly and the Ivy" arrangement he learned in piano lessons with Mrs. Gebhard.

This is for the boys and girls here at home and our brave boys fighting overseas. Sonny Skylar with Will Hall and His Orchestra bring you 'Santa Claus Is Coming to Town'!

Mom called from the kitchen, "Henry, please bring the sweet potatoes to the table!"

Walking past the living room archway, he saw Dad's tall form inspecting the tree. All the boys had decorated it together. Henry strung the colored light bulbs and hung the ornaments, smallest ones at the top and biggest at the bottom. James, home for Christmas from Nazareth Hall Prep, was always in charge of finding the perfect hiding place for the Old Ornament, the scuffed up glass ornament Mom brought from Iowa, that Kirk Kyle Jr. had hung on the tree that Christmas when he was six, before his January ear infection, and his February surgery, and his March death that was when

James was three and Mom was pregnant with Will. The ornament that Mom said had to be on the tree, and Dad too but he added, *Just put it where we damn well can't see it.* That was the rule. It was James' job because he was the next oldest after Kirk Kyle Jr. He was so careful with that ornament, like it was more precious than he was himself.

Dad and James had carried the tree home like always from Domeier's Store. It came bound in rope. But after the limbs were freed and had settled it was as wild a tree as any in the slough. James could always find a thicket of branches to nest the Old Ornament. And Will could always find bare spots Dad would let him fill with gobs of tinsel to sparkle under the colored lights. And when Mom called them to the dinner table, that was it. All arrangements and rearrangements were marked done and the radio turned off even if it was right in the middle of Doris Day's first verse of "Winter Wonderland."

Dad, at the head of the table, waited patiently while Mom asked James to lead the Christmas grace. Then Dad declared Merry Christmas and carved the turkey while everybody passed plates.

"We're fortunate to have a beautiful home and enough to eat. And it isn't luck that we have it. It's hard work." They all sat up straighter to show they were listening. "Your mom and I didn't have it easy like you boys do. She lost her parents young and her Aunt Helen raised her. I lost my dear mama, and my father sent me away to live with my Grandma Mammy who did her best. Your grandpa, my father, down in Arkansas" — his eyes met Mom's and she nodded — "we haven't talked much over the years. But he's getting older. And he needs to see you boys one of these days. He needs to see the family his son has made."

*

Dad gave the morning newspaper a crisp snap as they all sat down for breakfast. "Grace, we're going to be sharing our new state park with the Germans."

"Honestly, Kirk!" That was Mom's safe answer when she wasn't sure what Dad was up to.

"Now you see, boys" — he gathered them with his eyes — "we don't have enough young men to work the farms and the canneries and the poultry plants because all our working-age boys are over there in Europe fighting the Germans. So here's what you do..." He leaned in close, elbows on the table. Henry and Will leaned in like irons to a magnet. "You take all those German war prisoners we captured over there, and you bring them here to do the work. How much would it cost to pay a day's going wages to one hundred sixty workers? Eight-hour day, thirty-five cents an hour?"

A terrible quiet settled over the table until Dad said, "Henry?"

Henry tucked in his chin, eyes aimed at the gingham table cloth but really he was looking inward, looking, looking. "Four hundred forty-eight dollars a day!" he burst like a runner diving through the finish tape.

"Exactly right! And you can easily shave two-thirds off that cost when it's prisoners working, especially after you zero out housing costs. How? By housing them in the empty Conservation Corps barracks at Cottonwood River State Park." Dad sat back in his chair, eyes gleaming.

"You don't say, Kirk!" Mom said.

Henry's eyes gleamed too as he spread the currant jam onto his toast.

Will slid his chair from the table. "Can I be excused?"

*

In the middle of the summer of 1944, when the sun had drawn the prairie grasses tall to meet its warmth, drawn the trees' thriving leaves cupped and crowding upward from every reaching limb, when you crossed the Dump and came down the ridge to the ground that smushed and gurgled under your shoes, when you jumped puddles and galloped over fallen rushes toward the willow trees and cattails and the pond, the Slough was a wilderness. Farther on past the big cottonwood trees were the railroad tracks and Goosetown. And up the hill behind you was New Ulm. But you couldn't see any of that from down here in the Slough. That's what Henry loved most, you were in a country all your own. That and how the landscape changed every summer — the pond changed size and shape, puddles caught you by surprise where you could have walked high and dry last year, and a new-fallen tree gave passage to new ground.

"Gee whizz!" Victor exclaimed, mouth open wide.

Henry landed and steadied himself. A perfect landing on the boulder in the middle of the pond after leaping from the trunk of that new-fallen tree.

"Man, now you're cookin' with gas, I didn't think a kid from up the hill would do anything like that!"

Standing atop the boulder, Henry looked up into the blue, blue sky with the sunshine glinting every color of the prism through his eyelashes. He hadn't been trying to prove anything. He was just playing the way Victor was playing, welcoming Victor's way of having fun. And somehow, with that leap, he had proved everything.

Some of the Saint Mary's boys stopped playing with Victor when they heard he was a Goosetowner. *Nobody who matters lives down across the tracks* — they'd say. And it wasn't just Goosetown. The kids up the hill on Summit Avenue didn't play with the kids just below them in Wallachia. And Northside kids didn't play with Southside kids. And Catholics didn't mix with Protestants, and neither mixed with the Turnverein. Dad had been barred from the father-and-son breakfast for James' Saint Patrick's Troop, first because he wasn't Catholic and second because he had been seen entering Turner Hall where the members didn't believe in God at all. That was the end of Boy Scouts for the Crossland family. As far as Henry could see, the one and only thing that separated Northsiders and Southsiders was the numbering of the streets. First North, Second North, Third North, versus First South, Second South, Third South. That was all it took, it seemed, to come between people in this city of eight thousand seven hundred and forty-three. And when something made so little sense, Henry's solution was to do what Dad would do — ignore it. He called to Victor. "Let's see you beat that leap!"

"You're on!" And Victor launched laughing, splashing into the pond.

*

Most of them came home. Some didn't come for a while. Some never did, or came home with part of them gone. So some families were never quite the same again. Maybe nobody was. The biggest war ever had ended with the biggest bombs ever. And even after it was over, Henry read the news about the army testing even bigger bombs. But even for all that, nobody could deny that by the next spring, the sidewalks of Minnesota Street and the seats at the Lyric Theater and the tables at Kaiserhoff Restaurant on a Saturday evening were filled again with young grown-ups who'd been missing those four long years.

*

On a May morning when the green on the trees seemed to have popped into being after the night's rain, James sat at the foot of Will's bed and Will at the head. James was nineteen, Will sixteen. Henry looked on from the bedroom doorway. He was twelve. Somehow his brothers had become grownups while he was still a kid.

"Come on in and close it, Henry," James said. He was almost fatherly, almost motherly, as if he might reach for Will's feet with care and begin to wash them. That was how James was changing. He was home from seminary for a little while, after his second year of what Dad called priest college.

"Are you doing it for the right reasons?" James asked.

Will squirmed, then smiled that amazing smile that was Dad's confidence and Mom's sparkling blue eyes all in one. Will was changing too. His toys sat untouched while stacks of magazines rose from the bed stand: *Collier's, The Atlantic Monthly, The New Yorker.* And while books multiplied atop his dresser: *The Adventures of Tom Sawyer* was first, then *The Holy Bible.* And when Mom gave Will the pair of bookends for his fourteenth birthday, two years back, the space between bookends — which was infinite really, if you thought outside the limits of the house and the planet Earth and everything beyond — that space seemed to open up a universe for Will. *Moby Dick, The Great Gatsby, Of Mice and Men, Pride and Prejudice, Paradise Lost,* and right next to the *Bible,* the one whose long title didn't fit on the spine like the others: *Circular Letters of the Very Reverend Basil Anthony Mary Moreau, Founder of the Religious of Holy Cross.*

"I can belong there," Will said. "You belong, you have a place in the church, something Mom is proud of."

"If we can't have Dad's love then maybe Mom's, or maybe at least we can get God to love us." James tilted his chin down, then looked up at his brothers. "When I was in fifth grade during the depression — Henry you weren't in school yet, and you were in first Will — the eighth graders decided one day they didn't want to go back after recess. They sat along the fence and refused to get up. A sit-down strike, just like the meat-packers down in Austin and the Ford plant workers up in Saint Paul. Most of the littler kids followed suit, but we had a test that day and I figured that if I was a good boy who did what he's supposed to, then I'd surely get a good grade." James paused, watched and waited just long enough for Will to chuckle in expectation. "You guessed it. I failed the test, miserably. I felt let-down and confused, but that meant I was starting to think, to question things. I now believe — and I could be wrong, I've been told that enough times — but I believe we don't earn God's love by being good. We can't, because God loves us always, no matter what. That doesn't mean everything is always going to be okay, at least not what I think is okay like passing that test. It only means we're loved. And we can help others by loving them the way God loves us."

Will's eyes moved to the dresser, to the one book one whose long title didn't fit. "I'm going to belong in the church like you do, James. I'm going to share God's word and God's love."

"I'm not going to stop you Will. You've got another couple years of high school to think and pray. You decide. I surely won't stop you."

James shifted his gaze. "What about you Henry, what are you going to do?" What was it in his eyes now? So loving before, so measured in thought, and now so sharp and ready to judge like Dad.

"I'm going to be a math teacher."

Will's eyes widened in delight, opened up like those bookends on the dresser. But James' eyes only sharpened. "You never felt like I did in fifth grade, did you Henry, like you had better do what's expected, like you had to earn everybody's love? You go ahead and be a math teacher. See if the smartest boy in the little school in the little town of New Ulm is the smartest boy out there in the big world. It won't be easy. God always loves you, Henry. But His plans may not be the same as yours."

*

As foretold that Christmas Eve in 1943, the family that Challys Crossland's son had made piled into James' 1936 Ford on a warm July morning in 1947. Dad had decreed it and so it was that they set out on the two-day drive to Dallas County, Arkansas.

James at the steering wheel couldn't seem to wait to put miles between himself and Dad. Henry in the passenger seat could hardly believe that he was on his way to the colorful places on the roadmap on his lap. He focused hard, determined to make sure they got onto State Highway 68 and followed it past Mankato onto Highway 22, on down between Blue Earth and Albert Lea and onto U.S. 69. Will called out from the back seat, "I wonder how fast this jalopy can go?"

James' voice was matter-of-fact. "One hundred and twenty-four miles per hour."

There was absolute silence in the car. And then a riot of laughter all around.

"Okay, okay, it was a one-time thing!" James shook his head and put it in gear.

Highway 69 took them across the state line and through Iowa's flat endless cornfields punctuated by towns where a diner with burgers was an easy pitstop, onto U.S. 65 and by late afternoon to their halfway point, Warrensburg, Missouri.

Next day they crossed the Arkansas state line after Branson, and now it was the endless hills and forests of the Ozarks. Little towns, Bellefonte, Leslie. At Choctaw Henry directed James onto Arkansas 9 South, through Formosa, Birdtown, Solgohachia, towns where the word "WHITE" or "COLORED" topped diner doors, nonchalant as a sign spelling out hours. Across the Arkansas River and alongside Ouachita National Forest. More little towns, Williams Junction, Crows, Malvern, and into Dallas County. At Princeton they took Route 8 West and County 205.

Just outside Sparkman, Henry followed the map the best he could, supplemented with Dad's hand-scripted directions to a place he knew a lifetime ago. The paved road turned to gravel. The gravel road turned to dirt. The dirt road ended at the railroad tracks, no more road to follow. James shifted down to a stop, foot on the clutch, other foot on the brake, and stared at Henry. His mouth was set closed and his cold blue eyes said, *Look where your thirteen-year-old map skills brought us.*

They were all worn by the drive. Two long days, rarely topping fifty miles per hour, sixty on straightaways when Will was at the wheel, crawling at twenty miles per hour through every one of the hundreds of little towns. They were baked by the sun in their little tin can of a Ford, eighty-some degrees the first day according to the diner's thermometer, ninety-some degrees the second, and the wind through the windows hardly whipped five degrees off that. But it was really just James. All he could do as a weapon against the hurt was to take a swipe at the favored child, the one who was born free and clear, well after Kirk Kyle Jr., in a different house, in a different state, in a place where Mom and Dad were ready to look forward into hope again. Henry didn't even fully understand it. He just knew it was different for him than it was for James and Will. And different meant, it was the strangest thing, that Henry, the one who didn't try to fit in, was the one who did. With Mom and Dad at home. With the kids in town, where he was the only one born in New Ulm, the only one who wasn't an *Auslander*.

"This is the right place," Henry said as a statement of fact.

"The right place?" James was now less sure of himself.

"It should be one of those houses beyond the tracks." Henry pointed over the grassy, scrappy field where two lonely houses cast long afternoon shadows.

They entered the worn wooden gate, wound through an obstacle course of broken barrels, a wagon James said was like the one that delivered ice to the old house in Ottumwa, wood piles, and rusted iron things you couldn't even say what they were. There were garden beds between the two houses, or were they two sheds? An antique tractor stood guard in an overgrown field beyond the bigger shed, and beyond that stood a row of gnarled oaks, and beyond that, the hills.

Henry was drawn to the door of the bigger shed. Why did he do it? Was it because it looked safer, more likely to be uninhabited by the strange man they were sent to meet? He knocked nervously, desperately hard. A deep bellow sounded from inside.

"That's the barn, fat-head!" Will laughed.

Meanwhile James was already leading the way to the other shed, the actual house. He knocked, and they looked at each other.

"See if it's open," Will said, and James gingerly opened the door. "Hello?"

"Put the bat down Cora. I told you it was them." A white haired man leaned back in his chair at a long wooden table and summoned them through the half-open door.

Even seated, you could see he was a little taller than Dad, so wrinkled, so thin, but wiry like steel, the strange man with the strange name, Grandpa Challys Crossland.

A woman, white hair pulled back in a tight bun, leaned the baseball bat in a corner and disappeared into the next room.

"Cora, will you get these boys some milk!" The man called after her. "Cora's my wife. She milked old Bess just before you come, so it's fresh."

She served three tin cups of foamy milk and gestured to the wooden chairs. Henry and James sat with their cups, marveling to be drinking milk warm from the cow.

Will gulped his cup where he stood beside the table, gestured for a refill but she was already gone. He sidled toward the other room.

"Who's the middle one augering about the kitchen doorway?" Challys asked.

"That's Will," James said apologetically.

"Tell him the food out here is same as the food in there, so he ought better set himself to table." Will found his chair fast like when Dad called him William.

Challys tipped back a bottle of Coca-Cola while Cora served a china plate of watermelon slices and a basket of bread.

"I baked the acorn bread at sunrise" — she said — "Should still be fresh enough."

"Acorn?" Will echoed.

Challys stared at Will with eyes dark and sharp as Dad's. "I reckon you sighted the stand of oak trees as you walked to the house? Run to town, boy, if you want store-boughten bread."

"Where do you get your watermelons?" Will asked. Henry watched James cringe.

"From the gettin place, boy..." Challys smirked, then chomped into a slice. "That is a melon! Homegrown," he declared. "Hope's got bigger ones, but harken boys: A Hope melon'll cost you a rough diamond" — his dark eagle eyes focused on Cora — "but hasn't a scrap of the flavor held in this little gem."

"Honestly! You'll never cease courting if you're Moses' age!" Cora shook her head and retreated to the kitchen.

"I reckon you boys know about the diamonds in Murfreesboro? Or what do you boys know?" — He eyed Will then turned to James and Henry — "Well it's true enough about the diamonds, but never mind. Company men fixing to get rich quick have gone broke instead. I'll tell you this: Treasure makes a fool. Work and wisdom make a man."

Challys reached for the bare lightbulb hanging from a wire above the table and screwed it tight to illuminate the shadowed room.

"Kirk's boys...from away up the Mississippi, away up in Polar country. The Crossland family can't sit in one place. I could chart our peregrinations with pencil and paper for you, and it would be a goddamned spider's web. My daddy and mammy both came from Missouri, and his daddy from

Alabama and his mammy from Tennessee. Cora and I dwelt a spell in Oklahoma. And there sits your daddy in a fancy company office away up North. What parts you boys will set down to work in I can't predict."

"Our dad lends money to farmers..." Will blurted, but he saw the look on James' face. Henry looked down at the table with a peek at the old man. Challys shook his head, beyond disapproval, and turned his attention to the kitchen. "Cora, will you bring out...."

"Yes your lordship!"

Challys stopped cold. His eyebrows, pepper black to the salt white of his hair, arched up and he chuckled and coughed and chuckled, then confided in a low voice. "That means I have to watch myself. See, my mammy, Martha, who raised your daddy, it's the blood of her mammy that runs back to George Calvert, Lord Baltimore. If you ask me, I say royalty is like treasure, it's for fools. I fed a family hauling logs those twelve years I shared with your daddy's mammy Caria, bless her, before the world that God made took her from me..." — Henry watched uneasily as the old man, the stranger, his grandfather, choked back feelings as old as the century — "those twelve years I hauled logs, I never missed a day, not a day of work, and took care of my family."

Suddenly Challys was drained, more ancient than his seventy-three years.

"What did you need, Challys?" Cora asked, hand on his shoulder.

"I can't remember."

"Do you boys have a place to stay?" she said.

"Get a room in Sparkman," Challys exhaled the words like a leaking balloon. "Might better suit your city tastes."

The boys scooted back in their chairs but he stayed them, his raised palms settling firmly to the tabletop.

"Hold fast boys. I have something to say. A man makes a living, and a woman keeps a family. Do you understand what I'm saying? Your daddy, my boy Kirk, seems to think a man can tend to family at home and tend to work out in the world all at the same time. Two places at once — Mr. Einstein'll tell you that can't be. Heaven forbid Kirk should ever...and I say heaven forbid... ever find himself bereft of his children's mother — I know he lost Kirk Jr... just like Caria and I lost our first, before Kirk was born — but when you lose your wife..."

Henry looked away from the dark eyes.

"Then it all tumbles down and you've lost your children too. I'm sorry, Cora. This ain't your calamity." He half-turned to her but the hand on his shoulder dismissed any worry.

"Boys, that field out yonder, the one with the tractor. It wasn't always weeds and scrub. A score ago it was tomatoes and beans, tall as the younger one here." Henry felt his face flush red. "Then in the latest war we grew hay for the cattle men's cows. Whatever we grew, we got by. When you own a farm, even a little one, you own your life. *A man best own, lest he be owned by another.* Cora taught me that. You know what, Cora? I reckon my mammy knew that too except my daddy drank the means to do it, done drank and pissed away every hope and means."

"I reckon she did know it, Challys."

"You see boys, my daddy never owned nothing after he was shed of the farm. Thence onward he was a bartender and his own best customer. And I reckon drink is like fame and treasure. When you get what you lust for, you lose all else in the bargain.... That's all I've got to say." He looked worn but satisfied as he clasped his hands and leaned back in his chair. "Cora, see these boys out the door will you?"

She wrapped the bread in a cloth, a quick sweeping motion. "You shan't go hungry," she said and opened the door to the humid darkness.

"You boys catch the scent of rain?" Challys stood like a hunting dog. "I foretell a frog strangler of a downpour — make that fore-smell!" he chuckled and coughed. "Come morning, you boys best get on down the road directly, and if you know mountains, which I reckon you don't, you best peel your eyes for washouts in the hollers."

Next morning while mist clung to the wet hillsides, the family that Challys Crossland's son had made exited the Ouachita Motor Inn and piled into the 1936 Ford.

"I'm done with Sparkman, done with New Ulm," James muttered as he shifted into reverse. "Done with fathers and their fathers before them" — Henry glanced to Will sprawled in the backseat, Will whose eyes and ears were blinking open as James carried on — "Lord, Your will be done, You know better than I, but get me home to Saint Paul, Minnesota!" James shifted forward and accelerated out of the parking lot.

"Actually, me too," Will said. 'Except take me to Notre Dame, Indiana."

Henry was ready for New Ulm, to bike around town, practice his putt at the country club, brush up on his algebra for sophomore year at Holy Trinity. He opened the roadmap to chart the way home, when a picture popped into his head, the globe on the living room table. He closed his eyes, turned a sheaf of pages and plunked his forefinger — Hmm. Richmond, Virginia. His mind was still turning as he paged back to Arkansas, Route 9.

Nomad

Boston, January 3, 1981

"**H**i Barbara! ...I am so ready... Yeah, it's gonna be great... I'm on my way baby! Good...good... I'll be there about seven tonight..." Mary boarded the crowded bus in downtown Boston, northwest-bound for Bellows Falls, Vermont. A get-away to Barbara's new bed-and-breakfast was just what she needed. The Greyhound coach was crowded but quiet in the early morning hours. Quiet thoughts, sleepy heads, tender voices murmuring. There was an open seat beside a mother and toddler daughter, nowhere else. She settled in and focused her gaze out the driver's front window.

Once out from under Boston's towers, the transformation into forest farmlands was quick and final. Walden Pond and Concord. The tree-topped hills grew higher, looming gray-blue on the changing horizon. Whole stands of birch trees. Snow-dusted hills became undulating ranges, dotted with ancient cabins and farms. How many paintings finished themselves before her eyes every minute, every mile that passed? The bus, full to capacity, strained upward. "Fitchburg Junction!" the driver called. A few passengers disembarked. The mother and daughter squeezed past Mary to join their family in the open seats at the back of the bus. Mary exhaled. Her shoulders loosened and she stretched her legs.

More disembarked at Fitzwilliam and the remaining travelers spread themselves across the empty seats.

Two in the afternoon. The forested hills rose higher and her ears plugged as the bus climbed. The towns became smaller but still remarkably close together, as if huddled for warmth. Her penetrating gaze swept the faces across the aisle, the faces behind her. The weight of a brow, the curve of an eyelid. A busload of lives and portraits, of hope and worry and release. Men and women dozed. Children, sprawled, were dreaming. The windows fogged and ice crystals crept across the glass.

The driver's call roused her, "Bellows Falls!" She stood and swayed with the bus's turn into the little depot, tugged her bag from the overhead rack, stepped down to the pavement, and inhaled the crisp winter air. Gentle hills all around and there, across the canal, the town. Her bag was packed with dirty laundry, no time before leaving home, up until two in the morning finishing a poster mockup that she threw in the trash when she realized the deadline was already past. Rules and deadlines and who even cared if your design was the best? And Phillip. She was so ready to love him. But all year long in the little room on Beacon Hill he fussed and grumped over his grad studies, wallowing in his money and Harvard education without it ever bringing a glimmer of inspiration or happiness to his life. Finally he was as square as any Boston blue blood. She laughed to herself. Robert had said Beantown would bore her silly, a tease of radical art, but uptight and pompous after all. He was one to know about pompous, Robert, the big Orleans fisherman who never fished a day in his life. Why was she so ready to give her life over to a man who had nothing to give her? Man, oh man, was it time for her to find her own way, her own city. *Saint Jude, forces, heaven, whatever... I need a place to live and work.*

She crossed the bridge and followed Canal Street — it narrowed as the four and five story buildings of old brick and wood and stone rose on either side. A laundromat! Saint Jude found that for her anyway. She scrounged the bottom of her bag for coins, threw the load in the washer, and walked on down to the Square, which was really just a beautiful quirky old street, not square at all. And there was Andrews Inn, everybody in Provincetown knew it, the A-House's northern brother. She shook her hair back, all eyes on her, no longer the skinny string bean of girl who had left college and home for the East Coast. The decade had endowed her still slender form with graceful curves and the poise of a woman. Guys with guys studied her for a gesture, a style, a new way to be everything they longed to be. Girls with girls secretly locked eyes with her, then turned to their partner with a kiss that discharged all the energy of that fleeting flirtation. For a moment all the world was love and she was its axis. God, the hurt that shot through her heart and she downed the tequila and her heart warmed and she laughed with the bartender, a man who would never want her but hot as could be.

"I'll be back after the dryer cycle at the laundry. I'm quick, I turn it on full heat."

"Ouch! You're a fucking doll, where have you been all my life! I'm pouring your next one right now honey, so you better run!"

Nine o'clock that night, she was at the lodge. Ten minutes walk up a curving wooded road from town, winter stars above.

She stamped the snow from her boots and stepped inside. "Oh Barbara, it's beautiful! And warm, thank God!"

"I've done a lot of work on the place this year. Come on in! The kitchen is all redone, I'll be preparing meals in here but you can grab a snack or make coffee any time. And if you want to really warm up..." Barbara ushered her through an archway to the dining room where logs crackled and sparks danced in the fireplace.

"Oh baby, you know just what I need." She hugged Barbara, held on a little too tight. Barbara hugged her close, then pulled back and looked into her eyes. "You just need to let down and tune into your own heart."

"Hey!" A low voice, a lanky man in a leather jacket and jeans walked into the room.

"Oh my god, Barbara said you might be coming." She hadn't seen Chris since New York City ten years ago, her first way station, the first time she could say Sandusky was behind her, could never catch up to her.

He swept back his blond locks, rested an elbow on the mantle like he owned the place. "Been a while!" he laughed. "Anyway, I'm here for a change of scene from the City, looking to recharge. You look great, Mary."

Damn him. Her heart was an all-in jam session, no idea what she wanted to think or feel, she couldn't stand this part of herself. She smiled her sexy welcome smile. "We can recharge together."

*

Mary rolled from her sleep and looked at the clock: seven in the morning. Somehow after supper she had escaped to her room alone, to journal, to draw, to slow her spirit, slow down. The last thing she had written before sleep. *Perhaps I can take this opportunity for some reshaping of various sorts.* Whatever that meant.

Slippers on, she padded out to the living room. At the window her spirit was flooded with a blue glow. Between the black leafless trees of the woods, the blanket of snow reflected the lights of night, spotlight, moonlight, star.

She whispered. "Neon forest." Wind whispered back. A rush against the window. A drawing was forming, lines and strokes, tracing outward, the very path the limbs had followed from sapling to old oak, growing toward life. Her spirit treaded over the snow, not breaking the crust, traced deep into the forest, into the light and the dark, the blue and the black, until the whir of the distant highway waked her to the polished wood floor where she stood. She shivered, the beauty of it, rubbed her fingertips along the cool leather of the hardbound sketchbook in her hand. She had swept it up from the night stand as she rose from bed. Old-fashioned gilt-edged pages. *Anything Book* read the trademark on the back. She sat in a comfy chair by the window, neon forest in view, and filled a page with first impressions of the day. Her pencil sketched light lines and dark. Forest. The strong tree trunk in the foreground, spruce needles tracing across it. More trunks fading to background. Wild little lateral branches and twigs. Fallen logs. Her pencil stopped.

It was so quiet. Why was she the only one awake, the only one who couldn't wait for day? She exhaled, and in that moment her body relaxed and her eyelids felt heavy again. Soon enough the new day would begin. But first, back to bed, to dreams deeper than sleep.

Tangled, why was it tangled, blanket around her legs, thrashing, darkness growing to light, whiter than light, a blinding nothingness of voices and rustling that was nothing to do with her, they hardly knew she was there. Lines tracing toward her, thickening, darkening. The warmth inside, her ball of glowing warmth, glowing life, rose above her. Thickening claws swiped, snatched, faster. No, no! No! The glowing warmth distant, fading. Her big brown eyes, tiny beating heart. She knew what was next, please wake, please wake. She saw, below her breasts, her belly was a gaping dark hole.

Startled upright, blanket and pillows strewn around her, the lodge, yes, Barbara's lodge. Someone sobbing. Her own voice sobbing. "Alone, alone, alone..." Could she ever cry the word enough times to speak the full meaning. Quieter. "Alone, alone..." To lose the meaning, say it enough to lose all meaning. To obliterate a decade of wandering, running, stumbling, leaping toward a life in the void.

Eleven years ago she had walked across the quad, hand-in-hand with Marie, always and forever her best friend, walked together in the thrust of springtime. The scent of flowers laced the air above the campus, and it seemed to hold a sense of beginning and possibility. Her tummy not even showing yet, her baby.

It wasn't what anyone would call the right time. The middle of sophomore year at Dayton, the middle of her graphic arts studies, single, not even in love exactly. And no, she didn't even know his last name, she admitted to Marie, the beautiful boy who gave her this fullness of life, this fullness of heart she had never known before. "You'll try to find him and talk to him, won't you?" Marie had pleaded. "He'll do the right thing and marry you."

In the rush of feelings all she could say was, *I don't want to be pitied.* What she really felt was that marrying because she should, because he should, would be a trap for them both. The expected thing to do wasn't the right thing to do. Mother and Father, even Marie, dear Marie, would never understand. That her baby wasn't a mistake to be explained and excused away. What happened was life and love, hers and her baby's, not something bad or sinful. She felt a world opening up, a world of people loving people, exploring ideas, exploring art, exploring each other, doing their own thing, their own way. The boundless parties sharing love and opening minds with music and drinks and hits of whatever was handed around — it wasn't reckless. It was freedom. It was love. And she didn't need anyone telling her what to do with the love growing inside her. But they did tell her. Men and women. Her family. And people she didn't even know.

She sat in the cold office of the unwed mother's home on Carroll Avenue. Out the window, the heavy snow of a Minnesota November. Opposite her, behind a massive wooden desk, the social worker filled a notebook. Father Stan, Mother's uncle in Saint Paul had arranged everything. A favor to the family. An act of charity.

"How far along are you?" the woman peered over her reading glasses, volleying questions from behind a screen of safety.

"Seven months, I believe." She wanted to sound mature, self-assured.

"Have you received prenatal care?"

"No." She sank a little in the hard wooden chair.

"Have you consumed alcohol or drugs during your pregnancy?"

"Some." It all felt so horrible, so shameful, as if she were on trial before God.

"Who is the father?"

There it was, the dreaded question. She knew his first name, Ronny, that was all. And her own principles dictated that even if she knew his full name, she wouldn't betray him. His name was nobody's business.

"I don't know," she said. And even as she said it, she felt a pang of guilt. She would always know him as the special young man who touched her soul that night. This simple lie was her sin, her shame before God, if He was even listening.

The snow deepened into the month. One by one the young girls she met there, who she comforted and who comforted her, disappeared to Saint Joseph's Hospital. Each thought their story was unique, the suffering theirs alone. Yet each told the same story, her story. *No one ever explained what was happening inside me, what would happen when the day came. Catholic Services knows how to handle these situations. My parents said no one must know. I was sent to my aunt, my grandmother, my mother's best friend. I was kept indoors, never allowed to be seen during the months of my pregnancy. No one in my hometown would ever be told the truth.*

Every nurse who entered the room and leaned over Mary's bed or the other girls' beds repeated, as if their words should be a comfort, that the baby would be taken by a family who had everything she didn't have, a married home, a solid income, standing in the community, who would give the baby a better life than she ever could. Was it even true? Father and Mother had all those things. And she appreciated all they had given her, but knowing for the first time in her life the love of a mother for her baby...can anything be more important than that?

You will go back home afterward — the social worker counseled — *and pick up your life exactly where you left off before any of this happened. Do you understand? Can you imagine how damaging it would be if you were ever to interfere in the adoptive family's new life with the baby? You would never forgive yourself for doing such a thing to them, to the baby. Do you understand? You will move on, you will forget, you will make something useful of your life.*

On December 8, 1969, on her twenty-first birthday, three days after her baby girl was born, she committed the most unnatural act she could imagine. A decision made for her, for both of them. But it was her hand, the pen in her hand. The brief moment she had held her daughter in her arms at Saint Joseph's Hospital, her tiny fingers had clung to her almost as if she'd known they would be separated.

There could be no penance, no forgiveness for this. And if God chose to forgive her, she might wonder what kind of a god he was.

A decade of wandering. Across the corn fields and factory towns to the coast and New York City. Then Philly, Baltimore, Norfolk, Charleston, Savannah. A nomad along the shore. The ocean was her companion, the vast blue she'd imagined from Winnebago Beach, where the lakes could lead you if only you followed. She found a name in a magazine, Zadora. When you don't know where you're from, any name might be yours. Mary Zadora. Finally it was the Cape in Massachusetts that called her. A world away from the pain of that horrible December long ago.

And why she had left the Cape, left Robert in Orleans — well she knew why she'd left him, but the question was, why to be with Phillip in Boston? What was she thinking? Love? Big city culture? More opportunities, more paid work? She hadn't found any of it. And whether it was Beantown that was too square or just Phillip, it was over. After Bellows Falls, all that would be left would be to pack a duffel bag with her clothes, her art supplies, her treasured collection of feathers and seashells, her handmade jewelry, her coffee brewer — there really wasn't much else — and leave the keys and a letter on Phillip's bed. She wasn't the type to walk out without at least leaving a letter. Everyone deserves an explanation.

She splashed her face with water in the lodge's shared bathroom. There it was in the mirror, her resplendent smile. She dressed and joined the others in the dining room.

"Another serving?" Barbara was trying to keep up with Chris' bottomless-pit stomach.

He lifted his plate. "Keep it coming!"

Mary made a face that made Barbara laugh all the way to the kitchen. And there sat Prince Charming, blond hair straggling over one eye and down his cheek. Mary couldn't stand how he chewed his pumpernickel bread, smacking his lips like kisses. Poached egg yolk smeared on his chin. She might as well be dining with a donkey.

"Barbara, I'm done with Boston."

"What! You're convincing Phillip to move up here?"

"I'm done with Phillip."

Chris looked up from his eggs.

"I need to put some water between me and this crazy land. I'm going back to the Cape."

After breakfast it was a hike in the woods. Mary, Chris, and Barbara. After lunch at Miss Bellows Falls Diner swiveling on the counter stools, it was Brattleboro and the bars. After dinner it was Doc's Bar in Rochester where the three of them shot pool and filled water jugs from the beer tap. And two in the morning it was Bellows Falls again. "How did we even find this place?" Mary mused. Barbara steadied herself and pierced the keyhole like a bullseye. "I live here, remember?" They stumbled laughing into the lodge and stomped the snow off their boots in the living room, then stumbled into the kitchen for one more drink and where the hell did Barbara disappear to, and it was just Mary and him and the kitchen table, and the counter, and the slippery tile floor.

*

Six days of quiet mornings and wild evenings on these tree-covered hills. Mary breathed it all in one last time before boarding the bus for Boston and then, the Cape.

The morning after that first night with Chris, she had felt like such a loser. Lost to yet another man. But maybe he was just what she needed. Oh god, she was pretty sure that was what she had said to him, naked on the kitchen table — *Baby you know what I need!* She cringed. But really, she did need it, as a consecration of her breakup with Phillip. Break up and break out! There were a couple more nights with Chris, but by Wednesday, nestled in the woods, cabin fever had set in and mania ruled the evenings, all three of them wrestling, screaming, tickling, laughing, joking, giggling, and totally flipping out.

The bus maneuvered out of the depot, crossed Bellows Falls Canal. She opened her sketchbook and wrote. *My spirit is fiery, eager to learn, to translate, to love, eager to burn like the eternal flame. Above us it glows. I need to learn what my heart already knows.*

*

Duffel bag in the overhead rack, Mary looked out the window of the Cape Cod RTA bus, then leaned back in her seat. They had passed Harwich, and in ten or fifteen minutes she'd be looking for Robert's truck in the parking lot of Roundabout Gas at the Chatham rotary. She had left the letter for Phillip.

Now she would collect the few paintings and books she had abandoned at Robert's.

She had met Robert two and a half years ago by the simple accident of choosing the Land Ho! Diner for lunch. It was her last day of unemployed freedom, she thought, before starting as a deckhand on a fishing boat, a day boat called the Plenitude.

She took a stool amidst young men who tore into their sandwiches and tipped back their bottles, and old men who savored their soups and nursed their beers, and older men who savored their whiskies and nursed their soups.

The waitress set a plate in front of the young man beside her and announced, "Cape Cod Reuben, bowl of chowder."

"Clam chowder, elixir of the gods!" He caught the waitress's eye — "and served by a goddess!"

"When I hand you the bill you'll say I'm hurling lightning bolts." She set a menu in front of Mary. "Start with a drink, honey?"

"Newcastle, please." Mary flipped her dark curls and asked him, "What's in a Cape Cod Rueben?"

"Miracle of the sea. Fried cod...or other white fish...and coleslaw with tartar sauce."

"I'll be catching the contents of your sandwich, starting tomorrow."

His smile froze as if hit with an icy gale. "I'm sorry?"

She was ruffled, puzzled, tried to pull herself together. "I'll be a deckhand on the Plenitude starting tomorrow."

"I'm really" — he disintegrated into laughter. "I'm really sorry but...oh my god, that's...I'm sorry. It's just that, you're not from here are you! Not with that America's Heartland accent of yours!"

The waitress set the bottle in front of Mary. "What'll you have honey?"

"I'll have one of those." Mary flashed a defiant nod his way.

"I hope you mean the Reuben and not him."

Mary melted into laughter.

"Ouch!" He shook his head. "I'm taking a beating today!"

"As you ought to."

"I'm Robert. And what do the corn fields say when they whisper your name?"

"They say, *Mary, this guy Robert is full of himself.*"

"Mary, then. Well Mary, I give you a week, no more," he said.

"Where in hell do you come up with a week?" she was unanchored.

"The only reason I give you that long...hear me out, hear me out...is because I saw the lightning in your eyes when I said *America's Heartland...* That's it, there it is again, like a nor'easter brewing on the horizon. You're a lady to be reckoned with!"

She had wished way back then, so wished he had never said, *I'll give you a week.* It was the most miserable, filthy, exhausting, all-consuming work she had ever done, and the only reason she did it for eight, not seven but eight never-ending days was that she had to prove him wrong.

*

The gravel drive at the old house in Orleans crunched under the tires of Robert's pickup until the final scatter as he pulled to a stop and shifted into park. "Welcome home, Mary. It's been a while." She gazed at the little house while he gazed at her. "It sure as hell has," she said.

They had lived together more than a year in this old house inherited from his parents. Robert wasn't so much living there as squatting — all the family furnishings in place, his grandmother's china, his mother's antique collectibles, his dad's library of medical books.

Mary had taken pleasure in bringing the house to life, her own latest paintings on the walls, fresh linens on the bed, home-cooked meals in the kitchen, whatever she could do without disturbing Robert's sense of order. It wasn't out of sentiment that he kept everything as it was. He was a man who lived simply. He didn't need or want much. But what little he did need he acquired through collecting, and he used what he needed and sold what he didn't, and the house was, in a sense, a windfall of collectibles the likes of which he might never see again. Name any item, useful or useless, and he knew where to find it. The house was a well-ordered inventory, and the inventory moved only when he was ready to sell it. So she got used to things never changing on the one hand, and randomly disappearing on the other. One day, it was the library, the entire medical library, gone.

"Those books were fascinating," she had said. "Did you ever really look at them? The anatomical drawings — the muscles, the bones — had an amazing sensitivity. No one draws like that any more."

"I admit, you make them sound very special. But this is special too." He had led her down the basement stairs and opened his arm in a dramatic sweep. "A half year's supply of Newcastle beer!"

She didn't dare try to convince Robert that some of these treasures were worth keeping. He had his way of doing things and not even she could influence him. They were both strong willed and more and more their wills had clashed. The late-night arguments were a downer.

One night she had stormed out, driven to Provincetown not even knowing why. On a bar stool at Piggy's her eyes met Phillip's. He was everything Robert wasn't — intellectual, articulate beyond the realm of one-liners, well-mannered. He was a man who had it all pulled together. He actually had twenties in his wallet. She didn't even care about money, little prints on paper that lacked color, originality, but that somehow everyone had to acquire. She didn't care except that she was tired and here was a man who could take care of everything. It didn't happen all at once. It took a week before she was living with him on Beacon Hill. But in the end, Phillip took care of everything except her spirit. He teased her with hints of beauty and love, a script that life had taught him, not a life he owned, not a life he could give. He pulled himself together tighter and tighter and tried to pull her along with him, puppets dancing on his blank stage and, sorry baby, but that was the end of that.

And even though she wasn't coming back to Robert, not in that way, the fact was that she wasn't only coming back to pick up her things. She needed a breath of freedom, Robert's sea spray of wonderful nonsense. He never, in the years they were together, never tried to control her like Phillip did. Despite all Robert wasn't, he really was something rare to find in a man. He was a friend.

"Mostly the house is still the same. But you're going to love what I've done with the living room." His boyish grin. She leaned over and kissed his lips. "Let's see it then. You going to help me with my bags, kind sir?"

At the front door, he paused for effect, then opened it.

"Oh my god," Mary laughed. "Oh my god."

All the furnishings that belong in a living room were banished to the walls. A credenza piled with tools, a sofa piled high with coats and rags, planks of wood stacked against the French doors to the garden. And in the middle of the room, where all the living room things should have been — "I can't believe you," she said — there it was. A boat.

"Don't judge it just yet. It's not finished. I still have some things to work out."

"I'll say." She walked around it, smiling so big she felt she might burst.

The overturned boat stood on a wooden framework with a long beam that ran the length like a spine. He ran his hand along it. "What do you think of that strong back? Northern white ash. She's a New England Dory." Planks of wood, stretched from end to end, were glued and clamped.

"Those clamps look like a flock of seagulls roosting!"

"A boat builder cannot have too many clamps," he grinned.

He had always talked about it, building a boat. He talked about a lot of things. But now here it was. She could see the childlike pride in his eyes, an innocent pride that she loved.

"I always knew you could do it, Robert." She held up a bundle wrapped in a plastic bag. "I have a surprise for you!"

"Fresh from the sea?"

"Clams! I picked them up at Chatham."

"Just like old times."

As darkness fell, Mary carried the steaming tureen of chowder from the kitchen and placed it on the wooden table in the dining room. With a flick of her lighter she lit the candle.

"You want another beer?" Robert asked as he popped the cap off a Newcastle.

"How about a classy dinner? Red wine?"

"That's my Mary!" He returned with a bottle and corkscrew.

"Is this the last of your grandmother's china?" She ladled the steaming chowder into the crackled porcelain bowls.

"I've held onto it longer than some of the other inventory, I can't say why. But I see another question in those dark eyes of yours."

"When I moved away to Boston, did you miss me?"

"I survived your departure my dear, and I am surviving your return as well."

She pulled the spoon from her soup bowl and flicked a splat of chowder. Got him, right on the chin.

"Damn it, Mary!" he belted as he pushed back from the table, angry as the phrase broke from his lips, but as he got to "Mary" he chuckled and shook his head and wiped the chowder from his chin and said it all over again but soft, "Damn it Mary."

She shot him the defiant I've-done-nothing-wrong look she always did. His same dry humor. His same anger. The same way they would never be right together and never be completely apart.

"You were right about Phillip, you were right about Boston. They're not for me."

"So, Boston's out," he raised his glass, then tipped it back for a swig. "Beantown, land of opportunity. I made plenty of mistakes in life, but at least I never got suckered into moving there."

"Every job interview, every art grant seemed to fall apart in the end. I just don't understand what they're looking for."

"They're all bastards. You're an artist Mary, you're not one of them. Join me at the marina! We could make some good finds together! You wouldn't believe what litterbugs our storied seafarers were — anchors, chains, rudders, buoys, old propellers! Turn them into sculptures and I'll sell them to the highest bidder!"

"You are resourceful. My seafaring man."

"As long as the Cape shore is well in sight!"

Even as he laughed at himself, she could see how he soaked it in: *My seafaring man.* He loved playing the part.

"I'm settled on Provincetown, Robert. It's the only place I've found where nobody minds if things don't quite work out. Everybody does whatever it is they love to do."

"I cannot argue. Provincetown dances to the rhythm of the sea — tide and storm and calm. I even venture a hope. That you can be happy there."

Next morning they were at Land Ho! Diner. Betty made her rounds with the glass decanter. "More coffee?"

Mary and Robert looked at each other across the condiments and the glass ashtray overflowing with butts.

"Last one?" he asked.

"Last one." She searched his eyes in a quick sweep as they leaned back from the red-and-white-check tablecloth while Betty filled their cups. Mary waited for Robert's signature banter, the usual fountain of teasing flirtation and charm, and Betty waited too, but for the moment his swaggering style was gone.

Mary raised the cup to her lips with Robert in her gaze.

He looked down, then met her eyes with a reassuring smile.

"I'm leaving you again, Robert."

"I know, darling. It's what we do. You always know where to find me."

The entry bell rang. Robert waved to the new arrival.

"Damn," Mary said, not quite ready to be finished. It was Joyce, her ride up Cape.

Premise

Indiana, Fall 1955

After the gray, smokey skies of Chicago — he had never driven through a city so endless — and after the stagnant gray stink of Gary, Indiana, the skies gradually diluted to a pale blue wash above the chartreuse green countryside along U.S. 20. He pushed up his horn-rimmed eyeglasses with one finger. Wind was the only sound in the car's cabin. He could have turned on the radio. But that wasn't how Henry Crossland traveled. News or music wouldn't leave room for what was in his head. It wasn't a conscious choice. It was just that once he started watching the road open before him and roll under him and the thoughts began rolling through his mind, it never occurred to him to do anything but think. The University of Notre Dame du Lac was sixty miles ahead. Will was there. And the next step toward Henry's dream, the dream he'd followed first to Saint Edward's University in Austin, Texas. Dream was Katie's word, what a doll she was. Maybe his word was fascination.

It was fascination from the start. There was always another kind of numbers to learn. In first grade he had sat in the back of the class writing numbers from one to one hundred. Count as high as you like, they were called the counting numbers. Next he learned about zero. Zero and the counting numbers together made the whole numbers. Zero wasn't just an extra number, it was a number that changed what you could do with all the others. Without zero you couldn't subtract three from three, or three thousand from three thousand. And every few grades he was learning yet another kind of number that, when you bring it in, changes what you can do with all the rest. Bring in the negative numbers and you have the integers to subtract any whole number you like from any other. Then the fractions too and you have the rational numbers to divide.

He learned more at Holy Trinity, the irrational numbers like pi and square root of two, and still more at Saint Edward's. What would be next? It seemed there was no end, always a new way to solve what you couldn't solve before.

It was different from Dad's way of seeing numbers. Dad was trying to solve problems too, but they were problems like how to make money for State Bond and Mortgage by giving a farmer the loan he needs at the right time, the right amount, and the right interest rate. And as complicated as that seemed to Henry — something he could never solve — the fact was that the only mathematics Dad ever used was the rational numbers and the operations of addition, subtraction, multiplication, and division. In other words, elementary school arithmetic. All the other complexity Dad solved with intuition, a gut feeling that pretty well never failed him.

Henry knew that feeling too, something taking shape deep in his mind when he was learning a new formula or a new number system. Even before he grasped it, he felt the aesthetic rightness and knew that he would grasp it. You could say it was like knowing the beauty, then the meaning, like hearing the leitmotifs in Der Ring des Nibelungen the summer of 1949. Dad had let Henry and his friend Victor drive up to the Cities, as a graduation present, when the touring company from the New York Metropolitan Opera came to the University of Minnesota.

And Henry started to realize that must be what Mathematics is all about. When you can turn a feeling into a written formula, then you've got a method that anyone anywhere in the world can use to solve any problem, as long as they know the right numbers and operations. That was what he wanted to learn, and he wanted to teach other people to do it too.

It won't be easy, James had said, sitting on Will's bed that spring day at the end of eighth grade. Maybe James should have been talking about his own path to the priesthood. He was ordained four years ago now, and he admitted to his brothers that already he had spilled the beans on a few occasions, let on to various pastors that he had doubts about some of the Church's doctrine. Father Lachaise at Saint Peter's in Richfield had responded with the best advice, not to let formalities get in the way of ministering to the flock. *You earn your respect as a man, and respect for the priesthood will follow.* More often he was told to set doubt aside and learn discipline and obedience, and before long the reassignment would follow — to Saint Olaf's in Minneapolis, Saint Joseph's in Red Wing, Saint Leo's in Saint Paul.

That was how the Church's doctrine was a world away from Mathematics. The farther Henry advanced in his studies, the more the professors welcomed questions. And another difference. New number systems let you do something you couldn't do before. Every development in Catholic doctrine, when there was any development at all, seemed to specify something else you could not, must not, do.

Must and must not. Every day of his childhood and teen years, he lived in danger of failing God one way or the other and that meant the danger of spending eternity in Hell. God wouldn't condemn him. There would be no one to blame but himself. His own acts, if he wasn't careful, could destroy the charity in his heart and thereby turn his heart away from God. Even as a child he had to guard against any grave sin, any transgression of the first, second, third, fifth (that's right, the fourth is not a grave sin), sixth, seventh, eighth, ninth, or tenth Commandments, because these transgressions were an offense of grave matter against God. And no, there were not merely nine rules to remember. The Church specified, for each of these Commandments one or more sinful acts, some fifty in total, which if committed willingly and with full consent, were mortal sins. *If we sin willfully after having the knowledge of the truth* — Saint Paul warned the Hebrews in a letter they must have wished they didn't open — *there is now left no sacrifice for sins.* In other words, nothing less than God's absolution, granted by the priest in the rite of penance, could save you from Hell. Laugh if you want to. But it wasn't funny. Mom would never forgive him.

As a teen he particularly noted the Ninth Commandment, which included the sin of Lust — *a disordered desire for, or inordinate enjoyment of, sexual pleasure.* In those early years he hadn't had any sexual pleasure, but he was pretty sure he had felt a disordered desire, definitely inordinate. Even worse, under the Sixth Commandment *You shall not commit adultery,* he now understood a sin he had never understood back then, the sin of masturbation. The shame of temptation in the quiet darkness of his bedroom, the fear of temptation in the solitude of the bathroom, the excruciating internal interrogation exposed relentlessly to a God who knows every man's heart: Was it willful? Is there any possibility it might not have been? Was it with full consent? How could it not be? And after all, adultery was, he had to think, sinful because it was a theft of another's privilege or the betrayal of a spouse's trust. It was a social breach. How did it make any sense that masturbation was adultery? But the priest screened from view within the cramped confessional booth did not tolerate questions.

And all the while, from high school on, his mathematics professors wanted questions, demanded questions, and lauded his criticisms of the needless length or complexity of a mathematical formula.

He got a little turned around in downtown South Bend but found his way up North Michigan Street, onto Angela Boulevard and Notre Dame Avenue. He would find his way to Will's Holy Cross Brothers residence first, make a plan for the night, then in the coming days visit the Math department office and figure out rental housing for the year. Beyond the chartreuse trees, it loomed in the distance, glistened in the late afternoon sun. The famous Golden Dome. The graceful figure at its peak caught a flare of sunlight — Our Lady of the Lake, Mary, Mother of God, her hands outstretched. From Mom's arms into Hers.

*

Maybe James had been right after all. Out of line, but right. It wasn't going to be easy. Being the math whizz at Holy Trinity didn't help. Being an "all As" math major at Saint Edwards University didn't help. That only made it harder as Henry nodded in nervous agreement while his graduate advisor, tapping a ball point pen on the paper-strewn gray metal desk in Notre Dame's Nieuwland Science Center, so new the scent of paint still wafted the hallways, explained that Henry lacked any foundation in mathematical theory. *Our undergrads know this material. You can't do graduate-level work without it.*

One more year sitting in undergraduate courses. After all the commencement day celebrations at Saint Edwards last May, his hand reaching for the diploma, Bachelor of Science in Mathematics, eyes scanning the audience for Mom and Dad as he left the stage. And Katie's smile of wonder back home in New Ulm that summer. He must have seemed like some kind of living proof that you could leave that little wedge of prairie and its eight thousand seven hundred citizens and come back to tell about it. That is, if you even wanted to come back. After four years at Saint Edward's, now he was "out east" in Indiana. She was starting her own academic venture at Bryn Mawr College in Pennsylvania. Where would she be after her four years?

He had known her as one of the neighborhood kids when the Crosslands moved to South State Street the summer of 1948, after his first year at Holy Trinity. Katie Meichner. She was the little fifth-grader who lived a block away on Washington Street, who strolled the sidewalk nonchalantly, blonde hair loosed in the August breeze, her three cousins, girls her age and younger, trooping beside her. She had a way of stealing a glance at Henry across the street, suddenly self-conscious as she reached toward her black and white oxfords to pull up her Bobby socks. As soon as the littlest girl shrieked — *A boy!* — they all bolted giggling, Katie too.

Henry realized eventually that she was the same girl he had seen at the country club. The Meichner's, like the Crosslands, were a golf family. So he wasn't too surprised, his first summer home from college in 1952, when he and Katie were paired in the Guys and Gals Mixer Tournament. He was nineteen, she was fifteen. They lost by a shot on the ninth hole. He asked her out to a movie and ice cream the next weekend to celebrate their *almost* victory. "She's awfully young," Mom had said to Dad. "In Arkansas they'd be marrying, not just going for ice cream," was Dad's plain response.

In Mom's worried remark, Henry heard more than just a caution about Katie's age. He heard her mind turning over the many risks to the Sixth Commandment. Fornication for example. Not likely in his mind. Lust, yes. Masturbation afterwards. That was a genuine concern.

After the early movie — *Singin' in the Rain* with Gene Kelly and Debbie Reynolds, Katie liked it a lot — they walked up North Minnesota Street to the neon sign: *Eibner's Dining-Bakery-Ice Cream-Candy Smorgasbord.* He felt proud to be holding a girl's hand. He hadn't dated much in high school, and strangely he didn't feel that much more grown up than her. He actually felt a bit nervous. About making a good impression. About keeping his guard up, morally. They took a table in the ice cream parlor. Over chocolate sundaes he told her how in his high school years he used to work here at the ice cream counter, though that didn't seem relevant now that he was in college. And he told her how the townspeople hid here in the cellar during the Dakota War eighty years ago, when the Indians set the town blazing, though everybody knew that already.

"I think you're brave to go all the way to Texas to follow your dream," she said and took his hand. That was how it all started.

All through his Saint Edward's years, summer break at home in New Ulm, there were more movies, ice cream, bicycle rides to the country club. He tutored her in math, and that always earned him a kiss. She discovered books in high school, and read to him from classics that could have come from Will's bookshelves. Even as she was growing up, catching up to adulthood, the age difference mattering less and less, she still looked into his eyes with the same pride and wonder as on that first date. And now he was admitted to graduate studies at Notre Dame University. With the one caveat, two undergraduate courses. *Real Analysis,* which was the study of limits and series. And *Modern Algebra,* which meant the theory behind algebra. He knew something was missing those four years in Austin, Texas. It was a good school, founded by the same priest who founded Notre Dame in Indiana — the Reverend Father Édouard Sorin of the Congregation of Holy Cross. Will had written from Notre Dame: *You'll qualify for the two thousand dollar scholarship, I know you will, and that's half your ride through college!* Will was a Holy Cross brother now. And, like Dad, he had a good eye for a bargain. And part of the bargain was that Saint Edward's math teachers were mechanical and electrical engineers. There wasn't a single mathematician on the faculty. And there wasn't a shred of theory in the lessons. Henry could apply the formulas others had created, but he didn't know how they created them or how to create new ones. He didn't know how to be a mathematician.

*

He closed the Real Analysis textbook, turned out the lamp, and stretched out on his bed. What would Katie say when he arrived by train at Bryn Mawr next month for Thanksgiving weekend, when he told her he was still taking undergraduate classes? Would the pride and wonder evaporate? *I thought you were a graduate student?* He rolled, the blanket seam neat across his chest, unrumpled by each restless turn of his body.

There was a tightness in his muscles. He rolled to his back, thinking about the first vertebra at the top of his spine. Only the thought, and now he sensed the muscles in his neck relaxing. Only the thought, and he relaxed the next vertebra, and after a time the next, and continued to the very last.

He woke to the alarm clock as dawn faintly illuminated the small bedroom on Eddy Street. He had a routine by now. Into the bathroom for a quick wash and shave, comb his hair which already at twenty-one was like a monk's rim around a bald top, get dressed in slacks and a button-down shirt, then to the kitchen where he pulled three slices of Wonder Bread out of the bag, covered two with grape jelly and one with peanut butter. He wrapped the sandwich in tin foil for lunch, then downed the slice with jelly and a big glass of orange juice. All before Greeley woke up.

Luke Greeley, a biology professor, was his landlord and housemate. Part of the routine was that Henry helped Greeley dress for the day. There was a lot that Greeley did for himself. But with no left arm to speak of and a short right arm with only three fingers, there were some things he couldn't manage. So, as Greeley said, why not a symbiotic arrangement? Henry saw the notice on the bulletin board at Nieuwland when navigating the long hallways his first week. *Free rent, off-campus shared housing. Assist biology professor with various daily tasks he cannot perform due to phocomelia.* Some of the tasks were easy enough. Drive him to campus and back a few days a week. Shop for groceries. Other tasks would have repelled some would-be renters. Help him dress in the morning and undress for bed at night. Help him unbutton his trousers to go to the bathroom noon and evenings. Just unbutton, the rest he managed himself. For Henry all of these tasks were easy enough to do because they were acts of charity, exactly the kind of charity that Jesus gladly would have done if He were here now. And He was here, in us. It didn't even matter whether Jesus was God or simply a man — something Henry had started asking himself after a course on evolution at Saint Edward's. What mattered was that Jesus lived an exemplary life of moral principle and compassion, a life Henry would try to live in his own way.

And it wasn't as if the arrangement was all sacrifice. There was a lot to learn from Greeley. His perseverance in the face of obstacles. His dedication to science and to the scholarly life.

"Mathematics!" Greeley mused one evening in the living room as he grasped the neck of the brown bottle for a slug of beer. Henry liked cans but soon understood they were out of the question. Three fingers wrapped a bottleneck.

"Your field is the lingua franca of the sciences, more so as we progress through the present century."

Henry nodded, eager to hear more.

"A convergence of the sciences is gathering speed. Look at biology. Twenty years ago Niels Bohr suggested we biologists take a look at the principles of quantum physics." Greeley chuckled, "So of course physicists started doing it, because they were the ones listening to Bohr! We're so segregated, you see, but it is changing."

"All the fellows I play poker with at Nieuwland are physicists!" Henry confided and raised his bottle of Budweiser.

"Convergence!" Greeley toasted. "It was the physicists, like Schroedinger and Delbrueck, who started applying physics to questions of the mutability of genes and their role in heredity." Greeley paused. He must have seen an unspoken question in Henry's eyes. "Reduce biology to physics, you're wondering? Well, Schroedinger imagined you could. But Delbrueck was more creative about it, he applied the models, the mode of thought if you will, to laboratory biology. He started breeding bacteriophages, for God's sake! A biologist at heart!"

"Bacteriophages..." Henry echoed uncertainly.

"Viruses that attack bacteria. Valuable because they reproduce so fast." Greeley tipped his bottle for a draft. "Today's fruit fly! To say nothing of Mendel's peas! I won't bore you, but it was Hermann Muller who first put Drosophila melanogaster, the fruit fly, in front of an x-ray. Now in the last few years with the work of Hershey and Chase and Watson and Crick we know emphatically we need to look to DNA, not proteins, for heredity. DNA carries the instructions to create life itself. I'm sorry, I'm going on and on. But what about mathematics, our lingua franca? What are the instructions for creating new mathematics? Or put another way, you may solve an equation perfectly well, but how do you test the validity of your formulas in the first place?"

"So you're getting at theory?"

"Verus quidem! Theory and the validity of the theory itself. What's the basis for that?" Greeley adjusted his eyeglasses and sat back in his chair, watching Henry. Was he expecting an answer? Or was he satisfied merely to have asked the question, to have triggered a reaction in Henry's brain, a chain reaction that might continue for a lifetime.

*

When Henry got off the train at Bryn Mawr Station, he was excited to see her but nervous too....

When he didn't see her, not anywhere on the platform.

When he dropped a nickel into the pay phone and dialed her dorm, and she said "Come meet us at the Campus Center. Walk up Morris Avenue to New Gulph Road. You'll be here in fifteen minutes!"

When he found the Campus Center thirty minutes later, escaped inside from the chill November wind, and Katie waved from one of the many tables of women poring over books under the high-vaulted ceiling, and the girl and guy with her smiled and waved.

When she threw her arms around him, almost theatrically, but didn't kiss him in front of the others. "These are some of my friends!"

When he didn't have to say anything at dinner about his undergraduate courses, didn't have an opening, didn't get to tell her about the beautiful greens at Burke Golf Course on Holy Cross Drive.

When she told him "You don't have to stay the whole weekend if you don't want to. It's hard to explain. The world is so much bigger than I ever knew."

*

He walked past Sacred Heart Church, down Corby Drive to the foot path around Saint Mary's Lake. Two lakes, side by side on the Notre Dame campus, one named for Mary, one for Joseph. He walked in the lacy shade of the newly leafing trees and the pines that lined the shore. Will lived in Carroll Hall, the Holy Cross Brothers residence at the west end of the lake. The sky a pale blue. The lake a pea green from the shores to the murky green-blue at the center. Not like the little lakes in Minnesota that shimmer blue through and through.

He looked across the mute calm of the water. Thursday next week would be the last exam of the spring semester and last undergraduate exam of a lifetime. His bonus undergraduate year — Will's goofball name for it made it more bearable — was almost done. After Thursday he could say to anybody, plain and simple, *I'm a grad student.* He wanted to say it to her. How she used to look at him. But when he walked alone down Morris Avenue, out of Bryn Mawr campus last fall, he knew. Everything he was and everything he'd accomplished — none of it was ever going to matter again, not to her, the one he wanted to tell every little discovery to, every little success. He could almost feel the chill wind strike his skin even now. It was the first time he could remember ever feeling like an outsider, like he didn't belong. *Is that what it feels like, Will, when you talk with Mom and Dad? Is that what James feels too?* He looked again to the path opening before him and disappearing under his feet, his gait fast and steady around the curve of the lake.

*

"I told mom about the science of evolution," Henry confided as he sat forward in the leather chair in the Carroll Hall lounge. "I didn't know how she would react, but she listened, like she was willing to consider it. I'm wondering about a lot of things. They say an apple doesn't fall far from the tree, but I'm still falling."

Will, dressed in his black habit and white collar, leaned back and opened a Life magazine to a color photo of hundred-foot royal palms lining a boulevard in Los Angeles. He gave that lusty laugh of his. "The taller the tree, the farther you fall!"

*

Spring 1957

The living room at Eddy Street was the perfect balance of old-fashioned homey and bachelor pad easy-going, probably because Greeley was both — old and bachelor. "Knowing the foundations of your field is so important! Why don't they teach it in your department?" Greeley asked from the comfort of his big leather armchair.

"Some mathematicians don't care about foundations, I guess. And that's valid. They start at a certain established point of theory and say, *Where can we go from here?*

"True enough, true enough."

"I always want to say, *But wait a minute, how did we get here?*" Henry said.

"Precisely! And you know why I keep bringing it up, don't you? It's because *you* keep bringing it up! Whenever we talk, your mind seems to go to the root of things. It's almost an innate need in you. Maybe it really is innate! We don't yet entirely know what the genes do, and what they don't!"

Greeley had touched on the topic occasionally since that first late-night conversation in the fall of 1955: Henry's quest for foundations. Each time

Henry had waved it off with a promise he would talk with his professors. But the Mathematics faculty weren't really interested in talking about it. He had tried to start conversations in that moment after class when most students are herding out the door, and one is waiting nervously to ask for an extension, and a few step up to pose a challenging question. It was graduate school after all, and the professors liked those questions. But his questions elicited oblique responses. *Let's focus on the interchange of limit operations first, shall we!* Or *Maybe you'd like to add a few more to Hilbert's Twenty-Three Questions!*

"My professors say it strays into mathematical logic," he explained. "A specialty, shall we say. And none of the math faculty specialize in it."

"Listen to me, Henry, now it's my turn to get to the bottom of things. If nobody in the mathematics department specializes in logic, then who do you suppose does?"

"I suppose it's more a matter of philosophy."

"Ergo: You have to find a class in the Philosophy Department!"

"No, I didn't mean... Well, I don't know, maybe." His gaze disengaged from the outer world, he focused into an imagined conversation with the chairman of the philosophy department — whoever that might be — until Greeley's voice pulled him back.

"Another round to celebrate our breakthrough!" Greeley raised his empty bottle, three-fingered, then raised his eyebrows in mock candor. "Do you want to serve or shall I?"

*

Henry attended Mass every Sunday at Sacred Heart. And about every other Sunday he entered the confessional booth. *Bless me Father, for I have sinned. It's been two weeks since my last confession...* He respectfully heard the admonishments and penance imposed by the priest, whether delivered in a tone of pastoral care, grave disappointment, or careless boredom. It was the boredom he could hardly stand. Why was the priest taking it less seriously than he was?

*

There was a coolness and a solemn peace in the long dark hallways. Door after door of empty classrooms. Summer, only a few students remained. Mostly grad students. "Hey, where have you been? I've been waiting for you." Henry had barely crossed the threshold into the graduate math study hall and there was Burt, motioning him to hurry, as if they had plans and Henry was late. Burt was a year ahead in the masters program, a head shorter than Henry in height, and was a gushing jet of energy and brains. Burt had fervidly circled Henry for days that first autumn a year and a half ago before finally swooping in and demanding an in-depth discussion of differential equations and what Henry thought of the girls at Saint Mary's College across Highway 31. Henry hadn't paid any attention to him those first days, and it was almost as though Henry's indifference was the very reason Burt insisted on being friends.

"I've got an invitation you can't refuse," Burt announced as Henry joined his study table. "Ready to say yes?"

"I don't know."

"I'm inviting you to a beach party where you're going to meet a beautiful girl. Are you gonna spend all your nights playing poker with the physics guys and gabbing with your one-armed landlord? You a homo?" He punched Henry's shoulder and laughed.

"What would be wrong with that?" *We're all human* — Henry thought to himself. *Logically anyone you name can denote the individual 'human being.' That's the underlying identity. So if anyone is okay, then everyone is okay. Or maybe it was better expressed as a relationship of parts to the whole....*

"You paying attention?" Burt smirked. "What's wrong is, you need a girl. Louise's younger sister is visiting from Syracuse. Ready to say yes? She's pretty and single. Say yes."

"I might go but..."

"Just say yes. Lake Michigan is less than an hour away. How many times have we invited you to Bridgman Beach and every time you've had an excuse? You like your Minnesota lakes right? All ten thousand! Listen, you'll think you're home on the shores of Lake Superior except here you won't catch a summer cold!"

"I've never been to Lake Superior."

Burt slapped his hand to his forehead. "No girl. Never seen the Great Lakes... Saturday, Bridgman Beach!"

*

Theirs were the only voices in the house, the kitchen where they lifted tea cups to their lips was the only lighted room. Burt and his wife Louise had gone to bed. The other guests had gone home hours ago. It was only Henry and Genny, Louise's younger sister.

"I was always the one getting into mischief, even more than my brothers. Now Louise, she was always the goodie two-shoes!"

He echoed, "...the goodie two-shoes."

"Except the day, she must have been eight, when she sneaked a dollar out of Mom's pocketbook and bought a hundred penny mints at the corner store!"

From the winds of Lake Michigan to the winds of childhood. They had spent the day at the beach. Genny was animated, vivacious. But shy and uncertain too. A rush of expressions across her face. Delicate and slender, she must have weighed a mere hundred pounds. She hardly made a splash when she dove into the waves as he waded waist-deep — she said the water soothed her legs, the pain a remnant of a childhood bout with polio. "You're lucky to be walking," he said. She laughed it off — "Luck of the Irish!" — and peered across the sand. "Dunes at a lake, I can't believe it! You'd like the Atlantic shore at Coney Island!"

When the four of them emerged dripping from the surf and sprinted up the sand for a picnic lunch under the sun, she unfurled her colorful towel nonchalantly, strategically, beside Henry's.

He'd been set up, no question about it. And maybe he should be. He had been alone a year and a half now. And as little as he cared about Burt's juvenile taunts, he was starting to feel like some kind of outcast, invisible to the women of the world even while they were perfectly visible to him — the Saint Mary's girls who visited campus, the town girls around South Bend.

Now at the kitchen table this beautiful woman was telling him every detail of her life. "Can you imagine, a hundred mints! Mom marched Louise down to the cellar, opened the door to the furnace, and threw the whole bag into the fire." She tried a faint laugh, a strangled sound in the quiet house. "Louise was sure Hell would be just like that furnace, and I'm sure it is, only worse. I'm scrupulous about confessing my sins. *Back so soon?* the priests all ask. But I am determined to remain pure in God's eyes."

Henry nodded, remembering the day last month when he confessed and listened and stepped out into the filtered red, gold, and green light streaming through the stained glass windows of Sacred Heart Church — and knew it was the last time.

"I wanted to become a nun when I was in grade school. Oh, I shouldn't even tell you, but one weekday my mother gave us girls, Louise, Margaret, and me, a quarter each to buy our Catechism booklets. When we came home Daddy stared us down as we took off our shoes in the hall. *I saw a most interesting sight driving home from the paper tonight, just in the last hour! For Pete's sake it may have been a mere seventeen minutes ago!* He made a big story out of it. *Crossing the bridge I saw three of the purist, most innocent little girls the Heavenly Father ever planted on Earth, skipping along the sidewalk licking ice cream cones!* He went on and on. I was so ashamed. It was my idea to spend the money on ice cream, and he knew it. He always knew."

"We live a lot of our lives in shame, don't we?"

"God forgives, if we confess and are truly sorry." She seemed to steer him away from the path he was starting down. He relented.

"What will you do once you get your degree?"

"I'll be a mathematics professor somewhere, maybe even here. Last year I started leading problem sessions at the university's National Science Foundation Institute for High School Teachers."

"You're teaching high school teachers!" she marveled. "I would have liked to teach some of my teachers a thing or two!"

"You didn't care for their teaching style?"

"I just can't stand sitting at a desk and being told every moment what to do. People aren't robots! And I don't like tests, they make my stomach do turns. Sister Thomasina could see me shaking in my seat. She excused me from class and let me walk along the brook behind school while the other kids were taking the test. I just wished I could tell them all — Stand up, drop your pencils, let's go outside!"

He laughed with her. She made everything seem so light, the scolding from her dad, her acrobatic stomach, and dreams of rebellion on test days. But he also knew why the furnace still burned in her memory. He had lived with that same fear and shame all those innocent childhood years. He saw how she suffered even now under that burden. It made him angry. His decision to stop going to confession had been a simple annoyance at the limited insights of the priests, not an anger like this. He pressed it down, didn't let it show. He just knew she was an innocent, free-spirited young woman who didn't deserve anything less than wonder.

It was four in the morning, just the faintest light through the kitchen window when he said good night, and good morning, and drove home to Eddy Street. And it was almost as though the conversation never stopped, just moved from the kitchen table at Burt and Louise's to his writing desk at Greeley's, letters back and forth from Syracuse to Notre Dame, the time between constrained only by the speed of the Postal Service. Across the weeks and months of handwritten flirtations, adorations, and confessions — she thought he was a real dreamboat — there was more, a revelation.

It had been stirring deep inside, he couldn't say how long, the irresolvable contradiction between free thought and blind faith.

Dad was a free thinker, a self-made man of principle who made his own rules, didn't care what anybody else expected him to do. He believed in a higher power, that was how he said it. But he was the one who decided what that meant for his life.

Mom was a devoted wife who knew what Dad expected of her. And she was a devoted Catholic who never missed a Sunday Mass or a meeting of the *Women's Congregation of Christian Doctrine*. She taught the boys devotion to God through obedience to that doctrine.

Henry was their son, and that was his problem. Everything in him leaned toward free thought. In many ways he made his own rules. He befriended whomever he wished in elementary school, bicycled carefree through the Wallachai neighborhood the other Southsiders feared. In high school he understood, maybe better than his teachers, that number systems were practical man-made inventions, and that what men have made they can unmake and remake. Without that freedom to question and remake, mathematics would be nothing more than the counting numbers.

But Henry was equally inspired by Christ's life of service, a life he was taught was inseparable from the Sacrament of Penance, a doctrine that couldn't be questioned, whether it made sense or not. Even that day he walked away from the confessional booth at Sacred Heart Church, it was Confession he walked away from, not his Catholic faith.

All these years Dad and Mom had been a contradiction he couldn't resolve. Like an integer divided by zero, a problem whose solution is undefined, which means that everyone has agreed not to solve it because solving it would break a relation you really want to maintain — between division and multiplication, between Dad and Mom, between what he felt inside and what he was supposed to feel. Yet somehow, miraculously, Genny was the solution. He might have lived the contradiction forever, suffered through, carried the cross. But he wasn't going to let her carry that cross. It had to stop. A terror swept him. He couldn't let go of everything Mom had taught him. He held his head in his hands, then tucked in his chin, stared into the universe of the wooden desktop, and reached for his pen.

He wrote, as a starting point, the essence of what Mom had taught him:

Premise — We must confess and repent our sins, in order to acquire God's forgiveness, in order to preserve the charity in our hearts.

To preserve charity. In mathematics he always dug down to foundations. What is the problem the formula is supposed to solve? Confession is supposed to solve the preservation of charity. He thought back to Saint Edward's University, how Brother Elmo Bransby instructed the students at the opening of each year: *Charity teaches everything. It shows a man his place, gives him a point of view. It is the key to happiness.*

Amazing. *We must confess,* wasn't the premise at all. It was a method. The fundamental premise was: *We must preserve charity.*

Okay, define charity: *Charity equals our relationship of generosity and compassion toward God and our fellow men.*

If he simplified the terms. *Generosity and compassion toward God and our fellow men equals...love.*

...then he could simply write: *Charity equals love.*

And it came back in a flash, what James told him all those years ago, sitting on Will's bed in New Ulm. *We don't earn God's love. God simply loves us.* Love was the point of everything. That's why Jesus healed the sick, multiplied loaves and fishes to feed the hungry, gave his life for us. And in the Sacrament of Charity we love God by loving others.

Confession was a rule book, boundless rules about what not to do. Love was a purpose, a purpose you could fulfill in infinite ways. He tossed the paper in the air. "Throw away the rulebook!" He sat awe-struck, then promptly gathered himself, tidied up the wild feelings, pursed his lips, and nodded to himself. And burst out laughing, laughed until tears formed. Problem defined and solved. Dad versus Mom, free thought versus doctrine, Genny's intolerable suffering in that bizarre box, the confessional. He was his father's son, his mother's son, and his brothers' brother. A free thinker and a Catholic devoted to the Sacrament of Charity, and his next act of charity was to rescue Genny.

He returned to the path he had started down in the kitchen that night with Genny, the burden of guilt and shame we live under, the assumptions we make that this is eternal and beyond question. *We went to confession as far back as we can remember, didn't we? —* he wrote her *— But my mother told me one day that she never went until the age of twelve, and some started even later. It was only Pope Pius the Tenth who required children of all ages to confess sins. It was a new idea.*

And over the months of letters that followed he offered her a Catholicism rendered in the same freedom and elegance he found in mathematics. Freedom, elegance, charity. A life in mathematics, a life in Christ, and a life with her. Her jet black hair. Her lips, red even when the lipstick washed away in the Great Lake Michigan. Those eyes, my god, Lauren Bacall couldn't match those beautiful eyes, doe-like under delicate brows. And the energy, the outpouring on the pages of her letters. Burt had nothing on him now. Okay, Burt was married. But that wasn't where Henry wanted to be. There was something he had to do first. Become a mathematician.

*

As a late summer rainstorm swirled outside the windows of the classroom in the philosophy building, a big, stooping man with short gray hair and penetrating eyes stood at the black board in black suit and tie. He spoke carefully: "Id is vil nun ded in de zet deery" — Henry, in a chair in the back row, strained to hear English in the thickets of consonants — "de felwing deerim is prwable..." Maybe he shouldn't have registered for this course. When he asked around at the philosophy department, they told him Boleslaw Sobocinski was the man to learn from. They said mathematical logic was his specialty. And they said he was Polish and had an accent, but... Henry surveyed the profiled faces seated ahead to his right and left. He saw snickering glances, boredom, disbelief, terror. And a few faces set in concentration, determined to penetrate the thicket and find what was inside — he was going to be one of them. He focused on Sobocinski. "Eed is indrissing do nud en enelgs foormla foor de mooldipligazion..." Henry gulped nervously, and then something wonderful happened. Something that had to happen. He could have predicted it and saved himself the past ten minutes of terror. Sobocinski faced the blackboard and chalk dust rained down as he wrote swiftly and effortlessly in the formal language of mathematical logic, formulas written and read the same way everywhere, in every country on the globe. Henry bent to his notebook, quick glances to the board, and dulled his graphite pencil to the strokes and curves and dots of the professor's chalk work.

*

In the candlelight of Rocco's Italian Restaurant, Henry looked into Genny's eyes and let it out, let her know how he felt: "I'm very happy to see you again."

"I'm happy to see you too."

He smiled and looked down at the red-and-white check tablecloth. It was easy to say what he wanted on paper. His letters had become more expressive as July warmed into August, more poetic as September matured into October. And now, Thanksgiving weekend, here she was across the table for two, close enough to touch. In fact he'd noticed her left hand resting open on the table between them.

"Your letters have been wonderful," she said. "I feel like we know each other as if there were no distance between us."

"I agree."

"And you're almost done with your classes now, you said."

"My Masters coursework, yes. I'll finish in May. Then comes the hard work, the doctoral seminars and my dissertation."

"And you'll be a professor. Starting a career, and I'm sure, a family of your own."

"Yes," he stumbled.

*

Henry trudged across the quad under a swirling snow. Lake-effect was what they called it here. In New Ulm it would have been just any old December snow. He stumbled over an icy ridge as he stepped onto the plowed sidewalk. As he steadied himself, hands outstretched, the ring on his finger flashed before him like a foreign object. He found his footing. Learned to interpret Sobocinski's spoken English almost as well as his chalkboard logic, and completed his final Master's courses in Topology and Complex Analysis in the spring. Started his doctoral dissertation in the fall. And right in the middle of it all, that ring had slipped onto his finger.

It happened that November evening a year ago at Rocco's. No, she didn't force him to ask her. Not directly. She was simply farther along than he was. She pressed him discreetly about his plans and watched him expectantly and the waiter served the lasagna and...they were engaged. Mom was so pleased, so proud he was starting a life of his own even though she said it made her cry.

Genny was a princess in her flowing white gown that August morning in 1958. He watched her father walk her up the aisle under the vaulted ceiling, summer's early morning light filtering down in a shower of red, gold, and green, Sacred Heart Church, where he still went to Mass every Sunday. He actually did go to confession one more time. She insisted they partake of the Sacrament of Penance before their wedding day. The last time for him, and very nearly the last for her.

They lived in surplus World War Two army barracks erected on the edge of campus a decade ago. Vetville was married student housing. Two bedrooms, a gas heater in the living room, a Ringer clothes washer in the kitchen, and a clothesline outdoors for drying in all seasons. A home of their own — all their own. "Those curtains have to go!" Genny declared. The ones Mom had sewn for his freshman year at Saint Edwards.

And a baby all their own. There had been no girls but Mom in the Crossland household in New Ulm. But Henry's first was a daughter. Margaret. Her eyes bluer by the week as a smile burst into being. Her happiness could hardly be contained, happiness at everything. Did she even see you amidst the wonder of it all? He didn't know much about babies. He voiced his opinion about the timing of naps only once and then decided he had better leave matters to Genny. The household was her job, mathematics was his.

*

His doctoral thesis, "Contributions to Mereology," was published. It started from Sobocinski's proofs of several key theorems. The proofs were valid but complicated, and were proven under a very strong hypothesis. You could say Sobocinski used too much firepower, slogged indomitably through procedural steps to victory. Henry weakened the hypothesis but still proved the theorems. And he proved them in fewer steps. Truth and elegance. And that made a doctoral thesis. By the time Luke was born, Henry was an assistant professor at Notre Dame and the world was publishing him. The *Journal of Formal Logic* and *Journal of Symbolic Logic* in the U.S., *Fundamentica Mathematica* in Poland, *Methodus* in Italy, *Logique et Analyse* in Belgium.

"So you're famous," Genny said.

He smiled, paused because he didn't want to contradict her. "Famous with some mathematicians and logicians."

*

Baby Luke. What a rage, what did he want! Genny plugged the screaming mouth with a pacifier — *doesn't it soothe and calm?* — and the tiny bundle spat it projectile across the room in their new off-campus home on White Oak Drive. As soon as his arms and legs would obey him he struggled to be free of her embrace, better roll and crawl than be restrained by arms and hands not his own. And on his own, he grasped at the world, bent it this way and that, and lived in the world he made.

Everyone was moving on. Burt and Louise were raising their kids in Pittsburgh, Burt on the math faculty at Carnegie Melon University. Will was in Palo Alto, California, teaching English at a Holy Cross Brothers high school under the palms and eucalyptus trees. He wrote to Henry about great flocks of heron flying over the Bay, bars and restaurants in San Francisco, surfing at Santa Cruz. *And I don't even want to talk about the surfer girls! Lead me not into temptation!* Will, same as ever.

And on a muggy August day in 1962, there in Genny's arms was James. A mop of black hair. His eyes fixed on everyone in turn, on Genny, on Henry, on little Margaret, and baby Luke. How he looked at you! Quiet and probing. He watched everything, watched and listened to the world around him as if he was trying to decide what he should do about it.

Christmas on White Oak Drive, Henry unwrapped a box from Dad and Mom, his globe. *Now you have your own children to share this with.* He set his fingers onto the Pacific Ocean and turned — not his Dad's vigorous spin, but a thoughtful turn like Mom darning a sock, like Genny browsing fabric for new curtains. Quietly, under his breath. "There's Perth."

Secret

Saint Paul, Minnesota, December 1969

I n the sweet warm water, rocking, flipping somersaults. Dim light, shifting. Her voice, rumbling through the water. Rush, into the dry air. Water again. Cold water. Strange voices. Where... is... her voice?

*

Bloomington, Minnesota, September 1976

Catherine's attention strayed from the teacher to the window. Out there, yellow tinged leaves rustled, like the newspaper pompoms she made with Mister Rogers. The sun never quite as high in the sky as it was in North Carolina. They were back in the north now. She was born here in Minnesota, Mom said, but babies don't remember. And she didn't. It was all new. The other first graders wiggled at their desks, the teacher's voice steady like the September wind. She tried to pay attention but wanted to be outside, tennis shoes on the curving blacktop path home, tossing a pebble from the wooden railing over Nine Mile Creek, fish mouths opening at the water's surface, when a single word brought her back.

"Adoption. We're going to be talking about it today. Does anyone know what adoption means?" Catherine straightened at her desk. Eyes dark as droplets of India ink, waves of deep brunette brushed her shoulders, held to the side by her favorite yellow flowered barrette. Even though she knew very well everything that word meant, she didn't raise her hand, didn't want the other kids to know that the teacher was talking about her.

She had always known she was adopted, and that it made her different. She wasn't born to her mom and dad like other kids were. And even though she had another mom and dad somewhere out in the great big world, Paul and Heidi were her parents.

"...so the adoptive parents go to pick out the baby," the teacher continued. "Adopted children are special, because out of all of the other babies, your parents chose you." Catherine beamed. She had never thought of it that way, that she was chosen.

Instead of her usual stroll home, she ran. Couldn't wait to ask Mom. Ran over the creek and around the foot of the big sledding hill. Up to the crest, her leg muscles burned beneath rust-colored corduroys until she jogged down the other side and home. She swung open the door, breathless. "Mom, mom!"

"What is it?" Mom asked from the second floor landing, a stack of folded hand towels cradled in her arms. Lucie raced down the stairs and circled Catherine's legs, purring.

"Today Miss Smith talked to us about adoption."

"Oh?" Mom's voice lifted cautiously as she reached the lower landing. Her eyes were lakes of pale blue. Her blonde hair was neatly combed straight and tucked behind her ears, except for one strand that hung out of place.

Catherine's eyes were lit with wonder. "What was it about me? Why did you choose me instead of the other babies?"

"Well" — Mom's eyes looked a little unsure — "You were the only one there!"

*

Behind the white house with black shutters in Minnesota, all the backyards met in a big grassy field that Catherine wanted to run through, but she was never sure where the line was between her yard and the neighbor's, or if she was allowed to cross it. She ran around to the front. "I'm going to Freddy's house!" She hardly heard Mom's voice behind her — "Catherine!" — as she darted down the blacktop driveway to the grass along the curb, because it's not safe to be in the street. Lawn, concrete, lawn, blacktop, lawn again. She rang the doorbell, panting. Freddy appeared, his pudgy face checkered through the screen door. "Before you can come in, say purple!" Each time it was a different word, always with an R. Back in North Carolina, she sounded just like everyone else, and it was Mom and Dad who sounded different.

"Puhple."

Freddy laughed with delight. "C'mon in, let's play Duck, Duck, Gray Duck!"

*

Home used to be, until the summer before her seventh birthday, the red brick house on the edge of the woods in Durham, where Mom ironed Dad's shirts while watching TV and where Dad drove every morning to Duke University. Dad said he was doing his post-doc, and Catherine imagined his blond head shining brightly in the sun as he sat on a dock with a big post at the end of it, but she wondered what he did out there all day.

Each night when Dad came home, Mom called from the kitchen "Hi Paul!" and he called back "Hello Heidi" and set his briefcase on the laundry room floor, which was a long way down because he was so tall.

"Hello Catherine!"

"Hello Paul!" she answered as she spun the little golden numbers on the briefcase's lock.

*

Sometimes she went with Dad to Duke Gardens, where they walked under giant trees called magnolia. The white flowers smelled lemony and were as big as the palm of your hand. In autumn she plucked shiny red seeds from its scattered cones and wrinkled her nose at the smell. Dressed in mint terry cloth, she stepped up to the concrete ledge circling the goldfish pond. Heal to toe, she was on a tightrope around the little pond you could almost jump across. But Dad's blue eyes looked serious behind his horn-rimmed glasses. "I don't believe that's what the ledges are intended for!"

Mostly Catherine's world was in the woods behind the house, climbing trees, jumping over roots and fallen branches, spotting baby trees just a foot tall that she imagined were a forest to the bugs. Bees buzzed in and out of the white and yellow flowers of the honeysuckle. She pinched and pulled the sweet center from the flower and touched it gently to her tongue, then blinked into the sun at the pine trees towering above her. They swayed together in the wind, tall bare trunks with bunches of needles at the top. Sometimes she had itchy bumps on her arms and legs. *It's poison oak,* Mom said, lathering her in calamine lotion. As soon as the lotion dried she was back in the woods, her tanned face flitting from determination to wonder and back.

The other girls played indoors — Barbie dolls, tea parties — but she ran wild outdoors with the neighborhood boys. Playing tag, racing around the tree trunk until someone called, Ollie, Ollie in come free! The boys were as wild as the rabbits and squirrels. They even peed outdoors without a care in the world. One time she tried it herself, shorts down to her ankles, squatting in the back yard, and Mom caught her through the kitchen window. "Catherine! You get in here right now!" She yanked her shorts up but wondered, if the boys could and the animals could, why couldn't she?

*

Outer Banks, North Carolina, June 1975

Catherine ran to catch the foamy surf as it rolled up the sand, then spun around in the rough grains to watch her footprints wash away until you couldn't even tell she'd been there. Her skin was already browned from summer sun, a splash of freckles across her nose.

Grandpa tromped over the sand in yellow shirt sleeves and tan pants rolled above his knees, and Grandma wobbled along in a red and pink checkered blouse and slacks — their usual everyday clothes, nothing different for their visit from Saint Paul, Minnesota to the Carolina shore.

Mom called over the wind, "I don't know how you can enjoy your first visit to the ocean dressed in that."

Catherine dug her toe into the sand and peeked down at her red-white-and-blue top of X's and O's that she liked so much, especially with the Cracker Jack sticker she pressed on like a badge. She looked to Mom as they caught up and passed her, and Mom said, "Keep up now Catherine. You know our usual spot, we're almost there."

Summer had just begun and there were hardly any people. She stopped where she was and watched the bathers wading out into the water. With hunched shoulders, they lifted their arms like birds ready to fly as the cold waves rose up their bodies. She let her eyes follow a wave, squinted as it crashed on the beach, spray and swoosh, and watched little shells tumble back to sea. She chased one, held it up to the sun, a pretty pink you could almost see through. A tiny clam was sealed safe inside. She threw it back into the waves where it wanted to be.

It was then that he caught her eye. A grandpa maybe, a grownup a little older than her dad. She knew she wasn't supposed to stare, but she watched him as he stood there, his one leg crossed over the other, hand on his hip. He looked down to the sand and then out to the water for a long time, like maybe he lost something. She wondered if she could find it. Foamy water swishing around her toes, she looked out as far as she could see and there was only more water, more waves rolling in from far away. She waded in, hunching her shoulders like the others, and the water pulled at her ankles, and pushed, and pulled at her knees. She wanted to go farther. The waves were big. "Catherine!" Mom sounded mad, and she turned and just then a wave knocked her rolling, water up her nose, salt in her mouth. She stood and ran up the sand, her skin tightening in a frosting of salt, and she peeked back at the sea just one more time.

*

Fall leaves rustling in the wind, the bell chiming at the gift shop door, the brush of pant legs, Mom's keys jingle-jangling from the brass ring on her wrist, strangers' voices inside the shop. She followed Mom past a rack of postcards, a shelf of ceramic mugs, and a lighted case where Catherine saw something beautiful. She peered in on tiptoes at the shiny crystal figurines. Each one had so many little sides, reflecting blue, green, and gold like lights on a Christmas tree. The tiny crystal ballerina dancing pirouettes, the colors beaming. The tiny crystal bird taking flight. A beautiful dream suddenly broken by an awful silence. Something missing, the jingle-jangle of Mom's keys. A jolt of fear. Only a moment had passed. She ran from the lighted case down the aisle, no one. Down another, a strange man looked up from a bottle filled with colored layers of sand. Down another aisle, her heart pounding. She couldn't breathe, couldn't cry out the word, it was buried in her throat, *Mom!* She was being pulled away, into a giant dark hole, inside herself. Until a voice, a voice somewhere said. "Are you lost?" Her eyes blinked into the light and she saw a plastic name tag on a woman's blouse. She got the words out. "I think my mom left me."

"Oh, don't worry sweetie, your mom must be here somewhere."

The shop door chimed, Mom's keys jangling. Catherine was embarrassed by her mistake, but so relieved to see Mom again.

"What is it Catherine?" Mom looked concerned.

Her voice shook. "I thought, you were gone."

"I was just next door for a minute. Didn't you hear me tell you before I went?"

She didn't hear. But it didn't matter. Mom was there.

*

Summer of 1976 when they first moved to Minnesota, it didn't feel like such a different place. She still jumped out of bed every morning knowing, from the moment her eyes opened, all the things she wanted to do. Climb and jump and hunt for colored mushrooms and baby trees and flowers and bugs and bees. Search the grass for four leaf clover, then turn to the sky to spy shapes in the clouds. What was different was the fall into winter, so quick and so deep in the north. Halloween morning she woke to see frost sparkling white on the lawn. By Thanksgiving everything was covered in snow — lawns, treetops, rooftops — and by her seventh birthday the December air was so cold that her nose burned and her wet hair froze stiff like icicles.

Christmas Eve, before midnight mass at Saint Matthews, it was cookies and presents at Grandma and Grandpa's house in Saint Paul where the tree in the living room cast a glow of colored lights on the gifts below. She peered through the tiny stained glass windows to each side of the fireplace and watched the snowflakes swirl in the streetlight. She ran to the kitchen window. Mounds of snow, more snow than she had ever seen before. Her eye followed a flake as it floated down and took its place among the others, it sparkled like a diamond.

*

Every evening the pressure cooker rattled and it was meat and potatoes and canned corn and the grapefruit that Mom called salad. Catherine's eyes fixed on the cooker as it shook and hissed, steam billowing from the coin-like medallion that crowned the lid. It probably dreamed of cooking a rainbow of vegetables, the ones Catherine saw in the grocery aisles, but didn't even know their names. She was sure one day it would explode and spray hot potatoes across the kitchen. But it didn't. It cooked them again every night like it was supposed to. Finally the rattling was done, and they took their places around the dinner table.

"Well, Heidi, we're nicely settled in I'd say." Dad spread his napkin on his lap.

"Honestly, Paul, I'm glad to be home in Minnesota again. Catherine, this is where we got you. Well, in Saint Paul anyway."

Catherine imagined herself on display, a lone manikin in a store window, the only one there. She pushed aside the pork chop and scooped a forkful of mashed potatoes.

"And Dad's starting the new year with a new job. Paul, what is it called again?"

"Sorensen, Conti, and Sullivan. They're really on the cutting edge of medical law..." Dad cleared his throat. "The bioethics committee meeting was very lively today."

"I don't know how you figure out those complicated questions."

Dad leaned back in his chair. "To understand if it's ethical, you need to understand the level of risk involved, and that's where you get into the interesting part, the medicine."

"Don't tell me you're thinking of medical school after all those years seeing you through law school."

"Dad?" Catherine interrupted, "Can you cut my pork chop?" Dad's thick fingers with big knuckles delicately carved the pork into petite squares smaller than a dime. She swallowed a square. It was the only way she could stand to eat it. "Mom, may I have more potatoes please?"

"Finish your meat first and don't even think about feeding it to the cat."

"The meat crackles when I chew it." She nervously pushed her tongue into the space of her missing tooth, and Lucie's tail curled around her ankle.

*

Mom was staring at her paper list. She always stopped inside the shopping mall's big entrance and stared a while before she was ready. Catherine waited, undid and redid her barrette, and eyed the shiny earrings under the spotlights in the jewelry store window. She peeked in the doorway, slipped inside, climbed onto a stool, legs dangling, and waited for the woman who helps the customers.

"Are you getting earrings sweetie? Is your mom here?"

"She's coming." Catherine swung her legs back and forth and scanned the black felt display card for her favorite pair. Mom rushed in, "Catherine, hold on!" Catherine held on to the stool. Whew! She felt the swish of cold over her earlobe and smelled the funny smell before the poke. Mom shooed her out the door when it was done. "For goodness sake, Catherine, where did you ever come up with that idea?"

Catherine twisted the stud in her ear, "I wanted earrings like you!"

*

The mechanical hum of the garage door rising, the clink of the laundry room door handle, the thud of Dad's briefcase on the linoleum floor, Mom's voice from the kitchen — "Hi Paul" — Dad's footsteps climbing the stairs. All unseen, all behind the wall as Catherine sat at the family room coffee table where she dabbed glue to the blue felt eye and stuck it to the sock. Today their project was a sock-puppet dragon. Mister Rogers was her first best friend.

Each day he showed her what supplies she would need and gave her a few minutes to race to the kitchen and her bedroom and back to the coffee table where she followed Mr. Rogers through each step. "Now," he said in his gentle voice, his accent like hers, though hers was changing after almost a year in Minnesota. "Put another dab of glue on the dragon's other eye."

She heard Dad's footsteps on the stairs and his smart blue eyes peered around the pocket door, "Hello Catherine." He always changed into corduroy pants and a sweater when he got home from work, just like Mr. Rogers, except Dad's projects were tightening the hinges on the cupboard door and mowing the lawn on Saturdays. "Hi Dad."

Mom and Dad's voices were a mumble in the kitchen. The pressure cooker hissed and rattled and she could picture the steam bellowing. Mom's voice got louder. "I'm not sure I'm giving her what she needs. I'm not even sure I know what she needs." Catherine rose from the coffee table, sock dragon on her hand, and peeked around the doorway into the kitchen. "They told us when we raise her from an infant...I don't know. Why isn't she more like us?"

"She does march to a different drummer," Dad said. "We're giving her a good home. I suppose it's just in the genes."

Catherine glanced down at her jeans and ran back to the coffee table. Mister Rogers sat on his bench, his dark blue sneaker with white laces in his hand, and he said that all real animals have histories and that he likes to think about those kinds of things. And he sang his Good Feeling song.

*

"We're going to Grandma and Grandpa's," Mom said. "Bring something along to keep yourself busy." Catherine found her paper and colored pencils.

Sprawled on her tummy on the wooden floor in Grandma's kitchen, her eyes angled to the paper inches away, her mind deep inside the world she was drawing onto the page. It was a book. She'd made a picture book all her own. Little creatures in the woods, mushroom houses with tiny doors and windows. Atop the stem she drew a plump mushroom roof, colored it red, leaving empty white circles for polka dots.

"Here Catherine." Grandma set a bottle and a plastic wand on the kitchen table. Bubbles. Out in the yard Catherine blew through the wand and watched the bubbles drift in the breeze. One tiny bubble floated up and up. She kept her eyes on it as it rose, and for a second it was lost against the sky until she spotted it even higher, when the bottle was ripped from her hand.

"My turn!" Teddy howled. He was the boy down the street, the same age as Catherine. He always wanted to play when she visited. But he didn't seem to know how to play nicely.

"I'm not finished," Catherine said holding the bubble wand behind her back.

Teddy grabbed at her, then dug his dirty nails into the top of her hand, leaving a line of bloody cuts. She wanted to run after him, almost did until she saw in the corner of her eye the pink barrette dangling from her hair. She plucked it out, popped it open with her teeth, stuck it in at her temple and smacked it closed, all with one hand. She stomped inside and showed Mom what he had done.

"What happened?" Mom asked.

"It was Teddy, he dug his nails into me."

Mom's face wrinkled. "Go wash your hands. You should know girls play with girls."

Catherine swished her hands under the bathroom faucet, winced as she soaped them. Stared at the cuts she got from playing with a boy. Maybe she should play with the girls instead. She liked Barbie's clothing, how the pieces of cloth were sewn together, even if her naked body was strangely odd with its plastic bumps. But she really just wanted to be outside.

*

Every summer they packed the car for the long ride to Grandma Lind in New Salem, North Dakota. Mom and Dad stayed with Grandma at her apartment, and Catherine at Aunt Lillie's across the lawn, and, well nobody stayed at

Aunt Ulla's. Catherine and Aunt Lillie stayed up late playing cards at the kitchen table — very grown up. When heavy eyes and yawns finally overcame her, Catherine pulled the covers to her chin on the pull-out davenport in the living room, and in the morning she waked to the sweet smell of donuts frying. Aunt Lillie knew how to cook. And how to knit. In the afternoons Aunt Lillie taught her how to push one needle through the loop on the other. Catherine passed the yarn over her needle as Aunt Lillie smiled and nodded. She imagined her birth mother would be like that. If she ever got to meet her. There was so much she wanted to know. She was going to ask Mom someday. She just wasn't sure how.

On the second day Dad said, *Let's go say hello to Aunt Ulla!* That was when Catherine and Mom glanced at each other, and for that moment, she knew that she and Mom were thinking exactly the same thing. Even for all the family hospitality, there was something intimidating about the Lind's. Catherine timidly followed Dad to the apartment at the end of the long hallway. Aunt Ulla stood at the old iron stove, her wild gray curls bursting from the top of her headscarf, bright blue eyelids and red lipstick, her stump leg wrapped in towels where a foot should be, while steam billowed from the boiling potatoes over blue flames, and smoke streamed from the glowing red cigarette that dangled from her lips.

Even Aunt Lillie was a force to be reckoned with Dad said. Back when she and her husband owned the restaurant, a man walked in with a gun to rob the place. She grabbed him by the ear and threw him out. *You ought to be ashamed!* she said and slammed the door. Dad was the gentle one, though he wouldn't be in law, Mom said, if he didn't have that piece of Lind in him.

*

Fifth grade gym class, it was a race the length of the pool and back. At the end of the first length she flipped and pushed off the wall, held her breath as her arms sliced and legs fluttered, her body smooth like an Outer Banks pelican riding a wave. She grasped the wall and popped up, chlorine stinging her eyes. A second later Dennis Manning popped up beside her, looked at her stunned. She couldn't believe it, she beat a boy. And not just any boy, but the most athletic boy in her grade. She looked away to hide the hint of a smile.

Bloomington Athletic Association after school she corralled the puck with her stick and raced down the polished gym floor, pigtails flying. Floor hockey. She heard the center from the other team call out, "The Indian girl! Stop the Indian girl!" They raced alongside her, closing in. There was Patti by the goal. Catherine shunted it. Patti whacked it. *Goal!*

Back home she peered into the bathroom mirror at her dark eyes, her dark hair parted in the middle, gathered into pigtails. Her skin still golden brown from the summer past while the other girls' skin was a white made of pinks and blues. Maybe that's who she was. Maybe she was Indian.

*

By sixth grade she and Patti had been best friends for almost two years. They invented their own secret code, an alphabet of symbols. Catherine could write it almost as quickly as regular words and pass a note to Patti that the teachers couldn't decipher. Summer days they swan dived into Patti's backyard pool, raced laps end to end. And when they should have been sleeping, they talked into the night on their walkie talkies, Patti's house just one door down. On the way home from school, they tightrope walked atop the mounded snow that lined the boulevard after the plows came through, slid down to the driveway — "Scoop up some snow for slushies!" — and rushed for the door as the icy wind whipped.

Inside Patti's it was Captain Crunch, homemade snow slushies with Kool-Aid, Casey Kasem's Top 40 on the radio, the two of them singing and swooning. "We're going to be teens next year!" Patti struck a pose.

"Is that what teens look like?"

"It's exactly what my older sister looks like."

"It's just an age, you know. You turn from twelve to thirteen."

"It's a feeling too. The feeling boys are looking at me."

Catherine turned red, not even knowing why, and they burst into giggles.

"Come to the den!" Patti changed the subject, kind of. "Let's get style tips from my mom's magazines!"

Patti's dad, just home from work, was relaxing in his living room chair with a beer and a game on the TV. Catherine quietly studied the dimple on his chin from the sofa in the den where Patti flipped noisily through magazine pages. It was the same dimple on Patti's chin and on her little brother's chin. And Patti's older sister had the same lift at the tip of her nose that her mom had. Maybe Patti had a little lift too. They were all related by blood. What would that be like?

"Oh my god" — Patti looked up from the magazine — "My mom says we have to go to the Westergaard's for dinner Friday. I hate being out with company. You feel like there are all these rules to follow, like you can never just be yourself."

Catherine raised her shoulders. "I think I always feel that way."

Patti scrunched up her face and laughed. "You're just weird Catherine, maybe that's why I like you!"

*

Catherine lay with covers up to her chin, surrounded by her animals. Her big brown Teddy Bear, her white Seal with black eyes, and her favorite, Kitty, with the pink felt dress and the bell inside the end of her tail. She heard Mom's footsteps in the hall. "Mom, will you come in and say goodnight?"

Mom appeared in the doorway. "Goodnight then, dear."

"Can we talk a little?"

Mom plopped on the edge of her bed. "Okay, and then it's time to sleep."

"I was noticing at Patti's that she and her dad both have the same dimples on their chins. Does it matter that I don't look like you or Dad?"

"Well, you don't look like us because you're adopted. Why would that matter?"

"I was just wondering if, if maybe it means we don't love each other the same as people who look like each other."

"Of course we do, dear. We love each other the same as anyone else." Mom kissed Catherine's forehead and stood from her bedside, "Good night, Catherine. Don't let the bedbugs bite."

The door closed. In the darkness, the familiar dread crept in. Why did it always feel like this at night? So final, so lonely. She pulled her knees tight to her chest, wanted her heart to stop pounding. Lucie leapt from the floor and curled up on her ribs, her nose almost touching Catherine's, her purr rumbling. She petted Lucie and kissed the top of her head. "Do you remember when I found you in a box at the door of Southtown Shopping Mall? Thank goodness I found you." Eyes closed in the darkness, she felt the warm rumble of Lucie's purr and drifted into sleep.

Catherine woke to the winter sun, a pale gold through her bedroom windows. Downstairs Mom was writing in her appointment book at the kitchen table.

"Mom?"

"Yes dear."

"Do you have any information about my birth mother?" There, she said it. She had wondered forever but didn't want to hurt Mom's feelings.

Mom raised her brows, hesitated, then set her pen squarely on the notepad. "I do. I have a document from Catholic Services. I'm not sure where. Maybe in my dresser."

Catherine followed into the bedroom where Mom pulled an envelope from the back of the bottom drawer. And from the envelope she pulled a sheet of paper. "This is it." Catherine opened her hand, grasped the page, peered into Mom's eyes — "I'll leave you to read it," Mom said — and alone in the room she settled cross-legged on the oriental rug and peered for the first time into the world of her birth mother.

> *Birth Information for Catherine*
>
> *You were born at 4:25 a.m. on December 5, 1969 at Saint Joseph's Hospital in Saint Paul, Minnesota. Your birth mother named you Michelle Louise. You had black hair, blue eyes, and a medium complexion. You were described as a "very alert, attractive child, seems to be a little colicky." Your birth mother signed consents to the termination of her parental rights, and you were released from the hospital to a foster home on December 8, 1969. On that day you weighed 7 pounds and 8 ounces. On January 23, 1970 you were placed in the adoptive home of Paul and Heidi Lind. Your adoption was finalized on July 9, 1970 and your legal name became Catherine Anne Lind.*

It had always been, *you were adopted...when we adopted you...*like her life started then. But here it was, in an official paper: *You were born...you were Michelle Louise.* Already, before adoption, she was somebody, with a mother. She read on —

Your birth mother was born in 1948 in Ohio. She was adopted and knew nothing of her genetic background, including her nationality. She was 5' 6" tall, weighed 145 pounds, and had a medium build. She had dark brown hair, brown eyes, and a light complexion... She was in good health and expressed concern about your well being. She was a college student at the time of your birth... outgoing and bubbly, above average intelligence, talented in all areas of art.

Your birth father was not identified.

Her birth mother was adopted, knew nothing of where she came from, just like Catherine. Her birth mother, out there somewhere, was concerned about her.

Building Blocks

Accra, Ghana, West Africa 1971

T he cabin lights flickered on, lighting the overhead compartments and the seatbacks in upright position. White and black heads turning, eyes tired and blinking as the metal seatbelts clinked open. The oval windows were dark except for a few lights glaring outside.

James' blue eyes were steadfast on Mom for instructions, when to stand and what to carry, but Mom was busy making Luke wait, he wanted to jump into the aisle, and waking Kelly, she was only five, and instructing Margaret, who was the biggest and helped out with things. Dad, who already asked the stewardess to get Mom's crutches from the back, watched Mom too and glanced back and forth down the aisle to know when was just the right time to pull the big suitcases down from the bins.

James' ninth birthday was two weeks ago, August fifth, right in the middle of everybody choosing what to pack and what to leave home at White Oak Drive in South Bend. President Nixon was going to China, and the astronauts were riding around the Moon in a rover, and as for Ghana, how do you decide what you need for a whole year! *Will we need this in Africa?* Dad said, *We won't be able to carry it all.* And Mom said, *I don't think we can buy it there, we'll have to bring it!*

They bumbled heavily down the narrow aisle — even Mom carried bags because she knew how to load all kinds of things on her crutches — and at the open cabin door the thick wet heat of night swallowed them and they steadied themselves down the metal stairway to the tarmac, and the voices and languages and smells and bodies and clothes were a different world, and that was all he knew of it because at night, random lights in the darkness, you have no idea what place you've come to.

*

He opened his eyes to bright sun through slatted glass windows, big fan blades circling slowly overhead, his pillow damp with sweat. Mom and Dad and the other kids were sitting up, looking around, and there was a knocking on the bedroom door of the rest house where they had stayed the night.

"Doctah Crossland! Da breakfast is ready, and I take you in da van to university!" Dad's new job, a Fulbright grant and one year's leave from Notre Dame to teach at Cape Coast College. He would be one of the few non-African professors there.

They filed into the dining room through one door and a column of ants filed in through the other. Ants and sun and heat and birdsong — the whole outside was inside, and Mom said in her emergency voice, "Oh my God, Henry this place is infested!"

"Cool!" Luke shouted. "Look at them all!"

"It's okay, love," Dad began.

"This is outrageous," Mom said, and Margaret joined in, "Atrocious! But it is somewhat interesting."

"Is this our house now?" Kelly asked, looking up at Mom with tired dark circles under her big eyes.

*

The van rattled down the middle of the highway to miss the worst holes, then jolted along the side when a big truck raced toward them, and back to the middle again. Dad was in front with the driver whose hair was short like Dad's — everyone had short hair here, no afros — and his skin was as black as black construction paper. Dad's bald top was like a lightbulb next to him. James leaned his head of black curls against Mom, too hot, then leaned back against the cooler vinyl of the back seat with Luke and Margaret and Kelly. He watched the green rush by, so many leaves on so many trees, sometimes a few wood or concrete shacks with tin or palms laid on top for a roof, a broken down truck with five men crowding under the hood, and farther on people walking in the orange dirt by the road even though it didn't look like there was any place to walk to. A man in a long red T-shirt that came way down over the top of his dark pants, a couple of ladies in colorful dresses to their ankles, four more men in long T-shirts — let's see, green, red, white, yellow — and another lady... He looked up at Mom and raised his voice just above the engine's grind, "What's that big thing on her head? It's as big as she is!"

"Dat a way you carry da heavy ting!" the driver called back to them. "You no have a car, you still gotta carry da heavy ting!"

James shrank into Mom, he was talking to her, nobody else.

"That's what I call using your head!" Dad said, smiling. Oh, no. James watched for the reaction. Sometimes people didn't like the things Dad said. But the driver bellowed, "Ahaha! Use your head, dat's right!" Like Dad understood and knew exactly what the lady was doing.

Dad nodded. Not the worried Dad of White Oak Drive who rushed to get everyone to school before work while chewing those mint things for his stomach. But a Dad who made people laugh. James smiled and closed his eyes and let his head bounce on Mom's shoulder, never mind the heat.

It seemed hours later that the van stopped in front of a concrete-block house on a gentle sloping hill, white concrete stained yellow-brown by the weather. This was their house now. Up the hill behind were palm trees like the ones in Grandma and Grandpa Crossland's yard in Sun City, Arizona. Up a scrubby hill to the left was another stained concrete house. To the right, a side yard with a garden and a big leafy tree gave way to jungle. And in the front yard by the door was a small tree with long things like string beans hanging from it. The palms were the only trees he recognized. No white oaks here.

The house's roof slanted up from both sides toward the middle, but in the middle the roof gave way to open air and the solid front wall gave way to open concrete blocks that let the breeze through — and framed by those blocks was the front door, just opening.

"Welcome, welcome!" A tall man in tan shorts and a fancy shirt, colorful patterns, curly-cue embroidery around the collar, motioned them to come in. A black man, but there's no point saying it because everyone was black now. He had big bright eyes and a wide mouth, wider when he smiled, and his hair was a small American-style afro, not short like everyone else's.

"De steward take care of you now," the driver explained and shot a spray of words across the yard, and the steward nodded, singing, "Thank you, okay, thank you!" in a way that said, *No more instructions please, I'll take it from here.*

*

James woke in the room with slatted windows on opposite walls. The jungle they called *the brush* out these windows and the concrete courtyard out those. He felt sick from the long trip. South Bend to New York — *That's the new World Trade Center, there just below the wing,* Dad had said as they approached JFK while James peered down the aisle at the stewardesses in their landing seats, the gentle eyes, the curls of hair, knees under skirts, remembered the scent of their breath, different from Mom, as they had leaned in with airplane dinners. New York to London to Rome to Accra and the rest house and this house. He was so tired that first night, but he couldn't sleep because the night noise never stopped — crickets was all he could think but ten times louder, all kinds of chirps and buzzes and rustles. And something else, later into the night. A deep pounding rush, over and over, that he felt more than heard, the last thing he remembered before waking.

Groggy he opened one door adjusting his eyeglasses, it must be the girls' room, then the other, a short hallway past the bathroom to Mom and Dad's room, and then Mom called from the courtyard, "James, we're all in the dining room for breakfast!"

He only now grasped the odd fact that to get to the dining room he would have to go outdoors. Half the house was the three bedrooms and bathroom, with a door from Mom and Dad's room to the open-air courtyard. The other half, across the courtyard, was the kitchen and a large living room with a dinner table at one end.

"What if it's raining!" he guffawed as he sat, roused from his usual timid quiet.

"Then you carry an umbrella to breakfast!" Dad answered.

"Did anybody else hear the sound last night?" James asked, as Margaret motioned to Ignatius the steward, "Might I please have just a tad more jam?"

"The crickets kept me up all night!" Mom said. A tone of moral disapproval, if that could even apply to bugs.

"I think I heard the ocean," James said.

"I heard it too," Dad said. "The Atlantic is only a mile away."

*

Every morning was Saturday. There was no school. He could still hardly believe it. Mom said he needed the break, and she and Dad needed the break from the morning struggles back home. So they brought books from home and got more in Accra. *The kids can read and teach themselves,* Mom said. His favorite was a big science book from London called *Fascinating Facts.* If you stared at the row of red birds on page nineteen and then closed your eyes, you saw a row of green birds in the blackness, and that was because light makes an impression on the part of your eye called the retina. Mom made the right decision. School back home at Edison Elementary had been horrible. All year long, first grade and second grade, Mom and Dad knew he didn't want to go, but they kept making him. They said it was the law. He hid behind Mom's wheelchair, it was a wheelchair back then, while Dad reached around on one side, then the other, getting madder because he had already taken Luke and Margaret to school, and now he and James would both be late, James for Edison and Dad for Notre Dame. Dad didn't yell but he got really red. And before you knew it they were pulling up to the curb outside Edison Elementary, the sidewalks and chain-linked playground empty and quiet, grades one to eight inside at their desks, it was obvious he shouldn't be there, too late to be there, he wasn't getting out of the car — he dreaded the desk, kids he hardly knew, raising his hand to use the bathroom, watching the clock on the wall tick minutes and hours, wanting all the while to build Lincoln Logs on his bedroom floor, examine his Stars pocket guide, memorize the temperature of red giants, sip spoonfuls of consommé soup in the kitchen with Mom while Kelly sipped milk from her bottle — he made a last try to explain why he shouldn't be there, and then he got out and — Dad shouldn't have done it — Dad reached across and shut the car door and sped away. He ran after the car a little, screaming *stop.* And he wiped his cheek and walked inside, down the empty hall to his classroom. It wasn't one time. It was every few days, all school year. Now that home was a town called Cape Coast, there was no such thing as school. And except for the drive to Sunday Mass at Saint Peter's Seminary, the whole family crammed into the VW bus that went backward in Drive and forward in Reverse, there was no schedule, no clock other than the big round sun and the steady movement of Ignatius' hands in the kitchen and the song of his call to mealtime.

Breakfast after sunrise. Everybody at the dining room table. Hot cereal or fried eggs, oranges that were green outside but sweet orange inside, James breathed the jets of mist as he peeled it, and toast and jam. Not Smucker's. It was Wilkin and Sons Strawberry Conserve with a shield and crown on the jar that said, *By appointment to Her Majesty the Queen.*

When the sun was high, lunch. Spaghetti with meatballs in tomato sauce with homemade rolls and butter, followed by mangoes in a calabash bowl.

Dinner at sunset when the sky was pink and he was tired from going in circles in the brush with Luke, both thinking they were lost when really they were always by the house but couldn't see it through the leaves, tired after running on the dirt road from the circling vultures that probably never even noticed them, tired and ready for the comfort of night. James loved the smell of fish frying and white rice and big dark kontomire leaves cooking, and he couldn't have known it then, but it was like the red birds on the retina. Every day the rest of his life he waited for the smell of rice.

But he did wonder, "Why is he making our food, Mom?"

"Ignatius knows this kind of food. And I don't mind letting someone else cook for a change!"

Every day Mom was sewing curtains and bedspreads from batik she bought at Kingsway in Accra. Or reading long books: *The Forsyte Saga, The Good Earth, Pavilion of Women.*

"A cook comes with the house," Dad said. "A washman too. If we don't keep them, they don't have a job."

So Ignatius Echetabu came on his bicycle at sunrise every day but Sunday. On Saturday's a little later, his bicycle heavy with baskets of all the good things he liked to cook. The fish and chicken went into the freezer and the rice went into a glass jar in the cupboard. All safe from the cockroaches. The butter and conserve went in the fridge where the cockroaches positioned themselves around the lid until Ignatius flicked them off with his finger to scurry across the floor at super speed. Mom whisked the sandal from her foot and smacked them, but they were little tanks. It took four hard smacks to kill them. "Heavens to Betsy!" Mom said. Margaret said, "They are utterly pernicious creatures." Ignatius laughed. "So much worry over cockroaches."

Dad said Ignatius was Ibo, a tribe from Nigeria, a country to the east. A tribe was people who all belonged to the same group, and they recognized each other by the markings on their cheeks. You wouldn't believe it, but they made the marks with a knife. Ignatius had the marks, but he still smiled.

Kofi Nalikem, the washman, had different marks. He was Ewe, from Togo. He came on foot, barefoot on the dirt road, every week, waved hello, put his basket of things in the shed behind the house where he stayed overnight, and then he washed and ironed for two days. The first day he washed the laundry in the bath tub, wrung it with his hands and hung it to dry on the lines in the courtyard. He had big arms and shoulders and only wore shorts, no shirt, on washing day. The second day he wore shorts and a button-down shirt while he ironed and folded all day. His iron was actually made of iron, and he heated it in a coal fire in a little metal box on a metal stand in the courtyard.

Kofi hardly spoke any English, unlike Ignatius who spoke very well once you got to understand him. Dad said the family before us must not have talked to Kofi. He said it with the lifted chin and straightened shoulders that meant it was a disgrace. But Dad talked with him every week. Even so, Kofi was quiet and said only what was important to say. He told Dad, as he warmed the iron in the coals, that people in town were whispering about Juju magic. "Some dey afraid, some not."

"Do you believe in Juju?" Dad asked.

"Myself I don't believe," Kofi said. "But if you believe, it works."

*

Voices calling, singing, shouting. Motors grinding past, cars and lorries that looked like they were put back together too many times. People all ages crowded past each other in the outdoor market where the Atlantic threw salt clouds over the town and palms but couldn't wash away the rot of noon fish and chicken and goat cut and laid out in the market stalls, where big hands worked fast and rough and customers didn't just pile food in front of a cashier to pay. No. They stared close at every fruit and every slice of meat and haggled prices and shouted back and forth and laughed and filled their colorful reed baskets with dinner for their families.

*

Mom saw Kofi's bare feet and how the villages on the beach along Beulah Road had thatched roofs and walls made from palms and, who knows, probably just the beach sand for a floor, and she said it was inexcusable they had to live in such poverty. *Look in their eyes and tell me if you think they're poor,* Doris had said. She was British and her husband taught at the college like Dad. *In their eyes you'll see what soul means.* Mom was offended. "Does she think I'm stupid? Who does she think she is!" Mom was right that happiness in your eyes doesn't mean you don't need anything. Maybe Doris said what she said so she doesn't have to help anybody. But as Dad drove the VW bus with the whole family bumping down Beulah Road, James leaned into the wind while the thatched villages rushed by, huts with roofs and walls matching the palm fronds that swayed in the sea breeze above them, and between the huts, paths to the ocean surf, and crowds of singing men pulling huge nets from the waves, lines of men, feet dug in the sand in a tug-of-war with the ocean itself, scattered men in the crashing waves gathering the ocean-end of the nets, and farther out long wooden fishing boats, no sails or motors, gently rising and falling, and he felt like he was rising and falling out there too, and he wanted at least some part of what they had.

*

September and October the heat gathered and the rains pelted. Giggling huddled dashes from the bedrooms to the dining room, eyebrows dripping. And the mugginess of that first August night was nothing compared to Thanksgiving when Ignatius baked a whole chicken to stand in for a turkey and the family bathed, each in turn, before the meal so that at least they would sweat clean sweat around the dinner table. And by Christmas the rain was less each day but the old rain still lived in the dirt and the palms and the brush and there was no break from the hot heavy air. Dad was the only one who said, "I don't mind it."

James didn't mind it too much because the big round sun was setting, everything was pink, and this was Christmas Eve. He and Luke and Margaret and Kelly waited in the bedroom side of the house while Mom and Dad finished wrapping and decorating across the courtyard in the living room. "Our turn to shower!" Luke said. It was a two-person job. They stood in the tub and took turns mixing the cold faucet-water and the boiling hot kettle-water into a plastic pitcher, took turns pouring it over each other to rinse.

"Are you boys ready!"

He and Luke froze like a game of red-light-green-light, stared at each other, mouths open. "They're ready for us!" Luke said. And they mixed the last pours — *Careful!...I AM being careful!* — and laughed as they struggled damp into their clean clothes and rushed to stand beside Margaret and little Kelly at the bedroom courtyard door, waiting, waiting, until the bells rang out, Mom's Christmas bells, and they ran across the twilight courtyard, the Christmas tree lights shining out the living room's slatted windows.

A hand-puppet washcloth with a friendly lion on the front, a Matchbox red metal semi truck, a book for kids his age called *Page Boy of Camelot* — his three presents, each a total surprise, each alone more special than the pages and pages of Sears Roebuck toy planes and cars and parking garage sets he always worried over for weeks on end back home, all the cataloged marvels he so desperately had to get that it almost ruined Christmas before Christmas ever came. And now, in the split house in the hot brush on the dirt road where they made their own Christmas tree decorations and their own manger scene figures of Mary and Joseph and sheep all cut from construction paper, where Mom carried hot kettles from the kitchen to the bathroom, where Ignatius boiled drinking water on the stove, where millipedes long as your finger walked their tiny feet along the floorboards and lizards small as toys darted out from light fixtures to snatch bugs from the walls, where there was only a staticky radio and no TV and to buy anything at all like the things back home — well basically you just couldn't, unless maybe Kingsway, hours away in Accra — now these three gifts in James' hands were a wonder. And the simple things of that Christmas mixed and multiplied and the stories of Camelot became construction paper kings and queens and knights in an English countryside of linoleum tile plains and swirled bedsheet moors.

*

It was a morning a couple of weeks after New Year's Day. Mom couldn't get the BBC from London, only the GBC from Accra, and it was only military band music and a careful, serious voice they called Colonel Acheampong. *The new government is a military government which will rule with advice from certain eminent civilians in the country. I would like to emphasize that this coup was not initiated by the Armed Forces....*

Lying in bed that night he heard the high-pitched hum, mosquito, and pulled the sheet over his head and it was like being inside a pan on the stove with the lid on. The window screens were metal wire in a simple across-and-updown pattern, tight enough to stop birds and monkeys and lizards and snakes, not tight enough to stop mosquitoes. He listened for the hum, hoping not to hear it, and instead he heard a sound, above the distant pounding of the Atlantic, a sound he hadn't heard since November. Drums, far away. On and on, patterns and tunes changing but never stopping. In November Ignatius had said, *That's the talking drums, the Ashanti people are telling each other that Cassius Clay beat Buster Mathis.*

Tonight the Ashanti people must have been talking about Colonel Acheampong. In the afternoon Kofi had told Dad not to go to the market in Accra. *Dey taking mens to da beach and dey shoot dem. Maybe dey don care who you are. Better not going.*

James liked the drums in November, but now he wished it was only the ocean and the mosquito.

*

"Let's gedam going!" John Adonfo shouted to the men around him, raised the curved sticks like long wooden candy canes, struck his drum *ba da bom,* another man got going *ba da bom, ba-da-da bom,* and they all got going, the seminarians from Saint Peter's, the drummers who drummed Amen before Communion at Mass, but never like this. The courtyard between the bedrooms and living room got going, pounding cow-skin, ringing brass as loud as the Atlantic at Elmina, waves, how many waves, one done and another, how long between, between one and another, he couldn't predict but perfect, it was perfect. On and on they drummed.

"Henry! Somebody's at the door!" Mom called. And Dad opened the door and they all came in, and more came in, and more.

"Henry, get the Fanta bottles from the fridge."

"It's not nearly enough, love."

"We've got to serve them something!"

"Why are they coming inside our house, Mom? And they're dancing!" James was shy and amazed.

"They hear the drumming!" Ignatius sang and laughed. "They hear it miles around!"

*

Umaro Mousa wrapped up his things, everything he had laid out on the living room floor for display. A bird carved from cow horn, miniature people made of brass, leather satchels, ebony boxes in-laid with ivory, a mahogany mancala board with tree nuts, wooden masks that looked part human, part antelope, always with a bird carved on top like it was pecking the forehead. He wrapped it all in his plain, rough fabric and stowed it in baskets he attached all over his bicycle the same way Mom could carry anything on her crutches. He stood up, tall, wiry, not young or old, and he said, with a look that meant he knows things, knows when there is danger, "I am late."

The traders came to the house every few months, our house. On bicycles that they rode through towns and forests and across borders. Umaro was Hausa, from Nigeria. Dad didn't haggle prices with him even though haggling was normal. Dad said he had the fairest prices and the best quality. Mom served bottles of Fanta, and Dad and Umaro talked about the lives they lived. James thought maybe Dad could feel himself on the bicycle in the brush. And after talking and trading, Umaro always said goodbye before sundown, especially when there was no moon. When there was no moon, you couldn't even see the road under your pedals.

Dad looked concerned now, like Umaro. "It's the new moon. I'll drive you, just to where you're spending the night."

"No, no, my bicycle..."

"We'll put it in the VW."

Mom was a nervous wreck all the while Dad was gone. It was black out the windows of the bedrooms and James saw her march with crutches into the courtyard again and again to peer through the breeze blocks.

"Thank heavens!" she finally said, headlights sweeping the courtyard and motor clunking silent. She opened the door and seemed right between scolding Dad and hugging him, but he stopped her with the words, "Love, you've got to bring the kids out here. Turn off the bedroom light."

Hand in hand they filed out the door beyond the little Tamarind tree into the mysterious darkness. Everything lost in black — house, tree, brush. It was only the sky you could see.

"That's the Milky Way," Dad said.

"You mean from there, all the way to there!" Luke must have stretched his arms wide with excitement but you couldn't see him.

"Impressive!" Margaret's voice said.

Kelly's said, "I don't think it's milk."

James gazed into the faraway glow that was beyond a world away and heard Mom say, "It's beautiful, love."

*

When they came back across the Atlantic, it wasn't to White Oak Drive, the house that held his earliest memories.

Looking out the big front windows from the living room couch into the branches of the oak that stood at the bottom of the hill below. Squirrels ran out the branches, jumped from the tips to another branch. You could live in a tree. Cars went downhill as far as the front yard and then slower uphill. The yard filled like a tub when it rained and Mom said flood water was dangerous. She came from the kitchen and sat beside him looking out the window, and he liked that. But when she asked, *Penny for your thoughts?* all he could say was, *I'n know.*

He remembered crawling slowly, heavily across the dining room floor, like a real Brontosaurus in Luke's dinosaur book.

The burn when he picked up the darkened lightbulb from the basement floor, dropped it, his hand red and hurting. He didn't know a dark bulb could be hot. Mom's ointment. And how proud Mom was when he told the story a week later, opening one hand and pointing with the other, there to there, to show where it burned. He had never explained anything that way before.

He remembered the glow of green moss, the smell of dark dirt, wet bark, leaves fallen from the trees. Dad raking a big pile to set on fire. *Stand back everybody!*

Running with Luke under the shadow of the oaks, sunshine poking through, across the big field made of all the backyards from their house to Bill, Tom, and Joanie's house. Everything you saw around you changed as you ran and ran.

He remembered he and Joanie, both six years old, stretched out on beach towels on the grass. He imagined this must be what kids meant when they said their older brother had a girlfriend.

And hiding with Luke and Bill from Tom during War because Tom was older and you knew he'd get you. Tom was kind of scary because he didn't listen to his Mom and Dad who never seemed to be around, some other way of being a family, but Luke said Tom always had neat ideas for things to do. Sometimes it seemed like James was the only one still hiding with his stick gun and he didn't know where the other kids were and he was glad when he heard Mom's voice call across the big field, "Luke, James! Dinner!"

There was one other memory, from so, so long ago now. He had run out into the dark hallway, he had to get to Mom and Dad's room. He stood at the side of the bed, tapping Mom's shape under the blanket.

"What? What it is?"

"I had a dream."

He never dreamed it before and never again. One time was enough for a lifetime. He stood in a night-black world surrounded by huge white blocks. Huge, heavy, jumbled blocks, a wasteland of pieces that were supposed to be something but weren't anything at all.

"I have to make a city out of them."

"Honey, you don't..."

"It's too big, but I have to."

"You don't have to. It was a dream, honey. Go back to sleep."

All of that was a dream now because, when they came back from Cape Coast in the summer of 1972, it wasn't the house in the woods. It was a house on Whitehall Drive, and that name, if you picture what it means, that's what it was like. A plain one-story house, with a plain yard. No White Oak woods. No Beulah Road surf.

In the new house, Dad settled into evenings and weekends correcting tests and paying bills at the big oak desk in the living room corner or reading textbooks in the gold upholstered chair, legs crossed in a way that didn't quite look comfortable. You couldn't talk to him because his only answer was, *I have to prepare for class.* He was kind of back to the worrying Dad with ulcers.

Still, the new house had a long front walkway you could race Hot Wheels down like they were driving on a real highway. And the rooms were filled with the familiar old living room couch and the antiques from White Oak plus the mahogany Ashanti stools and ebony busts and bronze masks from Cape Coast. It was a new place for their old things, and their old games. The King Game they played in Cape Coast grew with more knights and damsels and peasants and invading Saxons James read about in his book *Medieval England.* Luke began building a little cardboard fortress but stopped partway because he got a new idea. He drew lines and flaps he could cut and fold to just the shapes he wanted. Kept drawing and cutting and folding and gluing, for days and days. And none of them could believe it, the castle that took shape on the family room floor. Four feet tall, a hundred rooms, surrounded by a turreted wall with towers. Dad called the *South Bend Tribune* — "I think you'll want to see this." It was in the newspaper the next week.

*

In the fall the old plagues came back, colds and flu. And school. None of the reading he and Luke and Margaret did in the split house in the hot brush on the dirt road in Cape Coast, none of what they learned living on the other side of the Atlantic meant anything to the school administrators in South Bend. They had missed a year and were enrolled in the grade they had missed. James was starting third grade at age ten, a year older than everyone in his class. Thank goodness it was Tarkington Elementary, a different school where nobody would recognize his embarrassing situation.

He didn't put up the fight that he used to. He was old enough to know that he had to go. He even liked it when Mrs. Walensky told them, *Now everybody, arrange your chairs in a circle!* and they read aloud about a ring of cattle rustlers out West. And in fourth grade, when his family moved from 1029 to 823 Whitehall Drive, which brought him back to Edison Elementary, it was still okay because nobody remembered him any more. He browsed the library shelves, found a book about roads the Romans built across Europe a thousand years ago — you wouldn't have expected something like that, way back then. And in fifth grade he wrote a Halloween story and read it to the class. They liked how the purple flowers at the Egyptian tomb kept reappearing as a mysterious sign of danger.

But through it all he still couldn't wait to get home to his own library, *Encyclopedia of Animals, Our Earth, The Lord of the Rings Trilogy,* and his own games. Over those years from third to fifth grade, the King Game gave way to Animals, where two-inch-tall plastic giraffes, lions, and toy soldiers mingled with cut-out paper four-legged space aliens. And no matter what kind of creature you were or what you were made of, you were a citizen of the make-believe cities and nations, living in cardboard houses, driving cardboard cars, flying cardboard planes. He and Luke measured, cut, folded, taped, and glued them all. Soon James could look at a sheet of cardboard and see the shapes that would fold into car cabins and plane fuselages. Rrrrraaaw! He raced them and flew them all weekend until the dread of the next school week filled the places that the day's sun had fled.

Sunday morning the downturn began. Wasn't school all week enough? "Luke, brush your teeth!" Mom set her purse next to the front door and turned to James, buttoning the top button he could never button no matter how he tried. "When we were your age it wasn't just Mass, we had to go to confession!" Dad started to correct to *every couple of weeks* but he stopped when Mom's shocked eyes said *Don't contradict me in front of the kids.* "The entire Mass was in Latin," Dad said. James joined in the grimaces. "Were there drummers back then?" Kelly asked, and Margaret vigorously shook her head, "There were no drummers, you're thinking of Cape Coast." Dad slipped into his jacket, "I told Father Callan last week about the drummed Amen at Saint Peters Seminary, but it didn't make an impression."

The fact was, the only good thing about Mass was that it was one hour instead of six, and one day a week instead of five. In other words, it wasn't school, the place James had learned to put up with but just plain couldn't when he was sick, which was a lot.

Every cold or flu that went around, and worse. He still had the white marks on his arms from chickenpox in fourth grade when he saw and heard Margaret and Kelly in the family room but then realized nobody was there — it was the fever, Mom said.

He hated being so sick. But here was the thing: He couldn't help being sick. And when he was sick, alongside the sore throat and fever, it also saved him from the thing he dreaded every morning, being thrust out into the world.

At home, he just plain fit in, in a way you couldn't explain. It wasn't that they always got along. Margaret listened to Carly Simon with her bedroom door shut. Kelly played in her room or joined James and Luke's games. She told Mom when he and Luke were bossy. And James didn't like it when Luke said his Animal country had bombed James' and that James' country couldn't counter-attack because of Luke's anti-aircraft system. *It's totally impenetrable!* Luke declared and fingered his eyeglasses higher. But he and Luke reveled in making paper national flags for the Animal Olympics Opening Ceremony and using a dinner spoon catapult to see who's marble went farthest in the shot-put competition. At home everybody had their place.

Somehow, outside home, nobody made any sense. The boys in fifth grade joked. *Dave let one! Did not! Did so. Whoever smelt it dealt it!* They made friends out of those words. Or the morning he stood looking out the classroom window, kids milling around, free for the last minutes before the drill of the bell would send them scurrying to their desks. Fred sidled up to the window. "I'd rather be out in that sunshine! You know, by the time we're grown up, nobody will have to work." Fred had never made much of an impression before, but now it seemed like he had something to say. "Machines will do everything for us. My dad says it's going to be a paradise."

James turned his head away, his brows scrunched up. That was the stupidest thing he had ever heard! He looked back to Fred. He didn't say it. *With nothing to do why would you even want to be alive? What's better than reading his Stars pocket guide? Dad writing his math papers? Men singing fish nets out of the sea?*

*

The trees at the edge of Thomas A. Edison field trembled the tiniest bit in the September breeze. Behind him, the shouts of play. Sixth grade. The girls were getting taller and talking about boys. The boys were pretty much still stuck on farts and solving questions like whether the ball was in or out, and who cheated or *Did not!*

Recess was almost harder than being in class. If he was an outcast, it was because he'd cast himself out. Nobody blocked him out. Nobody teased or bullied him, and if any boy tried, then the other boys, who weren't even friends, stepped in. *Leave him alone.* He wasn't outcast. He was...apart. Not part of whatever world the other kids lived in.

He bent down to the patchy grass field. Bare dirt between the clumps. He bent closer, listened to the breeze and traced his finger through the dirt, felt the grains of soil push away, a path through a miniature jungle. Until the drill of the bell, the sound that stopped everything. The whole school building was a giant brick alarm clock. All the games on the playground fell into confusion. Some kids froze in place, mouths open as if the unthinkable had happened. Some threw a last ball. James stood from the grass and walked to the line that formed at the door and filed into the hallways where kids pulled textbooks from metal lockers and hurried to their classrooms.

"Ready for practice this afternoon, Lisa? I want to see a classic Teng goal in the first quarter!" Mr. Zimmer's voice, the gym teacher.

"I can do that, Mr. Zimmer!"

James peered secretly beneath lowered brows. It was her. Taller and more beautiful than ever, silky black hair down to the middle of her back. Lisa Teng, from first grade. She must be in seventh now. It was the teacher-student banter you only saw with middle schoolers. He had forgotten until just this moment, the night in Cape Coast he had a dream of a beautiful girl with long dark hair. She wore a long white dress and he stood beside her in a suit and they were married. Lisa closed her locker and strolled past his line, the line of little sixth graders. He looked away. He didn't want her to remember him.

*

Spring 1977

"Mom, I don't feel good." Last fall it was bronchitis. And now on a spring morning before school he couldn't even get a spoonful of Cheerios down his raw sore throat. "You're burning up." Mom felt under his ears. "And your lymph nodes are swollen. You're staying home."

There was always something freeing about those words. He flinched as a sharp pang pierced his temple. Freeing and crippling. Flu would keep him home from school a week for sure. But it wasn't just a week.

"It's mononucleosis," Dr. Chamblee said, when James hadn't gotten any better. "Four weeks of dedicated rest. He's not going back to school until May ninth."

James was silent as he and Mom crossed the asphalt parking lot.

"You're going to be home for a while, James." There was a little upturn in the corner of Mom's lip as they climbed into the Ford station wagon.

"May. Is that the end of the school year?"

"Very nearly."

He went back to finish the final weeks of school before summer vacation. But the letter from the principal made it clear. Sixth grade wasn't over for James. *Due to your child's extended absence, albeit for legitimate reasons of health, your child is failed and required to re-enroll in sixth grade in the fall.*

Dad read the letter to him, and James planted his feet, "I'm not...going... back."

*

Henry settled back in the chair at his big oak desk, the one corner that was his in Genny's showcase living room, a corner for his own thoughts. He knew the moment James had said it, that this was not just another I-hate-school day. It was a new day. A reckoning. August would be James' birthday. Imagine a fifteen-year-old repeating sixth grade. Old enough to be a ninth-grader and advanced enough in his knowledge too. The kids really hadn't lost any ground the year away in Cape Coast. Their arithmetic was probably as good as most kids their ages, what they learned about the world was beyond what most would ever know, and after that year teaching themselves, they had never stopped reading and studying. Just now James had completed four weeks of English grammar assignments in four days, to near-perfect scores — that's what he had done to catch up after the mono. *James isn't going back* — Henry's own words now, his own stand on the matter. But if that was the premise, how was this argument supposed to unfold? Attendance was the law, period. And the school administration had the authority.

That night, he talked with Genny in bed. She was ready to march into the principal's office, write a scathing letter to the school board, telephone the newspapers. So much fiery energy at half-past eleven. He loved that about her. But her reaction was almost a whole second crisis. When she had finally fallen asleep, his heart was still racing. He imagined the vertebra at the top of his spine, relaxed the next, and the next, and at the eighteenth the wash of relaxation released a tide of realization — He already knew what to do. They had done it before, gone where the school board couldn't touch them, overseas.

Home from classes the next evening he announced, "I checked the Chronicle of Higher Education. There are two math jobs in Saudi Arabia where I could teach in English. There's one in Venezuela too, but that would be in Spanish."

Genny's eyes widened, like the day he'd told her about Cape Coast. "And Notre Dame will give you a leave of absence?"

He blinked. He hadn't thought that far ahead. "I'm sure they will. They did for Ghana."

"You had a Fulbright grant, and you were a department favorite. Now you're dealing with O'Casey. He doesn't know a thing about your mereology.

All he cares about is those young professors he brought from Yale. I hate how arrogant he is!"

"I know love, I know."

Genny deflated and leaned back against the kitchen counter, a buttered casserole dish and box of macaroni noodles behind her. "We have a family, Henry. How can we go anywhere if O'Casey..."

"He will, love. He'll give me the leave." There, he'd said it. Like declaring the sun would shine. As if he could will it so. And then he waited anxiously to see if the sun would make a fool of him.

When O'Casey sat there at his gray metal desk in the Nieuwland Science Center shaking his head — "No, not granted" — Henry tucked in his chin a moment and delivered the only response he could imagine giving. "I guess I'll have to quit."

A faint grin dawned on O'Casey's lips, "I guess you will."

As he put the key in the green Ford station wagon to drive home and tell Genny, it wasn't at all like the sun was failing. He lifted his eyes to the rearview mirror. Clear. Backed out of the slot and put it into drive. The Crosslands always found a way. He wasn't a fool. He was free.

Petal

Bloomington, Minnesota 1982

Catherine traversed the steps of the dimly lit corridor to second floor. Seventh grade math class with Mr. Bosko. At the landing, about to climb the half flight is when it happened. She winced as the big hand swiped past and landed with a crack on the books in the arm of the boy next to her. They scattered and skidded along the shiny terrazzo floor, tumbled down the stairs. A ninth grader's hand, a giant to the seventh grade newcomer who stooped and gathered the books frantically, hoping the whole incident would go unnoticed in spite of passing laughter. Catherine couldn't stand it. Why would the big boys do that to the younger kids? Somebody had to show them they couldn't get away with it.

From that day on she cradled her books in the vice grip of her left arm as she walked the halls between classes at Oak Grove Junior High, her dark hair in two long pony tails bouncing over her shoulders, her shoes pinned with colorful friendship beads Patti had given her in those last days of sixth grade. It was a new world, a big school, and there was no question about it, she felt a little unanchored without Patti who had gone on to Olson Junior High. She hardly saw her any more. Nobody to talk to about this crazy new world. Nobody to laugh with and sing along to Casey Kasem. Nobody to tell whenever that day would come, and she knew it would, when she would show the older boys.

*

She dived into her studies. Shop class where she crafted wooden coasters. Math where Mr. Bosko said, *Fractions are friendly and express division.* Science where Mrs. Hermann and the class huddled under the cold night sky, *Look, there's Orion.* Home economics where she baked an apple braid pastry and knitted a scarf, a Christmas gift for Dad, in pretty gold, green, and rust with tassels knotted at each end. Orchestra where she toted her violin case into the back seat of Mr. Morelli's Ford Pinto, her carpool ride. Mr. Morelli was onstage, his running commentary made her giggle. She marveled at his ease behind the wheel, the speedometer hidden by a homemade cardboard sign that read *KEEP COOL.* Just riding in that car with him at the wheel made her feel free.

*

At the landing her eyes darted. Nothing. She started up the stairs, determined to get to Mr. Bosko's classroom without any trouble. Crack! The big hand came down on her books, and when they didn't fall or scatter, the ninth grade boy with the curly brown locks stood there stupid, confused, amazed. Her dark eyes zeroed in on him. She waited. Waited for his apology. And without a word he turned his back to walk away. A hot rush flooded her chest and her muscles tensed alive and her fist thrust deep between his shoulder blades. He choked, turned around stunned, was shocked that it was her, this slender young girl breathing hard, ponytails in disarray, her poofy mohair sweater off-kilter revealing the strap of her training bra. He walked away, but she didn't care because his jaw had dropped and he couldn't seem to figure out how to close it. No one ever took a swipe at her books again.

*

When day lilies bloomed and cottonwood leaves quaked in the summer breeze she felt something changing. She was nearly a head taller than the boys her age, and she spent most days in her bedroom with a book or outside in the grass watching the cumulus clouds float by in the deep blue sky. That was when she felt a trickle down there. *What in the world was that?* She ran inside the house and into the bathroom, pulled down her shorts and it was, oh my god, it was blood. Surely it would stop. She washed up and discretely snuck to her bedroom for a fresh pair, ran outside again, lay down in the grass and looked up at the clouds. She wanted to forget, but she couldn't, and then, oh no, there was the trickle again. Back inside, she knew what she had to do.

"Mom, I think I'm dying."

"Oh for heaven's sake, Catherine."

It was all humiliating. And it wasn't a one time thing. It was going to keep happening for the rest of her life. Nothing would be the same any more.

She ran outside, tried to run normally with the big pad in her pants, flopped down on the grass and peered into the blue. A cumulus cloud changed shape as she watched. Stretched, thinned, evaporated. And over there in the empty blue a tiny wisp formed, spread, ballooned. How had she never seen this before?

*

Now she was a ninth grade girl among ninth grade boys. And nothing had changed about how she thought a ninth grade boy ought to act. If they wanted to know what she expected of them, all they had to do was try something stupid and she would show them. Not a fist in the back. Just a no-nonsense answer and a stare that made most boys raise their hands and chuckle and walk away. Boys are stupid. But do they all have to be stupid? She didn't want them all to walk away.

She tried talking to Mom one night. Mom was so busy during the day ironing in front of the television and making meals in the kitchen and vacuuming the house edge to edge, that nighttime was the only chance to ask her anything. And then they were all at dinner, and then Mom was washing dishes, and then... "Mom?"

Mom stopped at her bedroom door. "What is it dear?"

Catherine could see how tired she was. "I guess it's nothing."

"It's probably not nothing if you called me over."

"It's okay Mom. I love you."

"I love you too dear, sweet dreams."

She could have talked to Patti back in elementary days. But three years into Oak Grove there still wasn't anyone she could talk to. Why was it so hard to find a friend? She walked home from orchestra practice under the dark bare limbs of the boulevard trees, the iced sidewalk glistening in the first lamplight of evening. She wasn't ready for winter and the letting go of summer loves — wren and nuthatch, quaking green cottonwood, honeysuckle blossom and morning glory. Yesterday the grass vanished under a mere inch of snow. More would fall every week until no one even remembered what grass looked like any more. It happened to everything she loved. She stopped in her tracks, slid a fraction. The speed skaters on television last February popped into her head. The Winter Olympic Games, Sarajevo. She folded one hand behind her and scissored the other, feet pushing out behind until she hit a dry patch and spun and laughed and caught her breath and strode into winter, her hands finishing out the last graceful scissor swishes of her Sarajevo sprint.

*

Sadie Hawkins was coming up this Friday. Girls were supposed to invite the boys to the dance instead of the other way around. Everybody lived by mindless rules. They couldn't break a rule unless someone declared: Today the new rule is that you must break the old rule! Even so, she wanted to go to the dance but just didn't know how to ask. She'd seen Carl in the hallways, his dimpled grin as they passed. She liked that he liked her, but what would she say, how could she ask? They talked together in the halls between classes and she nodded and said yes. And he mentioned the dance and she nodded and said yes. And finally, he said it. "Are you going to ask me to Sadie Hawkins?"

"Yes."

"Okay do it."

She breathed in, and breathed out, and breathed in again before she could say, "Will you come?"

"For damn sure."

She smiled and felt like she was glowing red all over.

*

The house held the chill of the winter night even as the pale sun shone gold on the wooden railing. Catherine scuffed down the stairs as coffee trickled from the automatic drip. She didn't pop awake any more, not like she used to. It was a labored process. Dad greeted her entry into the kitchen with an enthusiastic, "Good morning Catherine!"

She grumbled, unsure herself what words she was trying to form, and plopped into a brown vinyl chair at the kitchen table. When his slippered feet did a little shuffle dance on the linoleum in front of the stove, it drew a smile from her. On the counter were a mixing bowl and a carton of eggs. And on the stovetop, a frying pan. He took a stick of butter from the fridge.

"What are you making?" she asked.

"An omelet."

She watched him crack an egg with one hand.

*

It made her laugh to think of it. When she was little, she had made up her mind she would never marry, for the simple reason that there was no way she could kiss a boy in front of a church-full of people. That all changed when she met Carl. It had been over a year since Sadie Hawkins and she never imagined sweet sixteen could be this good. He was her best friend, that one special person she had been looking for. They liked doing the same things. In their tennis matches she perfected her one-handed backhand. In photography class, in the red glow of the darkroom, he stole a kiss. At Koblend's Pharmacy she watched from the cash register as he stocked shelves, and she giggled when he flashed his dimpled grin.

*

Tomorrow was the first day of her last year of high school. She had already been accepted to the College of Saint Benedict. Her dark waves flowed below her shoulders and freckles sprinkled her cheeks. The August sun warmed her back as she sat beside Carl on the grassy bank of Nine Mile Creek. Twisting his class ring around her finger, she threw a pebble into the creek a little too hard. It wasn't their first argument — his drinking, his lies. And the party last night. He didn't invite her but called at one in the morning, loud music in the background, asking for a sober ride home. She felt like his mother, not his girlfriend.

He was just like all the other stupid boys. He still wouldn't admit he had cheated. "I was drunk, I thought she was you." She was beyond feeling heartbroken, tired of his betrayals, his childishness. He leaned back on his elbows, his biceps stretching the cuffs of his polo shirt, and he chuckled with that dimpled grin. "What are you going to do? Break up with me?"

She gave the ring one last twist and dropped it into his palm. "Yes, I'm breaking up with you." And she was on her bicycle, peddling around the foot of the sledding hill and up to the crest, leg muscles burning. Her coral Esprit sundress rippled as she picked up speed downhill, the wind in her hair.

*

The first week of school, she walked into second hour photography to a crowd of classmates laughing, hands over open mouths, huddled around a piece of paper posted on the wall. And beneath the paper sat Carl, leaning back on two chair-legs, snickering. She took a closer look: It was the letter she had handed him yesterday, asking for a peaceful senior year. Naively she had thought he could be mature, thought they all could be mature. Even the teachers stood in their office doorway watching and whispering. Her chest was on fire. She snatched the letter from the wall, glared at the teachers, and stormed out.

Things needed to change, and fast. Second hour became breakfast at Pannekoeken Huis where she and Julie talked over coffee and lemon poppy seed muffins. They had met just this summer. Why their paths hadn't crossed when they lived just two blocks from each other and went to the same high school, she didn't know. Sometimes people just come into your life at the right time. After coffee, they sneaked through the school parking lot and into a side door for third hour and the rest of the day.

*

Catherine sat at the desk in her bedroom, pen in hand, her journal before her. She and Julie had found a solution for second hour, but that didn't change the fact that she was over high school, over the petty social groups, ready to leave it all behind. In the spring she would graduate. College would mean new places, new people, finding her own way in the world. But that was a year away. She wrote, *My last year at home, how will I get through it? Stay busy!* She started a list — *Try out for the school soccer team. Work and save money. Search for my birth mother?* She gazed out the window into the lamplit suburban night. *If only I didn't have to wait, if only I could escape.*

*

She made the junior varsity soccer team, one piece of her plan in place, but at scrimmage Carl's grudge followed her onto the field. She jumped for the ball and three girls converged on her midair, knocking her to the ground. It was Mindy, she wanted Carl. Didn't she know she could have him? Catherine walked unsteadily to the locker room, nauseous, flashing lights. But she wasn't going to quit. Not soccer. It was her release, a field where she could run, block, score. Where bruised or beaten, she could always wrestle control from anyone who tried to take it from her.

Bruised, sore. Her knees had been giving her trouble, but they were worse now. Coach knew what to do. He wasn't just their coach, he was a professional trainer, knew everything about sports medicine and used only the latest equipment. It was a deal he had made, he said. He would take the assistant trainer job with the Itascas professional soccer team if, and only if, they donated the equipment to Eisenhower High.

She sat on the edge of the hot tub, bubbling water glowing infrared, and recessed her knees into the soothing warmth. Every day after practice she soaked, and there were others soaking, and they weren't high schoolers. They were five or six years older. It began with small talk, "In for the magic sponge, eh?" His accent was British.

"Are you serious, Coach?" — it seemed to her like some kind of joke — "The Itascas use Eisenhower's hot tub?"

"It's where the equipment is. That was the deal!"

Add it to the list of things she never thought she'd be immersed in: second hour Pannekoeken Huis, and post-scrimmage rehab with the Itascas. It wasn't long before she was invited to a game, her name on the guest list. It was the ridiculous perfect escape from the nightmare her senior year had become. While classmates mingled within their high school circles, she and Julie went to every Itascas home game, hung out with the players in the stadium suite afterward, appetizers and drinks on high cocktail tables, no chairs, no IDs.

Julie sipped her cocktail, eyeing Bryce Grant. Out of uniform and freshly showered, dressed in black with the constant cigarette between his lips, bantering with fellow forward, Collin Craig. "They really bottled it." Collin said. Bryce downed his shot. "Their gaffer'll be giving them the hairdryer treatment about now!"

Julie was after Bryce the moment she saw him, flirting, vying for his attention, and even though Bryce was untouchable, her affections never waned. Catherine didn't have anyone in mind. She was immersed in the experience, fascinated by the guys, not so much older than she, who were different from everyone she knew, otherworldly. Not just England but Australia and South Africa. She looked across the table to Julie, "A lot better than high school, huh?"

Julie nodded, her eyes still glued to Bryce. Bryce, like a tall magnificent bird, his hair a plume flowing down the back of his head. After the suite, it was dinner at the Mediterranean Cruise Restaurant followed by a party at one of the player's apartments until daylight.

*

She rang up a bag of prescriptions at Koblend's and heard the door clink as another customer walked in. No, it wasn't a customer. It was Carl. He mock examined a package from the shelves, didn't even look up while he said, "I slept with Mindy last night. Man, was she sweeeet!" He cocked his head, and there was that dimpled grin that used to charm her. Now it made her embarrassed. Embarrassed for him. An Itascas midfielder was parked outside. Her ride. Carl had no clue.

*

Every home game it was the usual story, "I'm sleeping over at Julie's tonight," and she and Julie were off to the Itascas game. Halfway through the season, a new forward was signed to the team. He was brought on to score. The announcer over the intercom, "Gooal! Another by Bo Juric." Raising his hand in a number one, Bo leaned into the embrace of his huddled teammates. Bo was his Americanized name. Jersey number 23, no taller than she, fast, agile, determined. After a game one night she met him in the stadium suite. He spoke only a sliver of English with a thick East European accent. Sitting beside her at the Cruise, he swept his hand over his dish in offer and smiled, a conversation in gestures more than words. As she slipped into the passenger seat of his brand new Volkswagen Golf, shiny black, she could see how proud he felt. He had never owned a car. Her hand touched his, his knuckles wrapped around the gear shift. "It's a beautiful car Bo."

At his apartment they lay together on the floor and talked into the night. "What is your real name?"

"Bozidar Juric."

It was hard to interpret. "Bozidar Yourich" she repeated slowly. "Tell me, in your language how do you say *hello*?"

"Bok." When he smiled his eyes curved like crescent moons.

"What is your home like, where you live?"

"The sky, it open, hills around." His voice was gentle and his openness drew her. "On night I look on window. Mjesec — how you say on English, moon? — he shine hills like day."

Pictures formed in her head. A place she had never been now felt like somewhere she knew. They were together just the one night. It ended as easily as it had begun. But she was different now. He opened the world for her. "Sretno. It mean good luck." His eyes curved into moons.

Mountains

Maiquetía, Venezuela 1978

J ames leaned back his tired head, crammed in the backseat of the taxi
with Luke, Mom, and Kelly, airport lights flashing in the night, the
warm breeze disorienting after the January snow in Syracuse that
morning. A ten hour flight after a five month stay at Grandma Lancer's
house while Dad petitioned by phone and in person at the Venezuelan
consulate in New York to get the visas — *Come back after lunch. Come back
tomorrow. Come back next week.* Thanksgiving and Christmas at Grandma's,
months of strangers' questions about why they weren't in school. Margaret
was a college student at Notre Dame, but the rest of them were in school
limbo, which was way better than school. Dad studied Spanish all the while.
He didn't speak any at all when he accepted the job in August after Saudi
Arabia fell through. Dad could do just about anything that was hard to do. In
fact it seemed like that was what he did best. In fact it was kind of annoying.
Nothing could ever be the simple thing, the expected thing. James struggled,
a little more than he really had to, to free his arm from behind Luke's
shoulder.

It was a comfort anyway to see Dad in the front passenger seat, speaking
Spanish to the driver. Dad had flown across the Caribbean two weeks ago to
set up housing, had met them now at the airport gate in Maiquetía, bent to
kiss Mom in the wheelchair as she patted his cheek, her shyness about the
public display, and herded family and luggage into what he called *el
porpuesto*, the taxi.

James' irritated fatigue made him want to close his eyes, but he felt
something in the breeze, smelled something in the air where the Andes meet
the sea, and when the taxi driver turned on the radio's tenor cry over
strummed harps and ringing cowbells and hit the gas, James was moving
through space and all he could do was listen and watch and sway. Lanes,
signs, one-way, two-way — none of it was what the driver was seeing. Dad

asked something about "no entre" and pointed to another lane like maybe that was where they should be. "Es lo mismo!" the driver said, which must have meant this was the right way. Mom's voice rose in alarm, "Henry, tell him to slow down, for heaven's sake!" But as James felt the car sway with methodic acceleration into open space and melodic slow-and-swerve through traffic to acceleration again, he knew, without knowing anything, that the road was the map and the cars were the signs and the song on the radio was the ride.

*

In the darkness, you have no idea what place you've come to. In the dawn, as the others stirred from bed, James gingerly pulled aside the hotel curtain, opened the sliding door, and stepped onto a balcony to another world. A great wall of lush green mountains rose before him, glowing green in the morning sun. Laughter and shouts, car horn and birdsong echoed up steep hillsides adorned with tile-roofed houses and concrete high-rises. A new day on the edge of the Andes.

*

From the night lights of Maiquetía, to the dawn green mountains of Macuto, to the evening blue hills of Cumaná and the red-tile-roofed stucco houses of his new neighborhood. Cumaná Tercera.

He and Luke slept the best they could on the aluminum-frame canvas cots. Kelly had a cot in her room and Mom and Dad a mattress on the floor in theirs. The crate of household goods hadn't shown up at the port, and the university hadn't paid Dad, so they camped out with handouts from the other professors. A dining room table and living room chairs were something to hope for. Mom called it *bare bones decor.*

In the morning, waking late, James walked the polished stone floor, down the hall to the front of the house. The floor was cool against his bare feet, but when he opened the front door the air was already hot. He looked across the small front yard to the steel-bar gate in the concrete wall. Every yard in the newly-built neighborhood was walled, some topped with steel spikes, some with glass shards, some like their own with polite red tile.

Out there an occasional car pulled from the curbside and rumbled down the street past boys and girls who bantered and laughed and strolled in twos and threes. Little kids in white tops and blue pants. Teens in blue tops and white pants.

"Dad thinks you can probably attend high school here," Mom said, standing beside him at the door. "He's talking to the principal."

His heart sank. "Do we have anything for breakfast?"

"Dad thinks it's a good way to learn the language. You can start by auditing, just listening in."

Okay, first thing: after half a year of freedom, school was back. But second thing: he wasn't repeating sixth, he was starting high school. Three girls in uniform, his age, long black hair, strolled down the street, hips swaying like Ginger on *Gilligan's Island*.

*

The steel-bar gate. Every house had one. It was the gateway between your house and the rest of the world. Out there, three boys walked down the street. One, dark skinned with slick black hair, juggled a soccer ball on his knees, casually like flipping a coin, while he bantered with the others. He glanced to the gate, then the others did, but they kept on walking. Out there the afternoon streets were noisy with kids, and in the evenings the gates opened and the front stoops came alive with families taking in the twilight breeze. The young and old rounded the blocks, visiting gate by gate, talking, singing, playing music.

It was different from Ghana where people kept to themselves, they didn't approach you. Under the palms of Cumaná, people expected more, expected you to say *hello, how are you,* answer questions. All in Spanish.

The woman from next door peered in the gate, beckoned to Mom while James and Kelly helped arrange flower pots on the porch.

"De donde vienen ustedes...la familia?'"

Mom turned on her crutches and smiled tightly. "God, I wish Henry were here! James..."

He stood from the pots and stepped hesitantly toward the gate. "I don't know what she's saying, Mom."

Within seconds the boy who James had seen with the soccer ball and the girls from the corner and a boy from across the street had gathered.

"Son norteamericanos."

"De los Estados Unidos? Ay, que lejos. Porque vienen aqui?"

"No se."

They seemed to be talking among themselves, which took some of the pressure off.

"Uni-estates America?" The boy with the soccer ball smiled past James to Kelly, who turned bright red.

"Sí," James said. "United States of America."

The boy smiled at James and gestured to himself. "Me llamo Estelio... Yo, Estelio."

*

In the Saturday noon sun of Cumaná, a high sun that stung your skin, he was kicking around a soccer ball with boys his age, and the boys were flirting with girls his age, and the girls weren't just girls any more, they were women. And it wasn't just their bodies, it was how they talked and dressed and walked. Dark eyes, or sometimes green or blue, that said vayate and vente at the same time, voices that sang sweet or husky phrases, long black hair, or sometimes brown or blonde, that flowed over tiny tank tops, tight jeans moulded to swaying hips. They knew they were women, they wanted everyone to know. Nothing in South Bend had revealed this new world to him. The question was: If girls were women, how was he supposed to be a man?

Luke knew how. Within a week of starting school at the liceo, blue shirts and white pants, Luke had a girlfriend. In the same week, James had gotten one classmate's full attention, she was by his side every moment, and she was pretty and friendly, but of course he could hardly say anything to her, the Spanish was still all so new, and one day she laughed in a way that made her mouth look huge and somehow he wasn't attracted to her any more, which was just stupid — but the point is that in the week Luke got a girlfriend, James blew his chances.

"You'll meet another girl at school," Mom said. And maybe he would have, if things had worked out differently. By March, six weeks in, James and Luke faced a daily gauntlet of classmates pleading for help on English assignments, English tests performed at a tilt for other eyes to see, English papers written start to finish — a growing volume of work, on demand. James could hardly walk the liceo's halls under the pressure of it all, his shoulders tightening, knees stiffening, as if he might seize up and stand paralyzed under the demanding gaze of his classmates. That's when Dad said they could stop. He said they shouldn't do the other students' assignments and not doing their assignments probably would mean being ostracized — which always made James think of ostriches, but that wasn't the point — and that meant that high school in Cumaná, for its own reasons, wasn't going to work out any better than elementary school back home. Dad hardly seemed to mind. "I have to get to class. You boys, give the Renault a push to get me started." The old French clown car with miniature tires whose engine wouldn't buzz to life until James and Luke jogged it to a start.

*

Henry's feet gripped the hard wet sand, walking the slant where the spent waves slowed and spread and retreated. Playa San Luis. He liked to walk the length of the cove, traipse up and over the arm of hillside that reached to the sea, then walk the length of the next cove and over the next arm of hillside. The first semester had been harrowing. Standing at the front of a classroom of Spanish-speaking graduate students, his stomach wrenched. Yes, there was the universal language of mathematics he scrawled on the chalkboard — he was South America's Boleslaw Sobocinski. But then came the questions. Was the young woman by the window asking him about the logic of the formula or about the number of questions on next week's exam? The day he caught one single word of a long question and instantly somehow realized that the context — the time and the place and the person asking — filled in for all the other words, that was the day he realized he was going to be okay. And beyond that, he was free. He never realized how trapped he felt at Notre Dame, trapped by the convenient opportunity to teach at the famed university where he had studied, trapped because it was the good job that paid the bills. He never realized until O'Casey pushed it in his face with that self-satisfied parting smile. Genny was a handful that evening. He understood. She was scared. He wasn't. It was an intuition like his dad's. Henry tripped on a piece of driftwood and stood motionless under the tropical sun as a chill shot down his spine. Disbelief. At what he had done. A family of four to support. His career had only just begun. How long might it have taken to get another job...thank God Venezuela came through. He breathed the sea spray and felt the wet sand under his feet.

The crate never came to port, they were still little more than campers in their house. And nobody at the university had been paid in two months, which didn't seem to surprise anyone. But they made do. And the camaraderie he saw — how the first faculty to get paid shared with the rest, knowing the others would do the same for them the next time — it was something he hadn't seen since he was a boy in New Ulm during the War.

The puzzle that remained was the kids' schooling. Really James' schooling. The whole family studied the Spanish conversation book and the Spanish-English dictionary. He was tutoring the kids in math. They were reading the novels Genny brought in her suitcase, and others lent by the few U.S. or British faculty. He knew that whenever the family finally returned to the U.S., Luke and Kelly would fit back into the school system okay. But James. He was the one who couldn't tolerate school any more than it could tolerate him. He was the one who arrived in Cumaná already two years behind his grade according to the official paperwork. They needed paperwork, official paperwork, that said he wasn't behind. Jerry Robins in Geology had told Henry about correspondence courses from the Calvert School in Baltimore. Funny, it was even James' middle name, Calvert. He'd talk with Genny. She'd know what to do.

*

James listened to the bouncing bass line that sounded from the end of the block. Una fiesta. From a distance the bass was a hum, a noise, because he couldn't hear enough of the other instruments to follow the melody.

"C'mon!" Luke said.

"I just have to comb my hair."

"Then meet me over there!"

"No! Wait!" James felt a surge of fear, finding the right house, asking to be let in, what if he went to the wrong house? "I'm coming!" he shouted and caught up with Luke rounding the gate.

The house on the corner was a real home, fully furnished, decorated with rugs and paintings and potted plants. Lived in. It was packed with guys and girls dancing. And now he could hear the music, all of it, salsa blaring from the stacked speakers. Clave beat and the bouncing bass, the chorus calling out. *Pretenciosa!* Conga beat and the bass line, trumpets calling till you're dancing. *Mentirosa! Pretenciosa!* You had to sway, had to move your feet, but when he did, he saw their faces snickering. Some guy he didn't even know smiled assurance, but that made him feel even more pathetic. They were all so comfortable moving their bodies. He felt the music in his mind, but his body was stiff. When somebody handed him a plastic cup of Coke with ice and...wow...rum — he just leaned against the wall. Leaned and listened and watched.

Young teens like him, grown adults, even some grandmas and grandpas. No matter the age, the couples danced close, bailando juntos, in sync, all romance and flirtation, knowing smiles. Some of the teen girls danced like in a dream or a trance, mouth half open against their guy's shoulder. Good grief, the guys' shirts were streaming with drool.

"Asi la chica muestra que se ama el chico." Estelio, sweating and catching his breath explained it to James.

Estelio knew how to be a man. When the warm evening breeze carried relief from the day's stinging sun and rustled the palms south of Calle B, where you could walk the dirt path down to a shack bodega for a soft drink, Peksi, no matter if it was Pepsi or 7-Up or Frescolita, the same breeze carried music, and a young man with blackest hair and greenest eyes and red-brown skin carried the music in his hands, in the cuatro he strummed, and in the pureness of his voice. Following him, a growing wave of young men and women, listening, singing, wanting to be wherever he was. He was Estelio.

"It shows she's in love," he explained.

"Verdad?" James found it hard to believe.

Estelio wiped the wet shoulder of his own shirt and blew a kiss to a girl across the room. "Sí, claro que es verdad!"

"Wow," James said.

"Se dice ua-o!" Estelio laughed to the others and joined his girl on the dance floor as a bright blaring trumpet chorus called out from the stereo speakers.

James is the kid who says ua-o. It was true. He was the odd one here. Not Luke, who found a goofy, friendly way to dance, to fit in. Not the guys hoping for drool and the girls deciding who was worthy. Think about that. Drooling saliva to say *I love you.* Who knows how these things get started, but it works as long as everybody knows the signal. It could theoretically be a smile, a yelp, a snap of the fingers, a stomp of the foot, or a puddle of drool. He shuddered. But he might feel differently if it came from Yurima's lips against his shirt, her body pressed against his...but on the other hand, he didn't really know, when you get there, what you're supposed to do next. Maybe that was the real problem. He didn't know exactly, even at this age, how it worked. Mom had always given little warnings — about diseases, about it being immoral or disrespectful. But Yurima. He wanted to talk with her, and kiss her, and cuñar se whatever that meant, and be by her. On a couple of evenings Mom had called him out to the front patio when Yurima came to the gate to visit. But he had been so flustered he couldn't think of anything after *Buenas! Cómo estás?* and he excused himself within minutes. Yurima didn't come by again after that.

He could still do it with the girls in the magazines, when nobody else was home. Borrow a teen magazine from the stack in Kelly's room, then in his room marvel at the precious face on the cover of *Seventeen*, green eyes red braids, blue eyes blonde waves, brown eyes black curls, the delicate brows, the red lips. Already feeling good from the cover, he could stretch out naked on the cold polished stone floor, what a feeling that was, and flip through the pages, more girls, ads with girls in bras, girls in panties, ads for feminine products with girls wearing nothing, girls facing modestly away but still wearing nothing... wearing nothing at all... nothing at all... Oh god! Whew. Wow. That was one of the best yet.

*

The faintest light through the slat windows, and birdsong. Luke was still asleep on the other cot within the gray glow of the bedroom's plaster walls. The stack of new books from the Calvert School stood fortress-like on the table. James sat up, aluminum frame creaking, and paused on the edge to let the quiet settle in again.

A half hour later he was walking out the entrance of the neighborhood onto Avenida Bolivariano and into the dawn. He had left a note on the dining room table, *I'm walking to the sea.*

He only had to find the way. In Macuto it would have been easy. Green mountains towered above one side of the city, the sea surf lapped the other side. But here the mountains stood low and blue in the distance, shrouded in cloud. Sometimes you couldn't even see them. And as he looked up and down Avenida Bolivariano, he realized. All of these places called out their names in the sky above. Heavy clouds named the mountains even when you couldn't see mountains. Bright open sky named the sea. He followed the sky. On Whitehall Drive in South Bend everywhere was the same. It was a desert of nondescript houses on nondescript streets. What would it mean to walk around the block, or around twenty blocks? White Oak, that was a neighborhood of places. Uphill either direction from the flooding driveway. Streets that curved under woods. The strange hill the older kids biked down, *Killer Hill,* that dove sharply down to the busy traffic of South Bend Avenue. Places mean that something happens. You get tired going up or maybe scared zooming down. You're in the clouds or in the sun, in mountain winds or a hazy sea breeze. You start to learn what happens in one kind of place versus another. And place by place you can put together a picture of everything.

He followed the avenues that followed the sky. Bolivariano north, the avenue he knew best, the one he walked every week to Supermercado Todos, carrying four heavy plastic grocery bags home to the family as his scrawny South Bend arms formed respectable biceps and his child body awakened to a young man's.

From behind him now, a porpuesto slowed, "Centro, Centro, Centro!" A lonely driver, nobody going anywhere yet. James shook his head, waved it on — "No, no, gracias!".

Avenida Nueva Toledo west, following the sky, the morning sun rising higher, more people on the streets, starting their day like any day. But it wasn't just any day. Over the spring and summer he had walked the barrios with Luke and Estelio and the other boys, out on their own yes, but going wherever Estelio and Luke wanted to go. Today he woke with the sea in his thoughts, the thought of how near it was, wherever exactly it was, and that he could get there, be there, himself.

Somewhere near Avenida Universidad, wanting to break harder west, he crossed the Bebedero canal and tried a dirt road shortcut and — how did he even get here? — he was wandering a dump, some kind of city dump. Piles of debris everywhere. The sky had no name for this. In the tiny world he'd entered there was no horizon but the scrub and trees and fences that seemed to surround him. It was now that he thought of water. He didn't bring any. He brought his Cédula identity card and five Bolivares in coins. At least he had that much sense. But now back to the shadeless dump radiating with the sun's rising heat. He needed a view, so he climbed the highest pile. There, over the hill — that seemed to be the way out. He clambered down and toward the escape route, trudged over a hill grown with thorny brush, and followed one street and another and another and oh my god, the ocean, the breeze. He staggered through the sand to a food cart where two men were just firing up an arepa grill.

"Una Frescolita, por favor." The cream soda he loved.

"Da me bolo, chamo. Veinte-cinco céntimos."

He handed over the coin and drank. And another and another as he staked his place in the sand and peered across the blue-green waves.

He stripped off his shirt and shoes and dove in, floated in the hills and valleys of water and body surfed to shore. He inhaled the salt laden air, the sun's heat on his skin, the waves pushing and pulling. Cumaná was teaching him what Cape Coast tried to — to be alive in his body, alive in the world around him.

*

The fortress, the stack from the Calvert School. James lifted the little hardcover on top, *The Growing Vocabulary*, turned the gray fabric binding in his hands.

Authors' Preface: This book is designed to help those who are awakening to the pleasure, beauty, and power of words...

The authors signed with their initials and *Santa Barbara, California, July 25, 1940*. That's where and when they wrote their message to whoever might read this book, even a sixteen-year-old boy in Cumaná decades later. A stack of books, every one filled with beautiful words. *Tom Sawyer, World History, Methods in Mathematics, Frankenstein, A Treasury of Poetry*. The fortress of books was his. He would go through it stone by stone. Build his own fortress from it.

After two years caminando por las avenidas, nadando en la playa, escuchando la música, the rumbling jetliner climbed steep above the waves, and the great Andes ebbed below the horizon. And when he started school again in August of 1979, he wasn't repeating sixth, wasn't repeating anything. He and Luke had passed the high school equivalency exam — high school, done — and at seventeen he was a freshman at Holy Cross Junior College, sitting down to the traditional welcome meeting with Brother John Driscoll. After a year or two he and Luke would transfer to Notre Dame.

Light

Provincetown, Cape Cod 1981

They all talked about the light. It seemed to emanate from within. Not a sunlight that shines on the world, but a glow, a solar afterglow that emanates from the sea itself, effervescent on the face of the world, on sky and cloud and sand and rooftop. Provincetown is lit by the Atlantic.

*

She swept the long dark curls from her face and lifted the pastels from the box, one by one, held each to the afternoon light, let the color find its facet in her mind, turned the stick sideways to read, Carmine. Scattered over the drafting table at the window that faced the bay, she put Red beside Carmine, then Vermillion, arranged them like spokes of a wheel, radiating from a multicolor center: Minium, Orange, Yellow, Emerald Green — no academic color wheel, it was a wheel of real pastels ready-to hand — Cyanic Blue, Ultramarine, Violet. She opened her sketchbook.

*

By October she had traversed Commercial Street hundreds of times, and would thousands of times again as every Provincetown year-rounder did. Commercial Street on the water and Bradford Street a block inland together defined the town, running parallel for three miles, connected by little cross streets like rungs of a ladder.

Arriving from Orleans in January, Joyce behind the wheel, Mary had bounced in her seat — "Take me down Commercial!" — and Joyce, blue eyes and ruddy smile under a mop of sandy hair, had wheeled the Dodge down Snail Road to pick up the easternmost reach. "You get the full tour, honey, East End to West." Joyce's voice was gruff and tender all at once. "My place is up Blueberry Avenue."

Mary beamed at the very sound of the words. Let New York City have its Fifth Avenue and Boston its Mass Ave. "Oh Joyce, thank you, thank you for letting me stay with you."

"I was wondering when you'd figure out you're supposed to live here. We're gonna tear it up, honey. Welcome home to Helltown!"

Piggy's, the OC, the A-House. They did tear it up, late nights to early mornings. Margaritas, music, marijuana. She was thirty-two and desperately ready to live. It was a blast, a release, a little messed up. Her mind reeled with the wantonness of it all. So many amazing people, living their lives in truth, far across the bay from Boston, on the narrow arm of land that reaches for the Atlantic and curls back, motioning to America, *Come away, they won't look for you here.* Women, men, men-women, women-men. Painters, actors, writers, singers. Fishers, scavengers, schemers. Dreamers. Her sketchbooks filled with faces, faces filled with everything that's in us, the good and the bad and what doesn't even have a name, but it has form and gesture and color. January into March, images and emotions rampant and unorganized. She needed it all but she needed something more. It was a portrait in profile, half missing. Joyce's life of partying was balanced against her routine job at the wharf — the other half. Mary was awash in Joyce's party, Joyce's blow-off-some-steam, but for Mary it wasn't ever just a party. She was drinking in everything life could be, sketching a swirl of possibility and now she had to paint from the sketch, make something important happen, art, and enough of a living to keep making art.

As spring's empty streets under stormy skies warmed to summer's sardine-packed streets of tourist throngs, she walked Bradford and Commercial with the eyes of a year-rounder looking for her next rental. White picket fences, dainty seawalls against the tourist flood. Flowers in dots and dashes, orange, violet, blue. A flush of roses over a trellis, red, yellow, pink. Seas of English ivy at the foot of a sculpture. Cottage houses, each a creative patchwork of repurposed rooms and salvaged parts because Provincetowners always did-it-themselves. The only constant was the cedar shake roof and siding that shielded most every home, top to bottom, from squalls and salt air. The town was buffeted. Sea storms and tourist waves.

Joyce had taught her — after cursing her out for forsaking Blueberry Avenue, and kissing her and apologizing — taught her there were rental tides bound to the seasons. Tourists flowing into the coveted shore rentals in summer as year-rounders flowed out to inland streets. And year-rounders flowing down to shore again in autumn as tourists flowed off-Cape.

*

The season had turned, fall was in full force. Gardens had lost much of their color, rose stalks bare of leaves and blossoms, bare of everything but hips and thorns, even while seas of ivy still flowed over the ground.

It was the one house that stood out from the rest, the two and a half story yellow clapboard house with the mysterious bust of an angelic woman mounted above the front door. Everyone called it the Figurehead House. Waves of long brown hair, paint peeling with age, flowed over a yellow cloak with green trim fastened by three black buttons at each shoulder. In her hands she cradled a wreathe, her sea-blue eyes raised to the sky, watching. Watching the sea for the ones who had gone out, the ones who might still come home.

Anyone you meet anywhere could be someone you've lost. Any face you see, even a face she had sketched...could be.... She pushed back the tears. She never did ascend the tower at Our Mother of Sorrows. But she did watch the faces at Winnebago Beach, recorded them on paper, first in crayon, then pencil. Watched in hope for the one face that might be her mother's. But now, mother herself, she watched broken, in hopeless desperation. The old church's name rang a horrible truth she couldn't have imagined back then, sitting in the pew while the priest told of prophets, kneeling in prayer, standing in song. She hadn't known the name of the church was a prophecy, her own life to come. Mother of Sorrows. She would watch, secretly, forever, for the big dark eyes and tiny face. And for a little while, someone would watch with her. The wooden woman in the yellow cloak.

*

Afternoon light splashed across the drafting table. She gazed out the third-story window, across Commercial Street, past the bare limbs of a large tree, through the ever-present telephone lines strung between poles leaning this way and that, and over the rooftops to the bay. Her room was a soft yellow, the floor, broad planks of fir. Her pastels and watercolor paintings covered the walls. Gauze fabrics from Ruthie's Boutique, diamonds in earth-tone colors, warmed the ceiling.

The fading gold of late afternoon startled her to action. She grabbed a pencil and sketchbook, threw on her lambswool cloak from Ruthie's, and raced, her feet skimming the stairs down to Commercial Street, and whisked toward the sun and West End. The telephone poles cast long shadows. There was only a little time before the sun would slip under the sea.

It was just past Pearl Street that she saw his lean, muscular figure. Bellbottom jeans, deer-skin leather vest over the black turtleneck, his dark hair pulled back in a ponytail. He stood in the open doorway of his storefront office, shoulder against the wall, slate black eyes fixed on her. She didn't have time for this, thought of crossing the street, wobbled as crisscrossing thoughts broke her gate.

"Hey Babe. Where you headed in such a hurry? Got a hot date?"

She melted into his voice, wouldn't let him see it. "Tommy Raven! I'm off to West End. For a painting I've had in mind."

"Looks more like you're going to sunset," he glanced to the sky, then set his gaze on her again. "Meet me for a drink at the OC later?"

Tommy Raven had done well for himself. An architect with a busy office on Commercial. Joyce said he was pure Wampanoag. Mary just knew he was pure Tommy Raven. She gave a quick smile over her shoulder. "It's a date." With a flip of her hair, she hurried on down Commercial, curls bouncing on her shoulders.

She glanced through the doorway of Old Colony Tap as she passed. It was an everyday bar where fishers and washashores shook off a long day's toil when work was to be had, or a long day's worry when it wasn't. The room was nearly empty, just Wilson and Joyce on their stools at the bar. She waved to Mark, the P-town EMT, who was ducking in after his shift. Later that night, the dimly lit room adorned with nautical artifacts — a ship's wheel, a life preserver, heavy jute ropes, old photographs of fishermen — would be crowded with boisterous year-rounders.

Mary tousled her hair and danced her hips at the sight of Georgie through the front windows of West End Salon. Sandy bangs nonchalant over tailored eyebrows, he worked his magic, scissors in hand, the salon filled with people waiting to be beautiful.

Off Commercial, she walked toward the shore, slipped from her shoes as pavement turned to cold sand that pressed between her toes. She traversed the scattered mussel shells, then lifted herself atop a retaining wall where she could look down along the bay. Swift and sure she sketched the curve of shoreline shrinking into perspective, and a third of the way along, the towering Pilgrim Monument. She sketched boats and buildings and notes — *greenish blue, cyanic blue, blend horizon* — and the light was gone.

She dashed in under the big neon sign *LOBSTER POT*, about the only neon sign in town, flashed her neon smile to Sam in the steaming kitchen and Bev who took her take-out order. Fifteen blocks and three flights of stairs brought her home, her safe place where she could let down and come off the stage. She peeled the plastic lid off the clam chowder, and between spoonfuls she worked pastel into the sketch, white and ultramarine into the monument, yellow at the edges, and a foggy white-cyanic blue into the horizon. She showered, scrubbed the pastel from her fingernails, and damp-skinned, coaxed her Ruthie's candy red leather dress over her body, only the tiniest panties, no bra, the strapless dress too sleek for anything more. She turned before the mirror, slid her hands along her hips, smoothed her tummy, leaned into her reflection. On her eyelids she painted a shimmering violet, on her lips a red blush. Out the door she blew a kiss to the Figurehead, buttoned the lambswool, and raised the fur collar against the Atlantic chill.

The OC was a steamy cocoon of joy. Regulars around wooden tables leaned into a point of conversation, then fell back in laughter against their heart-shaped wire-back chairs. When the lambswool dropped from her shoulders, all fell quiet for a beat until she smiled and greetings rang out all across the room. She caught a glimpse of Tommy Raven at the bar with his buddies. Ignored him. She mingled, waxed dramatic and comedic, spoofed Ronald Reagan, leaned into kisses from friends of many months or minutes, drew smiling eyes from every corner, wrapped herself in what felt like love.

"Hey, I thought we had a date." Raven at her shoulder.

"Everyone saw me walk in, and they all knew enough to say hello. What's your excuse?" She punctuated her challenge with a smile.

He raised a brow and looked deeply into her expectant eyes, "Say hello? Is that the right word for what I want to do to you?"

My god, she couldn't believe the things he could say. "You're wicked!" She feigned offense, a mask for the flare of anger in her, and started to walk away, then spun on her heel and put her lips to his ear, "I'll have a tequila, with a lemon twist."

"One shot of Cuervo, coming right up." She caught his arm and pulled him close, "You looking for a high quality date?"

"I'm the wicked one? How about an 1800, top shelf?"

His hand grazed her thigh as she released him, and she breathed deep as she watched him walk to the bar.

Across the room — this was too much — Tommy McNulty, tall and lean, his blue eyes sparkling, pushed from the bar to navigate through the crowd.

"Mary Contrary, all alone, a rare moment."

"McNutty!" She reached toward him and felt her hand slip into his. Somersaulting butterflies flitted inside her — those dimples, the long dark hair that seemed to dance in wisps across the shoulders of his quilted plaid jacket — she had always been drawn to him, never quite knowing what it was, not just one thing, everything about him.

"And you, why are you alone? Where's Sandy?" she asked.

"She's back with the carpenter, her old boyfriend."

"Oh, Tommy." She searched his eyes for a sign.

"So where are you living these days?"

"I found a room at the Figurehead House."

"Ah, the Figurehead. You know where she came from, don't you?" he asked with a lift of his chin, ready to laugh.

"Where? Tell me."

"She was floating in the Indian Ocean. Gone for a swim! Captain Henry Cook's whaling schooner came across her."

"Are you serious?" Always a story to tell, he was a man who reveled in life's nonsense.

"More than a hundred years ago. Cook brought her home to Provincetown and mounted her above the front door of his house. You know, just about every house in Provincetown is part boat."

"Incredible!" She bobbed happily in the safe harbor of his story, then saw Raven returning from the bar.

He made eye contact with McNulty and gestured toward Mary with the two drinks.

"Is one of those for me?" McNulty asked.

"Funny guy, McNutty," Raven stared through him, then thrust his arm between the two, handing Mary the tequila.

"Excuse me!" McNulty chuckled. "I'm off to the bar!"

She nudged his arm and winked and saw his eyes dart to Raven. All these funny signals, checks and challenges men toss back and forth. Raven's eyes gleamed triumphant: challenger defeated, prize-woman conquered. But she had her own secret stash of signals to play before the night was over. They were two fiercely independent souls, she and Raven. Sometimes his raw intensity toppled her senses. Other times her dramatic twists left him off-kilter. Their friendship was living theater, tragicomedy, a play of love and loss that finally was just that, play. And that was where she drew the line. She would never let herself or him walk away in pain.

"So, how did the drawing go?" He raised his glass to her. "Did you make it to West End before sunset?"

"I did! The monument, the boats on the bay. The light was magical!"

Raven nodded. "Like the light of the Riviera, always changing."

"The setting sun steals away one palette and hands you a whole different one. I'll show it to you when I finish. What are you working on?"

"I have a design going for some rich New Yorker who wants a place in Helltown. There goes the neighborhood!"

She laughed and he joked and they drank together, then mingled on into separate circles. And there was McNulty standing in the corner near the door. Manly one moment, an innocent the next. Always McNutty.

"That's quite a dress you're wearing," he said, "I can hardly take my eyes off you."

"Those sparkling eyes..." she said. "A shame about Sandy. You're a man who shouldn't be alone."

"Now you're scaring me!" He laughed. "And flattering me." He kissed her cheek, and she marveled how Raven seemed to smell it. Out of nowhere Raven's arm wrapped around her waist, and he leaned in and whispered, "Let's blow this joint and take in the stars above the surf."

"I love the sound of that," she said full-voiced and turned to McNulty, "Tommy, come with us to the beach!"

McNulty chuckled and looked at Raven who was smiling at the floor, shaking his head.

"Let's go!" McNulty said.

"Let's go!" Raven echoed, conceding to fate.

She reached out a hand to each of them, each offered an elbow to escort her, and Mary and the two Tommies blew the joint, arm in arm.

They paraded out onto Commercial, into the cold quiet of an off-season night. A dark alley between two buildings led them to the beach. The backside of Commercial, spare light from bayside windows shone on the sand revealing the white surf crashing, and out on the bay a delicate line shone across the water from the lighthouse at Long Point. The backwash fizzed as it retreated, saltwater thick in the air. Beyond the surf, a big undulating darkness ever darker and darker until there was nothing she could see, and yet the sound of the shifting waves still reached out to her.

Raven's eyes met hers, his voice low and husky. "I can't give you what you want. But I can give you what you need."

She hated how he could do this, sweep her up so easily in stupid words that any man could say, but when he said it.... She glanced to McNulty, raised the fur collar to her cheeks, and looked up the hill to the lighted monument. "Even in the dark of night, the monument is there."

"Provincetown's permanent hard-on," Raven said.

"Oh, stop," she laughed. "Anyway, I thought that was you!"

"Enough, enough!" McNulty chuckled. "I'm starting to feel inadequate! Time for a drink. I have a bottle of Scotch at my place. Anybody game?"

"We're game," she darted in.

Inside the Bradford Street apartment, McNulty lowered the lights and laid an LP on the turntable, the J. Geils Band. Raven pulled a joint from his pocket, cocked his head to the side, lit it, and held it out to her. She sidled close, took the joint and drew in long and slow, then motioned McNulty to join them. He set three Scotches on the end table, sat beside her and took a hit. She smiled into his smiling eyes, then leaned to Raven and exhaled from her mouth into his.

"Oh my god, it's that song, Centerfold!" She jumped from the couch at the synthesized bagpipe riff and handclaps that could set any room on fire. She danced for Raven, swooned, spun in red leather waves of rhythm, push and pull, hemline riding up her thighs until he pulled her down, nestled her in his lap. Swaying with Raven, she took McNulty's hand and pulled him, not Raven, up from the couch. Amazed to be the one, he stood and she felt the gentle touch of his fingertips on her back as their bodies moved in rhythm. His gaze shifted from her eyes to her lips and to her eyes again. He pulled her close, his heartbeat resounding through the second skin of her dress.

She kept one eye on Raven, who had grown quiet and still and wild, like an oak rooted in the burning forest, burning motionless. She knew what he felt, knew the anger was nothing compared to the arousal.

Oh Mary, she said to herself, in confession and prayer, as she released McNulty and locked eyes with Raven, danced to him, took his hand. He stood, stood before her, and she kissed his lips. His hand in hers, she led him to the bedroom. And just at the doorway, before passing through, she looked back to McNulty, dazed on the makeshift dance floor. She reached her hand lovingly toward him, beckoned him to follow. "Come. It's your bedroom, McNutty."

*

Blink, blink, blink, the strands of light came to life, a towering skirt of lights, top of the Pilgrim Monument to the bottom. "Happy Thanksgiving!" Mary cheered amidst the sea of shouts and car horns honking.

*

January 1982

Dear Mother and Father, The start of a new year in Provincetown. I know it sounds a lot like Providence, but I just want to let you know I'm actually in Massachusetts on the Cape, rather than Rhode Island, in case you ever want to plan a visit. And the business card I enclosed in my last letter was something I designed for Down Cape Specialties. So the work I'm doing is more like art design for advertising — I'm not actually hired staff at these businesses. Anyway, I love it here, there is so much beauty to draw and paint. I don't know if I told you last month that I handmade and sold several Christmas cards, mostly pastel drawings of snow on the dunes. Lately I've been making coats out of blankets. I've sold three of them now. I made myself a bracelet today out of a silver butter knife, pounding and bending it until it fit. It polished up into a beautiful piece, maybe another direction I can go. My love and energies to you and Kit.

She marched briskly down Commercial, averting her eyes from the OC and the Crown and Anchor, avoiding Masonic Place and the A-House, determined to make it to the post office and back without spending her last dollars or falling into the entanglements of free drinks. She gave up her one dollar bill and change for a container of sour cream at The Patrician and rounded the block for home.

As she stood alone before the stove in the shared kitchen of the Figurehead House, the healing aroma carried her right back to the warmth of Marie's mom's cucina. But this time, the recipe was Joyce's. Radish Soup.

In sauce pan, bring vegetable broth to a simmer.

Add fresh garlic and ginger.

Add shredded red radishes, and simmer until the broth turns a radiant red.

Serve with a scoop of sour cream and scallions.

She knew Joyce wished they could be something more than friends. Joyce had served her the steaming broth on Blueberry Avenue. Valentines Day. Some called it poverty soup because it was dinner when all you had in the kitchen was powdered broth packets, garlic and ginger, and a sack of radishes that were supposed to add life to a salad but had to stand in as the main course. That was Mary's kitchen tonight. Last week's inspiration — watercolor, of course, what other medium could capture the Cape's light! — had sunk her budget mid-month. Twelve paint tubes, five brushes, four sketch pads. It doesn't take much to sink when you're barely afloat. Rent would be late again. And dinner... *Stir while you pour, perfetto!* She breathed the steam from the bowl, breathed in everything Marie meant to her, everything Joyce meant to her as the radish swirled in the radiant red broth. Not poverty soup. Love soup.

*

And what about Alan? She stretched her slender legs luxuriously in the warm August sands of Herring Cove Beach, set her eyes on the farthest wave and her pencil on pad devolved from mindful sketch to doodling dreams. Where would the wave come to shore? How many others would merge with it? Would she lose sight of it along the way? Alan's head of dark curls, his head of dreams, an ocean of a man. He struck chords strange and beautiful, playing out with his band on Pond Road, a slight stoop to his hulk as if in apology for his height. Sabina invited her. Mary's age, she was a painter too. Hers was a family of sailors and fishers with Cape roots a century deep. Sabina knew her roots, knew her home, knew the out-of-the-way places. And in an out-of-the-way bar, there was Alan, rhythm guitar, playing the music of the spheres. She couldn't quite grasp him, the depth in his eyes, the quiet in his ways. He was a seeker like she was, a nomad, a wanderer. But where she darted, he lofted. Where she spun circles, he swirled great loops.

*

Mary swam back-crawl the length of the outdoor pool, her arms trailing droplets as they wheeled through the air and broke the water, pinky first, her body gliding beneath the stars. Just the twinkling stars above. All else was dark at the Atlantic Motor Inn, Truro. Alan worked the day desk, and the night desk readily waved him in for a midnight swim, Mary at his side. He sat on the pool's far edge looking somewhat dignified, somewhat high as a kite, swim trunks still dry.

She righted herself, water flowing from dark mermaid locks, and grasped the concrete ledge between his legs. "Aren't you coming into the water?"

"Coming into the water...plunging into the water, oh definitely...you see nobody even knew about Pluto until Clyde Tombaugh in 1930..."

"Your music is cosmic. I never would have guessed you were studying the cosmos." She scissored her legs, hand on the ledge.

"For a new book, oh yeah, reading heavily in cosmology, planetary histories. There's a whole spiritual thing, shamanistic, Kabbala, Buddhist, ultimately its Buddhist. I have notes from two hundred articles, Lamont Library at Harvard, they know me from the stacks. I'd like to take my research, my notebooks, travel the seas by freighter. They take passengers..."

"Don't you dare sail away!" She launched from the wall, another lap with the ease of a childhood passed in the Lake Erie surf.

She righted herself again, dripping, wondering at the fact that he was still talking. She scissored in the pool in her hot bikini, and he was still talking.

"I think the planets might have an answer. Planetary histories. Something to send a larger resonance through the human ego-body politic..."

"Would you like a blow job?"

"A larger, a larger..." He chuckled. "A what?"

She unclasped her bikini bra, submerged to peel off the rest, plopped it all on the pool's edge, and launched herself in slow motion, a slow back-crawl, her form gliding through the glassy blue to the other side and back until she righted herself at pool's edge, heaved herself up, arms resting on his thighs, and peeled back his swim trunks.

"The thing is, Mary, I'm an employee here...Oh lord, oh lord almighty... This isn't Provincetown, oh, Truro's not as, ugh, open...oh baby!"

She smiled her innocent I've-done-nothing-wrong smile and launched from the wall. Another slow lap across the pool and back. "Hi again."

"Yes, hi. Jeez Mary. You are Queen Hijinks." His trunks were on now, but he was smiling up at the stars.

She laughed, a little embarrassed. "So you're really a writer as much as a musician?"

He nodded his head — "Yeah, yeah" — and his eyes got big. "Let's just say I had a transformational experience..."

"Let's say that." She flipped her hair, pool spray, and pushed off from the wall again. His words sank in as she swam. Coming back from her lap, her eyes were dark and serious. "Tell me."

He nodded, tilted his head, mouth wide open and then the words tumbled out. "I was twenty-two, living at home after college. My dad was a salesman, had his own company, and he assumed I would take over running it." There was a hurt in his eyes. "Lord knows why he wanted to retire, he's still nonstop, board meetings and fundraisers all over town, award ceremonies, always the center of attention. My dad, I couldn't...the business was his path, not mine."

She touched his knee, a reassuring caress.

"He had no clue who I was, what I wanted. And there was no way — after what I experienced that day as I walked into my bedroom. Transformational. Changed in a moment, thrown to the floor. I had never had any desire to write. I got up from the carpet, and there it was, the yellow pad. My parents always kept it on the desk, like a desk had to have paper. It had been there for years, nothing ever written on it. I sat down to that yellow pad and wrote, hours and hours. Poetry, spiritual poetry. I've written every day since."

She held his eyes in the embrace of hers until her vision submerged under salty tears, rivulets down her cheeks.

*

He lent her his Korg keyboard. "Lambda ES50, electronic, very advanced, very advanced," he had said. He described everything with that sense of wonder. Whatever advancements it contained inside, its four octaves were enough for her to practice chords, create harmonies she could sing to. She'd always thought about it. She loved belting out lines in school plays. And the music she'd heard in New York a decade ago — Marianne Faithful in Greenwich Village, Patti Smith at St. Mark's Church — they showed her the power of word and harmony. Why not sing? Why not turn the poetry she penned in her sketchbooks into songs? Alan loved the idea and invited her to jam with him next week at *the Shrine,* his name for the makeshift recording studio in the little cottage he rented in Truro. "Work on your chords in the meantime," he had instructed. "Most of the guys I play with, me too, we can hardly read music, but we know the chords. It's all about the chords, know your chords and we can..."

"Coordinate?"

It took him a moment to catch on. "Coordinate? Chordinate, got it, I like that."

Thoughts of Alan accompanying her, she rolled a chord on the Lambda, her fingers finding their place with ease, a brushstroke in her able hands. *D Major,* she whispered.

*

Fall 1983

Mid-September, still sunny and warm, the tourists mostly gone. They coasted down Commercial in Alan's 1973 Chevy Malibu. Orange with white racing stripes. He looked so calm and cool, one hand on the wheel, other arm propped on the open window. Mary took a drag on her cigarette, exhaled in utter relaxation and gently flicked the ash out her window. "Want to go for a ride at West End?" he asked.

She giggled, shoulders scrunched, then threw her hair back. "Let's do it!" He nodded, a Mona Lisa smile on his face. It was their ritual, something they did now and then. Past the Art Ass and the OC, past West End Salon until they finally reached the very end of West End, the circle drive at Provincetown Inn. He steered the Malibu into the loop and stepped on the accelerator. "Oh baby!" she cried out as they laughed and looped, round and round and round.

*

Do I know you?

You say you're a lover from long ago
I don't remember one
Are you sure you haven't mistaken me for someone else?
Come on now think again
You say you loved me when...
Now I'm sure you've got it wrong
Because love is what flows out...
I don't know yet what flows in
You must have known some starry-eyed child
with bruises on her knees
instead of her heart.

*

She met Georgie in the stairwell, him on the way down and her on the way up after a morning sketching on the windswept winter shore. She whipped off her scarf and primped, her palms buoying up her dark curls. "I'll come downstairs later for a coif."

"I know you're joking, darling, but sometimes I don't know if you're joking." He swiveled at the bottom of the stairs, hair falling in platinum waves. "Whatever you need, darling." He winked. "You know I'm happy to do you any time."

She blew him a kiss and hurried on up the stairs, enveloped in his aura. The attic bedroom above West End Salon was a trip, her all-time favorite off-season housing so far, except for the Figurehead House. She had been here a month already, and it honestly felt like living inside a theater hall, all performance, always on. Georgie imbued the house with a tingling intensity. But beneath the glitter, he had a quiet depth about him and a heart of gold.

She didn't come back for the coif. She arrived home from the A-House about midnight, trying to stay out until the guests on the second floor, Georgie's floor, were asleep. Georgie's brother arrived by ferry that afternoon with his toddler daughter, so adorable, really. And all Mary had to do was sneak into Georgie's kitchen and brew a cup of tea to take upstairs. Surely they were all asleep. She filled the kettle at the sink quietly as she could, heard a baby's cry from the bedroom, turned off the tap, waited. She wavered, a strange rush over her. God, she shouldn't have done that third, fourth, whatever Tequila shot. She turned on the tap, just a little more water, and gently set the kettle on the stove, turned to high. She breathed out hard and leaned against the fridge, hand on her hip. And the cry sounded again. She stepped toward the stove, turned to the cupboards, stepped toward the fridge, pinball rebounding. Crying, crying, crying. She flung open one cupboard. "Where are the fucking cups?" Staggered, spun. Flung another cupboard open, heard the hinge crack. "Where are...the fucking..." — flung another open — "the fucking teacups!"

"God Mary, what's happening?"

"No, no, no!" She hurled a cup to shatter against the wall.

"Mary, it's me. Georgie. Can you hear me?"

"You fucking...you fucking...!" Everything she could grab, she threw everything. Ceramic burst into shards, scattered, struck counters, burst into slivers, slid across the floor. Crying turned to screaming behind the door.

"Enough Mary! Enough! My brother, my tiny niece... Mary!"

Her hand was bleeding. She was on her knees. Could hardly see through her tears. She looked up to Georgie's face, his hands were trembling.

"I'm so sorry, but you have to leave. Right now, Mary. Get your things. You have to leave."

*

How can I give you
a part of myself
to linger yet longer
than time itself?
Let me but give you
my spirit hold near
That way, my love, I'll
always be here.

*

Summer 1986

"Mary, hold still," Sabina pleaded. "I'm almost finished. You of all people should be patient with the artist!"

Mary mocked exasperation and lifted the conk shell to her ear again, eyes steady on the focal point across the room as she sat naked on the bed. "I love being just across the hall from each other. You won't move away for off-season, will you?" She closed her mouth, stayed still, as long as she could, and steadied the shell. "I can hear the party starting downstairs."

"Mary, stop talking! Are you even trying to sit still?" Sabina dabbed the palette and dashed her brush. "And just so you know, most people hear the ocean."

Mary dropped the shell on the bed, mouth open, a laugh ready to issue, but she set her jaw instead and grabbed a pillow and aimed.

"Don't you dare!"

"Right, artist at work." She dropped the pillow and they both reeled in laughter.

"Okay, okay, okay." Sabina's eyes focused and her brush dashed — "Shading above the eye...flesh tone in the cheek. There, finished. Santa mãe de Deus! Before you look..." She lit a joint and passed it to Mary.

"First you undress me and now you get me high?"

"I usually do portraits of my dog — he never says, *You made my nose too long!* So be kind!"

Mary hugged her close, took a hit, exhaled, studied the canvas. "It's beautiful, Sabina. And no stretch marks. I just can't bear to look at them." She went quiet.

"Oh Mary, have you ever thought, maybe thought to look for her?"

Mary gazed at the floor. "I pulled the ground from under her feet before she even knew what the ground was. And wherever she is, she's spent the past sixteen years stitching some kind of life together. Am I going to upend her life again? And why, so she can follow in my footsteps and live in poverty, bouncing from house to house? I have no right to knock on her door." She took a drag and stood from the bed, hand on her hip. "Do be a dear and hand me my panties!"

"Tears to laughs. Mary Contrary, I see where you got the name." Sabina flung the panties and Mary caught them and slipped them on in one motion.

"You know it's a Portuguese tradition, right? We love the nicknames. Before we knew it, everybody in the Province Lands was doing it."

"Amazing! I love this place." Mary slipped into her dress, silky violet satin against her skin.

"A place like no other. Cute dress! From Ruthie's?"

"Always." Mary pulled the side zipper. "Shit! It won't zip over my belly. Damn clam chowder. I should have stuck to salads." She pulled her sewing kit from under the bed, spread the seam with her fingers and ripped the stitches with the seam ripper, just enough to loosen the fit at the waist. Deftly she stitched it, tied a knot, and cut the thread with her teeth.

"Brava, my grandmother couldn't have done better!"

She slipped into the dress again — "I've always sewed, since I was little" — and pulled the zipper closed, turning sideways in the mirror and smoothing the fabric across her tummy. "What are you wearing?"

"I'll show you." Sabina disappeared across the hall. Mary penned eyeliner and brushed a glittering green mascara. Rose red across her lips. She stepped into her knee-high black boots. "Sabina?"

"Five minutes!"

She descended the stairs through a curtain of haze, Sabina at her side, and raised her hands in an embracing greeting. "Mary!" Voices in all keys rippled through the smokey haze of every incense. "I can smell the pheromones," Sabina leaned to her ear. "Stop it!" Mary laughed. No one could guess the flush of embarrassment she felt just then. No one had any idea what she felt inside. "It's terribly hot in here!" She vamped. "Can someone get me a drink?" Six party-goers stirred to their feet, three were stayed by the hands of their partners while three others, two men and a woman, slow-motion raced through the crowd of bodies to the bar cart.

"Looks like you won't go thirsty!" Joyce, demurely stationary, raised her tequila and Mary danced to her and drank from her glass. "I'll drink from yours and you drink from mine."

"Don't play with me, honey. I've had enough of these, you might find yourself getting more than you bargained for."

Mary embraced her in a gushing outflow of love for this husky, lusty woman, her friend and protector.

"All right now honey. You're as straight as a ballpoint pen. If you don't know that, I do. Go find yourself one of those man-beasts and have a good time." Joyce's kiss on her cheek made her feel like everything was okay.

Friends packed the ornate upholstered sofa and mingled in corners of the grand living room where the fireplace, empty on an August evening, was bookended by two tall glass-front cabinets showcasing Nelson's antique pewter ware. Most landlords kept to basics, and that's what the upstairs rooms were, but Nelson lived here too, and the common rooms had to be as grand as any ancient ship captain's home. Empty shot glasses littered the antique mahogany coffee table. Bodies steamy. Swinging, bouncing, swaying, grooving to David Bowie. Glam Sam, whose onstage persona Miss Apprehension was star of the *Like a Girl* revue swirled in a rose sequined gown. Outdoors and a block toward shore, summer tourists in T-shirts and baggy shorts packed Commercial, searching for more T-shirts and baggy shorts, scrambling past all things authentic.

"How is our assistant stage manager tonight?" Mary turned and there was Bette. Sweet Bette, a recent washashore just out of college. What a marvel to see the world as mostly good, to see the future in hope. Mary kissed her glowing young cheek. "Wonderful now that you're here. If only the title assistant stage manager came with a paycheck, or better yet a few lines onstage! Are you excited for opening night at Provincetown Inn?"

"I'm a little nervous," Bette said. "Have you performed in the Mayflower Room before?"

"Ah, the Mayflower Room!" Ginger punctuated her entrance into the conversation with a jet of smoke from her Embassy cigarette, her skin-tight python-pattern jumpsuit seemed to contract tighter as she gestured languidly in the damp heat of the crowded room. "For real grit, the grit stars are made of, you should have seen us at Caffe Cino!"

"Is that on West End?" Bette was wide-eyed.

"Greenwich Village, dear, Joe Cino's place. You probably weren't even born! And you met our Mary at the Provincetown Theater?"

Bette giggled. "You tell her, Mary."

"All right, can you picture this, Ginger? In a linoleum-tiled room at the Recreation Commission there sit seven adults, chairs formed into a circle" — Ginger's lips parted in a gasp of recognition as Mary recounted — "and the only ones talking during the whole hour are Bette, me, and the moderator."

"My god, don't tell me!"

"It's the Social Anxiety Recovery group."

"Oh my god!" Ginger put her hand to her mouth. "Dr. Freiberg's circle of horror!"

Bette was animated now. "And there sat Mary in unmatched socks, with feathers in her braids, and both of us talking nonstop..."

"And you with your violet glitter blush, Bette, and that's probably all it took to get us both committed!"

Ginger nodded. "I suppose there's been a Helltown party pooper in every generation back to colonial days." The gin and tonic swayed in the glass as Ginger gestured, "Look at these dears! Now here's the town I know and love!"

Three women paraded out of the kitchen blissfully naked. "We'll be back in a few," one announced. "We're making bread but there isn't any yeast!"

"Ladies, ladies!" Glam Sam, six feet of shimmering panache, opened his arms to corral them. "You'll spend the night in jail, ladies, and miss the rest of the party! I have the perfect dresses for you, with a little pinning and taping — wait here!"

"Where's Sabina?" Mary scanned the room. "Bette, I'll find you again. Ginger..."

"Circulate dear, circulate. I used to be the one who knew everyone, looks like I'm passing the torch to you."

Mary squeezed Ginger's hand and passed through the crowded kitchen where guests snacked from the ransacked cabinets while Wilson, Raven, and McNulty held their cards close at the kitchen table over two whisky bottles and a line of coke. Wilson, mustache and graying hair that shot out in all directions, was a pillar of the community, even though no one knew exactly what he did. "Boys, boys! Deal me a hand and save me a line!" Mary strutted into the next room to the fading sound of whistles and shouts from the table.

Quieter conversations brewed in the parlor, and there in a corner chair camped Anita, tangled dark hair with random gray wisps, beer cans clustered at her feet.

"Anita, sweetheart! You've found your safe place."

"Safe as any." Anita reveled in a long sip from a can of Pabst.

Muffled sighs of ecstasy emanated from behind the bathroom door. Love everywhere, love everyone. Down the hall a creaking noise from one of the bedrooms. She stood in the doorway, hand planted on her hip, and watched Bonnie and Sabina bounce on the queen-size bed as if it were a trampoline. As Sabina sailed up, lips parted in wonder, Bonnie sailed down, her loosened blonde bun flopping. Mary applauded, "Brilliant!"

A ruckus sounded from the front of the house. Voices chanting, "Free Peltier, Free Peltier!"

"Joyce is working the living room!" Mary said, suddenly sober. She joined the chant and led the others weaving through the house but by the time they reached the living room the crowd had swung from revolution to revel and David Bowie rang from the speakers louder than ever. Mary smiled reassurance to Joyce across the room and raised her fist in solidarity.

"Mary, where's that Bing boy you've been talking about?" Bonnie asked above the music. "I don't think I've ever met him."

Mary cupped her ear and repeated back, "Did you ask, what's Bing about?"

"I'm saying I've never met him, Alan Bing, I don't even know what he looks like!"

"Yes, I like him a lot, I mean... I'm not really sure what you're asking... the music is too loud."

Bette leaned in, "He lives here?"

Sabina explained, "Mary and I live here."

Mary laughed — "You could be saying anything, for all I know!" Her soul ignited, her voice rose, arms opened wide, hands gesturing, her face a changing mask of drama. "I could be saying anything, does anyone care, are we even aware of what we're saying half the time, I think I am, it's fine but no one listens or knows who I am, who we are, why we're here, somebody help us, help us say anything more than just to pass the day because what's the point of talking if you can't be saying something, Bonnie? Dancing, dreaming, saying..."

Bonnie's eyes lit up, and while Mary carried on, she overlapped, "What's Bing about what's bounce about when I bounced about the bed and didn't bang my head and who would bounce without a bed and ping-pong off the walls instead unless you're dead you'll bounce about..."

And Bette leapt in, "Say you? Nay pray you, he is dead and gone, lady, he is dead and gone. At his head a grass-green turf, at his heels a stone...oh, ho, that's all I know I should know more, stage manager, line, line!"

The three carried on wildly talking over each other without pause and gradually the room quieted, the whole rest of the room except the three and the LP on the stereo until — "Turn off the music" — McNulty's voice rang from the kitchen doorway and the music went silent and time stopped and she floated in the waves of blather, banter, spirits, muses, three partners upending the room in unending polyphony.

*

Autumn roses among the dunes, the hips, bright red ornaments among the flaming golden leaves and gray thorns, the shrubs afloat in an ever-changing sea of sand. She went to the back side, walked the dunes toward Peaked Hill. In December she would be — was it even possible? — thirty-eight years old. She still looked young, still drew the gaze of twenty-something men, and women. But she didn't feel young any more. Her body, her spirit, everything that could happen to you, everything people could do to each other. She wasn't the girl she had been, the girl Bette still would be for a little while longer.

Five days ago Mary had stood behind the governor at the capitol in Boston as he signed the official declaration, *October is Cape Seafest Month.* She was Seafest Committee artist — weeks of phone calls and bus trips down to Orleans — and she stood there with the Cape Planning Commission Coordinator and the Seafest Committee Chair. Three capable women, and a man who's talent seemed to consist in smiling and shaking hands. They were all supposed to smile the same stupid meaningless smile as Gov. Dukakis. But she wouldn't give the system the satisfaction. She waited for the photographer, watched his fingers rotate the focus ring, and just before his forefinger pressed the shutter button, that was the instant when she, bubbly Mary Zadora, planted her hand on her hip and scowled.

Men of authority. Father, governor, president, all the rest, answer to the system. She sketched it out in vibrant color on the chalkboard at the OC the night she ferried from Boston. Joyce raised a tequila and Wilson sat pokerfaced, surveying the fishermen as they grumbled and shook their heads. She just wanted them to understand that men do terrible things for greed and power, that we're not relieved of responsibility just because we're separated from America by the bay, the little stretch of sea the ferry can cross in under three hours. Didn't Jesus say the greatest commandment was, *You shall love your neighbor as yourself?*

There wasn't a lot of money in being the Seafest artist for a month. But come winter she knew security, financial security, for the first time since leaving Sandusky. As art director for Provincetown Magazine she handled client advertising budgets, did layout, paste up, and darkroom. She overflowed with ideas, a weekly full-page political cartoon strip, a new system for ad-sharing between area publications, a new layout for the magazine. They didn't want it, not any of it. They wanted budgets, paste up, darkroom, the familiar layout. Six months later they found someone who could give them what they wanted, nothing more. It was a blow. Not surprising. Just another step toward getting older.

She picked up odd jobs — store signs, flyers. This morning she had finished the menu designs for Adrian's Restaurant. Adrian was going to love the artfully rendered stalks of asparagus. She desperately needed the income to make the rent. Darrin, her latest off-season landlord, was running out of patience. *No more late payments. This is the last time.*

And then Alan. She tried to reach him. *You mean a lot to me. We're really good together. I love you.* What the hell kind of signal was he waiting for? They were such a musical match, such a match of mind and spirit. She thought. But then he packed up and moved on, back to Kansas City. "I don't need the Malibu," he said. "You do." He handed her the keys and boarded the ferry.

*

May 1990

It defied the laws of the tide. She was standing in an incredible second-story apartment with a view of Commercial out the front window and a view of the harbor out the back. It was the beginning of summer, and the owner was handing her the key, not reclaiming it.

"You're saving us, Mary. It's the worst possible time to lose a property manager, right when the summer crowds are moving in! You know where everything is. You've got our number in Boston. You gave her our number Toby?"

Toby raised his hands "I have nothing to do with giving numbers, you're giving the numbers, the keys, the...! I still think she's a member of the tribe — you're sure, Mary, you're sure? You're laughing now, I'm laughing. Ah...I could be wrong... Where did you say your people are from? Did she say?"

It was the simple question no one could imagine not being simple. Where do you come from? She wanted to say, maybe you're my parents, because for all she knew maybe they were. Flailing in the cold deep, she smiled. "My mother and father are Polish-American."

"Am I crazy now? Am I so crazy?"

"Leave the girl alone, Toby. The Kibbutz is your home for the summer," Sharon assured. "And we'll see how it goes, maybe longer."

The next morning, Mary put the coffee on to brew and stretched luxuriously before the harbor window. Three months rent-free for managing the property, and she could still pick up design work all the while. Arms stretched high above her head, she stopped cold. *Trash pickup. Seven AM, there's still time.* The morning passed like that, with flashed remembrances, the making of lists, the posting of lists on the fridge, on the broom closet. Then midday, a knock on her apartment door. She wondered who would be visiting and instantly realized, yet again, that she was the property manager. Someone needed something. She opened the door to a slender young woman, ten years her junior, who held a heavy case in one hand while the other pulled back a long black strand from across her bright green eyes. "I'm Elodie. I was told to pick up my key, the key for number four."

"Key, number four... You're right next door. I'll get your key. Do you have more things? Do you need help?"

*

On the other side of the wall Mary could hear the Smith Corona electric typewriter, morning fits and starts and...silence. She couldn't quite picture what kind of work this was. When she sketched, she sketched all the way through. When she journaled, she wrote, rewrote, all the way through. There it was again — the surge of key-clatter. Three or four seconds, a phrase or a sentence, and silence.

*

She walked Bradford down to the angled pavement entrance to Ruthie's Boutique and stepped inside to the familiar scent of laundry detergent and mildew.

"I'm in and out of the store room today — a whole new load of what-nots, I don't know where I'll put it all — let me know if you need anything." Ruthie rummaged, red-faced, through a crate atop a pile of crates.

"Thanks Ruthie." Mary walked the narrow aisles among dress racks, rolled the fabric of each dress gently between thumb and finger. Texture before anything else. Scratchy, surely polyester. Linen. Cotton. Silk. "Ruthie, do you have a used typewriter?"

Ruthie peered out from the store room, mouth hanging open. "Even with this new load, honey, no, I don't have any typewriters... But wait a minute, wait a minute..."

Mary stood perfectly still, a tingling sensation in the air.

"How did you know, Mary? I bought a plug-in typewriter last week and my old Remington is sitting on the floor, I've tripped over it twice already. Fifty dollars and it's yours."

The tingling turned to stone, to coal, to embers. "I'll organize your inventory. I know all about inventory from a salvage man I worked with in Orleans."

At home in the Kibbutz, she strummed stories from the keys onto paper. Stream after stream of clatter, punctuated by the thunk and ding of the carriage return. She and Ruthie settled on a week's labor at the boutique. Ruthie even threw in the precious little yellow pocketbook Mary spied seconds before walking out the door. Streams of story, thunk, ding.

*

She introduced Elodie to Piggy's on a rare evening when Elodie was free, when there wasn't a writers' gathering after the day's sessions at the Fine Arts Work Center.

She leaned toward Elodie's barstool. "I know it's noisy in here, but you seem quiet."

"Oh, am I? I didn't mean to be." Elodie looked down, took a sip of her Manhattan. "I'm sorry, Mary, I think I'm feeling inadequate. You know, I have a masters from NYU, I've published a handful of short stories, but suddenly I feel like a fake. I pluck away at my typewriter in slow motion, fighting demons at the first letter of every word, while you're on the other side of the wall, banging the keys with some sort of divine inspiration. I've written about two pages so far my whole time here. I just don't know if I have what it takes to be a writer."

"You do, Elodie."

"How do you know?"

"Because I've read your stories. I don't think I could ever use words like you do, it's like you're sculpting. A beauty in words that you know how to reveal." Mary's fingers traced lines on the wooden bar. "I guess for me writing feels like sketching. I sketch what's there in the world, what's there in front of me."

"But that's just it, Mary. When you're sketching, say the harbor, you're sketching something that's really there. I'm writing, trying to write, fiction. It doesn't exist, it isn't there in front of me. I somehow have to... And there are forms, there are tools of the trade, it's not like I can simply... Look I'm a writer and I can't even find the words."

"It's okay, it's okay, I know what you're saying. But listen, sometimes I draw a scene I imagine or remember, I don't even know which, and every grain of that scene is something I really have known before. Isn't it the same for writing? Places, people, the things people do, isn't it all there in the world around us? Even if it's fiction, don't we write what's real?" Something was stirring in Elodie, Mary could see it, but god, it wasn't clear if she was nearly okay or diving into a new anguish. "Wait a minute." Mary dug into her cotton satchel and opened her palm to Elodie. "Take these, I want you to have them. They'll help you find your way."

"Oh, Mary, I couldn't..."

"Keep them close while you write."

Elodie held the pair of clear quartz crystals to the cheap light of Piggy's. "You know I don't even believe in crystals."

She touched Elodie's cheek and swept the glistening tears onto her own finger tips. "Hold the crystals again. You can see the world through them." Mary held her own fingers to the light, edged in a saline prism.

*

Stumble, crash. She fumbled for her keys on the second-story landing. "Mary, you're so funny." Elodie laughed. "Let me." She eyed the two guys from New York who stood by, grinning.

"I am perfectly capable of opening my own door!" Mary dropped the keys, found them, wobbled to her feet, and waved them triumphantly over her head. "I am the stage manager!"

"Property manager?"

"Thank you Elodie. Property manager! Thank god, thank the forces we made it inside. Do we have anything to drink?" She plopped onto the couch and opened her arms to Elodie who cuddled into her lap and whispered. "This is all crazy, Mary." And Mary whispered — "There's nothing crazy about love, I wish it was just you and me tonight" — and finished her stroke of truth with the softest kiss on Elodie's lips. She did love her. Her beauty, innocence, creativity, but that wasn't even it. In the right moment of life, the right moment of night, there can be a chemistry, she had come to believe, a connection between two people that can't be explained, doesn't have to be explained.

Zack exhaled from somewhere deep down. "Smokin hot." But Mary just smirked — "They've never seen girls before!" — and she and Elodie burst into giggles while the guys nodded to each other like they were scoring some kind of secret victory.

"Of all the women I've seen, Mary, you have something special. I mean special. That's why I'm going to make you a star."

Mary focused on him as he pulled a bottle of Jack Daniels from his satchel. "You're already filming out on Race Point Road you said, so I'm guessing you've already cast your roles?"

"Beech Forest. Perfect setting for that little project. But I'm talking big. A big-budget film, my connections in L.A. I'm talking the Big Time, Mary."

"You talk big all right. Are you all talk or am I gonna see some action?" Elodie drew a breath of surprise but Mary was on stage now. She touched Elodie's hand in reassurance and didn't miss a beat. "Pour those shots boys, cups in the cupboard, and let's toast the night."

Mary gazed into Zack's eyes as he poured, and she raised her cup, "To art, to film, to love!"

"Here's to love!" Zack eyed his friend and wrapped his arm over Mary's shoulder as she downed her shot. He downed his and kissed her hard on the lips.

"You don't waste any time!" She made a comic face to Elodie, it was supposed to be comic, but Elodie's laugh was questioning. "It's okay Elodie sweetheart, I've got this."

"And I've got this," Zack's friend, she never caught his name, rode his hand under Elodie's mini-skirt. "You don't waste any time either." Elodie echoed Mary, looked into Mary's eyes, looking for an okay but it wasn't okay. Mary's mind raced as Zack pinned her on the couch and suddenly the words poured out. "God you're amazing, I want you, I want you both, you're all mine. Elodie, that problem you mentioned, you'd better not. Maybe in a couple weeks. You should go." Zack's friend pulled his hand away and stood back.

"What problem?" Elodie asked. "I don't understand Mary."

"You've got to go." She hated seeing the puzzled hurt as Elodie closed the door behind her.

*

Someone... Mary's head ached...someone was knocking. She eased herself from the bed, her hair a tangled thicket, and trudged stiffly to the door. She looked down, winced, a confusion of shame at the dried blood, blood and scrapes between her legs. She turned back to the bed. "I'm not fucking managing today."

"Mary? It's Elodie."

"I'm not here."

"Mary, open the door. I'm sorry but I'm not going away until you open the door!"

Her own words floated outside her. "Fuck. I'm fucking helpless. Fucking hopeless..."

"Mary!"

She pulled on a robe, opened the door, stood silent. Pulled back from Elodie's outstretched arms and Elodie's eyes filled with tears. "Mary. I don't really understand what's happening. Those guys, they did this? I heard the voices through the wall. I heard the sounds. Maybe that's what wild sex is supposed to be, I don't know. But I didn't like it. I wanted to stay, Mary, I could have helped you."

"I only wanted a night of love. And look what they've done. They've stolen it all away."

"You could have let me stay with you."

Mary trembled. "Do you think...do you think I had any power to stop them?"

*

Herring Cove Beach, gulls diving. She sketched a child, eyes closed, as if about to cry.

The Lobster Pot, dining room windows onto Provincetown Harbor. She sketched a heart, and from it flies a little heart.

Race Point Beach, south toward Peaked Hill. She pressed her toes into the sand and opened the Aquabee Super Deluxe sketchbook, somewhere in the middle. Atlantic light on a blank page.

*

Thinking of you
I try not to
It might somehow
Break the spell
Seeing life go as the spirits will
I try not to dwell
On fantasies of you.

*

Elodie, I'm not here.

*

July 1990. Midnight

"Okay, Bette, you answer me. What do I do? Another tequila to be okay? How many would it take just to be fucking okay!" Province Lands Road. Low scrub pine loomed in the headlights and vanished past the Chevy Malibu.

"Mary, I..."

"Betrayal! I can trust no one..." Her fingers tightened around the wheel, foot stiffened, the pedal retreated to the floor. "Too many wounds, oh god, too fucking many!"

"Mary, you're driving too fast..."

White sound roared through the open windows. She couldn't hear a thing, couldn't see beyond the red. "Why! What is the purpose! You know what I see in the mirror? A gash, a red gash where my mouth should be."

"Mary, it's okay, please slow down..."

"A razor scar like the scars crossing my belly. How can I turn any of this into beauty? God has chewed off my hands and demanded that I draw!"

"Mary, you're scaring me, please stop!"

Around the curve, the rubber screeched and the collection of mini stuffed animals tumbled from the dashboard. "I can't, I can't!" She skidded onto the gravel shoulder, ran from the open door, ran wild into the shadowed scrub brush under the cold night stars, fell to the ground, chest heaving. Felt Bette's hand on her arm. "Mary, it's okay, I'm here."

"No!" She clutched her belly. The faraway roar of the surf. A whisper. "No."

*

Race Point Beach, 1992

Night. The frigid salt wind buffeted her, shook her. The pounding surf crashed, rushed up the sand, lost in the next pounding crash. She gazed across the immense undulating darkness that had no horizon. It was too big to understand. Too big to fix. Not hers alone. She threw her hat to the wind, her long curls loosed and wild. Sea and sky and stars. Stripped off her jacket, hurled it. Couldn't stop. Stripped off her sweater and launched it flying. Blouse, jeans, every last shred of fabric, and released it into the wild darkness, the world's wind streaming through her. Toes dug into the cold sand, she gazed up the sky, the same sky her sweet one could see. Together they watched the stars.

*

O glorious advocate and protector, Saint Valentine. On Blueberry Avenue, on Commercial Street, on Commercial again. On Bradford and Cook and Pearl. On Center and Bradford again. On Atlantic and Commercial again and Winthrop Street. Every Valentines Day, there was only ever one. *Sweet one, big dark eyes so innocent, for god's sake forgive me, they wouldn't let me, I didn't know what to do, forgive me. I didn't want to.* She sobbed and rocked. *Didn't want to let you go.* Rocked slower. Something evaporating. Something lifting. Her eyes opened to the wooden floor boards, the latest room on Commercial, opened to the present, the everyday world that cared nothing about her cares.

St. Valentine, teach us to love, to find great joy in giving.

She stood from the floor — she hadn't even known she had fallen — opened a sketchbook. *No, no, not paper.* She dug oils and palette from a box, and a canvas no bigger than a sheet of stationery. At the golden mean, her hand deftly swept the curve of America's shore, the mainland across the bay as if seen from Jeremy Point, down Cape. The continent a narrow band of Pthalo green horizon bowed to the Earth's curvature, edged with Naples yellow shore. She brushed the narrow arm of land that reaches for the Atlantic and curls back to America and finally eastward again, Long Point's finger pointing to Provincetown Harbor. *Look for me here, sweet one.* She unscrewed Cadmium red, squeezed it right in the middle and filled the bay with a great Valentine heart — *damn that's dark* — and dripped turpentine and brushed until the heart glowed translucent. She swaddled the heart in Manganese blue waters and bathed the sky with the gentlest blend of Manganese and Pthalo and vaporous white cloud.

She stood back — always at this moment in a painting — examining, examining. She dabbed the heart and brushed red into the mainland horizon. *Who the fuck knows where Provincetown is!* White and black she dabbed from the palette and planted the Pilgrim Monument in one stroke, a short thin line pinning Provincetown on the map.

She examined. But this time, I have to tell you because you might not know, this moment, standing, staring, had nothing to do with the art of it. She dabbed black and white from the palette again and stroked up and down until the monument, still a mere two inches tall, became a weighty peg not a pin, and then it hit her. Reflection of the monument in the water. It will be a wriggle of black. But not any ordinary fucking wriggle. Gently she brushed. Waving, curving lines.

*

Mary dried the dishes as Joyce rinsed. A Saturday. She had called Joyce at noon to tell her she was coming over with makings for breakfast. Eggs sunny-side up, muffins from scratch, coffee. At the table they talked about all the usual things. Mary's latest menu designs, what one of the guys at the wharf said to Joyce and what she said back.

Mary toweled a dish and lifted it to the shelf, when it slipped from her grip — "Damn" — and shattered on the floor.

"Shit, I'm awake now! Don't worry yourself honey. It's not the Queen's china, it's just an old dish. You okay?" Joyce stood back while Mary swept the shards into a dust pan.

"That's the problem, Joyce. Am I okay? I paint, I party, I...I flip out. It's all about trying to be okay. I'm forty-three."

"Aren't you being kinda rough on yourself? You've had some hard knocks."

"I know. And I can't change any of that. It's about love, Joyce, the love we give to everyone around us. It's not whether someone loves us back. It's the love we put out into the world that makes us feel at peace."

"A stiff gin always worked for me. So what's gonna change in your life?"

"Maybe nothing, maybe everything."

Assay

Germany, January 1992

Rain streaked the train windows. Catherine followed the droplets as they spread and split, each making their own journey across the heavy glass. A snowless January was a wonder after trudging knee-deep through the bitter blowing snows of Saint Benedict College mere days ago in central Minnesota.

She opened her gaze outward, zipped the black leather jacket partway, snug over her light wool sweater, and traced the rushing spin of foreground, blur of shrubs, grasses, utility poles, out to the steady axis of horizon. In the middle distance clusters of tiny houses, smoke rising from rooftop pipes, punctuated the lush grassy fields. Were they the outskirts of a town? Or was each cluster a little town all its own? In the Old World of Europe, even in the middle of nowhere, someone lives there. She had packed a small bag, five hundred dollars cash, and her Nikon thirty-five millimeter camera for the month-long trip, J-Term, before her final semester of college.

Standing in the narrow window-side aisle of the passenger car, she flicked the ash from her cigarette, a falling ember bright against her black denim jeans. Carly would meet her at the Hauptbahnhof Frankfurt. The rhythmic rumble of the train lulled her. A train from another era, steel tarnished under a half-century of grease and soot. Who had walked these corridors? What life journeys had unfolded from Amsterdam to Cologne to Frankfurt and beyond?

A metallic roar poured through the door at the end of the car and the conductor entered. She squeezed herself against the window for him to pass but he stopped. "Fahrkarte bitte." Drawing the cascade of long dark waves to her back, she tucked the strands behind her ear and peered into his blue eyes. It took her only a moment to see that she was making the uniformed man nervous instead of the other way around. She pulled the Eurail Pass from the pouch inside her sweater.

"Danke," he said.

"Bitte schön." She watched him pass through the door at the other end, the metallic roar, open and shut. A sign loomed out the window, Haldern Bahnsteig, and spun past. There wasn't even a depot, just a sign on a pole on a platform. Middle of nowhere.

Miles and miles of scarlet wheeled outward to the horizon. So many poppies, you couldn't see where they stopped. A perfect photograph — rain saturates the color of everything — but she had left her bag and camera in the sleeping car, thinking only of stretching her legs. Down the aisle she yanked the handle and slid open the heavy door. The roar was loud as a thunderstorm as she stepped into the sheath of open space between the cars. Below her feet the heavy steel hitch shifted and strained, the tracks a blur.

*

Carly's smiling blue eyes, blue like a Minnesota sky, shone in the candle light as she raised her glass of Cognac. "Welcome to Frankfurt! Oh, we'd better toast our benefactors too."

Catherine followed her lead, toasted toward the three solid middle-aged men who nodded and leaned back in their chairs a few tables away, muted smiles beneath glinting eyes.

Catherine looked earnestly at her old college housemate. "Did they buy us drinks because we're Americans? Does that make us exotic?"

"I'd say it's because they're men. Eastern too. They've got that macho edge, even though they're gray! Tourists from the East are everywhere since the wall came down. I think the gesture is cute, as long as they don't come over to our table!"

Bozidar's words ran through her mind, *Moon shines the hills.* Eastern can also mean poetic. "It feels good to be here."

"I'm glad you're here too, even just for J-Term. I can't wait to show you around Frankfurt. It's really like home to me already. First things first, how's life at Saint Ben's?"

"The Morgue isn't the same since you graduated."

"Oh my god, the Morgue." Carly said. "I don't miss it. What kind of landlord turns an old funeral home into a rental house! And you're still doing photography. I saw the nonchalant shots walking here from the Bahnhof."

"From the hip. Nobody really notices so you get the candid shots."

"Candid! That's the word."

"Senior Exhibition is coming up. I want to capture what's left of the wall in Berlin. And back home I'm still shooting bands."

"Slip Twister?"

"Every Thursday at the Red Carpet. Paul, the lead guitar, introduces me like I'm part of the band — *Mike on bass, and Catherine on the Nikon!* I got some great shots by the railroad tracks outside Saint Cloud for their next album cover."

"They're hot. A little older you know."

"Like our benefactors?"

Carly snorted a laugh and stole a glance at the other table. "Stop it! They're basically grandpas!" Then her eyes focused on Catherine.

"What? What is it?"

"Do you think you could be Irish" — Carly asked — "with those freckles across your nose?"

"Aren't the Irish all redheads with porcelain skin, not dark like me?"

"Not at all. You could be Black Irish, the ones who mixed with sailors after the Spanish Armada shipwrecked on the coast."

Catherine absorbed the idea, added it to the long list of you-might-be's.

Outside the windows of the garden level bar, dark figures passed in the lamplit night. Inside the sconces cast an orange glow over the pale stone walls, and the room hummed with joviality and murmured stories while tables of guests cupped hands around goblets of brandy and wine. It was a world away from the bright lights of Saint Ben's cafeteria, the thumping music on the dance floor at The La, the crowded loneliness of the bar in Logan Airport, minds distracted from the life around them and from the life within. America. She hadn't realized until now, there was another way. "At home life moves so fast." Her eyes grew serious. "I like this better."

*

Minnesota, Spring 1992

Her final semester at Saint Ben's was a letdown after Germany. She got through it, graduated with a bachelor's degree in Psychology, got a respectable job as Housing Coordinator at a mental health drop-in center, Vail Place, and got an apartment of her own in Minneapolis. She hoped Mom and Dad were proud. The next thing on Mom's agenda would be for her to find a husband, good grief! Every guy she dated was a candidate for marriage in Mom's eyes. *What does he do for a living?* People just out of college are still trying to find their way. What could she say?

He plays lead guitar in a band you've never heard of, a band I've never heard of.

He journeys across the country working odd jobs and says he hopes to see the whole U.S. before his money runs out.

He smokes pot, he's very dedicated about it and I think he might become an important dealer someday.

He's an abusive ass and last night I finally just hauled back and punched him, he was still bleeding when I stormed out.

And the full-time job. It was a trap. In fact, she couldn't stand it. Her New Year's resolution for 1993 was to quit the respectable job and travel Europe again. By February she was in Amsterdam, everyone's capital city. She lodged at Hotel the Crown, a hostel in the red light district, spent evenings in bars packed with people from what seemed like every nation on Earth, afternoons in coffeehouses, plants in the windows, where coffee was second to space cakes and amnesia haze. Mornings walking, walking everywhere, marveling at the soggy fields where sheep huddled under reed huts while ancient windmills wheeled in the distance.

It was an absolute freedom that began with the flight east and ended with the flight west across the Atlantic. And if it had to end, she was determined it also had to begin again, every year. All she needed was employment flexible enough to quit every winter and pick up when she returned. Vail Place, the job Mom and Dad were so proud of, wasn't that kind of job — quitting was final. It was going to have to be a patchwork of places that expected turnover, and that paid in line with their expectations. Back home in Minneapolis in March, she staffed the listening station three evenings a week at Applause Records in Uptown. The pay was terrible but there were perks — no cover charge at the Uptown Bar next door and comps to First Avenue — Morphine, nothing but rhythm, the saxophones and Mark Sandman's homemade bass guitar poured across the checkered floor like rolling thunder, right into your body, and if you had nowhere to be on Christmas, Run Westy Run's annual show made for a wild night. She added a job as overnight staff for a group home for the developmentally delayed — Down syndrome, autism — where she was awake on duty four hours, asleep but on call six hours. And there was one more position she saw advertised in the Star Tribune — providing community support for mentally ill clients. It fell somewhere between the dignified stability of Vail Place and her low-wage work. If she could juggle it, this third job would give her enough to save every year for Europe.

*

Nine AM, a few hours after the group home overnight shift, she stood at the reception desk at Alliance for Community Involvement. "My name is Catherine Lind, I have a nine o'clock interview with Lourdes Casado."

Funny to imagine what would be going through Dad's head right now if he was the one interviewing. He would be determined to show he was committed to meet every expected obligation. She was determined to let them know she would be taking a month or two off every winter and that, naturally, the rest of the time she would do the work of a professional. If they couldn't deal with that, she had other places to be.

The young woman across the table in the small conference room, hardly older than she, peered over the top of her eyeglasses with self-assurance beyond her years. "I'm Lourdes. Everyone calls me Lulu. I see you have a BA in Psychology from the College of Saint Benedict. They have a good program there. But I see you lasted one year as housing coordinator at Vail. Did they kick you out? Or did you have enough of them?"

This was not going to be easy. "It was a good job, and I was good at it. I asked for a month leave to travel Europe, I'd gone the year before and knew I wanted to go back. They said no. So I quit and went to Europe."

Lulu laughed, the facade of authority cracking apart a little. She pulled herself together. "That takes some gumption. You'll need gumption here. But what happens when you get the travel bug again?"

"You let me go to Europe and then I come back to work."

There was no laugh this time. Lulu took off her glasses placing the tip between her teeth. "That's a new one for sure. We've got another week of interviews. You'll hear from us if we're interested."

Catherine walked out. More than anything she was disappointed because there was something thoughtful, something tender about Lulu Casado. She still had the group home and Applause, and she could always try temping.

But a week and a half later she got the call. She joined the staff of community support advisors at the Alliance.

It was the toughest job so far. The clients were diagnosed with mental illness and all living independently in the community, supported by weekly home visits. Living independently was the highest achievement for most of them before another ride on the ferris wheel — going off their meds, involuntary commitment, the half-way house. Even when they succeeded in clinging to independence, there was so much suffering and so little she could do to help. But she did everything she could. Visit the client's home every week. Make sure they were going to their day program, seeing their psychiatrist, taking their meds, keeping up on basic hygiene. It required a light touch, casual and conversational. *So what did you do last week? Oh, you took the bus, did you make it to your appointment with Dr. Kepling? Not quite? What happened? I know Dr. Kepling always helps you. Will you want to see her next week?* The conversation could take an unexpected turn at any moment. *So you took the bus out-of-state, where did you go? And why did you want to meet Jeffrey Dahmer's parents?* Sometimes it was a pattern of words and actions, or sometimes it was a single remark that demonstrated a threat to self or others. Those were the visits that ended with a call to the psych nurse for a seventy-two-hour hold. Sometimes it wasn't the client who posed a danger. One client's boyfriend cornered Catherine, blocked the door, his face red and shaking inches from hers, his eyes filled with rage, his mouth foaming — *She's my girlfriend, mine, not yours, that's why your dead, I'm gonna kill you.* He was hallucinating, off his meds, a psychotic break. She knew what to do. Not just her training. Something in her, an inexplicable sense that it was up to her, only her, to handle whatever came her way.

*

"You're finding the job interesting?" Dad leaned back in his leather chair, his graying head titled at an angle — quizzical, or quizzing, she couldn't always tell.

"I'm able to apply everything I learned from my psychology degree. And applying it in real life is much more challenging."

"It's no longer theoretical. Applied practice. That's the meat of the work at our firm. Medicine, science, life and death — when all those factors are at play, anything can happen."

"For me, my clients' independence is on the line. And our careers. And the reputation of the program."

"Exactly. It's a heady mix of social goods and personal motives. Institutional motives too, as you suggest." Dad was in his element. She loved connecting with him this way, in a give-and-take of ideas.

*

Her first leave from the Alliance, February 1994, she ordered a Pilsener from the Brazilian bartender at Hotel the Crown in Amsterdam and surveyed the tables of young people speaking German, French, Italian, and Japanese. And then there was the stocky young man about her height with the big mop of blonde hair in his eyes who plopped himself onto the stool next to hers. "Name's Alistair. Have you been long in this storied city?"

"A couple of weeks." Catherine's brows furrowed.

"Ha! You know what they say" — he sounded English like Bryce and Collin of the Itascas — "Come for the windmills, stay for the coffeehouses, and soon enough you'll forget your way home."

It was a stupid thing to say, really, but he kept on talking and before long they were at a table and he was complaining about those dodgy coffeehouses where potted plants fill the windows, if he wants a coffee, he wants a coffee, and explaining that he was taking articles to become a solicitor because he won't be some barrister sod doing whatever he's told. The night seemed to disappear down the drain.

"I've got to go." She stood from the table. "Have a safe flight home. I guess you won't forget your way."

He snapped his fingers and gave a double thumbs up. She laughed, shook her head, and walked upstairs to her room.

*

Morning in Amsterdam. She awakened with a plan for the day already in mind, like childhood mornings when she jumped out of bed to draw a horse, sew a pillow for Lucie, collect pine cones in the woods, that same exuberance even now at the mature age of twenty-four. She hurried downstairs to the ground floor. The sun shone through the entranceway, open to the bustling streets. There he was again. Loitering by the entrance. Alistair. She stopped, turned sideways, aimed for the stairway...no, she wasn't going to let his presence change her plans. She would sweep past him, right through to the street.

"All right? Going walkabout in the streets your Highness?"

Good grief. She barely made it over the threshold. "I'm going out for the day. Your Highness?"

"I think it a bit self-important, your willingness to sweep through the door without even saying hello."

"I'm on vacation, I'm exploring the city."

"Being on holiday, vacation as you Americans like to say, is in fact an argument for leisure, for taking your time to enjoy conversation, am I wrong?"

She felt her stomach tightening. Was something going wrong here, did she have to de-escalate his emotions?

He burst into a laugh. "Blimey, you look as though you've been cornered by the Keystone Cops. I'm joking my dear! I'm so sorry. Let me buy you a cuppa to start the day right. Coffee?"

She laughed. It actually felt like their own private joke now. "But no dodgy coffeehouses!" she said.

"Never!" He exclaimed dramatically and extended his arm.

They toured the city. He knew exactly where he wanted to go. The Rijksmuseum, the Van Gogh Museum, the Rembrandt House, people-watching at Dam Square, "Too many damn tourists," he laughed. Then shopping at De Bijenkorf. "Super posh, very high-end."

She was thirsty, worn out when they finally sat at a sidewalk cafe for tea. "I'd enjoy just walking the canals after this," she said.

"I thought that's what we just did! So tell me more about your father. You say he's a solicitor, an attorney, in Minnesota, The Twin Cities? Brilliant! What a market for solicitors you must have there across the pond, mega-corporations, mega-hospitals, a menagerie of mega-litigation!"

"I don't think my dad ever talked about it that way. He's more interested in the bio-ethics side of things. The Human Genome Project at NIH means all kinds of possibilities, but all kinds of complications too."

"Ethicist, ethicist, ethicist...If you say it enough times it starts to lose all meaning!"

She stared at him. From Prince Charming to King Goofball.

"Well Miss Lind, you must share your contact information with me. My flight departs at six this evening!"

"I have a rule. I don't date on vacation." She didn't know where it came from, just blurted it out and finished with "Have a safe flight home." As she walked away she heard his complaint replay in her head. *So self-important.* But she was free. She walked Haarlemmerstraat, turned onto Singel and remembered something in the guidebook about a cat shelter on the canal. There it was, parked among all the other barges: *De Poezenboot.* The Catboat. She sighed relief. This was her kind of sightseeing. And on to *De Bloemenmarkt.* The floating flower shop.

The next day she boarded the train at Amsterdam Centraal. Felt the rhythmic rumble as the train carried her to Munich where she walked the cobblestone streets among four-hundred-year-old buildings. Carried her south across Germany and through the towering snow covered peaks of the Alps. Church-spired villages cradled in valleys, board and batten houses, stands of spruce and fir.

In Slovenia she drank white wine from the vineyards of Ljubljana. On the hill crest, beneath trellises laden with grapes, she listened to the innkeeper's stories: how he had learned ten languages as an accident of his vocation, how over the years he had housed vacationers escaping boredom, refugees escaping danger, the infirm seeking health, the restless seeking whatever it was they were looking for. Catherine nodded to herself — whatever it was she was looking for.

She pruned shrubs at the pension in the Austrian town of Villach to pay for her room, pedaled her bicycle north through the forest, paused at her favorite spot beneath the fir and beech, alone in the quiet, filtered sunlight on her shoulders, then pedaled out to open sky and down, down a narrow roadway bordered by tall green shrubs, all else hidden from sight, until she came to a T, and it was as if someone pulled open the stage curtains as she came to a stop and peered around the hedge to the little shops and cafes of Urlaken, where the ruins of Landskron Castle stood watch from the hilltop as the daylight moon shone high above.

She visited Carly who was becoming more European by the year. Carly worked in Vienna now and had gotten engaged to a man from Germany. He wanted to live in America.

*

Minneapolis, March 1994

"You have a good time in Europe? Don't even answer, I'm already jealous." Lulu sifted through the file folder on her desk. "Back to business. I'm hearing that you've handled some tough situations on your shifts. That's what we hired you for. You said your dad is an attorney, maybe you got his steely reserve."

"Steely..." Catherine fingered the cuff of her sweater, eyes focused in thought. "My dad and I have always connected on an intellectual level. Maybe it's the logic, sorting the situation out. But I didn't inherit it from him. I'm adopted."

Lulu peeled off her eyeglasses. "I didn't know that about you, and here I am making assumptions."

'There's no way anyone could know."

"Have you met your birth mother?"

"I've thought about searching."

"I'm sure there is a lot to consider." She breathed deep and resettled her eyeglasses. "I'd like to talk more. And I actually do want to hear about your trip! It's almost five o'clock. You like Sergeant Preston's down at Seven Corners?"

Under the high tin ceiling, sunset through the west windows bathed the wooden tables in a pink glow. Catherine lifted a Newcastle, Lulu a Martini, "Cheers."

"What is that drink again? It seemed like the server hadn't heard of it."

"An Appletini!" Lulu said. "Vodka, apple liqueur, and lime cordial. I'm leading a cocktail revolution. Hasta la victoria siempre!" Her eyes were serious now. "Tell me, was it hard when you first learned you were adopted?"

"I've always known. I'm grateful my parents never kept it from me. And when I was eleven my mom shared the papers with me and, for the first time in my life, I read a description of my birth mother."

"It must have been a lot to take in at that age. In fact, that's about the same age I was when my mama passed."

"I'm sorry." Catherine reached across the table. Lulu clasped her hand with a gentle squeeze.

"My childhood ended then, right then. A child's dreams of what life will bring. As for searching, you will know if and when the time is right. All I can say is that if I could search for my mother and somehow bring her back...." Lulu took a sip of her Appletini and laughed. "My god, I'm inventing a new cocktail!" She lifted her eyes, full of tears. "Appletini with salt! Dios mío."

"Your love for her is right there." Catherine reassured.

"And you love your adoptive parents, true?"

"Of course I do. Most people seem to believe you only have enough love for two parents. But they have enough love for their siblings no matter how many, right? I believe there's enough love for our parents too, no matter how many." Catherine's gaze turned from Lulu to her own hands tracing the wood grain of the table. "But sometimes I feel a little lost. If you take a child from their biological family and place them into a different family, how can you not feel like something is missing?"

"My god, you're giving me a lot to think about, Catherine. We need to share more stories together. A boss isn't supposed to get personal. But god forgive me and board of directors forgive me" — Lulu burst into giggles and quieted and nodded. "Sharing stories is more important than any of that. Now tell me about your trip. Was it wonderful?"

"It was. The slower pace of life in Europe, the sense of history, it's a different way of living. I've been wanting to say, I appreciate the flexibility you're giving me, the leave every winter."

Lulu waved away the thank-you. "Listen, plenty of hires just up-and-quit after a year. If you're willing to keep coming back, I'm happy."

*

East Berlin, February 1995

She leaned low to the pool table, bridged her hand, angles in her mind. A swift crack. She left the pair of German sailors with seven balls on the table. She wished Lulu were here to see it. In daylight she searched for remains of the wall. The expanses of graffitied concrete she had photographed in 1992 were gone. Demolished or hauled away to museums. Here and there rebar sprouted from ankle-high concrete rubble like grasses among rocks.

From Berlin she trained to Prague, and by the end of a week she weaved with ease through the streets of Old Town on the south bank of the Vltava River. She had a mission. Actually her mom had a mission. "Can you find one of those infant Jesus figurines," Mom said on the phone before the trip. "Like the Virgin Mary from Lourdes I keep in the linen chest, and make sure the priest at Our Lady of...Paul! Paul! What is it our Lady of? The church in Prague? No, in Prague. Our Lady Victorious, that's it. Make sure the priest blesses it."

As she set out across the Charles Bridge under the gaze of sandstone saints, she could see Prague Castle on the New Town side and a church spire, and another spire, and over there another — but which was Our Lady Victorious? She pulled the folded map from the top pocket of her backpack. Walking down the long, treeless limestone corridor that is Karmelitska Avenue she found Kostel Panny Marie Vítězné — Church of Our Lady Victorious. But what caught her eye, and thank god she noticed before wandering the church, was the tiny storefront, *Infans Jesus de Praga,* on the other side of the street. The industrial steel door was rolled open for business and the infant Jesus, replicated in a wide selection of sizes, stood stiffly on glass display shelves, waiting to be purchased for loving transport to rectory offices, curio cabinets, and linen chests the world over. She had seen the statue before, an infant standing upright, wearing a crown, making a holy sign with the right hand and holding a globe in the left, dressed in a great conical robe. The whole image was something like a Christmas tree topped with a great star. Mom needed it. But was this ceramic thing what she needed? Wasn't it God that she needed? And whether there was a single god or many spirits who inhabited the world, was it even respectful to turn them into dolls? Catherine thought of all the books and idols and rules and beliefs the Catholic Church manufactured and the lesson she had taken away, intended or not, from the World Religions course at Saint Ben's — If every religion believes itself to be true and the rest to be false, then they must all be false. Not the god or spirits of the world, but the religions that people make, really that men make. She dutifully made the purchase. "My mother would like it, him, blessed." The clerk motioned toward the church across the street. Catherine half hoped a priest would shed light for her on the meaning of this seemingly meaningless exercise.

The walls outside the church were a simple mottled concrete but inside the marble and decorative gold were wildly ornate. It was awfully quiet. Empty. Her boots echoed a squeak and a man in black emerged from a hidden door.

Catherine swallowed hard, expected that to echo too. "Excuse me?" She said. "I'm sorry, are you a priest?"

His eyes arced into crescents, inverse of his smile, and he laughed. "I, the Reverend Father Rádsetoulal. You, my daughter, what help can I give?"

His eyes were too genuine, too full of real life. She loathed the question she had to ask, but she couldn't face Mom back home if she didn't. "Will you please...will you bless this?" She held out the conical chunk of painted plaster.

The familiar request. He exhaled a mumbled prayer and swished a quick sign of the cross. But then he looked straight into her eyes, "Come, you will see the catacomb!" He led her through the hidden door and down the stairs to narrow twists of tunnel into cavernous halls of glass-covered stone caskets. These caves held all meaning for him. "They build church. They Carmelite, some, they benefactor. They give all they have, to build and keep church. They are unsainted saints. Am I priest? I am nobody. We, whole church, are body of Christ." He swept his hand over the hall of caskets. "Who live before. Who live after."

Sun setting at her back, fog settling on the Vltava, the black statues of sand along each side of the bridge towered above her. They ignored the Vltava, the wild river at their backs, and watched her instead. She had hardly looked at them on first crossing, her eyes focused on New Town and Mom's errand, and in a way they had seemed like dolls, like bigger versions of the one Mom wanted. But with New Town behind her, and maybe because of the fog, they looked like people. As she neared the Old Town end of the bridge, she was struck motionless under the gaze of the Madonna, mild and caring, who cradled the infant Jesus in one arm, the other outstretched toward her. There was something in the Madonna's expression, a caring coupled with concern, an urgency, an untamable need beneath the surface. Seven years had passed since she first searched, when she found that she needed Mom or Dad's signature because she was eighteen, not nineteen. She couldn't ask them, didn't want to hurt them. She had every intention of searching for her birth mother again.

Footsteps on the stones. Only a few souls out on a winter evening as she walked under the archway of the bridge tower into Old Town. She followed the narrow, curving canyon of Karlova Street and finally emerged onto the lamplit cobblestones of Old Town Square. A clanging bell drew a small crowd bundled in coats and hats at the far end, drew her too, beneath the old Astronomical Clock she had seen in guidebooks but somehow hadn't gotten to in her week of explorations. The clanging bell rang from the hand of a mechanical skeleton as two little doors opened high above at the top of the clock. The twelve apostles emerged in the doorway one by one, pivoted to face her, then glided to the other doorway until finally the skeleton stopped its clanging and raised an hour glass, raised it, then waited in stillness while the clock chimed.

*

Minneapolis, Summer 1995

She set the grocery bag on the kitchen table. The light on the answering machine flashed, but first things first. Groceries into the fridge and cupboards, new inventory in the back, old in front just like Koblend's Pharmacy. On the answering machine, a young man's voice. Jamie, the guy from Uptown Bar. Striking blue eyes. Jaw length black curls. A few years older. A week after they had met, his arms wrapped around her and they swayed under the evening stars to Gary Louris's flawless phrasing, the Jayhawks live at Lake Harriet Bandstand. Sitting on the edge of her bed that night, Jamie played guitar and sang to her. She was head-over-heels until he looked into her eyes and shared his deepest feelings. "You look just like Darlene." He put his head in his hands. "Why did she leave me? And why can't I get her out of my mind?"

She deleted the message and glanced out the set of three windows to the garden in back, the apartment building's only garden, her garden. There was just enough time to water before the evening shift at Applause. Three years ago, her first summer in the building, she had eyed the neglected rectangle of scrub trees, weeds, and tangled plastic bags while taking the trash to the dumpster on the alley. Emil, the building manager, was tinkering with a drain pipe. She started the conversation. "It's a lot of upkeep, a building like this!"

"You said it. Especially when the owner doesn't want to replace anything. I have to gerry rig it all."

"You're the one who makes this a good place to live. I wanted to ask you, does this unpaved strip belong to the property, can I plant vegetables here?"

He looked at her matter-of-factly, "Anything would be an improvement."

So in spring when the ground thawed, she had turned the soil with a spade and planted tomatoes, beans, squash, and corn. She hammered in metal posts and wove a fence of chicken wire to keep the rabbits out. The corn was what surprised people. Cars slowed on the alley, fingers pointed. It required special care in a tiny plot like this. Every August she deftly broke the pollen-laden tassel from the top of the first stalk and touched it to the silk of each ear, then did the same on the next stalk, one by one until all were pollinated. It was almost that time of year again. For now she just had to keep the garden watered. She filled the watering can at her kitchen sink — a garden hose would have been nice — and carried it sloshing down the hall and out the back door. A man was lurking around the building. Not Emil. He eyed the watering can like it was an illicit device. "Who told you that you could have a garden?"

"Who are you?"

His eyes darted as if something in the vicinity might hold the clue to his identity. "Artie" — he hesitated — "I'm the building manager."

"Emil is the building manager, and Emil told me I could have a garden."

"Hmph," he grumbled and carried on.

A week later, she pulled her car into the parking lot after the overnight at the group home, and the moment she opened the car door, a man in a suit was sticking a microphone in her face. "Were you here when the brick wall collapsed?" A camera crew rounded the corner of the building and set up behind the suited man. She stared at the side of her apartment building, the exposed sandy under-layer where the bricks should have been, and the heap of bricks on the ground below.

"No, I was working overnight. I wasn't here."

"I was here!" A neighbor called from a second-story window. "I was sleeping and suddenly there was a huge boom!" His hands burst wide. "It was like a bomb exploding!"

The news crew scrambled to him. Thank goodness. There was only a couple of hours before she had to be at the Alliance. She pulled a yogurt from the fridge. Ate distractedly. She knew the building wasn't maintained as it should be. But this was troubling. How could she live in a place like this? She looked out the windows to the corn stalks. Everything upended.

*

She ignored the buzzer. Usually it was a package delivery, for someone else. One buzz and they were gone. But it buzzed again and then again. She glanced in the mirror, walked out into the hall to the entrance. She puzzled at the mop of blonde hair in the door's grille window. A puzzle piece completely out of place. A loud knock. She opened the door.

"Good day your Highness! All right?"

They walked, she wasn't sure how many blocks. "I still don't understand why or how you're here. You said you're at William Mitchell now?"

"Bill Mitchell College of Law I like to call it! A one-year postdoctoral program. I'll take your Minnesota bar exam and practice law right here in your fancifully titled Twin Cities. I saw you on the evening news, dreadful about the bricks..."

"But you only saw the news because you're here at William Mitchell College. That's what I don't understand. Why did you come here, right here, to study and practice law?"

"You told me you lived in Minneapolis, and your father was a solicitor, and I told you I wanted to have a go at law in America. Do you recall?"

She met him for dinner end of the week. He seemed to need a friend, alone in a new place "It's crazy that you saw me on the news. They didn't even interview me."

"Are we still on about that? You were in the background. Bloody slumlord," Alistair bellowed. "Waited for it to fall so he could file an insurance claim. Oldest trick in the book!"

"It's awful. The little kids from next door love to dig in that patch of dirt, right where the bricks fell. An hour earlier and they could have been killed."

Alistair shook his head indignantly, then furrowed his brow and snapped his fingers. "You should move into my building. That same sod owns it, Artie Pontiak — he must own a fifth of Minneapolis — but he keeps my building shipshape. Better part of town, you know. And if he doesn't we can sue him."

She laughed, not sure what to make of him. "Really?"

"Wouldn't it be bonkers to live in the same building! There's a flat for lease on the third floor."

"I like my apartment. Did you know I'm growing corn?" Her forefinger traced a line from her plate to the table's edge and she pinched the linen tablecloth between forefinger and thumb. "But it doesn't feel safe any more."

*

There was no place for a garden at Harriet Avenue, but she made the third-floor apartment all her own by setting up a darkroom in the pantry. Red light. Enlarger. Trays for developer, stop bath, and fix. Alistair's apartment was garden level, Number Seven. He had a habit of knocking on her door weekend evenings at the very moment she was trying to decide what to make for dinner. "Why not try your luck at Number Seven?" It always made her laugh, and mostly she said yes. It wasn't a bad thing having a dinner friend in the building.

She had to set some boundaries. No roasts, no kidney pie, no bubble and squeak. But once you got past the English dishes, he was a decent cook. Palak paneer, with spinach and cheese. Chana masala. He seemed to relish the spices — cinnamon, mace, cardamom, coriander, black pepper, cumin, bay leaf.

She washed the dishes, rinsed a plate and glanced over her shoulder to Alistair at the kitchen table. "That was pretty good. Where did you learn Indian?"

"All part of the empire. Was anyway. Like America. The monarchy must be doing something wrong, but I'm glad I got the spices right. Give those dishes a good rinse, will you?"

As if on cue water splashed through the window onto the kitchen table. "Bloody hell!" He jumped to his feet and yelled out the window, "Artie Pontiak! This is the second time you have sprayed your garden hose directly into my flat!"

"How would you like to not worry about there being a third time?"

"I beg your pardon." Alistair rebutted. "Would you like to explain the meaning of your clumsy threat?"

"Eviction!"

Alistair stiffened. "On what grounds?"

The voice outside the window shot back, "On the grounds of being a pain in the ass!"

*

Coconut

Mom was thrilled. "Thank goodness you've finally met someone with a good head on his shoulders."

"I haven't met anyone and I'm not seeing anyone, not him anyway. He lives in my building, that's all!"

"You can bet your dad won't complain about you seeing a lawyer."

*

June 1996

She was getting used to the idea of seeing a lot of Alistair. Not seeing him was pretty much impossible when he was just downstairs. And the fountain tour on bicycle. It was one of the nicest things someone had ever done for her. He grew up across the Atlantic, but after six months of frantic sightseeing he knew Minneapolis better than she did. He led her fountain to fountain, proudly introducing each.

"The Heffelfinger!" Arms outstretched, he laughed contagiously. Such a goofball. A little girl balancing on the fountain's ledge echoed him, "A Heffelfinger!" Alistair nodded toward a man and woman approaching over the freshly-mowed lawns of Lake Harriet. "Off with you, lassie, go find your mum!" The woman opened her arms as the girl ran to her, the urge, the need just beneath the surface of an ordinary gesture.

"Brought over from Italy before the Second World War! Thank you, Frank Heffelfinger!"

She laughed. He was a one-man show.

"Wait until you see the fountain at Loring Park. It's a giant dandelion, you'll be gobsmacked. To the bicycles!"

*

The pressure cooker. It was rattling when she and Alistair stepped inside and hung their jackets on the wooden hall tree. Dad and Mom were dressed up like it was Christmas dinner. "Well I hope you're hungry, we're having roast and potatoes," Mom said as Alistair snapped his fingers and gave a double thumbs up. And it was still rattling as Catherine joined Mom in the kitchen. "The potatoes are almost done," Mom said. "Would you take the salad out of the refrigerator, dear, and put it on the table?"

Catherine set out the bowl of orange Jello with mandarin slices and returned to the kitchen as Alistair's voice rose from the living room. "I told him, I don't need you faffing around, I'm the one'll do the faffing around here, I've earned it!" Alistair's laughter danced with Dad's rolling chuckle.

"Your father really likes him."

"Maybe he should date him then."

"For heaven's sake, Catherine. I don't know why you can't see an opportunity sitting right in front of you. Dad and I are trying to help you."

*

A New Year's resolution: 1997, get out of town. Last year she didn't have the time or the money for Europe. The move to Harriet Street, the hectic weekends with Alistair. She wanted the rumble of the train and miles and miles of poppies.

*

March 1997

She pulled a handful of silverware from the dishwasher while Mom scrubbed a pan in the sink. "Alistair's pushier than ever, Mom, since I got back from my trip. He wants to get more serious, but we're not even dating."

Mom dipped another pan into the soapy water and scrubbed. "Well you could have fooled me. And what's the problem anyway?"

"He wants to be exclusive. I'm just not sure he's right for me."

Mom shook her head. "Honestly, you young people expect to live in a perfect world!"

"I think people should be together because they're in love."

"I'm just saying that there are other reasons couples want to be together. You like him well enough, don't you?"

"He's done some really sweet things. But he can be really annoying."

Mom delivered her all-knowing look. "That's called being a man. And before you tell me I'm wrong, I want you to think about the value of a man who's smart and responsible and has a good career, same career as your father! He thinks Alistair is the best thing that ever happened to you."

*

Televisions hummed and bartenders pulled the taps at Sergeant Preston's. Half past five o'clock, the room brimmed with tables of young professionals and office workers, regulars lining the bar. Catherine spotted Lulu at a table sipping something filled with blackberries and a slice of lemon. "Another amazing cocktail?"

"Always! It's a Bramble. Gin, lemon juice, and a drizzle of Giffard Creme de Mure over crushed ice. There's even a sprinkle of sugar on top! Do you want a taste?"

"Mmm, delicious, but a bit too sweet. I think I'll stick with Newcastle." Catherine plucked a chip from the bowl, let it soften on her tongue. She tilted her head toward a question. "You know, Lulu, I wanted to ask you. You said you lost your mother when you were twelve?"

"On the precipice of adolescence, when you are finally ready to ask your mother everything, to ask her — How do I become a woman? It was fast. There were doctors visits, hospital stays. And it was over. Breast cancer. How can you make sense of that as a child? My father said, *You're the woman of the house now.* And I was. He went to work, I looked after my little brother and sisters, cooked and cleaned. At fourteen I got a supermarket job. Worked all the way through college. Any dreams I had, there wasn't time to give them up. They were gone. Poof! But what is that compared to what my mother lost, never to see us grow up?"

"Oh Lulu, she would have been so proud of you, everything you've done."

Lulu clasped her hands and peered into Catherine's eyes. "You and your birth mother both live with that loss. You lost each other. Maybe I'm a little dense, but I never considered that. You can still find her. But to be without each other the whole length of your life until now? Does it make you angry? Does it make you crazy?"

"Sad, I think. And I don't know anything about her or what she's like or where she came from. I don't know where I came from. Most people take all of that for granted."

"Catherine, I'm going to share something with you because I am finally grasping the void, the terrible void, you are feeling. There is one thing that I never lost, never can lose, and it is the one thing that sustained me all these years. My mama's love. Mothers all over the world are the same in this. She loves you. When you find her, and you will find her, God is my witness, you will know her love in the flesh. But even now her love is there."

Catherine nodded. "I know you're right. I do feel her love."

Lulu took a long sip of her Bramble. "Now I'm going to ask you something your birth mother surely would ask. Who's this guy you're spending all your time with? You have a boyfriend now?"

"What, you too?"

"Every other night you say you're meeting him for drinks or dinner. Isn't that a boyfriend?"

"Not really. I mean, we are spending more time together. I just don't..." Catherine scraped her nail at a speck of dry catsup petrified on the tabletop. "He's being really persistent."

"He likes you, and you evidently like him. And the problem is...?"

"God, you sound like my mom. I told her Alistair's annoying and she said he's a man."

"Eso!" Lulu raised her glass. "That's it! My Derrick gets on my nerves on a daily basis. And I married him anyway. If you want a man, that's what you get!"

*

They were going out several nights a week, joined by a growing circle of friends who were impressed, obsessed with his accent, his inane, irreverent humor. The more they crowded around him, the more he sought them out. The parties and dinners were nonstop. She wondered when it would slow down. But she enjoyed the dinners with Cheri and Cal. Cheri was at William Mitchell with Alistair, and while they talked law, she and Cal talked art. His paintings in oil, her photographs in black and white.

*

"These 1880s houses are bloody asymmetrical. It's crackers, really, but they've managed to convert lots of them to duplexes. See the two entrances on this one?" It wasn't unusual to spend a Sunday afternoon walking, she and Alistair, under the blossoming crabapples and leafing oaks of Uptown. It was an interest they shared. Cottage bungalow, Colonial Revival, Victorian. She had always loved the old houses. Everything she felt walking the old streets of Europe came to her on these not-so-old streets of Minneapolis.

"It reminds me of North London. Finchely, Willesden Green. This one's for sale. We should buy it." He said it just like that, while she squinted up into the sun at the ironwork of the rooftop widow's walk. She squinted at him. "What are you saying?"

"Think about it," he said. "No more dodgy landlords. We own it. No one can raise the rent or threaten to kick us out. Or attack us with garden hoses!" He laughed that contagious laugh of his. "Wouldn't it be bonkers? We live in one unit, rent the other to cover expenses."

"You want to live together?"

"Keep your hair on, the house is ginormous. It would scarcely differ from how we live now except we'll share the kitchen."

"And bathroom."

"How do you know there's only one bathroom until we tour it?"

She couldn't even afford the restaurant entrees he ordered. But there was something she liked about the idea of buying an uncared-for home, making it beautiful again. And something in her liked the financial commonsense of it. "I wonder if the rental would cover the mortgage?"

"We'll have to do the maths." Alistair was nonchalant. "I know you're skint. I've got the downpayment. You can pay me back once you decide on a career."

Her dark eyes interrogated him. "I have a career, my work at the Alliance."

"Pay me when you have a higher-paying career." He gazed up at the old Victorian. "Your own home. Think how proud your parents will be."

The next day they walked through the front door with a realtor. Catherine's eyes spontaneously traced the intricate woodwork of the ceiling moldings, the pocket doors. "Imagine how long it must have taken to carve this detail."

Alistair was inside himself, investigating, evaluating. He passed through the pocket doors to the dining room. "The floors are wonky over here by the fireplace."

She followed. "But look how beautifully the maple inlay contrasts with the wide-plank pine!"

Alistair was already through the next doorway. "This space could be my office." He pulled a tape measure from his pants pocket. "Take this end to that wall over there." She held one end to the wall while he walked across the room. "Eighteen feet. My desk can go here, and there's enough room for my file cabinet there."

*

By October they had removed the old wallpaper and freshly painted their unit on the ground floor. The second-floor tenants would be moving in next month. She saw possibilities in the tiny back yard on the alley, surrounded by chain linked fence and littered with gravel, trash, and bits of broken glass. She stole a glance at his stocky frame hunched over the computer keyboard in his office. Tried to gauge what it means to feel a partnership, not quite love. Fuzzy lines. Housemates, definitely dating, collecting rent to save for the next property, maybe a couple.

By December the yard was masked in pure white snow. In May when the ground thawed, Alistair worked up a spring sweat demolishing the chain link, then measured and cut cedar two-by-fours and constructed a serviceable wooden fence.

The landscape was her talent. Her skin soaked up the greenhouse steam as she shopped perennials inside Garden City, a pop-up tent store in a parking lot off Lyndale. She laid a circular path of gravel, and in the center she planted a magnolia. White blossoms, glossy green leaves, something she had always wanted.

*

When they didn't feel like walking up to Falafel King at Lyn-Lake, the two-story brick building with the big crown mounted above the door, they had dinner at the Mud Pie on Lyndale, which was practically their next-door neighbor. It was also her favorite vegetarian restaurant, really her favorite restaurant, with its laid-back hippie vibe, artful drawings on the menu, plants hanging from macramé, and cozy wooden booths. You could have dinner for two for under ten dollars. She loved the black bean taco. Alistair tolerated it, as long as he could wash it down with a half carafe of red wine.

She scooped the last of the black sauce from her plate and licked it from her finger. "Should we have the chocolate oats-cream for dessert?"

"Do you take me for a man or a horse?"

"A talking horse," she answered and excused herself for the bathroom.

As she washed her hands, she gazed into the mirror. Everybody was trying to steer her in the right direction, Mom, Lulu. Her stomach ached a little. Beans and hot salsa, no wonder. She studied the features of her face, the curve of her forehead, the arch of her eyebrows, her broad nose. She studied her irises, pools of brown and green. Within her pupil, she saw a reflection of herself. And a reflection within that. Her image repeated endlessly. But she still couldn't answer the question. *Who am I?*

*

They bought their second duplex in September 1998 on Pillsbury Avenue. Alistair passed the bar, making it official, he was a practicing attorney in the State of Minnesota. They walked the neighborhood in the evenings. "Now that I'm licensed, we should get out of the city, we could move to Roseville. Imagine us living in a rambler with an in-ground pool!"

They strolled on. Catherine turned to him, "Don't you love the beautiful detail of the old Victorians?"

"This one would be a money pit," he remarked. "Wouldn't you say?"

"It would need a lot of work." She felt good about her growing knowledge of properties and how to maintain them. And more and more she was looking at the grounds, how a house sits on the land, how the landscape accents the house. Composition, line, contrast. It was everything her photographs were made of. "The University of Minnesota offers a master's program in horticulture," she said.

"Career change?" He smiled.

"We'll see. It's something I'm thinking about."

*

December of the following year, Catherine turned thirty. Prince's *1999* met its expiration date, as Alistair put it, and faded from the airwaves. The Y2K predictions of worldwide computer crashes — *Stockpile your bottled water and canned food!* — faded away just as quickly.

They married on May 6, 2000 in the Van Dusen Mansion in Minneapolis. A cold front from the northwest clashed with the rising sun. May in Minnesota, you never know what to expect.

Alistair's father wore a top hat and may have completely missed the exchange of vows because he was talking law with Dad the whole time. His mother struck Catherine as a carbon copy of the Queen of England. Mom and Dad took on the luster of the Holmeses and seemed to shine brighter in their company. And how did she feel? How is a woman supposed to feel on her wedding day?

Alistair arranged a horse-drawn carriage ride through the city after the ceremony. A frigid gust blew Catherine's shawl from her shoulders, the horses snorted steam, and for a moment a shower of snowflakes whipped and swirled, crystals sparkling in the morning light.

*

Newly wed, they settled into a new house, a two-story 1930's Tudor on Edmund Boulevard, one block from the red-paved River Road that traced the bend of the Mississippi. Beyond River Road and the walking paths, a cliff of limestone tumbled down to the great river. She laid the blank sheet of paper on the dining room table in front of her. Alistair was hunched over the keyboard in his office — she shouldn't say hunched, it was his way of concentrating even if it made her tense. That morning she had done the books for the rentals and for his brand new law firm. This was her time. Her own thoughts, her own feelings, her own questions. White masses of cloud crossed the brilliant blue within the frame of the window. She had left the most important questions unanswered too long. She chose a pen, checked the tip, and inscribed the date, *17 September 2000,* then landed the tip in curving strokes, precise and deliberate.

Dear Birth Mother....

For thirty years I have wondered about you. As a child I imagined you at my bedside, the gentle look in your eyes, your fingers brushing strands of hair from my forehead. You brought me comfort. I have known for as long as I can remember that I was adopted and always knew I would find you, come to know you, and have you in my life...

She had postal mailed the paperwork and the five hundred dollar check last month to Catholic Services in Saint Paul. And yesterday she had received a letter back from Helen Quinn, the caseworker assigned to her search.

I will be handling communication between you and your birth mother. Let me explain the process we'll follow should she agree to contact.

The letter explained that both parties — daughter and mother — would write non-identifying letters to each other. The letters would offer an opportunity to describe expectations and get acquainted before having direct contact. She was to send her letters to the attention of Helen, who would then forward them to her birth mother. For a while, there would be this strange, deliberate barrier between them, but only for a while.

The reunion process is often likened to a roller coaster ride — Helen's letter continued. *Many emotions come to the surface, and it is important to have support at home in addition to whatever support you would like from me. Normally it takes about one week to locate a birth parent. I'll call you once I've found her. While I'm searching maybe you could draft your first letter. Good luck as you begin this journey. Sincerely, Helen Quinn, R.N.*

Catherine thought a moment and continued writing.

...I will begin by helping you know me. When I was a young child, I was described as friendly, polite, and happy. My world was outside: trees, sky, little animals. I had a pet cat named Lucie who was my best friend. As I grew older, I enjoyed soccer and swimming, singing and violin.

Throughout elementary and high school, my teachers described me as intuitive and bright. I was good at math and science but especially liked photography and home economics. I learned to cook and sew. Aunt Lillie taught me to knit. Barbie dolls never interested me. I preferred my collection of stuffed animals.

Since the day I was born you have been an important person in my life and you always will be. I have, of course, many questions. I would pursue the answers only if you were willing.

She wondered. How do you sign a letter to a mother you've never known? And at that moment, it hit her, the utter unknown she was entering into. Maybe her mother was in jail, or insane, or homeless on the streets, or dead. Or maybe, against everything Catherine felt inside, maybe her birth mother wouldn't want contact. She tried not to jump ahead. It would unfold as it would unfold and she would take what came. She decided to keep it simple.

Sincerely, Catherine

She read the letter, read again, then laid the pen on the table. She would mail it when she got the call from Helen Quinn.

The first days vanished. Every morning she rose with hope, excitement. Helen said it would take some time. If not today, then maybe tomorrow there would be news. News of a real person out there, not an anonymous document, not a childhood dream. A real person who looked like her, laughed like her — all the likenesses she observed in biological mothers and children. After those first vanishing days, each day crawled at the excruciating pace of the sun's journey across the sky. Busy though she was — making meals, washing dishes, mending clothes, doing the bookkeeping, listening to Alistair's daily monologue on the cases he argued and won or would have won if the judge weren't such a sod — all the while, every moment of every daily chore, her whole spirit was waiting, watching the sun, listening to the silence of a phone not ringing. And when the crawling sun finally impossibly reached the other horizon, she knew — *Not today. Tomorrow. Wait again tomorrow.* Until Friday rose and set, a week passed, and another weekend began, with no call. Emotions bubbled up and her mind raced ahead. She imagined the reunion, their embrace, never letting go of each other ever again. *Of course she'll love me. Of course she'll want me, because I'm hers.*

Monday. She dried the breakfast dishes, and she kept drying as the sound repeated, resounded, not in her mind, it was ringing from the kitchen wall. The phone. It was Helen. *I'm having trouble locating your birth mother. I think I will be able to find her, I just need a little more time, another week.*

Trouble locating her. What could that mean? Catherine didn't know, but she knew how it made her feel. Something was wrong. "No point crying over spilt milk when you don't even know it's spilt!" Alistair insisted. He was trying to help. But he had no idea what she was going through.

The second week crawled more slowly than the first. Morning hope cooled to evening resignation, and froze in the middle of night to fear. She slept fitfully, awakened again. And again. Until one night, Alistair sound asleep, she descended the darkened stairs to the dining room and laid out a clean sheet of paper on the table. A second letter.

Dear Birth Mother,

Now that I have described my childhood, I will share some information about my adulthood.

I have brown hair and brown eyes and medium skin color. I am five-foot seven, average weight, right-handed.

I consider myself to be intuitive, sensitive, and sincere. I am a reflective thinker, artistic and creative, free-spirited, determined, and stubborn at times. I am always busy.

I enjoy traveling, gardening, baking sweet bread and cookies. I'm in the middle of sewing a quilt. I enjoy many kinds of music. I feel drawn to the ocean and the mountains. I enjoy writing, going for walks.

She didn't know how to end the second letter. Normally a second letter would be in response to a letter received. But there was no letter. She decided to leave it as it was, without an ending.

*

She leafed through the incoming bills, separating them into two piles, one personal and the other, business. Two weeks had passed. There was no more watching the sun crawl across the sky. You can't live that way. She organized each pile by due date, oldest bill on top, then assembled the outgoing invoices. Her eyes scanned the sea of Alistair's must-have purchases: furniture crowding every corner of every room, making vacuuming more like a climb on the jungle gym — *Did you vacuum behind the chairs?* Trinkets blanketed the tabletops and bookcases, turning one hour of dusting into three. Even the kitchen cupboards were stuffed with collectibles, like the uranium oxide glassware they would never use. She sealed and stamped the last of the invoices. At the other end of the table sat her chemistry textbook, a prerequisite for the horticulture program. Elegant diagrams of atomic particles, electrons in concentric circles around a nucleus of protons and neutrons, orderly building blocks of the natural beauty she'd seen in the forests of Urlaken.

*

She dropped the grocery bags on the floor when she saw the red "1" blinking on the answering machine. She pressed the button and listened.

Catherine, this is Helen Quinn. Give me a call when you can.

She'd been holding herself back from feeling almost anything. Now a flood of every emotion swept her. She staggered, stared at the phone on the wall, lifted the receiver, dialed. Her fingernail nervously traced the groove in the island countertop where formica met wood. Helen picked up.

"Hi, Helen? This is Catherine Lind. I'm returning your call. Do you have news?"

"Yes."

That was what Catherine had been waiting to hear, waiting these two weeks to hear *Yes.* But there was silence after that one word. Helen's voice was low and quiet. "I found her obituary."

Catherine's insides dropped, like they were lying on the floor outside of her body. She was cold. Empty.

"I'm sorry," Helen said.

"Thank you," she said, listening from far away to the tremor of her own voice. Words that didn't make any sense as they left her lips. Her eyes flooded. It wasn't supposed to be like this.

"I had trouble finding her. The name in the obituary was different from the name in our records, but her social security number matched the death record. And when I contacted a friend of hers who was interviewed for the obituary, he confirmed it was her. There was no marriage certificate and it appears she never had more children."

Her obituary. Her friend. Confirmed it was her.

"There's a half page write up about her in the local newspaper. And I found an interview written about one month before she died."

"When? When did she...?"

"Seven years ago, January 1993."

Seven years. "Her name, what was her name? Can you...?" Her words a jumble.

"Her first name was Mary, and her adoptive surname was Tomczak. Her adoptive parents are deceased. But the newspaper stories refer to her as Mary Zadora."

Her name was Mary. Catherine's mind clung to the phrase. Forever she had been only *birth mother*. Now she was Mary, a real person with a life all her own. "And, am I right that my birth father is not named?"

"That's correct, I'm afraid she did not name the father."

"Is there anything more you can tell me?"

"I can tell you that Mary was an artist and that she lived in Massachusetts."

She and Alistair would be in Marblehead in October to visit Carly and her German husband Bernhard. "Where in Massachusetts?"

"On the Cape, in Provincetown."

Music

O'Shaughnessy Hall, Notre Dame University, March 1983

P
rofessor Hahn sat on the edge of the long seminar table as the students, all but one, noisily filed out. "James, I want you to finish this paper. I'll have to knock off a few points for tardiness, but I want to see where you're going with it."

James reluctantly held out his hand to receive the typed pages. He had half-hoped to admit defeat — *sorry I couldn't get it done* — and walk away. Instead he had to figure it all out. The late afternoon sun filtered through half-closed blinds, a pale amber gold, all else stripped away. "I just think Spengler's giving us an explanation of what he likes and doesn't like," James said. "I don't think it's anthropology to say rural life is soulful and city life isn't. It's all human behavior, like it or not."

Hahn heaved on his trench coat. "The age-old battle between natural philosophy and social philosophy." He sang as he hiked up his collar and walked out of the room, "*He says Naturwissenschaften, you say Geisteswissenschaften, let's call the whole thing off!*" From down the corridor James heard him call, "Show it to me when it's done!"

*

At Notre Dame, more than he could ever learn was there in front of him. Anthropological ethnographies, social philosophy, Christian, Sufi, and Jewish theology, theater, music, history, law. There to be examined and assembled piece by piece into a picture of everything he needed to understand — people, why they did what they did — that was anthropology. But first he had to figure out the anthropologists themselves.

Spengler was a lot like the new postmodernists who acted like they were scientifically explaining society while really they were all about what should and shouldn't be. But you can't figure out how society works if you're judging it the whole while. How could he write a paper about Spengler's method when his method was going nowhere? He'd have to stop hating Spengler while he finished the paper.

The old-style anthropologists, they were scientists, or at least what Hahn called "natural philosophers." The ethnographers were the professional describers of society. Their observations were the raw material for theory. The structuralist theorists sorted ethnographies into societies of similar kinds. And the functionalists examined one ethnography at a time, how the belief system and the social system fit together. It still didn't seem like enough to explain everything. The morning had been hazy spring sun. He watched a pale blue sky now as he walked Dorr Road through wetland wilderness and searched his mind for what it was the anthropologists, all of them, were missing. A wind swept from behind him and he turned to see gray clouds massing in the west, the day changing.

He walked into the classroom. Shakespeare Perspectives, at Notre Dame's sister school across U.S. Thirty-One, Saint Mary's College. Carol — tall, blonde, something gritty about her — eyed him and said loud enough for her friend, and him, to hear. "Love the fit on those pants, big time!" Her gaze dipped down. "Carol!" — her friend whispered — "Don't. He's a nice guy, leave him alone."

He didn't really want to be left alone. But what was he supposed to say? He found an open chair as the wind rattled the windows.

*

Pullman, Washington, June 1987

Two thousand miles west of Notre Dame, three years after the bachelors in Anthropology, James earned a second bachelors degree, music composition at Washington State amid the rolling hills of the Palouse. He studied Perotin, Bach, Beethoven, Bartok, Stravinsky. Wrote his own fledgling compositions, musical scores piled atop his anthropology books. Expositions, developments, recapitulations. Musical motifs woven in great patterns. It was like the premises, arguments, and conclusions of theory — but without words. Something you could feel in your body, not just your mind.

Dad helped him pack everything he owned into the Chevy two-door sedan for the long drive to Boston and New England Conservatory. Sweat beaded on their foreheads as the sun rose higher over Pullman amid the treeless hills. Mom was in Indianapolis for Kelly's graduation, a bachelors in

Political Science at Indiana University where Margaret was closing in on a Doctorate in Anthropology. Luke was making a life in set design and living by his wits in New York City. Before summer's end, Dad and Mom would fly to Malaysia for Dad's new teaching job. James took a final survey of the one-bedroom apartment on the hill above North Grand Avenue. "I guess that's everything."

Night fell as they coursed down Interstate Ninety along the edge of the Black Hills National Forest. After a late-night dinner they fell into a dead-tired sleep at the Rapid City Holiday Inn.

At breakfast James lifted a coffee to his lips, Dad an orange juice. "I can't believe I'm done," James said. Dad's eyes met his in what he recognized as a smile of connection, so understated that no one but family ever would have seen it. They quietly finished their eggs and toast, and suddenly Dad's ice blue eyes lit up. "Before we reach Saint Paul tonight, I thought we'd stop in New Ulm."

Interstate Ninety through Sioux Falls, across the state line into Minnesota. They would stay with Uncle James at the rectory of Saint Leo's Catholic Church in Saint Paul. But first the little prairie town that James had heard of but never seen. They came in on U.S. Fourteen, farmland all around, and entered the town in the wooded river valley.

"This is Washington Street, I was little when we lived in this house." Few words from Dad, little sign of what he was thinking or feeling. "This is State Street." A quiet concentration, that's what you could call it. And then a smile. "That's our old corner store. We used to walk down there for milk and bread. And candy." They parked by the little shop on South Minnesota Street. Domeier's German Store. The milk and bread were replaced by German imported steins, clocks, and Christmas decorations. But the candy was still there.

"Henry Crossland, is that you?" A woman with graying hair perked up behind the cash register. "I remember you and your brother Will. We were all just little then." Dad nodded matter of factly, "Yes it's me."

They were quiet now, driving up U.S. 169 toward the Twin Cities. Focused on Saint Paul and a good night's sleep before the next day's drive. "The exit for Interstate 494 East is coming up, two miles," James announced, map on his lap. As the Chevy cruised eastbound below Minneapolis and crossed York Avenue, James gazed south out the passenger window onto suburban lights punctuating the darkness along the highway.

*

Boston, Fall 1987

Estefan tipped back his bottle, then leaned back like he was going to say something important. "Griffin says it's all about grabbing the listener with spectacle, the bigger the better."

James shot up from his seat in the bar on Gainsborough Street. "What the fuck! That's PR, a circus! What does that have to do with making music!" He wiped the beer from his shirt with a napkin. Ji-Soo laughed and glanced at Dov and Estefan. Mosi took a long draught of his Dos Equis, undisturbed.

"You just made a spectacle of yourself," Estefan declared. "That got everyone's attention. Isn't that what you want your music to do?"

James shook his head. "No, it's not what I want my music to do. Music unfolds in time. Small changes in the rhythm and harmony are signs of bigger changes across the arc of the piece. That's what should be grabbing the listener's attention."

"I'm not convinced that listeners are going to pick up on all that," Dov said.

James thought a moment. "Listen, I'm picking up on it, and I'm human..."

Ji-Soo smirked. "More or less!"

"Funny," James said. "But my point is if one human is picking up on it, then others will too."

A subtle nod from Mosi.

*

Old brick-walls, wooden-floors worn by ninety years of feet scuffing, chairs assembled and rearranged, grand pianos wheeled in and out. In the classrooms of New England Conservatory he studied the music of Stockhausen, Cage, Ligeti. New sounds, new definitions of music. And still Beethoven, still weaving strands into great patterns. And new scores of his own. He sat silent in the audience at Jordan Hall while fellow students performed his song for soprano, cello, and percussion. *Rising, rising, make the high note! Too staccato on the cello line. Ah that's it, broader, open up, open up.*

Finale. The tense half-second of silence while the audience wait for the players to relax and bow and — thank god — there's the applause.

The first year at New England Conservatory everyone basked in the pride of arrival. Few were admitted, and once they had passed through the great doors of Jordan Hall there was a feeling of promise, yes, but also safety. A great hurdle crossed, all other successes and failures lay far in the future. James felt it. Everyone seemed to feel it.

The second year was different. A single year remaining to get it all right. And at the end of the year — real life, whatever that was that supposed to be.

Dad warned him off of trying for a university job with only a Masters. *Chances are you'll be stuck teaching as an adjunct. It's not really enough to live on.* Mosi, a year ahead of James, had gone on to doctoral studies at Princeton. Dov was aiming for U.C. Berkeley, Ji-Soo for Cornell. Estefan had enough of school. He was going to work odd jobs while playing out with his Brazilian band. Robert Ceely, James' composition instructor, wasn't much help. "I'll write a recommendation for you, but you should know that nobody likes my music so it won't do you any good. I'm kidding. But I haven't really kept up my contacts. That's what thirty years stuck teaching at the same school does to you."

James browsed doctoral program guides at the library. How do you decide? He wrote for admissions information and waited to see what would show up in the mail box at Langmaid Terrace, his apartment in Somerville. And by the time he finished reading the glossy flyers and detailed admission requirements — Harvard, Princeton, Berkeley, Cornell, University of Florida, a mishmash of possibilities — one thing stood out. One ridiculous, stupid thing. Almost every program required a piano sight-reading test, and every time he read the requirement he was struck through with fear. He could write a musical score. And he could read anyone else's score and play, after weeks of practice, a passable rendition of a sonata or fugue. But hunting and pecking his way through an unfamiliar score at an entrance audition? He would look like an idiot. In fact, it made him angry. Why should a composition candidate have to prove themselves at the piano? After all the music he had written, chamber trios for string and wind, songs for voice, solos for oboe, for harpsichord, for piano. After his deep explorations of musical form, from Gregorian chant to Beethoven to Lutoslawski. His contemplations of music as breath, music as the rhythm of body and mind.

After all that they would force him to sit in front of a faculty panel and hunt and peck the keys like an idiot.

And that, pitifully, was how he decided where to apply. One school only. Princeton University didn't require an audition.

All your eggs in one basket, Mosi had said in a late night phone call after the rejection letter. *I'm so sorry, James — What's wrong with those dummies!* Mom had said. *What will you do now?* Dad had said. James sat down to his Roland D-50 keyboard, his music, his mind, and played.

*

May 1989

Master of Music. While classmates entered the gates of Harvard and Princeton with that same pride of arrival they had felt at the conservatory, or walked into the classrooms of community colleges as adjunct instructors hoping to claw their way to full-time professorship, James took a lowly circulation job at the MIT Libraries, a job that would pay the bills and be so undemanding that he could funnel all his energy into his own interests.

It was two months after graduation that he and Estefan hatched the plan. Midnight at the Middle East Cafe in Central Square, they leaned close across the wooden table in the boisterous, heavy, aromatic swirl of alcohol and coffee and spice and too many young bodies packed together in the summer heat. "We have so much to share," James said. "But we're letting other people decide what we can and can't do. Let's do our own concert, our own music, invite other young composers." Estefan picked up the riff, "You and me, we arrange the gig. Everybody brings their own music, their own players."

In his seven-walled bedroom in the east tower of the old brick Victorian, Langmaid Terrace at the top of Winter Hill, the music flowed into his fingers on the keyboard and filled the manuscript paper with beamed notes every time he sat down to write. He swiveled from writing desk to Roland D-50, from pencil on manuscript paper to fingers on keys and back again. Every note, every phrase, every crescendo bore a load in the architecture of sound.

His rondo adagio for clarinet, viola, and string bass was a leap forward. Exploratory in its microtonal scale, sonically beautiful, tragic — he didn't mean to make it tragic — woven in classically rigorous form. And after that November concert at the First and Second Church on Marlborough Street across the Charles River from Cambridge, the music went quiet. He started a new trio to complement the rondo adagio, but the notes weren't right. Harmonic progressions led to the wrong keys. He switched to electronic composition, layering vocal and keyboard tracks on his Tascam recorder, phrases of poetry and philosophy from his penned journals, wild tunings and reverb programmed on the D-50. By the next spring it was just the mic and the Tascam as he sang his journals, punctuated with beats on the drum from Ghana and clangs on the saucepan from the kitchen cupboard.

*

Macroeconomics and sociology piled into the returns box at MIT's Dewey Library. Keynes, Marx, Pareto, Samuelson. He dug them out, wanded them in, paused over title pages, browsed introductions. Levi-Strauss, Weber, Hannerz, Douglas. Philosophy destined for Hayden Library piled in: Aristotle, Kant, James, Carnap. Art destined for Rotch Library: Kandinsky, Pollock, Basquiat. Shelving in the quiet of the stacks, he gazed across the thousands of bindings in rows upon rows from floor to ceiling, but in his mind was every one book — the architecture that made a hundred fifty thousand words speak one story.

*

"Take the train down, you gotta come!"

"I wouldn't miss it, Mosi. Or should I call you Dr. Kipruto now?" James marveled, a party down in Princeton to celebrate a doctorate. What a different life Mosi was living. There would be other music students there too, Princeton students, all on the verge of one success or another. *New England Conservatory! What are you doing now? Are you teaching in Boston?* It was going to be awkward. But what was so weird was that before anything awkward could happen, something amazing happened. A girl. Tall, redheaded, mystery behind her gray-blue eyes.

James had dated, tried to date, wished he could date so many girls over the years in Boston. Janay, sophisticated, slender, ebony skin. He met her eyes on the Orange Line platform at Sullivan Square and somehow knew he had a chance, got her number as the train pulled into Downtown Crossing, but when he brought her to a conservatory concert, her eyes were on every other guy. Ziying, smart and petite, a clarinet student from Singapore. She invited him to her apartment on Huntington Avenue, but when she rifled through his wallet for a condom that he didn't have, it was over. Celeste, from acquisitions at the library — beautiful feline eyes, but no intellectual chemistry, and yes, as far as he was concerned that was a real thing. There seemed to be infinite ways to not get laid. But tonight the room in Princeton was dancing, heating up. When she lifted the blouse over her head, camisole beneath, it was a lightning flash, every head turned. He danced with her, waited in the rain while she lingered over goodbyes, stepped soaking wet into her apartment. *I need to shower,* she said. He asked her name as the shower's spray streamed down their eyelashes. Veronica. They talked into the night. *You should really educate yourself about Derrida,* she said. As if educating himself wasn't the very reason he dismissed Derrida as rant posing as science. But it didn't matter. He took the train down every Friday for a month. The kitchen linoleum floor bathed in olive oil. The soft green moss patch under the backyard floodlights at two in the morning. It was ridiculous. Ridiculous that this could be a relationship. Because it did matter. Derrida. They didn't see the world the same way.

*

January 1992

He settled into the mahogany bamboo chair Mom and Dad had shipped from Ghana so many years ago, balancing a dinner plate of cold tofu, green olives, and raw broccoli on his lap and planting a bottle of Newcastle on the hardwood floor beside him. He gazed out the tall east window onto the sweeping townscape, down the twilight slope and away to the glistening skyscrapers of Boston lining the Charles River to the south, the darkened rooftops of Malden and Chelsea lining the Mystic River to the north, and across the church steeples of Charlestown to the little beacon of light on Massachusetts Bay — the control tower at Logan International Airport.

This evening what caught his eye was the string of seven sparkling lights that hung in the sky above the ocean — commercial airliners approaching the runways. He watched the string of lights loom brighter and lower over the bay as that distant beacon called to them.

Essence

Provincetown, October 1992

Mary dashed the final words in green chalk, then stroked an exclamation point with a fuchsia flourish and bowed. Enlightenment, she hoped. The OC erupted in hoots and cheers, resounding, pounding in her head. She groped seatbacks and friendly shoulders through the crowd. "You okay, honey?" Joyce hopped from her barstool and reached her hand to Mary. "I'm wonderful," Mary said. "I just need a tequila. No. Some air. Join me for a smoke, Joyce."

On the sidewalk she fumbled for her lighter. "What is that smell? It's making me sick." The lighter dropped to the pavement with a loud clink and the cigarette dangled from her lips and the ground moved and the pavement, she hit the pavement. There were voices all around. Joyce's voice — "Mark, get over here, it's Mary!" Too many voices. Mark kneeling, shouting, "What's she on? What's she on!"

*

I am learning to be free, learning to be a spirit. Sometimes it's hard to be a body.

*

"Joyce, it's Mary. I'm sending you my braids."

"Mary! What are you talking about? Never mind that, where are you? I've been going crazy trying to find you but they keep moving you around."

"I'm at the convalescence center in Hyannis."

"The convalescence center? With the seniors? Okay, one thing at a time. What the hell happened? You're looking a little ragged and we go out for a smoke and next I know, there you are flat on the sidewalk... It was awful Mary, you were like, having a fit..."

"They said I had a seizure. I've been having weird episodes. Stiffness or I'm dropping things or I'm seeing things."

"I know you haven't seemed quite right, but I wouldn't worry yourself..."

"It's a rare tumor, glioblastoma. It causes pressure on the brain."

"Holy fucking shit, honey..."

Mary waited. "Are you there, Joyce?"

"I'm here. You always were the rare one, always had to be different. Blasto-whatever you said. Is it cancer? Are you in treatment?"

"They'll do radiation first. That's why I'm sending my braids. But they don't know if they can operate. And it's growing."

"Holy shit. Does your father know, is he in touch with the doctors?"

"I made a list of everyone to call. You're the first. The radiation only slows it down, it might give me a year, they'll have to operate. Just when I'm finally getting my life together, Joyce..."

"Hang in there honey, you're a fighter. If anybody can beat this thing you can. Now the second thing. What's with the convalescence center?"

"I can't walk, Joyce.

"I can't believe this Mary."

"I'm paralyzed on my left side. I'll need care, during the treatments and after, but I don't have insurance. The social worker wanted to send me to a homeless shelter."

"Whoa, whoa, whoa! Now I'm getting pissed. They could have discharged you to me, Mary..."

"They can't..."

"I'll take care of you..."

"I need nursing care, in a facility. I'm going to have to be my own advocate."

*

Hyannis, Cape Cod, November

Mary watched the white-haired man next to her slowly, slowly lean forward until the tip of his nose was in his soup bowl. She leaned him back up, took a taste of her own soup and watched him descend again. She quickly swapped out his soup bowl for his dessert plate, a powdered doughnut in the center. At least he wouldn't drown. If she was decades younger than all her housemates, she wasn't so far behind them in many ways. Everyone at the OC chipped in to buy a good wheelchair, and she wasn't allowed to go outside unattended, not even on the center's grounds. She longed to be outdoors, walk on the beach, swim in the surf. It was a lesson she couldn't have learned any other way. To live every moment while you still can, sink your toes into the sand, before you've lost what you innocently thought was yours forever.

Bette brought crystals, taped them into the palm of her hand, read Shakespeare. Father sent a box with a note. *My thoughts have been with you since our last phone conversation. The enclosed prayer card expresses my daily prayer for your recovery. Mother and I presume that you have received the robe and slippers and will put them to good use.*

Five weeks of radiation done, one week to go. Then see if the tumor was small enough to take out. Such terrible headaches after the treatments. The morphine helped. And even though she knew she would never be the same, maybe after all was done she could walk on the beach again. Robert came with flowers. *You know, don't you, I'm going to take you dancing for your birthday!* He may have been joking, but she had a new goal for December.

Poor sweet Robert. He was baffled when she phoned him end of November to arrange her birthday visit to Orleans. "Mary, you're the strongest person I know, but you said you shouldn't overexert."

"Robert, I can do this. I'll have my morphine, I'll come in the van. It's too late to worry, mister fisherman. You already invited me." He laughed, he joked, he stammered, he choked. He conceded, "Okay, okay then, we've got a plan."

*

Orleans, Cape Cod, December 8

Freedom, the brisk December wind ruffled her scarf as Gloria, the nurse's aide, wheeled her to the van. The chair jarring as they fastened it for the drive, the sound of the engine, so many sounds, the vibrations on the road, sand, snow, and pine scrub flashing by on Route 6. She averted her eyes from the side windows, tried to focus on the distance ahead. The radiation was done. Thirty treatments. Without the shrinkage they had hoped for. They were assessing options. She reached to her forehead and was surprised even now at the touch of bare scalp. She didn't know how much time had passed. The crunch of gravel as the van rolled into Robert's driveway.

Pull it together. "I'm back! At least part of me!" Gloria eased her down the van's ramp.

"Happy birthday, Mary! And many more!" Robert's eyes revealed too much.

"Let's party!" She blinked at the flashes of light that no one else could see.

Robert held open the front door. "Let's get her inside."

She tried to straighten herself in the wheelchair. "Looks like the boat's gone."

"It sank a while back. Forty feet out. Maiden voyage."

Mary winced as she tilted her cheek toward his kiss. "A toast to my birthday?"

He looked to Gloria. "I'm guessing no tequila. Maybe a...coffee?"

"I'll have a sip of Newcastle. And give Gloria one. Just one Gloria!"

Robert returned and set three Newcastles on the coffee table. "I'm switching to Jameson after this one."

"I need this." Mary's eyes brightened. "To get out. Hear music. See people dancing."

"Or we can just party right here, but it's your birthday, you call the shots." He glanced to Gloria and smiled at Mary.

"Shots, that's it! Don't all be party poopers!" She laughed and reached, shaking, toward the beer. She stifled a moan as the pain grew. "Fuck it anyway. Gloria, my morphine. Can you believe what a basket case I am, Robert?""

Gloria rummaged in the pocket bag on the back of the wheelchair. "I told the nurse to dose you for the day. I'm sorry, but there's only one vial." Mary squeezed a drop under her tongue, let the sensation course through her. "Gloria, will you dig my makeup bag out of the pocket here and wheel me to the bathroom? I need to freshen up for some dancing."

At the mirror, she stared. *Is that me?* She focused all her energies on reaching her right hand toward the lip stick tube that Gloria held out for her.

"Let me, Mary."

"I can do it. I'll do it."

Pain everywhere, flashes of light. The sickening smell. "Gloria, Gloria it's starting..."

She heard breathing. *Why can't I lift my head? God it hurts.* Darkness opening to the bathroom lights. Robert. Her eyes held onto his. "Mary, maybe you need to go back."

Her eyes fluttered. *Robert, are you there?*

*

The three women, they had come to her before. She knew herself as the middle one. Her mother and her daughter beside her. *Not everything needs the answer you expected,* she told them, she needed to tell them. *The answer to Why did I give you away? can be, I will always love you. The answer to How can I live without you? can be, I will always love you. The answer to Why do I have to leave? can be, I will always love you.*

*

Bette's heartbeat. Bette lay in the bed beside her.

"You can take some of my warmth, Mary. Are you in pain?"

Mary shook her head.

"You look peaceful."

"I am."

"You've taken off the mask, and now it's just you. You're beautiful."

*

the nomad ever wanders
even as she lingers
by the river's waters
her heart cries to be moving
proving her life is meant to wend
over fields, round road's bend
her spirit then to send
her thoughts to wander on

*

Herring Cove Beach, Provincetown, January 23, 1993

Joyce stood firm on the slant of beach. Falling apart inside her insulated parka. Her hands were poised on the woven ring of alder. A clear tenor voice drew her eyes to McNutty, tall like a pier post, the dark curls beneath his knit cap flying in the sea spray. He recited from a crumpled paper in his hands.

"It is the middle, the cold hard middle of the off season. This is the time and place for locals. Born here or washed ashore, we are the ones who have made a life here, who breathe life into this barren strip of land as we go about our working days and crazy nights and crazy days and working nights. And we breathe out a last breath into this barren strip when we die. Nearly a month ago..."

He went silent. They waited.

"A month ago everything Mary was — art, love, possibility — she exhaled into this place and into all of us who live here. She no longer is the bearer of her own story. We carry her story now..."

Joyce's gaze drifted through the gathered crowd. Quiet conversation between these two, Mary's nurses. And among those three, Mary's lovers. She watched the eyes of that one search the horizon, that fog-swathed one from Truro whose name she couldn't remember.

Wilson stood from his folding chair. Behind him, parked on the sand, was his pickup truck, the hood topped with bottles of vodka, tomato juice, Worcestershire sauce. Bloody Marys. He wrapped a pen on the side of his tumbler and cleared his throat. His voice rang into the wind.

"This afternoon, to this captive audience of poetry sufferers, I should like to address a poem written by Mary's friend Ralph the Writer, fourteen lines of empty verse entitled...The Empty Bar Stool.

"So, on this January twenty-third,
in weather suitable for Admiral Byrd,
we gather here on Herring Cove Beach,
in tribute to a nonpareil Polish peach.
Cast among we swine, a pearl.
She was flowery, she was jouncy,
with her braids of brown a falling down
upon her Ruthie's evening gown,
with her sweet breath of Tequiler
cut with Sunkist lemon peeler,
she was not your Mama's apple pie,
she was a coconut."

And when Wilson uttered the last word of his proclamation, Joyce's hand brushed the alder that formed the hoop of the dream catcher — six long dark braids, decorated with gull feathers, trailing from the grapevine web. Mary's wish fulfilled. Joyce wrapped her fingers around the alder and lifted it, carried it trembling to the water's edge, her eyes met the sea. Boots in the surf, she was stilled. She didn't want to let go. Why should she have to? But the clouds that had hung heavy and gray seemed to open, hints of blue glinted through the gray, and the gray turned pink. Mary the water, Mary the wind, whispered. Joyce lifted the alder, a last glance at the braids, and turned it in her hand like a great frisbee. She hesitated. Then twisting her body to the side, she pressed her lips hard and with all her might hurled it out over the waves.

Sunset. Soft pink and periwinkle stretched across the sky, and a brilliant orange flame at the horizon multiplied on the faceted bay.

Angels

Cambridge, Massachusetts, 1998

Lunch break, Dewey Library. James sat beneath a boulevard tree on the wide grassy median of Memorial Drive. The Charles River glistened in the sun as the familiar old John Hancock Tower and Prudential Building stood sentry in the distance. He steadied the Au Bon Pain coffee cup on the grass and opened his notebook.

Dear Mary Douglas. He had to write to her after pulling *How Institutions Think* out of the returns box. He could still see her kind face under a graying poof of hair at the podium at Notre Dame. On the way to explaining her grid-group theory — yet another structuralist effort at classification — she did something unexpected and apparently unrecognized by anyone else writing in the social sciences. In fact it seemed like she didn't recognize it herself. She explained how individuals make choices and how they bargain for these choices through analogy. It came so close to a fundamental theory of culture. Confusingly close. It didn't quite coalesce. Did it?

I believe that your grid-and-group isn't nearly as important as the building blocks of bargaining and analogy you start from.

*

New York City, March 1999

Steam rose as Luke poured the kettle water over the coffee grounds into one cup, then the other. "We should stop by my studio after lunch. And I've got a video load-in at six tonight."

James nodded and looked across the crazy quilt of Upper West Side rooftops and water towers from the window beside the kitchenette. Luke shared the tiny apartment with three housemates.

"Hey, I've got to show you this." Luke set the coffees on the table and opened his PowerBook. "I built a website over the winter."

"What is that, exactly?"

"Take a look. Click the text here — or it can be an image — and another page opens up. You can make as many pages as you want. Look at the stuff people are putting up on the web. Old books and photos in the public domain, new research. Some sites are just link farms that link to other sites. Why don't you build one? You could publish your writing, your correspondence with old professors, whatever you want!"

On New Years Day in 2001, James launched Bhag.net, his own online magazine. He published bits of his own writing, and interviews with artists and thinkers. It was like magic the first time he typed HTML code into a text file, opened it in his Netscape browser, and stared at a colorful web page of writing and images. He played with information architecture and navigation, bought a digital camera to generate new imagery.

*

Cambridge, Massachusetts 2000

His eyes combed the shelves of the MIT Press Bookstore. In Philosophy an oddly titled book caught his eye: *Self-Consciousness and Self-Determination*. He carefully opened the book to the first pages of tiny print.

Originally published as Selbstbewusstsein und Selbstbestimmung, copyright 1979. He browsed the contents. *Lecture 1, Preliminary Clarifications. Lecture 2, Formulation of the Problem and the Program. Lecture 3, The Traditional Theory of Self-Consciousness at an Impasse.* Hmm, that language was interesting. *Lecture 6, The Way out of the Fly Bottle.* Unlike the postmodernists, whose ultimate point was always that we're trapped in cultural code, no way out, this author was bold enough to propose a solution. He carried Ernst Tugendhat to the checkout.

*

Tugendhat proposed that the self is not an unchanging object to be known by looking inside ourselves. Instead he proposed that the self is evolved through the procession of decisions we make throughout our lives, day-by-day, year-by-year. And if there is such a thing as free will, we have the opportunity to make future decisions that represent the kind of person we want to be. He closed the book in his lap, gazed into thought. Why weren't the anthropologists doing something like this?

*

James swiped barcode after barcode on the stack of books the economics student brought in for a third renewal, sticky-note bookmarks sprouting from the pages. "All due March 3!" he announced and turned to the overflowing returns box. Wedged inside, halfway down, he saw another author he knew from Notre Dame days, Clifford Geertz, *The Interpretation of Cultures*. The words came to him, something about the human brain being incomplete and because incomplete, flexible.

That evening James settled into the mahogany bamboo chair and opened Geertz. From Tugendhat's evolving self to an anthropology of evolving culture — how to get there? The problem was that the functionalists and structuralists were analyzing and categorizing a society at the moment the ethnographer observed it, just a snapshot in time, without ever asking — How did it get that way? Culture changes.

Geertz wrote that humans are animals whose genes stop short of adapting to one specific environment or another. Instead our genes leave us to figure it out. We can learn from experience and learn from each other. What we learn is called culture. It didn't seem like a radical idea, but it was a radical break from the majority of researchers who believed in determinism: the anthropologists with their social structure, the postmodernists with their cultural code, and the socio-biologists with their genetic code. The majority opinion left no room for free will.

James tapped the mahogany frame, stood, strode into his bedroom, the seven-walled room in the building's east tower. Turned within the walls. Something weaving together. Manic to find it before it vanished.

Geertz made room for free will. The human ability to experiment, learn, change our behavior is an evolutionary adaptation that allows our species to live in virtually any kind of environment. He gestured into the air. "So...so... essentially, humans evolved to the point that genes have virtually no role in human behavior. Geertz is actually making a radical case, a genetic case, for free will....and...." — he closed his eyes — "so listen" — he talked aloud into the living room — "No code making our choices for us." He knew people's choices usually followed patterns. But it's not a code. It's more like walking forward and when you hit a wall you have to turn. It's environment. It's still us choosing, but... He slumped into the mahogany chair.

*

Ziggy, a librarian? "Really?" James scrunched his face. Ziggy worked the Reserve desk, wanding books in and out same as James. And now.

"I'm enrolled at Tufts, the Master of Library Science program." Ziggy's smile told James there was a punch line coming. "I always wanted to be a scientist!"

"But you're serious?"

"I'm thirty-five," Ziggy said. "And I'm working alongside a bunch of twenty-somethings barely scraping by."

"I'm thirty-eight..."

"So what are you waiting for? Don't you want to be a scientist too?"

It seemed like Ziggy wanted James to jump on the bandwagon. Maybe so he could justify surrendering to a conventional life in a comfortable career. James wasn't jumping. If he did, how could he ever find time to read, write, think, weave it all together? Maybe what he was most drawn to in Tugendhat was the idea that who we are is the sum of what we choose to do. All James wanted was a book on his lap and pen and paper in hand, doing his own work.

He still couldn't seem to assemble the ideas in his head. He read and read. Cheney and Seyfarth, *How Monkeys See the World.* Aristotle, *De Anima.* Minsky, *The Society of Mind.* He wrote voluminous notes, condensed the books down to the essential ideas he needed. Building blocks. He could feel it. The Chan Buddhist notion of hua tou — word head, the opening, the flurry of inspiration just before a word is spoken.

*

June 2001

"Hey! James! How is everything!" Luke didn't call often, but whenever he did he always sounded like finding you at the other end of the line was the most amazing thing that ever happened to him. "What's happening in Beantown!"

"Not much. I did an interview with Jim Bellis from Notre Dame."

"Very cool."

"And I emailed some of my digital photos to another online magazine. I'm publishing other people. I want someone to publish me for a change. I haven't heard anything back yet."

"Cool, good you're getting your stuff out there. So listen, you like New York right, visiting here? How about living here? The lease is up at my old place and my housemates are scattering to the far corners of the city. Come on down and we can share a place!"

"Wow. New York City. That would be amazing. But I don't know."

"I'm signing for a loft in Bushwick. It's got a lot of potential."

"I'm just picturing every time we go to that juice shop in the East Village..."

"Juice shop?"

"You know it has the chalkboard menu with a hundred combinations and I don't know what goes with what, and I decide the hell with the chalkboard, I'll just have a small orange juice, and the barista points back to the board and says you have to choose from the menu."

"I'm not quite following."

"I don't know if I can handle New York."

"You can totally handle it."

*

Langmaid Terrace, Somerville, September 11, 2001

"They are saying it was a small plane, a small aircraft of some kind, it crashed just above the ninetieth floor, we're still waiting for more details...."

He moved the bowl of cereal from his lap onto the table beside the mahogany chair, cardboard boxes piled everywhere, and stared at the World Trade Center towers on the television screen. It was a few minutes before nine.

"That's the North Tower burning, you're looking at. You can see a New York City Police helicopter circling, but we are being told they do not believe a rooftop rescue is possible because of the intense heat and wind..."

The middle of the other tower exploded in flames. "That was another plane...This is a deliberate attack... Close to 50,000 people work in these two buildings...."

The South Tower collapsed, nine fifty-nine. The North Tower collapsed, ten twenty-eight. He picked up the kitchen phone and called Luke's number, *All circuits are busy.*

He started dialing Mom's number in Chattanooga, she would be waking about now, but no, he couldn't. You can't tell somebody who just woke up: The Twin Towers in New York fell down, they're gone, completely gone.

*

Luke unlatched the loading door of the rental truck outside James' apartment and hurled it ratcheting up. "Hopefully everything fits. Knock on Naugahyde!"

It was good to see Luke standing beside the truck, live and expressive as ever as the sun set over the top of Winter Hill. It took a while to load. Hands busy. Minds churning. Fragments of story. Luke was nowhere near the financial district the morning it happened, just one week ago. The sirens started as Luke arrived at his studio on Essex Street after an all-night VJing gig. He figured there was a fire somewhere in the Lower East Side. Until the sirens didn't stop.

It was almost midnight when the rental truck hauled across the Whitestone Bridge, Interstate 678, and Luke thumbed out the right-hand window. "There's Manhattan." James' eyes skimmed the blanket of lights, the city that always seemed too big, too fast, too everything to live in, that he wanted to live in anyway every time he took the train down from Boston.

"It's lucky we're coming down through the Bronx and Queens," Luke said. "Everything is still a mess in Lower Manhattan." After endless lighted expressways through endless night city, they double parked under the amber streetlights on Johnson Avenue in Brooklyn. Dilapidated two- and three-story brick and concrete warehouses.

"This is it. It used to be a factory," Luke laughed as they stepped up to the graffitied steel door. "And there's a Chinese import warehouse on the ground floor, forklifts and all!"

James knew the expected response was something like, *Wow, that's crazy, that is just so great!* He only said, "That's crazy."

The neighborhood, if you could call it that, was an industrial part of Bushwick rezoned and renamed Williamsburg Industrial Park. Across the street in back was Enquist Chemical Company, barrels of who-knows-what stacked behind a chain link fence. And next to Enquist was the New York City Sanitation Department fleet. Most people probably never give a thought to where all those white garbage trucks park at night — this is where. Across the street to the west was Waste Management Corporation — the fleet, the recycling plant, and football fields of whatever it takes to manage waste. All up and down Johnson Avenue, the same truly industrial cityscape. Above the ground floor's working warehouse, the second floor was divided into units, each with its own lockable door and a sink and toilet. Period. No conversion beyond the bare minimum.

Luke unlocked the door to Unit Five. James looked up into twenty-five thousand cubic feet of empty warehouse. A single room, thirty by fifty feet, with a seventeen-foot ceiling, and three ten-foot-tall windows on the north wall.

"We can build rooms, four bedrooms easily," Luke said. "One for me, one for you, and two more for housemates to help pay the rent. We'll go to the property manager tomorrow and add you to the lease." Luke squinted through his glasses into the emptiness, a grin beneath the furrowed brow, inventing something incredible.

"Aren't there are smaller units in the building," James asked, pointing uselessly toward the door and out of the remarkable space. "If we took one of those, we could pay for it ourselves. No hunting for housemates. And less construction."

"I've been in New York a long time. Trust me on this," Luke said. "This is our unit. I've already signed for it." They unloaded the truck until everything was safe inside the hallway. "We should get a bite to eat. Kellogg's Diner is open. It's on the L train."

"What time is it?" James asked.

"Uh, lemme check. Three in the morning!" Luke laughed. He loved to laugh — At working until three in the morning. At living in a warehouse. At nothing being what anyone expected it to be. There was a lightness in it. His laughter freed him from the bondage of expectations, and freed everyone around him.

It had been how long? Seventeen years since college, since they'd spent any time together beyond the few days at family Christmas, and then only when Luke could make it for Christmas, if a freelance job didn't pop up. Now they would see each other some part of every day, sharing the routine chores of daily life, grocery shopping, laundry, Kellogg's Diner for eggs and coffee, and another coffee and another. Taisho Restaurant on Saint Mark's Place for chicken yakitori and a sake, and another, and another. It was a funny mix of ordinary life and reunion party. In a very different way the whole City was a funny mix now. Ordinary life and trauma unit. Everybody was taking care of business like always. The subway trains were crowded. Kellogg's and Taisho were crowded. People streamed in and out of buildings, and cars and trucks streamed the boroughs' avenues, even while the news carried footage of candlelight vigils from around the world. The City was like a patient in critical care reading get-well cards and trying to look competent while nurses swap out IV drips and scan the monitors. The fact was, the City had been shot in the gut.

*

October 11, 2001

Wearing a light jacket, he crossed the Williamsburg Bridge. The sky was blue behind him to the east. The City was hazy. And there was the plume. The white smoke rising from downtown even now. He didn't have a plan except to walk there, to where it happened.

White dust coated Broadway, clung to the brick and concrete. He looked up. Twenty, thirty, forty stories and beyond, the white grime clung. At Cortlandt everyone was looking west, stopping and leaning at the barricades. He stopped where he stood. Two blocks away the steel arches rose in the smoke, and above the arches rose scant frames of windows, jagged and leaning, the steel frail, reaching up a hundred feet into the air and no farther. It was a shred of the northwest wall of the South Tower. You could look right through it like a picket fence. On the television there was a sound he had heard, a rapid-fire pop-pop-pop-pop-pop that continued fast and steady as the towers went down and the lives inside went down. Some had made a last phone call to a wife, a husband, a child. He glanced at an older woman beside him, white wavy hair like Mom's. He would have called her and Dad, and Luke and Margaret and Kelly.

*

He and Luke shared the cost of hiring a construction crew of five, shared the cost of lumber, hammers, drills, drywall, plaster. Shared in the ten-hour days of physical labor, sawing planks, cutting drywall. All the measuring and cutting and taping of childhood, the cardboard castles and villages, all full-size now. All cutting into the savings meant for rent and living while he hunted for a job.

"We'll need more lumber and drywall," Luke noted factually. James nodded agreement. He was deep in Luke's world, in Luke's city, in Luke's plans. He couldn't figure out where to draw the line. But it was hard to argue with what was evolving. When you opened the door to the unit you looked across the expansive space to a little seventeen-foot-tall apartment building on the other side of the room. Erected in the first month, a little building, in a room, in a big building. It was otherworldly.

"We still have to build the kitchen," Luke said. "And of course we'll need a bathtub."

*

In whatever words exactly, the voice at the other end of the line said, when he finally reached someone at the New School, "It's a university-wide hiring freeze. We'll keep your resume on file." October turned to November and the same freeze took hold across most of the City and much of the country.

He had to find work. That meant he had to strategize a viable resume. Dad's career had been straightforward. Start with a love of mathematics, study math, teach math, leave that job and teach math somewhere else if you want to. James' path was complicated. Start with a love of the pounding waves of the Atlantic at Elmina, the shadow blue foothills of the Andes at Cumaná, study anthropology, study music, get a library job, write music until the music goes quiet, pull philosophy, anthropology, economics out of the returns box at Dewey Library, move to New York City. And now? The bachelor's degree in anthropology was just any old college degree to most employers, proof he could read and write and make photocopies. The master's in music pointed to a job like adjunct music instructor, part-time no benefits. Fucking jobs. All he wanted was to do his own work.

*

How could the anthropology faculty at Notre Dame, or anywhere, find satisfaction in their patchwork of ethnographies, each of which examined life in one small community at one point in time — the Dusun of North Borneo in 1960, the Tewa of New Mexico in 1965 — without ever developing an overarching theory? When his term paper at Notre Dame analyzed the functional relation between a Cheyenne community's belief system and social system, his professors were thrilled. But he wasn't.

He imagined culture transforming through time, like a Classical sonata movement passing through exposition of themes, dramatic development, a recapitulation that's never quite the same as where we started. But while a sonata had a finale, culture kept forming and reforming. He saw it in the world around him. As far back as he could remember, Dad and Mom had talked about Catholic religious life becoming more humane after the Second Vatican Council in 1962. Mom wrote letters to Congress as the Civil Rights movement changed the way people thought about race. Dad's colleagues from Ghana said that the palm huts of Beulah Road were razed in the 1980s, replaced by concrete block houses. The "stable and cohesive" villages in the ethnographies were changing, pulling the rug out from under the anthropologists. And here he sat, November 2001, living in a half-converted warehouse in a city where neighborhoods change like the seasons. It was obvious. Theory had to explain an unfolding process, cultural change over time. Sonata or requiem, somebody had to find the music.

*

There were rat sightings, furry flashes darting among the piles of construction materials. Ben from Unit Ten down the long hallway, first tenant to move into the building, said that a cat was the surest way to get rats out and keep them out. So arrived the juvenile gray and white short-hair to Johnson Avenue. James named him Phoenix. As for rats, one kill was all it took. From then on occupancy was restricted to humans and one feline.

*

December. The industrial natural gas blower roared, warming the little seventeen-foot-tall apartment building inside Unit Five. While the main floor of the unit was still a construction site, James' bedroom with its raw plywood floor and fibrous soundboard walls was at least furnished as a living space with everything from his bedroom in Boston — desk, computer, printer, bookshelves, dresser. James sat down to his computer, hoping beyond hope for a message from the New School, from anywhere. And if not that, then maybe a hello from Kelly. What he saw in his inbox was the subject line, *RE: Photography submission for publication.* The message was from the editor of

Artzar.com, who said nothing about the digital photos James had submitted. Instead he wanted James to interview a major artist in New York City.

"Tell me who you want to interview and I'll make the arrangements," Alan Bing wrote. "It should be an artist here in the City, are you in the City?"

Artzar is in New York? Another lesson about his new home: Everyone is here, or has been, or will be at one time or another. It's only a small exaggeration. He had come across Artzar while searching the internet for an innovative online art magazine. He might have found a site based anywhere in the world, but it was right here in the City.

He knew who he wanted to interview. Chuck Close. But where did Close live? He did a quick internet search. Yep. There you go. Close was in New York City. Everyone was here.

James knew Close from the pages of *Art in America* magazine, an old 1972 issue at MIT's Rotch Library. He would never forget Close's remark: *I think we know what a blur looks like only because of photography. It really nailed down blur....* Close painted exacting portraits from photos, but he knew the photo, like the painting, was a mechanical artifact. Close was contemplating, how does a mechanical method make a picture, and how is it that we can recognize in any picture the thing it's a picture of? He was contemplating what it means to see at all. An artist with the heart of an epistemologist. That's who James wanted to interview.

*

Two weeks into the New Year, he entered a nondescript building he had already passed many times during these first months in the City. Mr. Stinson, Close's assistant, led him through a long hall, high ceiling, frosted windows, bountiful light. On the left a wall of books. On the right a huge four-panel portrait of Robert Rauschenberg. Through a double doorway he entered a vast space, skylit, where a mechanical easel held a large portrait in progress, oddly tilted at a forty-five degree angle. Tall windows yielded light from the left wall, and a series of daguerreotypes adorned the right. A big spectacled man wearing a long denim work apron over his long sleeves and trousers looked up and rolled his wheelchair closer to the long Formica table where two telephones and countless notebooks were scattered. Close gestured toward one of six empty metal chairs at the table. "So what do you want to know?"

*

Ten o'clock at night, snug inside the Johnson Avenue loft, he dreaded the task ahead. He slipped the manila envelope into his black leather satchel. From Notre Dame days onward, James had been the one to handle family business when Dad and Mom were abroad. And even though you could file electronically, Dad wanted to do the taxes, and Dad filing electronically was not going to happen. So James was mailing it all to Qatar, Dad's latest teaching post. He locked the graffitied door behind him. Head down, wind whipping his face, he trudged the two long blocks down Johnson Avenue to the trucker diner in the wedge between Knickerbocker and Morgan, then down Morgan to the L station where he dashed down the subway stairs like a prairie dog diving into its hole.

"Can you spare some change for a token?" a man at the bottom of the stairs asked. Torn coat, unraveling pants, grime in the wrinkles of his forehead. "I'm trying to get home."

James was getting to know the City and had already noticed the recurring *trying to get home* story. But nobody should be out in this cold. He dug into his coat pocket. A token was a dollar fifty, but he only had dollar bills. He saw thirty-five cents in the man's hand and that literal bent of his mind kicked in. "I'll give you two dollars if you'll give me that change."

They sealed the deal, which in hindsight James supposed was contrary to every New York etiquette imaginable. It's not a sales transaction. Either you give or you don't.

The L train to the E train, he watched the tunnels' darkness broken randomly by a fleeting glow of incandescent light. Outside Penn Station he walked across Eighth Avenue to the General Post Office and climbed the massive stairway framed with Greek columns and mailed the packet. He was back on the E train in no time, the homeward leg of his two hour roundtrip from Brooklyn.

At Fourteenth Street he boarded the L train in the bustling company of young people dressed in couples' dreams and loners' hopes, dressed for a night out. The train jostled. *Union Square station, next stop,* a recorded voice announced. At every stop the train doors opened onto another world, another part of the City, another moment of possibility. He leapt through the doors, and suddenly he wasn't on a two-hour round trip to the post office, he was on a night out.

He took the 6 train to Astor Place and emerged at the black steel Cube. From there it was a short walk down Saint Mark's Place, past the tattoo shops and sex shops and video stores, to Yakitori Taisho, where he and Luke had already shared dozens of meals and toasted numberless sakes. He descended the three steps out of the cold night and into the safe haven of the garden level restaurant. The grills behind the bar were alive with flame, and pots of soup spilled soothing steam into the dark narrow room. He stood in line, pressed against the wall as wait staff squeezed through the aisle between the guests waiting along the wall and the diners seated on wooden stools along the bar. A hostess motioned him to a newly opened stool and he sat shoulder to shoulder with the others.

"I'll have a rice ball with salmon, miso soup, and Nigori sake."

"Very good thank you," the waitress said in a flowing Japanese accent.

A glass window two feet from his nose separated him from the tall flames erupting from the grills. The cooks were mostly men, all trading counsel and commands in Japanese as their bare hands worked quickly, passing through the flames unscathed. He breathed the scent of grilled fish and chicken and pork, half satisfied and half hungrier. Watching the quick hands he noticed now, there were scars.

"Nigori sake thank you," the syllables rolled in a stream from her lips as she served him a short glass of milky, unrefined sake cradled in a tiny wooden box, the liquor overflowing the glass. He smiled into her eyes, not too much he hoped. He didn't want to embarrass her. He drank, letting the sweet grainy sake wash over his tongue. He should invite Alan here. Alan would love it. The theater of it, the language, the flames, the steam, the pretty face, snug in an underground hideaway.

Already during those intense weeks in January when he transcribed the Close tape and crafted it, under Alan's demanding, even overbearing, guidance from the runaway twists of live conversation into the logical order of a readable interview, he had started to understand that Alan was acting as more than a managing editor. He was a colleague as well, who seemed to hope that his own prospects might rise in tandem with his new friend's, that his experience might combine with James' talents to open doors neither one could have opened alone. And so a pathway was laid, and a random contact becomes colleague becomes friend and ally in the battle to gain a foothold in the world of professional writers and artists and web publishers and whatever else he and Alan thought they were becoming. A world where James could pay for an apartment that wasn't an abandoned factory.

She laid a plate before him. "Rice ball with salmon and miso soup."

More guests filed in. The guy beside him stood from his stool and swept on his coat, brushing James. "Sorry about that!" James nodded. There was no space, anywhere, for anything, without bumping someone. From the moment you entered, you were instantly communing with everyone around you. That was part of the magic. At Taisho no one ate alone.

The L train, just up to full speed under the East River, ground to a halt and the lights flickered off, then on again and the train jerked into motion, gaining speed, then easing, easing as it climbed from the depths below the river to the shallow sub-street level of the Brooklyn water front. When he turned the key in the lock on Johnson Avenue at one-thirty in the morning, he thought of the guy who had asked for a token. James had no job. What he had was enough savings to pay rent for the next ten months and because of that, he held a key in his hand. That was what made his night different. The key in his hand.

*

Kelloggs most days for lunch, Taisho once a week for dinner. The places Luke knew were the first ones James came to know, and those two he would keep even as the rest would fall away over the months and years, as he found his own way in the City. Kellogg's filled up fast at lunch time. Young hipster transplants from across the breadth and height of North America. Neighborhood natives, born and raised in Williamsburg, mostly Italian-Americans, Puerto Rican-, Dominican-, and Polish-Americans. And transplants from across the Atlantic too. Unhyphenated all-out Poles, Russians, Jordanians, Syrians, and Israelis. Greek-Americans were over-represented behind the counter — they owned the place. And amidst this selected mob of humanity you could find yourself waiting a long time for a booth or table. He liked the booths when he was with Luke. But when he was alone, which was most days now, he watched for an open swivel stool at the long Formica counter. The bustle of the wait staff kept him company as he browsed the big laminated menu of standard all-American breakfasts, standard all-Greek gyro lunches, and a few over-priced odd-ball specialties like Chicken Cordon Bleu or Broiled Seafood Combo. When the waitstaff rested their elbows on the counter for a moment, James shared tidbits of conversation about whatever was going on in the City, or out on the street, or here in the diner. And as the months passed, he started hearing his name announced as he walked in the door, "Jimmy!" and his usual order called back to the kitchen before he ever sat down.

Vasily, the middle-aged headwaiter with the heavy Greek accent and the sideways Brooklyn etiquette, shouted back to the cooks, "Two eggs over easy with Canadian! Today please!" He pushed a steaming ceramic cup in front of James. "Hey, here's the coffee you didn't have time to order."

"Man, it's raining like crazy out there!"

"Tell me something I don't already know," Vasily hurled back, a smile just under the poker face as the corner of his eye soaked up James' smile in return.

And for a while there was Ramla, the young waitress from Tunisia who spoke French and English and Arabic. By analogy with the Spanglish of the Nuyoricans, James tried mixing a little French into his over-the-counter chats with her, resorting to English when he had to.

"A refill...s'il te plaît."

"No! That's not how we speak French!"

"Ramla!" Vasily gestured with his chin to the empty coffee pots.

James peered over his cup at her graceful fleeting form rushing away. He picked up his toast, paused, then caught the eye of another waiter, a sturdy young guy with wavy black hair trimmed into a conservative cut, probably a member of the owner's family.

"When you have a chance, can I get some blueberry jam?"

"Hey! You're in Brooklyn now" — the waiter plunked a sealed plastic cup of Smuckers Grape on the counter — "It's jelly!"

*

"How long will it take to finish? Even just to get it to where we can find sublets?" James asked. He and Luke sipped cups of Cafe Bustelo brewed on the hotplate, as they sat at the big round wooden table in what would someday be the kitchen. Luke paused mid-sip. James smiled and they both

burst out laughing. *No idea if or when.* It wasn't funny. What was funny was both of them knowing exactly what was in each other's minds.

*

Hardly awake, before anything has begun, when everything is to come, he peers to the north wall windows and the morning twilight. The dark light that is only a reflected light. Sun not seen, rays cast from behind the Earth, but already striking the invisible particles that are the sky and reflecting from these onto landscape and city. There is no other light like twilight. And it is then, as he crosses the creaking floor of the big loft at Johnson Avenue, it is then that the chill breeze carries through the window screens a note, a high pulsing beep that repeats, and more merge with it, and the simple steady pulse multiplies, overlaps unevenly, layering in rhythm, a polyphony of undulations loud and near and soft and far, and the fleets roar into the streets, the great trash haulers of the City of New York.

*

Vasily and Ramla behind the counter, Tony or Frank or John, the brothers who owned the place, at the cash register. They were among the constants in his life apart from the less-and-less frequent crossings with Luke, and the occasional coffee or Scotch with Alan. Maybe that just shows how untethered he was in his new city even as it was getting to be less and less new. After lunch he walked up Metropolitan Avenue, under the Interstate 278 overpass, and past the black and white awning of that place called *Black Betty*. On Bedford Avenue, the funky hip main street of Second-Millennium Williamsburg, he browsed books at Spoonbill and Sugartown and stood at the door of Bliss Cafe until enough of the lunch crowd exited that he could grab a table and a coffee. Eventually he descended the stairs down to the L train to continue his journey on the other side of the river in Manhattan and, as the sun set, he trained back to Bedford to see what was going on. Young white hipsters dominated Bedford and mixed on the surrounding streets with Polish, Latino, Italian, and Hasidic locals. Or did any of them really mix? He walked back toward the diner, again under the black and white awning, curtains closed. Restaurant? Strip club? He wondered what it could be. He walked on.

*

The air was mild through the loft's screen windows. Funny how you could feel the freshness of spring even as the breeze wafted across the barrel-stacked yards of Enquist Chemical. The lock bolt clicked and Luke burst in the door, keys jangling. "Hey, just dashing in to pick up some clothes. I'm gonna be at the studio all week. My friend Androgenius is putting together a big art event at this empty retail space in Midtown. A lot of cutting-edge artists are getting onboard."

"Androgynous?" James tried to clarify.

"No, Androgenius, and yes, he's androgynous. He was born female but prefers to be called he. You can help me with my installation if you want. Or maybe show some of your photos."

James wrote text and selected images from his growing body of digital photographs to be projected on screens during the Midtown event. He was a novice, but he knew his photographs could offer a perspective different from everyone else, though maybe that difference was exactly his problem in life.

As the date approached, the hype from the organizers, including Andro, grew bigger by the day. The press release expanded like a hot air balloon preparing for take-off. He still didn't know what the event was supposed to be about or what he had gotten himself into.

T3 4PE@CE, successor to December 2001's ZE CONCERT 4 PE@CE -- Chashama -- Times Sq -- NYC, organized by Planet Generation (PG2M) and TeleTwinTowers, featured on PUNKCAST, a 4 day free meglamedia marathon in a storefront just off Times Square. Installations, projections, performances, forums, massages, food, and a full-on all night D'n'B rave on Saturday. Everywhere VCR-monitor combos playing different material, including the toilets. Polemics lushly remixed on multiple video back projections.

There's a planning meeting at the Pink Pony tonight," Luke said. "Do you want to come?"

"Yeah, of course." James thought he was already part of the show. "Didn't I give you my text and image files already? Do we know yet how they're going to be projected?"

"We'll figure all that out at the meeting," Luke reassured.

The sun had set on the five-story brick tenement buildings of Ludlow Street south of Houston, and inside the ground floor of one of those old tenements the night was just turning on. Amidst the murmur of conversation and clinking bottles, twenty men and women cobbled six tables together in the lamplit darkness of The Pink Pony Cafe. The huddled conspirators simmered and exploded in pronouncements, declarations, and self-displays of unimaginable hipness.

"It will be a meglamedia tribute to the interconnectedness of the world we live in." Mizz Fab, one of the organizers, painted the world with a sweep of her manicured hands. As James' eyes swept the tables, taking in the response, he met the ocean blue eyes of the woman seated beside him. Dark hair, milk-white skin, her graceful body shifted almost imperceptibly in her chair and she smiled.

"What kind of art do you do?" he asked.

"I dance. I choreograph. Performance art." Her voice was silken. She looked Irish, but maybe the accent was from somewhere else. "And you?" she asked.

A voice erupted from one of the tables. "The time is now for all the generations to come together!"

James looked to her again. "I write, I do digital photography. Sometimes I make music. How long have you been in the City? Are you from here?"

"I came four years ago from Auckland, in New Zealand. Have you been there?"

"The closest I've been is Malaysia and Singapore, visiting my parents. I moved here last year from Boston, but I've lived a lot of different places. I'm James."

"James," she repeated quietly to herself. "I'm Caroline."

"Tell me about your performance art."

"Dancing is moving through the world, it's what we spend our lives doing. It's a way of examining the world, what we perceive and what we think is real. When I dance I create part of what you perceive..." Her hand touched his, slipped into his, stayed in his.

Another voice intruded, it was Androgenius, standing with chin lifted and fists clenched. "Eet eez time to zink differently about ze planet. Zere eez going to be a revolucion. We are ze generation to have, to share, to be."

James' brow furrowed. "All these people collaborating is cool, but I'm not sure what it's supposed to be about. There is something not quite real in all of this."

"Not what you thought would be real?"

He didn't know if she was speaking philosophy or poetry but he liked her. "How do you like living in New York?"

"It has expanded my world, but not my living space. The apartments in the City are tiny. I'd rather be living in a country estate."

"I always pictured myself living in an old mansion with a big library," James said.

"Beauty, let me know if you find a good one."

Beauty. Her hand fit just right in his.

As the meeting closed and the artists poured out onto the sidewalk, he still didn't know whether he was in the show, and he hardly cared. He saw Caroline to a cab, and as she pulled her graceful legs inside and the cab pulled away, he fingered the cocktail napkin in his jacket pocket, making sure the neatly penned number was really there.

*

He wanted her. That he knew for sure. He watched Caroline's slender legs coil and spring with balletic strength, her hips roll with animal grace as she ascended the three garden-level steps from Taisho's door up to the commotion of Saint Mark's Place. Three beautiful steps. He was so ready to say the right thing, but before he could she blurted "I have a dance lesson tomorrow morning. I mustn't be out late."

Dinner had been a little rough already. Nothing like the flirtatious conversation at Pink Pony Cafe where the words had danced between them. Tonight at Taisho she was remote, in her own world. He tried to draw her out, but that was just it — effort tonight at what was effortless before. He turned to her at the top of the steps. Her face close to his while masses of other young people — he still felt young and she was — flowed around them. "Let's at least have a drink somewhere," he said.

"You know, I want to visit a friend if you don't mind a walkabout. He borrowed something, and I was supposed to pick it up but haven't had the chance."

He couldn't see how the errand fit with being on a date. But the alternative was to say *no thanks* and walk away. He wasn't going to walk away. They strolled blocks and turned corners and finally entered the vestibule of a six-story brick building somewhere in the East Village. He was still new enough to the City that he couldn't keep his bearings when it wasn't his errand.

She pressed the button under one of the mailboxes. "Kudy, it's Caroline, can I come up?"

"Come on up," the voice crackled over the hundred-year-old wires, and the inner door buzzed open. Up five flights of stairs painted so many layers of black you couldn't guess what was beneath, a lean man, black jeans and a red silk shirt, maybe in his thirties, greeted them. Wiry black hair crowned his weathered face, and his quick intense eyes examined James as they entered the narrow doorway. James waited, observed discreetly while Caroline and her friend exchanged clipped phrases.

"You have something for me?"

He shrugged and walked a few steps into the little room. "I didn't know you were coming."

She followed a step. "I was in the neighborhood."

"Not now. Come again sometime," he said still facing away and then turned to her with an expression that said nothing.

"Okay, right. Thanks," she said.

They descended silently to the street. The date, it almost needed quotes around it, had bottomed out. And from the bottom James grappled. He walked the street with her and watched her. She was edgy now. Maybe Pink Pony Cafe gave her safety in numbers, or a stage for performance that she needed in order to feel right. Or she needed a yes instead of a no from Kudy.

Her glance bounced from him to the cracked sidewalk. "I'm tired. I ought to go home..."

"Let's get a drink. I'm not ready to go home yet." His eyes never left her.

She focused on him, finally. "There's a bar we can go to, it's not far."

It was an ordinary bar. Not seedy. Not cozy. Not happening like Pink Pony. "I'll have a glass of milk," she said to him as they found a booth.

James walked across the room. "A Guinness and a glass of milk," he said to the bartender.

"Guinness and a what?"

"A glass of milk."

He settled into the booth with Caroline, drinks on the table, and took a draft of the creamy Guinness.

"You know, I don't so much want a milk. I do fancy a whiskey, on the rocks."

He returned to the bar. "We don't need the milk after all. Can I order a Johnny Walker Black on the rocks?"

"No problem."

He crossed the floor back to Caroline. As he set the whiskey glass on the table, she looked up at him, and his eyes read that something other than thank-you would issue from her lips.

"I don't know why I asked for ice. I prefer it straight," she said and waited.

He was supposed to say, *Fuck you, this is bullshit, you've been jerking me around all night.* But he didn't. His Celtic determination set in. He stood firm, feet planted apart.

He approached the bar again and clunked another rejected glass, brim full, onto the counter. "Can I get a whiskey straight instead?" he asked and reached for his wallet.

"I've got this one, buddy."

A free drink. He must be pathetic. It didn't matter. He wasn't going to walk away from her. With an acceptable tonic finally flowing into her veins, no dairy, no ice, Caroline lifted a shoulder toward him and rubbed it helplessly with her hand. "My shoulders feel so tight."

"Here." His hands replaced hers and his fingers pressed into muscle, tracing the curve of her strong slender neck and shoulders. She tilted her head and released a quiet sigh that drew him into the world she had kept to herself until now.

"I don't know why men and women can't just say what they want" — she quarter-turned to him, still looking down — "just say it."

He sought her eyes and she came to him. Her world gazing into his. "Can we go to your place?" he said softly.

*

He took the train to Lorimer the next morning for breakfast at Kelloggs. Still intoxicated with her scent, his finger tips tingling with the warmth of her milk-white skin. Between her elegant silken legs in the dark of night, it was strange how, when she whispered something at the height of it all and he leaned close to listen, she had said, "Just talking to myself, it's nothing." He was still shut out after all. In the morning they had kissed and caressed until the hour of the dance lesson, which seemed to be a reality. They parted without any particular plan to meet again.

"Jimmy!" Vasily met him at the counter with a fresh coffee, then shouted through the window to the kitchen — "Two eggs over easy with Canadian!" — and leaned on the counter. "Hey, this guy came in the other day..."

"Yeah?"

"The guy says, Gimme a bagel with cream cheese, so I give it to him. Then he calls me over again. This bagel's got no hole in it, he tells me." Vasily raised both hands in a can-you-believe-it expression, then leaned in close, "So I say to him, What are you gonna do — eat it or fuck it?"

James laughed. "I'm glad I don't have to fuck bagels."

"Count your blessings my friend. Count your blessings."

*

"This is what I want you to know." Alan ritually ripped open the sugar packet, a jagged journey through the paper's fibers, the white grains raining into his Veselka's coffee. Outside fleets of Yellow Cabs cruised down Second Avenue. "Something you may not have known before." Four more packets. Each the same journey, the same rain. "I know the librarian." His eyes, which were fixed on James, loomed larger as his head tilted into the thrust of the matter. "I knew her at the Museum of Natural History. So the librarian..." Alan sipped his coffee.

James sipped his coffee.

"She is now the librarian at the Universe Society."

James nodded, waiting to understand.

"There's a mountaineer, a Society member, these wealthy adventurers, and the Society wants him to write a book. But he needs an editor, really a writer, someone to interview him and put his words on paper. Like you did with Chuck Close, just this time it's a book, a whole book. You'd be his ghost writer. I'll give your phone number to the librarian. Tell her what you can do, like a job interview."

*

"We've got to get some sublets in here," Luke filled a glass of water at the kitchen sink and downed it. He had jangled his keys in the lock and rushed in just the moment before.

"It's July and we still don't have a working kitchen or bathroom," James said.

"Yeah, you're right. We'll need a gas range and full refrigerator. I know somebody who can install a shower." Luke scanned the unit as he gulped another glass. "Let me get some fresh clothes for the studio."

Over the month of August they finished the unit just enough to attract rent-paying tenants. It was always young people that answered the ads, usually women. One day, though, when James answered the door, there was a sixty-year-old man, graying hair, frumpy clothes. Somebody who probably had a reliable but limited income and just needed a safe, affordable place to live. James just couldn't imagine living with Mr. Frump.

*

"Don't order the Chicken Cordon Bleu!" Colleen laughed. "Some of the food here isn't very good," she whispered in conspiracy.

"I've noticed they're best with the basics," James said.

"Precisely, stick with the basics!" she nodded emphatically and gestured to the eggs and toast on their plates. "Right? I know!" she half-whispered, complicit in this privileged information.

He smiled into her sparkling brown eyes. She was a fraction taller, pretty and wonderfully girlish. He met her just a month ago at the Kelloggs counter, and already they had a standing lunch date, once or twice a week. She was a Williamsburg transplant from Connecticut, an artist who had graduated from the Parsons School of Design. She was more experienced in the City than James, but as an aspiring artist on the cusp of middle age hoping or wishing somehow to make a living in art, she was just as lost as he was.

"I got a new job," she nodded her head, affirming the news she was sharing. "I'm editing digital photographs for these two guys who sell celebrity shots to magazines like People and Vanity Fair. They're paparazzi!"

"Really?"

"You know that red carpet Style Awards event at Times Square last Thursday? It was on all the television channels."

"No, I didn't see it."

"I'm on a balcony ten floors up. The photographers are sending me the image files as they shoot them and I'm Photoshopping them on the spot — color balancing and clean-up — and uploading them to the news services. There were helicopters hovering fifty feet above me. Helicopters!"

What first seemed like good-natured bragging was starting to feel more like emotional upset steering toward breakdown. He tried to be a comfort. "What was that like?"

"It made me really nervous! I'm doing very careful work but I have to do it fast. You have to beat out the other paparazzi, they buy the first, best shots..."

"The news services...?"

"So you have to fix the contrast and the color and clone over anything that's obstructing even a tiny fraction of someone's face, and there are helicopters hovering over me. They were right over me, James!"

"That sounds really stressful."

"I know! And they sell these photos for a lot of money. I wish I was getting paid a little more of the money they bring in. Right?"

"How much are you getting paid?"

She deflated. "Fifteen dollars an hour."

"What!" He bounced up in his booth, his body language more expressive than he realized. But he was outraged in her defense. She was doing skilled work, and applying an artist's eye, something not every photo retoucher can offer.

"At least I'm getting paid to use my skills."

"That's true." He didn't want to add to her stress. "It's great you've got the work. It would just be nice if they could pay you a decent wage."

"I know. With the money they're making they could, couldn't they?"

He liked talking with her. And listening to her talk. She would talk and talk in circles and circles. It made him a little dizzy sometimes. But they always laughed, always had a blast in their little world in the diner booth. They talked about everything. About art, about jobs and no jobs, about relationships and no relationships. There was always a guy she was pining for or angry at or getting back together with. He watched the sequence of interests and attachments to see if maybe there would be an opening for him.

*

James walked down Second Avenue, coat zipped tight against the cold, and just below Tenth Street he walked into a sidewalk forest of Christmas trees. "We come down every year from Danbury," said the man in the peaked cap and earmuffs, the Connecticut tree farmer.

James brought home a five-foot Douglas fir to Johnson Avenue. He had arranged the Malaysian bamboo sofas and coffee tables on a large carpet on the loft's main floor. A living room in what used to be a hard-hat site. He entwined a string of colored lights and a string of white. They swirled up the tree like sparkling arms of the Milky Way. As he settled onto the small sofa, Chrystal, the new sublet, emerged from her room and settled onto the big sofa. A real Brooklyn Christmas. For the first time it felt like home.

Luke didn't see the tree. From the beginning, his late-night V.J. gigs and all-nighter grant deadlines had meant that he mostly slept where he worked, his art studio in the Lower East Side of Manhattan. He continued to pay his share of the rent and to store a half ton of gear. But beyond that, Luke had abandoned the castle.

*

James walked up the stairs of the L train First Avenue station into the cold wind of a February morning. Luke had come through for him, a part-time job as a gallery attendant at the Artists Alliance in the Lower East Side. Four days a week, eleven in the morning until three in the afternoon, ten dollars an hour. It was temporary but more than a blip. It would run until June, and that made it by far James' most real paid job since moving to the City a year and a half ago. Until now the employment high point was moving furniture at the loft of a semi-famous artist in Chelsea, one day only, for twenty-five dollars an hour. The low point was a one-night job steadying a ladder for an unknown video artist in the East Village who paid him in six rolls of quarters. *My uncle owns a laundromat in Jersey.*

The gallery, his new job, was a third-floor walk-up, not a well-worn path for art viewers. He sat at a small wooden table piled with printed exhibition programs, and he greeted any guests that managed to find the place, as they peered expectantly but tentatively through the open doorway. He studied the exhibition himself each day on arrival so that his mind was ready to offer insights. But mostly it was quiet. And in the quiet, pen on paper, artworks on the walls watching, he wrote.

*

The Seven train hurtled toward Alan and Susanna's home. Saint Patricks Day in Jackson Heights. It was a different kind of ride from the subterranean tunnels of the Six and the L lines. The elevated tracks above Queens sailed past third story windows, old brick warehouses and apartment buildings, until you finally disembarked and walked down the steel stairs to street level. The neighborhood was urban, diverse, but somehow not cosmopolitan. People of all colors busied themselves beneath storefront signs in English and Spanish and Chinese and Korean. But something told him they were all small town people. Was it the plain and casual way they dressed? Was it the pool halls and barber shops, car washes and laundromats? Where were the coffee shops and bars, the bookstores and galleries? There are neighborhoods like this in New York, where the world feels small even within the heart of the metropolis.

He found the address on a red brick apartment building. Susanna, Alan's wife, led him up the stairs.

"Mr. James!" Alan said. "Take off your coat, have a drink." Alan hung James' coat on the entryway hook and motioned to Susanna — "A green cocktail" — and to James — "Do you want one of these green cocktails?"

"It's Saint Patrick's Day, you've got to," Susanna said and disappeared into the kitchen.

"Nice place!"

"Yeah, Susanna found it. And her job pays for it!"

James asked. "Is she a writer too?"

"Oh no, no," Alan was emphatic. "Her work is not that work. Numbers, numbers that do not exist in nature, that you will not find in the motion of the planets." His head searched back and forth, mouth gaping speechless, until he threw his hands in the air, and surrendered to laughter. "She's a business woman, god love her! A business woman! Finance!" Alan ushered him into the living room. "These are some of my writer friends." Everyone raised their pint and shot glasses, some filled green, some a well-aged amber.

James toasted and scanned the room. "You have lots of original art on the walls."

"Yeah, oh yeah," Alan said. "This one is an early self-portrait, very early, by my old friend James Gurche."

James stood admiring the black-blue-and-white portrait, painted entirely in realistic stars and deep-space nebulae but with a pointillist twist. The stars, some large and bright, some small and dim, formed an image of the artist's own face.

"Big dioramas for the Museum of Natural History, the Smithsonian..." Alan said. "Oh, yeah, he's successful, very successful. Sort of an artist-scientist-paleo-visionary rock drummer. We played music together in high school in Kansas City."

"What about this one?" James leaned toward a portrait in primary colors, a woman with an inquisitive lemon yellow face, pale blue eyes with red pupils, and a red plume at the side of her head.

"It's a self-portrait by an old friend from Provincetown. Mary, a good artist, a good soul. Back in Provincetown."

"Can I get a photo of you? I brought my Nikon."

Alan scrunched up his face. "Yeah, uh, I'm not very good with photos."

"Here," James said. "This is a good spot. You need headshots for your writing career, right?"

Alan curbed his anxiety and assumed a dignified pose. James took the shot. In the background, on the wall, was the self-portrait of Alan's Provincetown friend.

Saturated with green cocktails, James leaned back and looked out the Seven train windows onto the City lights bound for Brooklyn, the accidental double-portrait stored in the memory card, in the camera, in his satchel. A seed buried deep.

Gift

October 2000

C atherine leaned back in the airline seat as they touched down on the tarmac. The engines roared, and the wind's force tugged the plane side to side. Rain drops streamed down the window as they taxied to the gate. Boston. And somewhere across the bay, the remnants of her mother's life.

When the chime sounded, seatbelts clicked open and passengers clogged the aisles. Alistair craned his neck beneath the overhead compartments and motioned her to push into the aisle. She watched as passengers pulled luggage from overhead bins and filed forward, let it all sort out until finally it was their turn.

They picked up their rental car, a Park Avenue, and navigated the lanes. "Mass. Pike!" Alistair announced, his hands tight on the wheel. "Look, there's a little picture of a capotain..."

"Wrong way!" Catherine said, as the Park Avenue merged seamlessly onto Interstate Ninety South and rolled to a stop behind a river of red break lights.

"Bloody hell!"

"We're supposed to go north to Route One-A."

Late evening, Marblehead. Carly and Bernhard stood in the open doorway of the stately brick home as Catherine and Alistair pulled suitcases from the trunk. Was it possible six years had passed? "Carly! Vienna seems like yesterday."

Carly embraced her. "And Frankfurt, Cognacs into the night. Remember our benefactors?"

Catherine leaned to Carly's ear, "Looks like we've traded them in for younger ones!"

Bernhard was delightfully German, both playful and deliberate as he showed off his newfound American free spirit. "Trick or treat!" He handed them each a bag of caramel corn. "Come, I invite you, in house!"

Alistair turned on his Buckingham Palace charm and inane humor and Catherine was glad to see the two settled with bottles of Sam Adams in the living room, where Halloween decor littered every tabletop. She joined Carly in the kitchen where a kettle was on for tea. They smiled, knowing there was so much underneath, bits and pieces they had shared by mail or phone, and everything they hadn't.

"I'm so sorry about your birth mother. You know her identity now, but... So you'll at least go and see where she lived."

Carly, always perceptive. Joy, sorrow, futility. *You know her identity. But.* The thing Carly maybe couldn't see was the hope. That's what was hard to see for anyone who grew up with parents, with the people you literally blossomed from. Catherine had lived her life as a cut flower floating in a vase. Mary was her garden. Even now she hoped she might take root there, at age thirty begin living the life that others take for granted, that others live from birth.

"I have her obituary. The caseworker sent it to me. And there's an interview too, a month before she died."

"So she was a local celebrity!"

"Yeah, she was an artist. She painted, did photography, made jewelry, knitted and sewed."

"She sounds like you. I mean exactly like you!"

"All those things I love to do, she was doing at the same time a thousand miles away in Provincetown."

"I'm getting chills. What do you think it means?"

"She's my mother."

Carly held out her arms and Catherine leaned into her embrace. "I'm going to meet her friends tomorrow. I phoned Bonnie, a friend named in the interview. We're meeting everyone at the home of a man named Wilson."

*

The Sagamore Bridge carried them across the Cape Cod Canal a little after one in the afternoon. Mary would have crossed this bridge. It was the first retracing of her steps, the chance to know something of what she had known. Tall grasses dominated the landscape, small groves of trees dotted it, and past Orleans, from time to time, there was a glimpse of sea. Small towns. Cottages of cedar shake, a church, a gallery, a lighthouse, and back to highway. Forests of juniper and white pine. Oak still holding their rusty autumn leaves. Closer to Provincetown, the vegetation dwindled to juniper, dune grasses, brambles of wild rose bare of leaves and blossoms. And as they drove the forests grew shorter, trees dwarfed to half their normal height, survivors clinging to the shifting sands of this very different place. Dunes shone almost white, opening to saturated blue sky as vast as the Atlantic, with wisps of white cloud painted across. And finally, a welcome sign along Route Six, not just a painted road sign, but a sign framed as a painting — fishermen on the wharf, the words *Welcome to Provincetown* scripted into the sky above the harbor.

They entered town on Conwell, turned onto Bradford, and after a couple of blocks, as the Park Avenue turned down Center Street, there it was, the monument. She held it in view — or it held her. Standing at the peak of the highest ground, the Pilgrim Monument had to be a daily presence to anyone who lived here. She imagined her mother rounding the corner onto Bradford, not the image she held as a child, the neat bun atop her head, but her real mother pictured in the obituary, long curls on her shoulders, a spark in her eyes. The monument holding Mary's gaze. Not a monument. It was a beacon.

They checked into the bed-and-breakfast and then strapped into the car again for the drive to Wilson's, unaware how quaintly walkable Provincetown was. Alistair maneuvered the Park Avenue down Center Street, swerving around parked cars, rolling bicycles, and frightened pedestrians. He cut the corner onto Commercial.

"Telephone pole!" Catherine blurted.

"Cripes! No wonder the poles are leaning, they've all been hit a hundred times. Good fortune I learned to drive on the narrow lanes of London!"

Outside the front door of One-hundred-fifty Commercial stood a frail man with a bushy mustache and gray hair sticking out like a heap of straight pins. The door cracked open behind, he watched, then motioned anonymously toward a gravel driveway overgrown with shrubs. Alistair's head shifted nervously side to side and just when the branches seemed to close in, there was a long scratching noise. "Brilliant, we nearly lost the car mascot!"

"That's a big car you've got," the man said. "I'm Wilson."

"Your big shrubs put a nifty scratch in the hood, and perhaps you would like to pay for..."

"Stop," Catherine demanded in a hush.

Wilson's yard was blanketed in English ivy, all else no more than a protrusion of bumps beneath the sea of leaves. A hand-welded sculpture at the yard's center was the sole survivor, gleaming in the afternoon sun. The cottage was a plain box with faded blue shake siding, a story and a half with two chimneys that stood sentry on the roof above the front door. The door, with double windows to either side, was framed with what looked like interior moulding reused on the exterior. And on the riser of the front step, a hand-painted sign, *Home at Last.* Wilson tossed his hand up in a gesture of invitation, turned his back to them and walked inside. Catherine stepped over the threshold, and her eyes swept the large open space, each corner dedicated to one thing or another. A lone table, maybe the dining room. Another space whose fixtures indisputably marked it as the kitchen. A painting on an easel, the studio. And finally, seated around a coffee table topped with pigs-in-a-blanket and cans of Busch beer, a circle of women, Mary's generation. They quieted and looked up from the sofa and assorted chairs.

A short stout black dog with wiry hair stood tensely and sneezed out the strange air the outsiders had brought in. "That's my Maggie." Wilson half bent to pat her and ambled on into the living room.

A rosy-cheeked woman sprung to her feet and the big loose bun of blonde hair atop her head bounced as she stood. "Come in. Come in and sit down!" She motioned them to the sofa with an energy wavering between caution and unbridled enthusiasm. "I'm Bonnie" — she burst — "I was in a dream talking to you on the phone! And now seeing you in the flesh!" She nodded to the others, who were leaning in whispers, and turned back to Catherine in quiet astonishment. "You're Mary's daughter. Sit, make yourselves comfortable."

"I'm so glad to meet you, all of you," Catherine said. "This is my husband Alistair."

"Delighted!" Alistair charmed.

"The British have come!" Bonnie declared. "We won't hold it against you." A wave of chuckles swept the room. Catherine was bemused to see Alistair speechless as he settled into a wooden chair, stiffly crossed his legs, and waited with pen and legal pad.

Wilson dropped onto one end of the sofa and Catherine settled onto the other and smoothed the worn fabric with her hand. Mary may have sat on this very sofa in years past. She studied the paintings on the walls, Wilson's signature in the corner of some, names unknown to her on others. She took it all in, the large single-pane windows, the massive fireplace at the room's center, its wooden mantel carved with cherubs, the firebox stuffed with trash. And a makeshift staircase of raw wooden boards, little more than a ladder, that ascended to the half floor above. Wilson followed her eyes. "End of the evening, I'll take you upstairs to collect your mom's things."

A sedate woman, gray hair tangled around her neck, perked up in her chair which sat at a slight distance from the others. "So you had a good trip? I'm Anita." Pleased to have joined in, she slumped back for a long sip of beer.

"Of course you had a good trip. I'm Ginger, dear." Her age was theatrically secreted beneath a leopard-print pillbox hat, platinum blonde spikes protruding from the edges, mascaraed lashes, and blue eyeshadow. She sat perched in a director's chair, its long spindly legs crossed like her own. "Your mother was always a good traveler."

Even as the obligatory courtesies unfolded and one or another asked how long the flight was or whether she had been to the East Coast before, the rest leaned close in pairs. "Doesn't she look like Mary!" and "Her flowing hair, it's Mary's in the wind when we'd go to sunset," and "It's so good to hear her laugh again!" She quietly welcomed the scrutiny, the surreptitious glances and whispers. They were answering the very questions she needed answered — What was it that made her her mother's daughter?

"Honey, she would have loved to be here. Your mom and I were best of friends, I'm Joyce," Her blue eyes were bright, and her hair drifted in gentle white curls to her shoulders, pretty despite too many wrinkles for her years. "The first place your mom lived when she moved here, was my place on Blueberry Avenue."

As one recalled a story, the others sat listening, adding a tidbit here and there, talking among themselves. Catherine watched and listened as the stories bubbled among them. Some of their comments were incomprehensible. They were speaking in the shorthand of Provincetown. Catherine loved it. She didn't know there could be such a place, a safe harbor for people who wouldn't ever fully belong anywhere else. Alistair cleared his throat and shifted in his chair.

Bonnie listened intently to Joyce, then burst forth with her own story. "Your mother was such fun! She ran in many circles. Her friends in one circle didn't know the others." The chorus of women nodded emphatically to each other. "She was the life of the party."

"Yes, oh, remember the parties at Nelson's house... Oh my yes," the chorus sounded, but Bonnie held the floor. "Now... now you all know that Mary and I would do this thing we called blathering..."

"Yes, blathering!"

"Our faces inches apart, talking hysterically..."

"Hysterical!"

"It was!"

"Hysterical!"

"...talking over each other so that neither could understand what the other was saying!"

There was giggling all around.

"The whole room would begin to stare" — Bonnie continued — "Watching, wondering what was going on!"

"I always thought it was just me who couldn't follow it," Anita shared from her distant chair amid an uproar of laughter.

"Every Tuesday morning..." — Wilson began. He had sat quietly listening, occasionally patting Maggie who stood by the sofa at his foot. Now he shared a story of his own — "Tuesday mornings, back in the seventies, Mary Zadora would enter the O.C. with her box of colored crayons and execute, on the chalk board over the juke box, a political cartoon." Joyce nodded, helping to nudge another raft of memories afloat. "Most of us yahoos didn't understand politics" — Wilson went on — "so Mary would explain it to us. Usually something about the Vietnam war. She drew and we drank and we learned a thing or two. So gradually, she became one of Provincetown's own."

"I can picture her" — Ginger said — "hair laced with feathers." Ginger recrossed her legs and raised a cigarette glowing at the tip. "Your mother, she was" — she took a long drag, exhaled, waited for the curtain of smoke to rise — "foxy."

"Sexy strutting Mary Zadora..." Wilson mused.

"I wove her braids" — Joyce's voice broke — "wove them with gull feathers."

"The dream catcher," Ginger added.

The room was quiet. Bonnie breathed deep. "It's almost like she's here with us, all of us together..."

Wilson patted Maggie.

"Never should have happened the way it did" — Joyce shook her head and sputtered — "Shouldn't have happened at all..."

Anita nodded sadly in her far-away chair.

It was as if they held Mary's spirit within them, even today, seven years after her death. The immediacy of emotions that swirled in the room — love, loyalty, joy, the sting of anger. Catherine longed to know her mother like that.

Stories spun to more stories, and Alistair sat with his legal pad taking notes. His comfort zone was washed away amidst this tempest of artists and free spirits who whirled at the fringe of society.

"There's someone I think you should talk to," Bonnie said. "Sabina Oliveira, a painter who knew Mary from her first years on the Cape. They roomed together at Nelson's. You can find her at her gallery on Commercial."

"Didn't Mary come in the early eighties?" Ginger asked.

"Eighty-one," Joyce clarified.

"Way before that, about nineteen seventy-eight," Wilson insisted.

"Well that's the thing," Bonnie said. "Over the years she came and went, but she always came back to Provincetown. This was her home."

In the hum of conversation that followed, Anita stood from her chair, hobbled to Catherine, and handed her a letter-sized clear plastic sleeve. "I went to your mom's room at the convalescence center after she died, and I found these things on the floor of her closet." Inside were papers covered with neat cursive handwriting, a folded denim cloth, and a pocketbook. The stories, the little plastic grab bag. All these gifts preserved only by the power of their love for her mother.

As the guests filed out at evening's end, Catherine followed Wilson up the ladder-like stairs to the attic. She paused at the top while he tugged the cord and a bare lightbulb flickered to life, illuminating the cramped space under clipped ceilings. To one side were pieces of furniture topped with an old table lamp and a bust of a fisherman. "That's my special collections." To the other side, a jumble of boxes and piles. "After she died I gathered as much as I could from her room. Couldn't stand the thought of it all being thrown out." He went quiet for a moment, ground his jaw. "It's been seven years and I've never gone through it." His voice fell. "Couldn't bare to, I guess. It's all yours now."

Catherine knelt to the floor. From this perspective, the scattered piles were mountains and plains. Vast, daunting, inconceivable. Sketchbooks, rolled canvases, papers, envelopes. There was so much, she couldn't possibly carry it all home. She wished there was more time, time to sift, examine, adore everything. She opened a sketchbook and flipped through the musty pages, an intricate drawing of mythical creatures brought to life in colored pencil, a graphite sketch of two men and a woman at a table, a page of scrawled cursive. Some of the rolled canvases were finished paintings, others were mere skeletons of what they were meant to be in a life interrupted. She would take all of the sketchbooks, only the most complete paintings, and... What was the shallow cardboard box, white with blue lettering: *Antioch Corporation?* She lifted the lid and pulled out a large-format photographic negative, held it to the lightbulb, tried to absorb what she was seeing. A radiograph of the brain, a shape that didn't belong there, the end of her mother's life. Alistair tapped his wristwatch, his nail *click-clicked* on the glass. She grabbed up loose papers, manilla folders, envelopes of who knows what from the floor around her, piled them on top of the box of negatives along with a stack of sketchbooks and motioned to Alistair to carry the canvases, hoping these fragments would help her construct a picture of her mother. The rest she would leave behind.

Late into the night she sat on the floor at their bed and breakfast, legs outstretched, sketchbooks laid open, papers strewn. Portraits, dunes, waves, names, dates, phone numbers. All night long, turning in bed, drifting in and out of dream. She heard water running. Alistair showering. She sat up. Sunlight lined the edges of the bedroom curtains. *Talk to Sabina Oliveira,* Bonnie had said.

"I tripped over your boxes this morning." He walked out of the bathroom, towel around his middle, hair pointing all directions. She had to laugh. "Oh funny is it? I nearly came to a sticky end. I suppose you would have been going through all my boxes and papers next!"

"Is that supposed to be a joke? It's not really funny."

"I'm quite simply recommending you spend some time among the living. We can go cycling today, see the sights — Town Hall, Pilgrim Monument, Winthrop Street Cemetery!"

"I have some bad news for you..."

"I know, I know, the cemetery — the pilgrims are dead. But let me ask you this, are you or are you not missing out on everything this vacation has to offer by sitting here and... Blimey, don't stare at me like that!"

"I know this was supposed to be a vacation to see Carly, but that's not what it is any more. I'm going to Sabina Oliveira's studio. Would you like to join me?"

"I'm going cycling to take in America the Beautiful. I recommend we reconvene for dinner. Until this evening Your Highness." He gathered his day clothes and disappeared into the bathroom.

Catherine walked east down Commercial Street. Maybe she shouldn't have said no. But how could she learn about her mother by touring town hall and an old cemetery where who-knows-who was buried? The street felt a little deserted. Probably the time of day, or the time of year. A lone man, muscular, with silver-streaked hair pulled back in a ponytail, was just unlocking the door to a storefront office.

"Good morning," she said. "I'm looking for Sabina Oliveira's gallery."

He looked at her with slate black eyes. "Wouldn't you rather see my architectural drawings?"

She laughed a mouth-wide-open laugh. His offbeat humor swept her instantly and she flushed. He allowed himself a hint of a smile. "You're almost there. Past Pearl, fourth door on the right, if she's open. It's not exactly tourist season."

The front room of Oliveira Fine Art was quiet and Catherine wondered whether she was intruding even though the door was unlocked. She gently treaded the creaking wooden floor and it struck her then, the scent of salt. Inside and out, the sea air was everywhere. She stood quietly in a quaint, rustic room whose white walls held just the right number of paintings, not cluttered, not sparse. Playful watercolors and oils of a black and white dog wading in the surf and running on the shore with a frisbee in its mouth. There was an immediacy to the strokes that captured the goofy joy of a real dog. Stylized, but absolutely real. She heard a panting sound. Beyond a half wall, a woman, maybe in her forties, sat behind a heavy wooden desk, and a large black and white dog lay panting on the floor.

"May I help you?"

There was a sensuous unfolding of her figure as she stood. And what was the concentration in her deep brown eyes? Catherine felt herself being examined. "Are you Sabina?"

"I am."

"My mother was Mary Zadora. I'm Catherine. She placed me for adoption."

"Mary's daughter."

The recognition. She saw it in Sabina's eyes. "You know me."

"She called you Sarah." Sabina looked away, busied herself. "Write your address in the guest book on the table, will you? I have some things I can mail you from my winter studio. Have you met Georgie?" She glanced to Catherine. "His friendship with Mary was complicated. Oh, Mary, Mary." She reached for Catherine's hand. "Georgie will love to talk with you. Walk down to West End Salon and ask for him. He's there all day, he never stops working. Night time, that would be a different story! Go see him."

As Catherine walked down Commercial, Sabina called after her. "You look just like her, amorzinha, just like her!"

Catherine waved and walked on down Commercial Street. Beyond the Lobster Pot, she paused at the intersection of Commercial and Standish where the sky opened, then followed Standish out onto MacMillan Wharf. It was like walking across water. She stood at the very edge, looked out to the bay, and squinted as the salt wind gusted white-caps toward her, endless white-caps birthed from the horizon's haze. Long hair whipping, she whispered to the water. "I'm here Mom. Can you hear me?" The wind buffeted her. "I'm sorry, I'm too late." A rush of spray, a ripple and swirl of foam.

She walked Commercial past Court, Winthrop, and Central to Atlantic Avenue. It was a two-story house, white with green shutters, West End Salon. Inside was a single open room, beauty chairs along the mirrored wall filled with customers in black capes. A young man at the front desk greeted her, "What can I help you with today? A new style or perhaps a massage? Or if you prefer a reading," his arm swept toward a heavy velour curtain. "There's a psychic in this room behind me. Something for everyone!"

"I'd like to see Georgie. Is he here?"

He turned to the first beauty chair and pointed with a laugh, "Georgie's right there."

Reading glasses perched atop spikes of blond. Silk shirt, skinny jeans, leather belt, all in black, there he was. Scissors in hand, he finger-combed the man's hair in a dance, the hair lifting and tossing like waves. "I'm Georgie. How can I help you?"

She was self-conscious in a room full of listeners. "They say you knew my mother."

His hands stopped mid-air. The man's wet head turned between her and Georgie until Georgie's mouth opened in a squeal, and he dropped the scissors on the tray and opened his arms wide, "Mary! Oh my god, you're Mary's daughter!"

"Would you have some time to talk with me about my mother?"

"Would I have time!" He gazed at her. "Meet me at the A-House at nine tonight — the Atlantic House, honey, Masonic, off Commercial. Mary's daughter!"

*

That evening after dinner with Alistair, Catherine toasted Georgie across the fireside table in the A-House's Little Bar.

"If your mother were here right now, we'd be in the Dance Club, her luscious curls bouncing." Georgie took a healthy sip of his Martini. "Hair can be the worst thing that ever happened to a person, but it can also be the best. I love how that first line gets people's attention, like oh my god, and then the second line is about what I can do for you, but I have to tell you, your mother had the most gorgeous hair." He reached across the table and ran his fingers through Catherine's waves. "I'm allowed to do this, I'm a professional. All I could do to her hair was make it gorgeous in new ways. But you're not here for a lecture about your mother's hair!"

"But I am." She laughed. "Do you know what I mean? I want to know everything."

"Well let me tell you, I was in love with your mother. We were the best of friends and she was the most kind, caring person I've ever known. She would do anything for you. Completely accepting, and that's something I needed. Isn't that just what everyone needs?"

"Did you hang out together?"

"My god, yes. She was the life of the party, kickin' it up, she had a real magnetism. Be it hairstyle or lifestyle, life is better on the fringe. The year she marched in the parade for the Art Ass..." Catherine scrunched her brows and he explained, "The Art Association, if you want the full name. So we went out afterward and she was wearing her flouncy white skirt and white leather boots and all eyes were on her all night long. I was so jealous!"

He took a sip. "Listen kiddo, I like to be Mr. Entertainment, but you have a serious side, your mom did too. Do you really want to know everything?"

"If I don't know everything, then I don't really know her."

"Okay, I have to tell you that underneath all the fun, she was also a deeply wounded soul. I'm sorry to say it, honey, but it haunted her, losing you."

*

November 2000

"It was wonderful meeting you, Bonnie, meeting everyone." Catherine held the phone receiver between her ear and shoulder as she loaded silverware into the dishwasher — *Prongs up, not down.* She could hear his words in her head. Out the window, a light snow dusted the boulevard oaks along River Road.

"It was a salutary reunion for all of us, dear. You gave us back a piece of our lives. Thanksgiving means so much more this year."

"I've been wanting to ask you Bonnie. If Mary and I had reunited, what would she have said?"

"She would have said, *You're smart and beautiful. And of course you are, because you're mine!* You're her daughter. She never stopped hoping that one day she would meet you. And the second thing she would have said is, *Do you forgive me?*"

"Really? Do I forgive her?"

"The regret weighed on her, on every aspect of her life, the regret that she wasn't there to protect you. She forever lacked focus, her mind was elsewhere. She had an extra beat in her heart, Catherine. For some it's art. For her it was you."

*

She lifted a hardbound sketchbook from the cardboard box, traced the letters of the title with her fingertips — *Anything Book.* She opened one sketchbook and another. Every time her mother had put pencil to paper, she had left a window into her life, a window for Catherine to peer through. First it was the subject matter that absorbed her. Sail boats on the water, musicians on a stage, a winter forest. Mythical characters whose flowing hair becomes the wing of a bird. Faces hidden within the froth of an ocean wave. A drawing of a loft room, brick wall, wood-beams, in the foreground an empty chair. The title, *Unfinished Business.* All were annotated, some combination of name or date or place or circumstance. *Bay Street, Savannah, 1972. Barbara sleeping. Robert. Alan at Pond Road.* Fragments of information. Her mother's friends in Provincetown were Catherine's first resort when she had questions. But often even they didn't have the answers. *I never knew a Barbara. Alan — I heard of an Alan, but I never met him.*

She turned a page to names in cursive, different names but all with the first name Mary. They were written without order such that they floated around the page like a pinwheel in the wind. *Mary Casey. Mary Oliveira. Mary Kaminska. Mary Zadora.*

And then it was the lines that absorbed her. Some sketches were delicate and full of life, and the place and date carefully documented alongside her signature. Other sketches were scribbly, jagged, unsigned. A graph of her emotions. Catherine closed the sketchbook, glanced to the rolled canvases standing in the corner of the room, she would get to them. She dug deeper into the cardboard box, held a wallet in hand, unzipped it just as her mother would have done every day. The routine acts of a living person. Catherine's fingers sorted through cards and slips of paper.

Eldridge Gallery

Don Walker, Manager, Oceanic Seafood Corporation

David S. Madden, MD, Provincetown Medical Building

CVS Pharmacy, Harwich, 1 or 2 tablets every 3 hours as needed for pain 12/08/92.

It was a wealth of documents beyond what some children would ever inherit. A wealth she would trade in an instant. But that was pointless. These sketchbooks and canvases and paper slips were bread crumbs along a path. They were everything.

*

In the mirror she examined the brushstroke of freckles across her nose, faded since childhood but still there. Her hair, loose dark waves highlighted red. She turned to the side. The gentle slope of her neck as it drew to her chin. Joyce had said, *If you wanna know what she looked like honey, just look in the mirror.*

*

Catherine opened Mary's pocketbook. Yellow leather with a clasp. Empty. Unzipped an inner pouch, and inside was a tiny one inch by one inch black-and-white photograph, an old silver gelatin print. A woman holding an infant sitting in a wingback chair, with a man standing behind her. Nobody looked like Mary, nothing written on the back. She turned the photo between her fingers as if the angle could matter. It was just a family.

*

December 2000

Sitting on the couch, her mother's box of things at her feet, and in her lap, a handmade card with a gray bunny with big pink floppy ears. Beneath the bunny, five words were drawn in her mother's hand in bubble letters filled with colored pencil. She was nearly shaken from her seat when she read — *I Wish I Was There.*

*

Catherine was thirty-one years old. She had never met, face to face, a living blood relative. Something beneath the surface.

*

An envelope dropped through the mail slot. From Joyce. Inside, a five-by-seven black-and-white photograph, the product of someone's darkroom. Mounted in the sand, a twisted branch of driftwood held a dream catcher whose long trailing braids lifted in the wind. The sun at the horizon blazed its rays across the waves and between the dream catcher's braids to enter the camera's lens. Catherine read Joyce's handwritten note on rice paper:

This dream catcher was made by me with six braids of Mary's hair, cut by her and saved for me during her treatments. Braids, turquoise, gull feather, grapevines, alder tree.

Joyce.

P.S. It now sails the seas.

*

September 11, 2001

The skies were quiet. Nobody was allowed to be up there. Nobody wanted to be up there. "It appears as though a small aircraft has hit the North Tower of the World Trade Center." The announcer's voice on Minnesota Public Radio was urgent but tentative. It all seemed impossible. A large plane, not a small one. Then a second plane, the other tower. Then, they said, it all fell down. Her hand was on her tummy. Five months along now. She listened at the desk of her part-time bookkeeping job. The job was Alistair's idea. *I'm studying horticulture and we have the rentals* — she had reminded him — *and we have a baby on the way. That's why I quit Alliance for Community Involvement.* But he had insisted, *Look at Cheri and Cal. Cheri's a mother and that hasn't stopped her from putting in a good day's work at a paying job. And while you're at it, cut your hair. A professional bob would enhance your prospects..*

Making a baby didn't come naturally with Alistair. Not for either of them. It was a labor of love. For the child to come, if not for each other. Mom and Dad were so excited for their first grandchild. Mom was prepared with two newborn outfits, blue for a boy and pink for a girl. But for Catherine, having a baby held a special meaning that no one but an adoptee could fully understand. Her own child would be the first living blood relative that she would meet. Her own child to embrace. The bond of mother and child, broken for two generations, would not be broken again.

*

The tiny baby flips of those early months had changed as Thanksgiving gave way to Christmas and Christmas to New Year's, changed to cramped effortful maneuvers, baby heels pressed hard into her ribs. Uncomfortable. But far better than the earlier kicks in the bladder when the baby had been feet down. Catherine made a game of the new feet-up position, pressing her thumb onto the tiny foot inside her and waiting for the baby to push back. Back and forth they went, playing push-push.

*

"Alistair!" She called from the bathroom as she stepped from the tub and dried herself. Earlier on the phone the nurse had said it was too soon to come in. *Take a warm bath, see if the contractions come closer together.* Great advice. Now she was about to have the baby in the bathroom. "We have to go!"

"I'm just packing the last things. I'm bringing Elton John. Which CDs do you want?"

"I don't want CDs, it's not a vacation!"

It was one o'clock in the morning. The snow blew with a fury and they could hardly see. Alistair gripped the steering wheel, driving thirty miles per hour on the highway.

"I'll never get accustomed to driving in this. We might was well be in the Arctic."

She squirmed in her seat. "Just keep us on the road, and keep moving."

"Blimey!" Headlights blinded them as they entered the Lowry Tunnel. A car ahead of them had spun out and sat facing the wrong way. He maneuvered around it.

The staffer at the ER front desk ordered a wheelchair. Catherine couldn't really sit, so they wheeled her half sitting, half standing through the bright hospital corridors as Alistair followed behind, luggage strapped over his shoulder and paperwork in his hands.

In the labor unit, Catherine lay on a small bench on her side, knees tucked, while the nurses buzzed around hooking her to monitors. A shorthand of concerned commands shot back and forth among the nurses. She caught bits and pieces, about not finding the baby's heartbeat, about the doctor being another hour because of the snow.

"Oh my god, this is not my life, this is not my life." Alistair was panting and pacing between the door and the bench where she lay.

"Can you straighten your legs?"

Catherine winced, "I can't."

"Did your water break?"

"No, I don't think so."

The nurse frowned. "Your water is broken." Another contraction. "Let's get you into delivery." On the delivery bed, Catherine puffed through the contraction.

"You'll need this." The nurse set a cup of ice water on the tray table beside her. "A resident will be with you until the doctor arrives."

The resident rushed through the door. "Let's see how you're coming along." He was disarmingly young. But his voice was sure and calming. "Fully dilated. Do you feel an urge to push?"

"Yes, but..."

"Okay, push."

She pushed. But it hurt, it already hurt so much. She was afraid it would hurt more.

"Push again."

"It hurts."

"I feel the head. If you push really hard, this baby will come right out."

She inhaled and pushed.

"That's it, that's it, there she is. You have a beautiful baby girl."

She mouthed breathlessly to Alistair, "Thank you for our baby." Olivia. Her eyes opened to Catherine, blinking into the light, such big beautiful blue eyes for such a tiny baby. So tiny. Her little face like a teacup. "I'm thirsty. Alistair, can I have my water?" She opened her free hand.

"Your water? I drank it," he said. "So sorry, nerves I suppose."

*

A newspaper clipping from Bonnie. Wilson's column in the Provincetown Banner — *Our Mary Zadora is a grandmother. Her daughter Catherine Lind gave birth to a healthy baby girl, Olivia, on January 15, 2002.*

*

Little Olivia was a wonder, ready for whatever the world had to offer her. There was a focus and depth to her gaze that told you she knew things beyond her young age. For the first time in her life, Catherine felt a sense of belonging. In Olivia's moods and gestures and expressions, she saw her own. And there was something else, hard to explain. When she looked into a mirror she only saw a face, but when she looked at Olivia, she recognized herself for the first time.

*

The crying started at about four in the afternoon and lasted through bedtime. Pretty much every day. *You were colicky too* — Mom told her — *so it's no surprise.* Mom understood what she was going through. While Catherine made dinner, Alistair carried Olivia bundled up in his arms around the block, then paced back and forth on the icy sidewalk under the bare limbs of the boulevard oaks and the winter violet green of the cedars. At bedtime Olivia cried through the nightly routine of stories and songs, and Catherine laid her in the crib — *It's time to sleep, it's okay, sleepy time* — and gently closed the door. Minutes later Catherine was back in the nursery, holding her, singing, rocking, walking, anything to calm Olivia as she cried and cried.

That was the exhausting routine. Until one day Alistair came home, gung-ho with an answer. "It's Doctor Mazur's proven method, *Your Baby Won't Sleep?* You see, if you come to her she'll learn that crying gets her what she wants. No matter if it's three minutes or three hours — you have to let her cry."

Catherine was skeptical. It contradicted everything she felt inside. It assumed babies just want attention. She's crying for a reason.

She tried it, sat on the wood floor outside Olivia's nursery while Olivia's cries rose to screams and after what seemed like an eternity, there was a second of silence while she took a breath, followed by a gut wrenching wail. Catherine felt all the agony Olivia felt. "This isn't right. She needs us, that's why babies cry."

"I'm sorry but I insist we give this method a chance. It worked for all the babies in Doctor Mazur's book, and it's going to work for our little Miss Cranksters too."

Two more agonizing weeks and Catherine put her foot down. "She needs us to help her, not ignore her. I'm done with this nonsense."

*

"Peek-a-boo again!" Lulu peered through her open hands. Olivia, nearly a year old, burst into giggles. "You find me every time Olivia! Here's your fishy, you want to get comfy on the sofa next to me and play with fishy? I'm gonna talk with your mom."

Working with Lulu at Alliance had been good. Being just a friend now was even better. "You're good with children." Catherine set a glass of rosé next to Lulu, and snuggled up to Olivia on the sofa. Snowflakes drifted outside the family room window. "You must have been a good mom to your siblings."

"I still am. We're all grown up now but they still need that motherly shoulder to lean on."

"You never told me what dreams you had to leave behind. Every time we talk it seems like we end up coming back to me before we get there!"

Lulu set her glass on the table and stood in the middle of the room. "I wanted to be a star!" She spread her arms. "Film, Broadway, the Oscars, the Tonys!" She bowed deeply. "Thank you, I couldn't have done it without... without my..." She waved away the tears. "Damn it, I was being so funny and now I'm ruining it!" She laughed and wiped her cheeks. "Oh, mama mía!"

"Oh, Lulu, it's not too late. Your mom would want you to be happy."

"Catherine, you're so sweet and I appreciate what you're saying, but nothing has changed. I still have to make a living."

"I guess I'm just thinking that your siblings are working adults. And I don't know, but maybe you could get by on Derrick's income while you see what's possible?"

"Oh god, Derrick. That's another whole story. I wonder sometimes if I made a big mistake. I feel like I'm always in last place. It's all about his plumbing business. He's got no time for me."

"Lulu, I'm beginning to wonder if I made a mistake too."

"Mistake? What are you talking about?"

"A mistake marrying Alistair."

"Well, you're not..." Lulu laughed. "You wouldn't divorce him, would you?"

"No, nothing like that. I'm just feeling like we don't have much in common, other than the business, and Olivia, of course, but we can't even agree on what she needs."

"Okay, hold on, hold on." Lulu set her glass on the table. "You and me, we both made our choices. They might not be the smartest choices in the world, but the world's not perfect. You've got a beautiful baby girl and a lovely home. The point is..."

"This is life."

"This is life." Lulu lifted her rosé for a sip.

*

Snow clung to the limbs of the big elm in the back yard, lined the fence, weighed down the branches of the evergreens. The air was still, the world silent except for the flutter of the sparrows. A flit of brown to the feeder and a splash of seeds to the ground and a flit back, they disappeared into the arborvitae. Olivia fourteen months old, lost in a bundle of winter bunting in the stroller, her dark hair curled around her face. Wide-eyed she observed the snow covered scene silently, pink nose and cheeks. Her eyes turned to the feeder at the sound of seeds splashing. Last night's storm painted a new layer of white, transforming muddy snowbanks and bare trees into a winter wonderland. The air was crisp, laden with the scent of crystalline snow. Gobs fell from the tree branches, plop, squish, joining the snow beneath the canopy. Catherine strolled Olivia through the footprints of early morning walkers who had paved a bumpy trail along the unshoveled sidewalk. Little Olivia bumpity bounced in her bundle. Catherine peeked down to her, "Do you like it?"

*

April 2003

"They've done it, they've actually done it." Dad had Alistair's full attention. "They've decoded the human genome. Well, eighty-five percent of it. The questions the Ethical, Legal, and Social Implications Program examined over the years are more urgent now than ever. It's no longer theoretical."

"Now the law has to catch up," Alistair said. "Isn't that always the way? Only when the facts bite us in the arse do the law-makers leap into action. A never-ending game of catch up!"

"Very true, very true," Dad's voice concurred.

Catherine pulled her chair in at the dinner table and adjusted Olivia's bib. "It sounds like those two are getting along just fine. Remember when I said maybe Dad should date him?"

Mom laughed. "Well he's yours now, like it or not." She set a big steaming bowl on the table and called toward the living room. "Paul, Alistair! Your stew is getting cold!"

Dad threw his arms in the air as he walked into the dining room, eyes wide with exaggerated alarm, "Oh no! Let's eat!"

"Honestly!" Mom smiled and shook her head.

*

She flipped through the pages of Mary's sketchbook. A typed letter — *The wind rises and falls in the last grip of winter as you drive into spring. Kansas City. Back into the perils that created the special person that you are...* It was a letter Mary had written to someone named Alan. And with the letter was a photograph of a young man walking a gravel road toward the camera, head down, hands in his pockets.

*

May 2004

This is life. Catherine woke to a chorus of whistling chirps. A flutter of activity was underway in the branches of the sixty-foot cedar trees outside the bedroom windows. Shadows landed on the walls, flitted away. She rolled to the edge of the bed and hoisted herself until the weight of her big belly, like Olivia's Weeble Wobble, sat her upright. Cedar waxwings. There must have been a hundred of them, coffee-brown feathers fluttering against the new green foliage as they dined on clusters of tiny blue cones.

A little singsong voice called from the nursery, "No climbing, no climbing!" Exactly Catherine's own words, her gentle admonishment to keep Olivia safely in the crib. She peeked inside and there was Olivia, one foot over the rail, chanting. She scooped Olivia into her arms, light as a waxwing. "Should we go downstairs Sweetpea?" On the family room couch, Olivia straddled her and pressed her little fingers into Catherine's belly, "Baby?" Catherine answered and Olivia repeated, "Baby." Then Olivia pressed her fingers into Catherine's breast, "Baby?" Catherine answered and Olivia repeated, "Not a baby." Back and forth they went. A new version of push-push. But when baby Leo came home from the hospital, in Catherine's arms instead of her belly, Olivia took one look and toddled out of the room. Suddenly baby was less fun than not-a-baby. She barely spoke to Catherine for a week. She, after all, was supposed to be the baby. But as the months passed, Olivia found a new role for herself: entertainer. Baby Leo's dark eyes were glued to her every action, blonde wisps atop his head, his wet smile

245

dripping with adoration. As Olivia's colorful toy mallet smacked the red, blue, and green plastic balls through holes, her dark curls bouncing with each smack, the balls rolled down the ramp to the catch box below. Leo squealed with delight.

When it was time for his nap, Catherine scooped him into her arms, a sturdy little bundle. Not a waxwing.

"The show is not over!" Olivia declared.

"He'll be back for another show after his nap, Sweetpea." She caressed the top of Olivia's head, climbed the stairs, and peered with wonder at this little boy who looked up at her so sweetly and adoringly, so lovingly, simply because she was his mother.

*

Catherine looked out the car window at the gentle hills as the two-lane county road wound through a scene so remote and beautiful — small farm fields lined with a rushing creek or a grove of trees, farm houses and silos in the distance. She turned to Alistair at the wheel. His eyes were tense. Had the responsibilities of married life, a home, and work drained the light from him? When they were younger he was goofy and it made her laugh. In spite of their differences, they came together in those moments, and each moment together created a relationship. Life moves you along its path. First to Alistair, then to Mary. Mary was leading her somewhere, but where? Catherine turned to the back seat. Leo was sound asleep. Olivia's eyes were wide. "Want some snack, Sweetpea?"

"Want some!"

As the car reached the crest of the hill, a vista opened. Forested hills of white pine, blue sky above.

*

No more musty cardboard boxes for Mary. Catherine had arranged the collection of sketchbooks neatly on the book shelf. She ran her hand across the fabric cover of one, pulled it from the shelf, opened it. A different drawing in each corner of the page: a lighthouse, a cottage in the dunes, a seagull at the water's edge, a cat poised on a split rail fence. She turned another page and there, in charcoal pencil, was an outline of Mary's hand. The lifelike creases of the palm were labeled in delicate, swirling script: *heart*

line, head line, life line. And beneath there was a scripted note: *thirty years for each line.*

"You only got to finish one line, Mom." Catherine touched her forefinger to the outlined forefinger and gently slid her hand into Mary's.

Plunge

New York City, April 2003

The tall windows at the Johnson Avenue loft flooded sunlight across the floor. James looked out across the roof of Enquist Chemical to the distant Manhattan skyline and the pale blue above. A simple delineation between one phenomenon and another. But as he gazed he saw that the blue of the sky tinted the great glass towers. And the city's smoke smudged the sky. It was what he felt every time he sat down to redraft, re-explain any element of his ideas. It was clear, until he delved deeper.

He puzzled through the afternoon at the desk in his bedroom, finally gave up and took the Morgan Avenue L train to Bedford. If the theory was going nowhere, he could have a go at life. Colleen always said he wouldn't find the right girl or the right job unless he got out there, opened himself to possibilities. *Sign up for classes* — she said — *You'll meet like-minded people.* He couldn't afford classes. Couldn't afford much of anything. So he strolled, wandered, hoped for... Who knows what?

The evening breeze wafted over him at the little waterfront beach up river from the Williamsburg Bridge. Couples sat on the boulders at the water's edge. He walked on. He smiled politely at the barista who served his coffee at Bliss Cafe, smiled politely at the Polish waitress who served his pierogi and chicken soup at S & B Restaurant. As he walked down Metropolitan under the black and white awning at Havemeyer, they were just closing the curtains. Probably not a strip club. But it didn't look like other bars or restaurants. He wasn't even sure it was open to the public.

Home at Johnson Avenue, he searched "Black Betty" on his desktop computer. No website. But he found a blog post, and yes, it was a bar, restaurant, and music club, open to the public. The young blogger wrote about being there on a Sunday night, Brazilian Beat night, two DJs and a non-stop dance party, guys and girls making out. He was shy and felt like a complete outcast and it was awful. He would never go back again.

James leaned back. The blog post was a map to treasure. Sit down to a drink surrounded by women, in a room that's dynamic, charged. As much as he loved Taisho's flames dancing behind glass, he was crammed shoulder to shoulder at his dinner station, and it was sheer luck who would sit next to him. But in a dance club you can mingle. At Taisho you're watching the show. At Black Betty you're in it.

Sunday night he walked under the black awning and swung inside. A narrow dining room lined with eight small tables was darkened and mostly empty. A young woman, a server he supposed, walked into the dining room from the kitchen at the back.

"Is it Brazilian Beat tonight?" he asked.

"Of course. They're spinning in the bar, through here."

He followed her. Black hair, petite with curves, self-assured. They squeezed past couples and singles, mostly younger than his forty years, who lined the wide archway, bottles and shot glasses in hand. She moved behind the bar backed with a gilded mirror and motioned him into the swirling pool of Samba dancers, their hips swerving and feet swiveling, all too fast to understand.

The first step to making yourself welcome at a bar is simple. Buy a drink. He carefully wedged an arm at the crowded bar, his hand a flag of presence, as regulars inhaled a breath and a drink before the next dance, before the hook from another Brazilian song drew a cheer and a whoop from the whole room and they fled the barstools. He marveled at the happening around him. And there she was, black hair, petite curves, his bartender. He fumbled, "Uh, do you have Guinness?" Her piercing blue eyes checked him out, she nodded and continued serving the patrons ahead of him. He was on her time. Tailored brows and mascaraed lashes. Slick black coiffured hair angled across her forehead and falling to her shoulders in curls and ringlets. She commanded the bar with a perfect balance of hipness and courtesy, charm and reserve, heat and cool. She was a seasoned performer at the height of her craft. He was starting to see that in New York City everyone is the epitome of something. It's what the City breeds in its natives and draws to itself from every point on the globe. She delivered the Guinness with a nod, swept the bills from the counter, and walked away.

He took a swig and turned to the room. An intimate space, yellow stucco walls, wooden beams, warm lights, shadowed corners, dancers swirling. A slender woman about thirty walked through the archway. He took another swig and watched her hazel eyes scan the room. Her red lips pouted down from the center and rose to a smile at the outer tips. She sat and crossed her legs on a cushioned bench along the wall and threw back her untamed red hair, letting it fall in cascading waves to her bare shoulders and to the blue and white gingham dress that crisscrossed her full cleavage, followed her curves closely, and ended suddenly near the top of her thighs. She uncrossed her legs, shifted sideways, gripped the dress below her hips in two fists and pulled the hem fractionally lower, striving almost impossibly toward modesty, then crossed her legs again. And all the while nothing that mustn't be revealed was revealed, not a fleeting glimpse of hidden silk or satin. He breathed deep just as a squad of dancing couples sailed like clouds across a gleaming mountain peak, and she vanished from view.

He tilted the pint to his lips and wondered how people learn to dance, learn the steps, feel like they know what they're doing so they can just relax and have a good time, instead of standing against the wall with a rum and Coke — the fiestas in Cumaná Tercera. The room was overfilled now as midnight came on and the DJs hooked the beat of the last song fading out into the sub-beat of the next fading in. He rode the wave of the music, the latest local hits of an era past and a city deep in the Amazon and a language like ancient Spanish, a smooth, rich, guttural Portuguese, the same language that half the crowd spoke together in this tiny lamplit room that was a valleyscape of earthly wonders in the heart of an old Brooklyn neighborhood.

He couldn't laugh at the young blogger now. He felt it himself, shy and a little unsure. But a man of forty knows you can't yet belong to a place you've just arrived. And the fact was, he was in love. In love with Black Betty. He would become a regular at Brazilian Beat. He would belong.

Every Sunday night he walked in the door under the black awning and through the archway into the intimate room that was the heart of Black Betty. Sofia commanding the old wooden bar. DJs Greg Caz and Sean Marquand in the nook at the far end spinning Brazilian vinyl. The black velvet curtains were pulled closed after dark as if to say to the passersby on Metropolitan Avenue, *We need a little privacy here, time to chill, son.* Eleven at night the room danced. Greg Caz was an African-American Samba brainiac with three-foot dreadlocks, and Sean Marquand was a white Samba prince as smooth as his French surname. Every year they flipped through LPs in old music stores for lost hits, not in New York City but on the side streets of Rio de Janeiro and Sao Paulo. The Brazilian Beat crowd was mostly Amazon transplants, mixed with a few white hipsters and a few local dealers who were sure to show up as the night got hot.

James still couldn't grasp the steps that passed so quickly. His new buddy tried to help him.

"One-and-two, two-and-two, bum-ba-bum. It's two-four time, but it's three steps in two beats," Sammy said, "like this" and Sammy's feet were a blur.

James met Sammy the third or fourth Sunday. He was a skinny young Jewish guy with black wavy hair and dark gentle eyes under a sporty fedora that he never took off and that dressed up his plaid button-down shirt. Sammy knew Samba, really knew it. He was a puppeteer, you know children's puppet shows at the park, and it worked okay for a living because he rented from his uncle, his family owned property in the neighborhood, and he paid the family rate, but anyway it was bum-ba-bum.

"Three in two," James repeated, "so a triplet across two beats."

"No, not exactly..."

James couldn't figure it out, but eventually he found a solution. "How about this? Does this look like Samba?" He moved his feet as fast as he could in some kind of pattern he could handle. It wasn't a joke. He wanted to find a way he could dance.

"It's not bad, well...you can do that." Sammy was generous toward everyone, and James could see, this is how they do it at Black Betty. Being hip meant knowing how to chill, respect, and get along. From then on he spent most of every Sunday night on the dance floor instead of the bar stool. Like Cumaná afternoons in the ocean waves, he was learning to dive in.

Spring blossomed into summer. The gallery job came to an end, and no job to replace it. But his Sundays were Samba. And something else. He was growing roots in the City.

*

Brooklyn. This is how we do it. Words matter. It's how to get along and get things done. Talking on the street with neighbors. At the diner counter with wait staff. At Black Betty slamming whiskeys with the Polish-American thug you never meant to meet. Give each word its due respect. Don't just speak it. Spit it off the tip of your tongue.

Brooklyn. A woman is open to eye contact at a distance of a block or two. If she likes that first contact, she'll offer a glance and a smile at a few paces before you pass each other. But there is next to zero chance of the close-up if you haven't worked the distance first. A man marks another man's presence and posture at two or three blocks, no eye contact necessary or desired. At a pace or two away, a passing glance of the eyes and an understated "hey."

*

July 2003

An email from Alan. *Hey James — The Universe Society is looking for a front desk person, part-time, maybe not much money, but here's the thing, I've been talking to Bridget, the librarian you did the phone interview with last year. She wants you to help with the website too, so could turn into something interesting. Send her your resume, highlight your amazing reception desk abilities AND your web experience.*

Three weeks later James was sitting behind a heavy wooden desk in the entrance lobby of the Universe Society on East Sixty-Eighth Street. The Society's Manhattan headquarters was a luxurious 1910 townhouse built like a Jacobean castle — glass-plated iron gates, gothic arches, hexagonal terracotta tiles. Maybe this was the old-fashioned estate he and Caroline had talked about that night at the Pink Pony. If he couldn't live in a mansion, he could at least work in one.

At the start of his shift on that first day, at twelve noon, the operations director, Chaz Berg, had led him through the entrance lobby, up three broad, shallow steps to an inner lobby with walls of rich dark wooden panels under a ceiling of heavy box beams. He pressed five on the hundred-year old elevator. "I like to start at the top and work my way down" — he quipped — "and if that conjures uncivilized thoughts in your head, your bad not mine." As that quip raced by another was already flying projectile. "The staff train in mountaineering — the elevator only goes to five so we have to hike the stairs to six." He swung open the door at the very top, "Greetings membership administrator!" — then swept his hand over his mouth to mutter a plainly audible aside — "membership muddler."

"Nice," Declan said. He was a smiling, burly, quick-witted man, plainly a New Yorker like Chaz, but not like Chaz. In fact, the two were lion and water buffalo facing off. "Chaz has applied for membership several times. I keep misplacing his application."

"And I keep misplacing your request for a raise. Meet our newest staff, James Crossland. He'll be watching the front desk."

Down the hall, Chaz opened his arms wide to present the Glory Hall. "The most valuable chamber in the building." Thirty by fifty feet of nineteenth century luxury, and luxury of a specific sort. The old fashioned hunting trophies began high on the walls, just below the rafters of the peaked ceiling, and roamed down the walls, corner to corner and end to end. The taxidermic heads of rhinoceros, water buffalo, deer, bison, caribou, wolf, antelope. Tusks of elephant, woolly mammoth, and narwhal whale. A bear skin, a stuffed penguin, a stuffed adult lion standing dead and proud on a big table top. And the people who lived where such beasts were found were represented by spears, harpoons, drums, and other so-called exotic artifacts of life beyond Europe.

They descended floor by floor. Fifth. "This is the Society's fabulous research library, and this is Bridget, our even more fabulous research librarian."

"Oh, Chaz, you're so sweet." While Chaz absorbed the appreciation, Bridget held out her hand to James. He noted the same carefully styled hospitality he had heard on the phone with her a year earlier. A tilt of the head and her copper-tinged bangs conspired with blue eyes and red lips in a coy smile that doubled as courtesy, "I'm delighted. We are desperately in need of your web expertise."

On the fourth floor he met the accountant. Her Russian accent was like bubbles emerging from boiling molasses — "If you have questions for filling your timesheet, please you feel welcome to ask me."

Third floor. "Welcome aboard, James." Blake Connor, president of the Society, was a tall, muscular man with a crew cut, a firm handshake, and a ready smile. Chaz couldn't hold back, "He's the one who signs your paychecks."

"Knock it off, Chaz," Blake was playful now. "Is he giving you a hard time already?"

Down the hallway from the president, Chaz nodded to the framed posters on the walls, faded announcements of Society events long past. "You see this poster? The guy prancing a tiger around the stage? Our founding members a hundred years ago used to bring back live exotic animals from their expeditions for public appearances. Today we'd call it earned media, back then they called it science." Never mind the animals, James thought. The Society itself was the exotic specimen he was interested in.

Chaz rapped on a closed office door. "Come in," a woman's voice from inside. The executive director stood from her desk and smiled with a reserve that marked her authority while her dark eyes examined the new addition. She was younger than James, tall with a short black bob. "I'm Saanvi. I understand Bridget is eager for your help on the website." She spoke with a precise and exquisite South Asian accent. "And of course Raymond, our custodian, is delighted not to have to cover reception any longer."

They rounded the stairs down to second floor. "This is the Cumberland Room," Chaz announced. "We present lectures to the public, for a fee naturally. Members get a discount, remember that when you're at reception. You're noticing the medallions. There are a hundred — approved expeditions only. Sir Edmund Hillary carried this medallion. Now you know who you're working for."

On the ground floor, Chaz pointed to the back of the building. "There's a full commercial kitchen. Grab a coffee, just don't get in the way of the caterers." The man behind the reception desk, Raymond, James assumed, waved to Chaz while a stout man in suit and tie stood stiff and indignant. "Mr. van der Meer here would like a word."

Chaz looked at James. "You're on your own, bub. Mr. van der Meer, come right in!" Chaz led the man into an ornate room directly off the entrance lobby.

"So you're the new fella? I'm Raymond." He shook James' hand. He was a tall man who spoke with a Southern cadence and a cultivated deference, and behind that, a sly smile waiting. "I don't know if Mr. van der Meer ever climbed a mountain," Raymond whispered, "but he pays the Society a mountain of cash. Anyway, I'm taking my lunch and then I have my other duties. You get a fifteen-minute break at three and you're all done at six. You ready?" He smiled, "Don't worry, I'll happen by in case you have questions."

*

Saturday morning. The loft was heating up as the July sun struck the Johnson Avenue roof, the exact reverse side of which was the ceiling of his bedroom, no insulation between. He hunched over the keyboard on his desk, writing, puzzling, writing again...Culture within the context of free will. He lifted his coffee cup for a sip. But how free? American culture promoted the idea that every person has complete freedom and independence of thought. Bombard people with advertisements — it's their own free choice to be influenced or not. Show employees what behaviors will get them promoted versus what will get them fired — it's their own free choice to be influenced or not. He believed in free will. But the idea of complete freedom and independence was too simple. Clearly there was peer pressure going on. That was it. Social pressure. We can choose whatever we want, but like Tugendhat said, there are consequences. Mary Douglas called them costs and benefits. That's the wall we walk into. That sets the patterns. But how does one pattern become the dominant pattern?

He wiped his forehead with the back of his hand, a sooty sweat, and stared into the pitiful little electric fan, and as he stared the fan stopped humming, unwound, and stood still. For an instant he was dazzled as if by magic, but then he looked to the power indicator on the phone-fax machine. It was dead too. No buzz from the refrigerator downstairs. In fact, all the sounds that normally pass for silence had stopped. The only sound was the forklifts rumbling under the floor. His eyes narrowed and he exhaled disgust. He had no idea what the cause or whose fault, but there was always something going wrong at the loft. He grabbed his keys from the writing desk, tossed a copy of *Science and Society* journal into his satchel, then jogged down the wooden stairs and locked the unit's big steel door behind him. He'd pass the afternoon somewhere with air-conditioning. A coffee at Kelloggs, a chicken soup at S & B on Bedford, and Black Betty would open at six.

*

Beneath the archway to his stool at the bar. "Andy! Make it a Guinness. Looks like I've got the place to myself."

"For now. It's still early. How is the new job?"

"Good. I'm mostly reception desk, but I also do some web design. Even a little bit of writing for the website."

"You get some satisfaction then, that's nice."

Andy tended bar on Thursdays. A sturdy, straight-ahead man, a pair of sharp blue eyes, he was all straight lines and right angles. His mouth, a short line, paralleled his square shoulders, and from the shoulders his arms hung like tools on pegs. He pulled the tap until the pint glass was one-third full, then let it settle a few minutes, then another pull and another few minutes. James waited for the final pull. "I never knew there was such an art to Guinness."

"One day" — Andy settled his elbows on the bar — "I ordered a pint in a little place in Peekskill, up near Bear Mountain State Park. The guy pulls the tap and steps away, comes back when the glass is half beer and half foam, and I'm watching this, oh it's gotta be a mistake I'm thinking, and then he sets it in front of me."

"What did you do?"

"I taught him how to pour a Guinness." Andy pulled the tap one more time and planted the glass in front of James, a swirl in the middle of the creamy foam top.

James took a swig. "What would you like to be doing?" He asked the question and then saw he'd taken Andy by surprise, Andy standing there with a rag in a pint glass.

"Oh, if I wasn't here?" He set the dried glass on the shelf. "I'd be shooting photos. That's what I was doing up the river at Bear Mountain Bridge. I like to find the views nobody was meant to see, an unintended vantage point. Other people miss it, you know, but I see something there. But I've got three kids to raise, and I can't make a living on that."

"I know. You're inspiring me and depressing me all at the same time."

"So have another drink."

"Oh my god," James shook his head and took another swig.

*

August 14, 2003

James opened the flatbed scanner. Digitizing old black-and-white photos from the Society's collection was now another one of his duties. The best part was being up on fourth, away from the reception desk. He spent a few hours every week here in the little office whose diamond-paned leaded glass windows looked down onto the second-floor terrace and into those spaces between buildings, unintended vantage points.

Wearing white cotton gloves, he positioned a fragile photograph over the glass. A white man in safari gear, flanked protectively by black men in leopard skins with spears. So different from Dad who sat on the floor with Umaro Mousa as they traded stories. He pressed the button and watched the line of light traverse the length of the scan bed...Shit. It stopped. He looked at the computer screen, gone dark. At Johnson Avenue a month ago and now here on the swanky Upper East Side of Manhattan. Maybe in New York City people were doing so many amazing things they couldn't be bothered with the basics. The hallway was dark except for sunlight from the office windows. He heard voices, a commotion rising. He gathered the photos into the folder and ascended the stairs to fifth.

"James," Bridget called as he opened the library door. "Come on in, join the party. I just phoned Raymond down at reception. He says the power is out on the whole block."

"Hey." Declan barged through the door. "What's going on? Are you yanking out wires, Chaz?"

"Yeah, yank on this, fat boy. I'm calling it a day."

Bridget looked at the clock on the wall: Four-ten. "What else can we do? We can't work in the dark!" She simmered with excitement, like school letting out early.

A stampede gathered force down the shadowed stairwell and they all flowed into the lobby. Raymond was just coming back through the front doors. "It's way more than the block," he said. Everyone stopped. "It's the whole city and then some. The subways are down, the traffic lights are down. I've got my van. Anybody that needs a ride, it's now or never. Grab a bottled water because you don't know how long it's gonna take to get home."

September 11 was less than two years ago. No one was sure how scared they should be about what was unfolding now. With two-thirds of the staff crammed onboard, Raymond steered down Sixty-Eighth Street and wheeled around the corner into Park Avenue gridlock.

"I'm walking. It's better than spending the evening with all of you." And with that, Declan was the first to bail.

"Y'all have to make your choice. I'll drive anybody who wants to stay with me," Raymond assured. "But I might get out and walk myself if it carries on like this."

James glanced at the other passengers and the street ahead. He always felt decision like a thrust, other options cut down while one stands. "Thanks Raymond, get home safe everybody!" He only knew he had to walk the sixty-eight blocks down to Houston Street, another five blocks to Delancey Street, and across the Williamsburg Bridge — the halfway point — then down through Greenpoint and Bushwick to Johnson Avenue.

He walked with the crowds. Manhattan sidewalks were always busy, he was used to that. But think of everyone in Manhattan getting off work at exactly the same time and pouring onto the streets. Not the cops suddenly on overtime, not the doctors and nurses tending patients under the light of emergency generators, certainly not the utility workers at Con Edison. But everyone else exited the darkened offices at exactly the same time.

He had been on long walks before. The two-hour trek from his Cumaná Tercera barrio to the sea. But today Upper Manhattan was more like the Franconia Ridge Trail atop the White Mountains, hiking with Estefan in his conservatory days. The city had become a wilderness. Everything was still there but not as the thing it was supposed to be. A car was a two-ton boulder. A skyscraper was a cliff-face lit only by the fading afternoon sun. What was happening was so out-of-the-ordinary that there wasn't any one mood that hung in the air. Uncertainty about what or who caused the outage, fear of what else might happen. And then the giddiness he had seen in Bridget. And there was another feeling too, something learned from September 11.

At Sixtieth Street a man in a summer linen suit stood in the middle of the intersection, stood in for the dead-eyed traffic lights hanging useless, motioned the cross-street vehicles through while holding his hand up to Park Avenue. He was utterly convincing in his command of traffic flow, this man who instead of walking home, swirled sweating in the middle of an historic traffic jam, one of thousands of simultaneous historic traffic jams up and down the five boroughs. No one was flipping him off. No one was honking. The solidarity born that horrible day two years ago was rekindled. The City would get through the blackout together.

By now any hopes of a quick restoration of power were sinking as surely as the blazing August sun. Yet there was a party getting underway, bars overflowing, people openly drinking on the sidewalks, in the parks. By the time he reached Twenty-Third Street, his water was long gone. He pulled out his wallet. Three dollars. He had seen people tapping buttons at ATMs, but the screens were black. And how many dozens of blocks still to go?

More parties on the benches of Union Square. He trudged past, squeezed between the gridlocked yellow cabs on Fourteenth Street, and continued down Fourth Avenue into the East Village. Two hours had passed. The pedestrian crowds were more random now, heavy on some thoroughfares, lighter on others. Ahead, people were stepping around an object in the middle of the sidewalk. A short bottle standing right-side up. Not a pee bottle, the omnipresent plastic bottles tossed to the curb from the backseats of taxis and car services. No, it was raspberry tea, vacuum-sealed. He marveled at the odds of it, and how a city of eight million multiplies the odds that even the oddest thing might happen. He drank it.

At Saint Mark's Place he cut east and then down Second Avenue to Seventh Street, Sixth Street, Fifth Street, Fourth, Third, Second, amazing, a milestone — First Street. Sixty-eight numbered streets crossed, sixty-eight blocks walked, almost halfway home. And here at Mars Bar, the bar with the bad-joke name, he bought a two-fifty Coca-Cola and left a fifty-cent tip.

At Chrystie and Delancey it was dusk, and apart from twilight the headlights on the gridlocked cars became, as far as he could see, the sole source of light anywhere in Manhattan. He made his way through the crowds with the Williamsburg Bridge in sight. The crossing to Brooklyn. The crowds thinned on the pedestrian walkway and the nightlight cars thinned on the bridge's roadway. Still crowds. Some in groups, talking loudly, flush with partying. Some alone and quiet like him. Over the dark river and finally the descent into a shadowed Brooklyn. Every street in every direction peeled off a few more pedestrians and a few more nightlight cars, until there were no more fellow travelers and there was no more light. There were voices. Murmurs from the open windows of the old brick tenement buildings, windows two and three and four stories up. Now louder voices from a candlelit doorway just ahead, four or five men and women lounging in folding chairs before a flickering light, hablando español, beer bottles and plastic cups in hand, and they glance to the street as they hear his footsteps, glance half-sighted into the dark. Their voices fade behind him. He looks up and ahead. He hasn't seen so many stars since the night, decades ago, when Dad called them to the front yard between the young Tamarind tree and the big Mango tree and they all stood gazing up into the glowing West African night.

"That's the Milky Way. The galaxy we we live in," Dad had said.

"If we're here, why is it there," he had asked.

"We're only in one piece of it, and that's the rest of it." And James had stared into the sky to understand.

Now he can find his way because the sky is stars, and the starlessness is buildings lining the street. By the starless shapes he knows Johnson Avenue. He senses the cracked cement sidewalk beneath his feet, steps down to the blackness of asphalt and up again. His legs heavy, but momentum carries him.

Footsteps. Face. A face walks by him. He saw no one until the face was two arm-lengths away. Now past. It's dark, but do you see what I mean? This is how it always is. People are always a little unknown to him, and before he can understand them, they have already moved on, maybe because he is unknowable to them.

The sky is stars. The starlessness is city. There's the Milky Way. And there's home.

*

2004

He had met Colleen less than two years ago, and now she was gone. It took the shine off the early-spring sun. They kept up by phone and email, still steady friends, but he was eating at Kelloggs alone again. Now he knew just how much he had looked forward to those weekly lunches.

It came up after the Christmas holidays, how she was paying rent down here in the City when she could be living for free in Connecticut, the duplex she inherited from her parents a few years ago. Her two renters, upstairs and downstairs, helped cover costs, but she did her calculations and found she would be decidedly better off renting out one unit and living in the other. And maybe up there she could find the steady work she had never been able to find in the City. *I'm tired, James. I need to go home.*

"Where's your friend, the tall girl?" Vassily asked.

"She moved back to Connecticut."

"Connecticut, Ohio, Oklahoma, that's what they do, they come and they go."

"I'm sticking around. I like it here."

"Me too," Vassily said, gesturing to the diner around them. "It's a paradise!"

Coconut

*

June

James navigated the website in the fourth-floor office, which increasingly felt like his office. Saanvi's eyes lit up as she peered over James' shoulder at the screen. "This is so exciting! We've had so many versions of the Society's logo, nobody knows which one to use any more. If you can help us with that..."

"We'll standardize the brand and design. And there's a lot we can do to make the website more intuitive, so members can find what they're looking for."

Day by day he rebuilt the website from the bottom up. Where does the webpage trip up the flow of the eye, where does the navigation thwart expectations, make you laugh when you aren't supposed to. He had learned more than music at the conservatory in Boston. He had learned systems — of harmony, of theme, of expectation promised, delayed, satisfied.

A website reflects an institution. He read expedition reports from the library. Observed members who strolled through the lobby in their finery, who huddled and argued and joked together, who reached out in handshake to an old partner or a new friend. Displays of pride and prowess, promises of partnership and new possibility — the world of commerce hitched to the climbing ropes of exploration. He quietly observed them, their motivations and worldviews, encoding it all in the website. He was still anthropologist, composer, and writer. His skills combined had led to a paying job.

At quarter to six o'clock he tested the last of the new Expedition Interview pages. All good. He carried the day's successes through the subway tunnels of Manhattan and Brooklyn into the night's dreams. Black Betty. Still the lamplit valley of wonder where anything was possible. But quiet tonight, no DJs, no band.

"James!" Andy pulled the tap while James took his stool. Around the bar's corner, where the DJs spun on Brazilian night, a woman tilted her head of braided blonde hair while turning the page of a book. At the top of the page's arc her eyes met his. She completed the arc and read on with a contrived concentration. He smiled to himself.

"Everything good, James?"

261

"Pretty good, I'm publishing more expedition content at the Society, giving the members more visibility for their work."

Andy set the pint in front of him. "Serve it up just the way they like it."

James lifted the glass. "Exactly. Cheers!" And as he took a draft, his eyes met hers again, and her eyes crinkled into a smile like they were sharing a secret. It was easy. Easy to pick up his glass and his satchel and walk over to the woman with the book.

"What are you reading?"

"Poetry. Czeslaw Milosz."

He couldn't believe it. She reads Czeslaw Milosz, and knows how to pronounce his name. "I like the richness of a life lived in two places" — James said — "a life made of two cultures, Lithuanian and Polish."

"You speak Polish?" she asked.

"I read the English translations. But Polish is your language?"

"Yes, Polish."

"How long have you been in Brooklyn?"

"Two years I am here, in Greenpoint. You know this one? Ars Poetica?" She pointed to a poem on the page, all Polish beyond the Latin title. "This means: In the heart of poetry there is a thing indecent..." — she glanced to him, then to the page — "...a thing comes from us that we didn't know about." Her eyes searched him.

And he melted then. The fragility of language, the heroic, doomed effort to know each other's minds. She wanted to know him, for him to know her. He smiled tenderly, "What brought you here from Poland?" The conversation continued over another round.

"I have a bottle of very good vodka at my apartment."

"Andy!" His hand swept in a circle to say *hers and mine together*.

Andy pulled a pen from behind his ear, scratched out the bill, slapped it on the bar and walked away. He had confided once how he hated watching James flirt with women on the customer side while he was trapped on the tending side. But if Andy had really been watching, he would know how rare tonight was.

At Union Avenue they descended the subway stairs, not to his usual L train but to the G for the short ride to Greenpoint. Inside the brownstone they ascended the stairs to her second-floor apartment.

"Sorry about mess. My roommate always have too many things lying around." She turned on a lamp, revealing a disheveled sitting room. "He is out of town this weekend."

A male housemate. That doesn't necessarily mean anything.

"You drink vodka?" she asked from the tiny kitchen off the sitting room.

"For a while I was drinking White Russians, but that's probably an insult to a good Polish vodka."

She yelped a laugh of surprise, surprised that he knew something about her, about being Polish.

"This" — she declared — "is Chopin Rye. No cream, no ice, no Russians!" She handed him a glass and raised hers. "Na Zdrowie!"

Probing what he heard, wanting to give her what she had given him, he spun from his tongue, "Nastrovyay!" and downed the shot. "Mm, that's good, very good. Frederic Chopin made a name for himself in Paris, but he was Polish, wasn't he?"

"Of course, one of our greatest artists. Many Poles fled from the Russian tyrants. We are free only fifteen years now. You know of Solidarność?"

"I remember seeing Lech Walensa in the news back then."

"Now we don't have to flee. We make our own music in our own Poland. I will play for you Kasia Nosowska. One of my favorite songs, *Cisza, ja i czas.* This means *Silence, I and time.*"

Electric guitar, a poppy, hypnotic syncopated four-four refrain. But in a minor key. Re, sol, do...fa, me. Re, sol, do...fa, me. Solo guitar four stanzas, and partway through the last stanza, the drums. It felt good, otherworldly, the lines descending slowly through the fast beat. He couldn't stop himself from swaying into it. He reached for her hand and they danced in the world they had found together. Her body warm against his, he was intoxicated with her femininity, her tender eyes, her tiny sweet lips. She reached to the lamp switch, and it was dark. In the darkness she led him to her bedroom.

She released the top button of her blouse and turned from him to the window that was now the only source of light, her silhouette haloed in the amber glow of the street lamp below. Button by button her hands worked, hidden from view until she turned to him, her bare breasts full and glowing as they passed through the amber halo and into shadow again. Her beauty waiting in darkness. His lips touched hers. The warmth of her skin shimmered within his fingers as he drew the blouse from her shoulders. He gently turned her again toward the light, traced the curve of her thighs and lifted the summer skirt above her hips. He yanked the scant silk panties to her feet, wanting her right there, as she watched the boulevard trees through the window, leafed boughs flirting in the breeze of the charcoal amber night. Instead she turned to him, her eyes bright stars, her skirt at her ankles. The wordless conversation of two strangers. He knelt and grasped first one naked calf and then the other. He raised his eyes to her, the glint of her own piercing the darkness, and his mouth stole, kiss by kiss, up her calves, her thighs, to the heavy perfume of her moist fur. He tasted her, kissed her, and tasted deeper.

"Not here," she said. "Take me to the bed."

Not here. He flinched. But as she crawled onto the mattress, he ripped off his clothes and followed. His thighs against hers, his fingers traced her delicate spine. She tilted her hips to him and he surged inside her. She gasped, then sighed as he grasped her hips and pulled her tight, felt her body echo his.

*

hey james, i'll definitely go to aurora (on grand and wythe by the williamsburg beach) tomorrow at three to have a brunch there. I had this big craving for their steak.

All week he had tried to reach her by phone. But instead there was an email.

if you would like to join me that would be nice, but only if it's convenient for you. i have to leave for my friend's farewell dinner at about five PM. let me know whether you can make it. i'm going to be there regardless. xoxo — Ewelina.

A two-hour date with a hard stop at five PM. *Regardless, xoxo.* They brunched at Aurora. A week later, coffee at S & B. And she was gone. Reverse dating. Sex on the first date, dinner on the second, coffee the third, and it's over. It happened more than once. That's why he gave it a name. Sometimes, of course, it didn't even rise to that level. Sometimes there was just a dinner or a coffee and nothing else. But when it did happen, he would awaken in a woman's apartment, look out the twenty-fifth floor windows onto the immense city, elevator down, and step out the glass door onto the streets of Midtown. Or awaken to feet passing outside a basement window, then step out the heavy metal door onto the streets of the East Village. A sampling of lives he might have lived if any one of these rare women were his girl.

*

July

Saanvi had been planning it for some time, but she still had to strategize how to sell the idea to the board of directors. "Declan used to have a membership assistant. I see an opportunity to leverage that. Let's put half your hours toward the website and the other half toward assisting Declan."

"That's possible," James hesitated. "But I'm a little concerned it won't allow me to keep focused on the website." It was a real concern. And another real concern, one that was obvious enough, was that assisting would chain him to the role of assistant — follower of orders, robotic performer of tasks — a role he had been trying to escape his entire adult life. But he didn't say that. He said, "You've seen the stats, the steady growth in web traffic since I took over, I want to keep us rolling forward."

"How about two-thirds web and one-third membership."

How often he had been trapped like this, unable to think fast enough, talk fast enough to dart from defeat. Low-level do-all helper was going to be his future at the Society, except for one thing. He darted, "Declan actually splits his time between membership and managing the IT vendors. Why don't I take over all the IT. I can handle the troubleshooting in-house that you used to contract out, and my wage is about half what the vendors were charging."

"Yes...yes, that could work."

And it did. He even got to title the role, a title that neatly tied the work into a single package to cinch the deal: Manager of Web & Technology. He was forty-two years old and finally working a full-time, highly-skilled professional job for the first time in his life. And better still, doing it in New York City. His pay was still below average for a web manager, but he could finally make a life for himself here in a city that everyone says chews people up and spits them out.

*

November

Eleven o'clock at night, home from Black Betty, he crossed Varick and there were Alicia and Craig, two of his neighbors, carrying a sofa out the steel door to the street.

"Are you guys moving? At night?"

Craig jerked his head toward the door. "Look at the sign."

"Condemned?"

"Fucking condemned, fucking bullshit property management, fucking bullshit city!"

That seemed to be about all he was going to learn from Craig. He ran inside up the steel stairs to the infinite corridors of the never-quite-fully-renovated-never-would-be residential second floor at Johnson Avenue. Unit doors were open, tenants milling the corridors.

"Welcome home!" It was Ben from Unit 10, first tenant in the building, first in command.

"What's going on?" James asked.

"The management company's gassing us and I'm gonna pull their guts out their fucking A-holes, that's what's going on. You missed the lunch-time visit from the FDNY. They evacuated the entire building for two hours for carbon monoxide. Two hundred ninety-two parts per million! That blows away every OSHA standard. The firefighters were breaking down doors to clear the air. Fucking unbelievable and we're paying a thousand a month to live in a gas chamber, you're probably paying more..."

"Two thousand, we're the biggest unit."

"Two thousand a month to bring your life to a premature end. This is the second evacuation..."

"The second?"

"Last week. You were probably at work. Now the building's condemned and we've got twenty-four hours to clear out. We're pooling resources, cardboard boxes in the laundry room, take what you need, share what you don't."

"Have you talked to Chrystal?"

"Your sublet? She's already gone."

"Shit!" James dashed down the corridor, turned the key in Unit Five. The long meow as he opened the door, and there stood Phoenix. "So you're still here!"

"Meow."

"We've got some packing to do."

He emptied the bookshelves, hauled the furniture down the stairs to the common room. Packed boxes. Then he stared at everything else. He sat on the bedroom floor. "How are we going to do this?" Phoenix circled without answering. "You're right, we'll just have to keep packing."

By nine in the morning he had arranged a van to move his things to self-storage on West Seventeenth Street in Manhattan end of the day. But he had to get Phoenix out of here, now. He lined a metal-wire utility cart with blankets, set Phoenix down inside it, set the litter box on top as a lid, and wheeled Phoenix to the subway.

After he parked Phoenix in his office, he went to see Saanvi. "Would it be okay if my cat lives here for a little while?" She looked up from her desk. He wasn't sure just how strange the question did or didn't sound. There was already a cat living in the library. "I'm in transition with my housing."

Saanvi took off her reading glasses. "I think we can do that, as long as your cat...what's her name?"

"He's Phoenix."

"I should think Phoenix can stay in the library as long as he and Mindy don't fight over food. Would you please let Bridget know?"

Phoenix was in. Nothing shocked anyone at the Universe Society. James still didn't know where he was spending the night, but his chances of finding a couch were better without a cat. He would take it one step at a time. He sat at his desk and picked up the phone to call Luke. Ringing, ringing, voicemail — and a flurry of doubts swept his mind, all the unresolved emotions about the loft. He had been led into another disaster, just like Notre Dame days when he and Luke enrolled in the same class and shared a textbook to save money, and when the exam loomed it was always Luke who had the book. But Luke had built up resentments too, blurted out in an unguarded moment that he had been overgenerous, paying his full rent even after all he was using was the storage above the kitchen. James left a message explaining what happened. Maybe he would connect with Luke later. Maybe it wasn't even a good idea. He picked up the phone again. Alan — A brand new baby, he wanted to say yes, but Susanna just wouldn't go for it, really so sorry. Sofia — She didn't think she could explain it to her boyfriend.

The twenty-four hours was up. Everything he could manage to pack and move was out of Johnson Avenue. Back at the Society, the evening's public lecture was getting underway. He was sweaty and grimy and kept his head down through the lobby. He used the back stairs instead of the elevator. He had to use the bathroom first thing. There shouldn't be much of anyone on the fifth floor at this hour. As he stood at the toilet, he eyed the clawfoot tub. The old luxury townhouse had full baths and even a kitchen. How long would it take to find a place? Probably not long. He had a steady full-time job, he could lay out a check for first month, last, and security deposit. He washed his hands and face and peered into the mirror.

From that night on, he didn't go home after work. There wasn't any home to go to. He sat at his office computer and searched apartment listings. His criteria were simple: Brooklyn, maximum seven hundred and fifty dollars a month. The results were not so simple: Share unfinished basement with four people in Williamsburg...Share two bedrooms with six people in Crown Heights...Studio apartment, six by ten, shared bathroom down the hall in Sunset Park. Guys looking to share with a girl, girls looking to share with a girl...

I'm working late, he explained to anyone who asked. There were usually a few staff around after hours for evening events — lectures, films, parties. James was just one more.

Of course there was the risk of being called on while you're in the building. *James, thank goodness you're still here. We can't get the laptop to connect to the projector for the film.* But when it was late enough that he was sure no one would come looking for him, he closed the door to his office, turned out the light, and spread his blanket on the floor. Early in the morning, before anyone but Raymond had arrived, he showered in the fifth floor bath and was at his desk impressively early in the morning.

A week passed, and another.

If it makes you feel better — Colleen wrote by email — *finding a new apartment is a New York way of life. Not only is everyone busy departing and arriving from all over the world, but the people already in the City move around the City too. Ah, the liveliness of it all!*

So lively that she had left town for good.

The situation was becoming awkward. Leaving at five after work to buy milk, cereal, bread, and peanut butter, and returning at six with his small bag of groceries. Or going out to meet Alan in the East Village or to Black Betty for a few drinks and returning at nine at night, finding Raymond at the reception desk for a night-time event. "Hello James," Raymond said with a wry smile.

"I have some work I need to catch up on."

"Mm, hmm," the wise custodian replied.

He started leaving at five and staying out late enough that the building would be empty when he came back. He sat in coffee shops or walked the streets or took subway rides, just trying to be someplace to kill time. It was easy to stay out all hours if he was drinking. But he couldn't drink all night every night. One night, walking Penn Station's underground mini-mall, he peered into one of the storefront windows dressed with clothed dummies and draped fabrics and thought, *That looks like a great place to lie down.* He pushed himself to keep walking. But he knew for sure now, he was homeless.

As November gave way to December, he couldn't face Raymond or Saanvi any more without coming clean. He walked down the hall to the executive director's office.

"Just an update on my apartment search. I haven't found anyplace yet... In fact, I've had to start sleeping here at the Society."

Saanvi looked up at him in silence.

"I'm sleeping on the floor of my office. Something's got to turn up soon."

"Well," Saanvi lowered her voice, "I'm actually doing the same. I'm between apartments too. All my belongings are in storage."

"Wow," James said. "I'm sure you'll find a place."

"Yes, I already know where I'm going, it's just not available for move-in yet. So, yes, that's fine. I'll let Raymond know your situation so he won't be surprised."

James didn't mention it was already too late for that.

*

"It's hard to find a good apartment in this city," the cabby told him. He rarely took a cab. But after a late night at Black Betty, he had no patience for the long subway ride back to the Society. The car raced up FDR Drive, the City's lights reflecting on the black currents of the East River.

"I found mine," the cabby went on. He was a little younger than James, maybe forty, a Near Eastern accent. "I met a kid who wanted a roommate. As soon as I moved in I told him, get out by the end of my shift or I come back and kill you. You want to survive, you have to know men's hearts." He eyed

James in the rear view mirror and James nodded simple commonsense agreement. People talked when he listened like this, quietly and without visible judgment. "I served with security forces in Egypt, my home," the cabby talked on. "We raided a rebel camp. While the others mopped up I guarded the prisoners. I shot one to put fear in the others. This is knowing men's hearts. My sergeant came back, angry. *You disobeyed my order, you will see the consequences.* What a prick, his head filled with rules. I looked around us and do you know who else I saw? Nobody but my hooded prisoners in the little ravine where we stood, him reprimanding me. I held a pistol to his head. *Pledge to say nothing or I blow your head off.* He never reported me. He knew I would come for him and my brothers would come for him. Problem solved."

"So you have the apartment to yourself now."

"Kid cleared out before I got home."

James looked at the meter as the car pulled to the curb on East Sixty-Eighth Street. "Here, keep the change." He climbed out and didn't look back. Everyone was here in the City. Not just Alan Bing and Chuck Close. Everyone.

Crossings

Minneapolis, December 2004

"**J**oan, would you hand me the corn starch from the cabinet above the toaster oven?"

"Corn starch, dear? You're changing a nappy, not making stew."

Alistair's parents were visiting from London, their first visit since Leo was born.

The phone rang. "Holmes household, Joan speaking. Yes she is here. And your last name? Hold the line. Catherine, a Lulu Casado is asking after you!"

Catherine held Leo by the ankle and in a flash slid the diaper beneath him, patted on the corn starch, and secured the velcro tabs. "There you go Poot-Poot!" She took the phone, "Hi Lulu, what's up?"

"I just have to tell you, I think I've got the travel bug. I mean, I wouldn't really know because I've never even left the state, but I think it's the travel bug."

"Okay, so what's your destination, sunny California or maybe a winter trip to Europe?"

"That's just it, you're the traveler. I don't even know how to decide where to go. "

"Maybe someplace where a bartender actually knows the latest cocktails."

"That's it, Catherine, you're on to something."

*

March 2005

The mail dropped to the floor inside the front door as it did nearly every day during Leo's nap. She could tell the volume by the rustle through the slot and the thump. Today a little more thump. She tiptoed past Olivia who was covered head to toe beneath her light green chenille blanket on the living room rug. "Joyce!" she whispered to herself as she opened the manilla envelope from Provincetown and pulled out a small fabric-covered booklet. And a note:

This is Mary's address book. It came to me after she passed. I forgot all about it until I came across it a few weeks ago, dusting my bookshelves. I was going to mail it right off to you but, well, it's kind of embarrassing... When I first received it, I erased the addresses because I thought I might use it myself. I never did, but that's why it's empty. Anyway, you should have it.

She turned page after page. Yellowed at the edges, roughed up, but strangely not empty. Smudges, sign of the act of erasure, filled the pages. And there was something more. Her mother had a way of pressing hard with the pencil as she wrote. Catherine could still read the ghost of her writing. It took weeks of painstaking work to decipher the names, addresses, and phone numbers, write them in her lined notebook, and verify them on the internet. Sixty-nine entries in all. She worked late at night while Olivia and Leo slept.

It was one of those nights that it happened. The house was quiet and Olivia and Leo had been asleep for hours. Even Alistair, who liked to stay up late shut away in his office on the second floor, had gone to bed. She sat at the desktop computer in the den with Mary's address book, her notebook beside her. Out the windows, snowflakes drifted under streetlights. She typed *Elodie Arquette* into the Whitepages search box. *Let's see...someone about the same age as Mary, somewhere on the East Coast. Elodie Arquette, age 67, Houston, TX. No, too old, wrong place. Here we go, Elodie Arquette, 41 years old, New York, New York. That's got to be her.* Catherine recorded the address and phone number. Next entry, Alan Bing. And that's when the doorbell rang. Her weary eyelids opened wide and darted to the clock on the desk: one fifteen in the morning. She rose slowly, sneaked upstairs to Alistair, and whispered tersely into his ear, "The doorbell rang!" He stirred. She rounded the bed to the window and peered out between the blinds, down to the front sidewalk. Nobody.

"Come on," she whispered, and Alistair pulled himself out of bed and followed downstairs. As she approached the front door, she could hear the doorbell buzzing. It did this sometimes, a steady buzz after it had been rung. Alistair peeked out the six-paned window in the top of the door. "No one's there."

"Are there footprints in the snow?" Catherine asked.

"No footprints on the stoop, none anywhere."

Alistair behind her, she reached out into the frigid night and felt for the doorbell button. It was stuck pressed in. She pulled it out with her fingernail and the buzzing stopped. She looked at Alistair, "How could it be pressed in if nobody pressed it?"

*

"I would like your expert opinion on something." Catherine's dark eyes interrogated Father Larsen across the dinner table. Alistair had invited him, quite certain the priest who had married them could offer useful guidance on how to make a successful and happy marriage. She knew what Alistair meant by that — not guidance for both of them but guidance for her. But as Father Larsen reveled in Catherine's baked salmon and roasted potatoes and she delved into questions of the meaning of the afterlife, the conversation took its own path.

"Of course, my child..." — Father Larsen laughed at his own formality, set down his glass of wine, and leaned forward empathetically — "Catherine, ask anything you wish and I will try to answer."

She told him the story. The doorbell. "There were no footprints in the snow. So no one could have pressed the button, yet it rang. I was working with my late mom's address book. I've been thinking a lot about her. Is there any way it could be her?"

He looked thoughtfully. "Spirits only visit when there is something new we discover from our experience. Was there anything you learned that was new?"

What she remembered most was feeling afraid. She didn't think Mary would want her to feel afraid. "I guess I can't think of anything new."

"In that case, I'm certain it was not your mom ringing the doorbell." He breathed a sigh, smiled, and reached for the bottle of red.

They talked into the night. "No need to call a cab, you can sleep in the den," Alistair offered.

In the morning, Catherine put the water on for coffee.

"Good morning" — Father Larsen peeked around the corner from the den and hesitantly entered the kitchen. "You know, I have to admit something. When I was in bed last night, just as I pulled the covers to my chin, I heard the doorbell."

*

New York City, December 2004

Sofia pulled the curtains, and Andy slid a Guinness over to James. "You find a place yet?"

James laid out his bills and lifted the pint for a smooth draw. "No, I'm still looking."

"A Makers when you can," a voice said.

"Johnny, hey!" James greeted the new arrival.

"Hey, Jimmer, good to see you!"

Andy set a shot of Makers Mark in front of Johnny. "James here is recounting his homeless woes."

"Are you serious?"

"Yeah, I've been looking three months now."

"Where are you staying?"

"On the floor in my office at work."

"Damn!" Johnny threw back the shot.

It was rare to catch Johnny alone like this. He usually had two girls on his arm. He wasn't a Latino macho, not an Italian stallion, not a Wall Street hotshot slumming it in hip Brooklyn bars. He was a thirty something white man with no apparent means of living, intelligent, soft-spoken, slightly balding. But he had a sort of blond Kennedy look about him and a strong gentle face. And apparent or not, he had means enough to have a good time. James ran into him every now and then, brief conversations while waiting for a drink. Nobody called him *Jimmer*, but Johnny extended the nickname one day and James accepted it. A bond — imperceptible, infinitesimal — was formed.

"Cause I'm looking for someone," Johnny said. "One of my housemates is away for a couple of months. It's available right now, well, let's say in two days."

"How much?"

"Three hundred a month. It's tiny. Like a walk-in closet. We share the kitchen, bathroom, living room. Beats the floor at your office." Johnny motioned for another whiskey.

Temporary but cheap, and no more hiding at the Society. "Where is it?"

"Hope Street."

"Where's that?"

Johnny pointed over Andy's head, like he was pointing through the liquor-lined shelves that backed the bar. "Right over there. On the other side of the block."

And so it was. Every weekday morning January into spring, James fed Phoenix, showered, dressed for work, and stepped out the door onto Hope Street, dignified in the dress pants and button-down shirt that Universe Society etiquette demanded. *Yes, I'm living in Williamsburg near the Bedford stop,* he could say to anyone who asked. He wasn't homeless now, there was nothing to hide. Or not as much anyway.

And every weekday evening he dropped his briefcase at Hope Street, then walked around the block to Black Betty. He could even go home after a drink and then come back for another later if he wanted to. The bar that had been his favorite getaway now became, in every sense, his living room. Because the fact was, there was just too much going on at the walk-in closet loft. There were four guys, counting James. It was cramped. It was dirty. It was chaotic. Everyone was drinking and, except for James, doing a lot more. It was a frat house. James was thankful to have a shelter where he could come and go as he pleased with no questions asked, where he was a legitimate paying sublet. But it had to be, and it was, temporary.

*

He was settled in bed, the little bed that consumed two-thirds of his room. Had he been asleep? But the noise now! A door opening and slamming, a crashing sound, the voice of Eduardo, drunk and raving. Something he had noticed on moving into Hope. Eduardo was always angry just under the surface. He was fighting a war up there in his lofted bedroom, and probably everywhere he went.

Now James heard another voice. Johnny's voice, whispering a shout, "Shh! You're gonna wake the sublet!"

"Fuck the sublet!" louder than ever, and more crashing and raving.

*

Maybe tonight he could finally get a good night's sleep. The tiny room was cozy in a way. James undressed, climbed into bed, turned off the lamp on the shelf, and pulled up the sheet. Music and laughter, the sounds of a party, coming from somewhere else in the building, maybe down the hall? He didn't even know the layout, didn't know the neighbors, hardly knew his temporary housemates. He wished... No, it was better to be in bed.

A woman's voice softly called, "Kitty, kitty!" He opened his eyes a little.

In the dark of the tiny room, a meow, and the slender figure of a woman sitting on the bed next to him, hand out-stretched, reaching for Phoenix. The party had spilled into Johnny's loft, and one party goer had strayed into the small dark room, following the pretty gray and white cat. James lay naked under the covers. Wow, a girl. *What should I do? What could I say?* He said the only thing he could think of.

"Hi."

A high-pitched scream and he saw the blur of a woman's figure fly from the dark room. He shut his eyes tight. Why was it he never knew what to say to a girl?

*

April 2005

What was the date of that guy's return, when the temporary sublet would be over? There was even the possibility he might not come back. James had kept searching apartments. Every place in his price range was as bad as where he was right now.

"Hey Jimmer, listen, I need to tell you, Brad is coming back sooner than I thought, in about a week. You already paid your second month, so I'll prorate it and refund you the rest. Sorry it's kind of sudden. He's been with us a long time, you know, it's home to him." There was no room to bargain. Brad was coming back.

*

James stared at his computer screen at the Society. The apartment showings he had gone to so far, it was young people looking for somebody like them to help pay the rent and add some spice to the house. Then he'd walk in. Old enough to be their father. Most guys his age could afford their own place or had given up on the City and bled back into America's suburbs. He knew. He had been on the other side his first year in the City, advertising for sublets at Johnson Avenue. He wouldn't rent to his father's generation and neither would they. He was the new Mr. Frump. God fucking damn it.

And then, Phoenix moved out. It was the strangest thing, and James would puzzle over it for years to come. Arriving home from work one day, the final week at Hope Street, he found the door ajar. Their apartment opened not to the building's corridors but directly to the street. He walked inside, ready to ask his housemates if it was open for a reason or could he close it so Phoenix wouldn't get out. But nobody was home. He walked up and down the sidewalk calling Phoenix's name. That night he randomly opened the door to see if the little figure was standing there, to listen for the meow above the nearby hum of Interstate 278. Home from work the next day, he posted missing cat flyers, posted them on South First Street, and Second and Third, beyond the orbit of Grand to Metropolitan in a neighborhood that was still new to him. He gingerly approached people on door stoops. Had they seen a gray and white cat?

Four months on Hope Street, Phoenix had curled up beside him every night, stalked the tiny apartment by day.

Sorry man, I thought it clicked shut.

Why did Phoenix walk out? Why didn't he come back?

Maybe somebody took him in, I wouldn't worry about it, man.

*

During evening events at the Society, James picked up a glass of wine from the serving table and mingled with the members in the second floor lounge. He wanted to learn who they were, what expeditions they were planning, what it all meant to them. And they had stories to tell.

L.J., a wilderness trekker who was a Wall Street executive. "Back in college I was hiking in the Poconos. Not exactly the big league, but it taught me, a New Yorker born and bred, that there are places only your feet can take you. That still fascinates me. Up and down the Appalachian Trail. The Chilkoot Trail in Alaska. The Gobi Desert where they might call it a trail but you're thinking, Man are you sure about that? The hardest places to go, it's the body you were born with that gets you there. Yeah, after a plane ride around the world, but you see what I'm saying? I've always hiked solo. No crew. Just me and my feet!"

Kurz, a mountaineer who was a tech company CEO. "Climbing in thin air at high altitudes, you take a step, breathe three breaths, take another step, breath three breaths, take another step. You don't speed up because you're

JOHN & ELIZABETH CLAY

excited or slow down because you're tired. You don't think about how far you still have to go. You just think about the next step, and the next three breaths, and that's how you get to the top."

*

Open up Craigslist in the browser, search Housing, take a breath, search Housing. He leaned back from the computer in his fourth-floor office, morning sun through the diamond-paned leaded glass windows. He was living at the Society again.

He dug his cell phone from his briefcase under the desk. Time for professional help. Contacts, Jeanette. She used to jump onto a bar stool at Black Betty and talk nonstop in that pretty voice. He basked in her beauty, her dark hair, the flash of her dark brown eyes. She was in real estate now, a licensed agent.

"Preferably in Williamsburg but it could be anywhere with an easy commute to the Upper East Side, no more than seven hundred fifty a month..."

"Seven hundred fifty?"

"Yeah, but every place I find it's a group of people and they have a very specific idea of who they're looking for and I just can't find a place." Now he was nonstop.

"Okay, let me see what's listed and see how we can work this."

When they talked again, she had a plan. "Everything at seven-fifty is what you've already seen. You really need to go to nine hundred and up."

"My old place at Johnson Avenue, I paid seven hundred fifty a month..."

"There's nothing at seven-fifty, you told me that, and that's what I'm seeing in the listings."

"Yeah...okay let's say a maximum of nine hundred and see what we come up with." James wanted to sound a little like he was still in charge of his destiny, but he wasn't. The New York real estate market was.

*

On a May afternoon, a Latino man about James' own age greeted him at the entrance to 99 Morgan Avenue in Bushwick, Brooklyn, seven long months and five short blocks from the Johnson Avenue disaster where the troubles had begun. The ground floor of the building was shared with the Velasquez Convenience Store and across the street was a metalworks called Century

278

Overhead Door Incorporated and a truckers diner pragmatically named Deli Restaurant.

"You must be James? I'm Enrique. You have trouble finding your way?"

"No, I actually used to live near here, just down Johnson Avenue."

"Great, come on in, I'll show you the place. It's all painted fresh."

The keys jangled in the door to apartment One-L, end of the hall on the ground floor. Enrique swung the door open. "I've been doing a lot of work around here lately. I want to make it nice, you know?"

It was like magic: Raise your maximum from seven hundred fifty to nine hundred a month, and the next day you can walk into a clean, secure apartment that's just for you, no housemates, no trying to show young rocker boys you won't be a drag, or convince young rocker girls that you won't be a creep. One room, twelve by twenty feet, with two tall windows at the end by the eat-in kitchen. A new refrigerator, oven with stove top, sink, plenty of cabinets. And just enough space for James' small sofa, writing desk, mattress, and bookshelves. The only other room was the bathroom — clean, in good working order, with still more cabinets. Like magic.

*

The four walls of the studio apartment on Morgan Avenue contained all he needed anymore. Except internet. The first month he had only his flip phone to connect to the world, and something new happened. At the end of the workday, instead of Black Betty, he took the subway to Morgan Avenue. There was something irresistible about arriving home entirely unburdened of the affairs of the outside world. He made a simple dinner of boiled rice and canned soup, he read as he ate and continued reading until he was ready for bed. Paul Auster's *Collected Prose*. Czeslaw Milosz's *To Begin Where I Am*. And as the summer heat rose, W.G. Sebald's *On the Natural History of Destruction*. It was a hot summer — June, July, August, September all hotter than normal. No record longest-ever heatwaves. Just hot, hot, hot, hot months that didn't break until October. As the days simmered and the nights became dark heat, no relief, the old brick building became an oven and the apartment felt unsafe. The bars on the windows barred the hope of installing an air-conditioner. Those sickeningly hot nights he showered in cold water as soon as he was home from work and then rose in the night, one or two o'clock, to shower again. On weekends he roamed from coffee shop to book store to anywhere air-conditioned. There was something about heat that thrilled him. A long echo of the years in Ghana and Venezuela. But when the heat resounds within the concrete world of the City, then something else happens. You pass into discomfort, then fatigue, and then into another world. He read Sebald's descriptions of German cities incandescent under waves of incendiary bombs as the Allies closed in on victory over the Nazi Reich. A world come to a place no one wanted, no one hoped for. Even as people said they wanted one thing, their actions, their actual choices seemed to pull in another direction. Recuperation of the anti. No wonder the postmodernists imagined an unseeable unsayable unchanging code that exists nowhere but governs everywhere. Was he already succumbing to the heat? Home from wandering the City, he absorbed the stunning relief of a cold shower, lay naked on his mattress, and closed his eyes.

*

"There's a box came for you. I put it in your office," Raymond said as James walked into the Society.

He lifted the heavy cardboard box from his desk. *Science and Society* journal. Finally. There was a note from the editor and fifteen complimentary copies. Volume 70, Number 3. "The Deep Difference between Labor and Use-Value, James Crossland." His article was published, nationally published. It wasn't his theory. It was his correction of another author's misinterpretation of Marx's theory of value. This was the first time he had ever been published. In a kind of dream he opened an HTML file and keyed in the title for the latest report, just in. *Medallion Number 47, Ancient Signs of Cyanobacteria.*

*

Minneapolis, May 2005

Morning had been such fun marching down Bloomington Avenue in the May Day Parade, colorful costumes, fiddles and brass, cow bells ringing, the crowds waving from the curb. Olivia in her homemade papier-mâché owl mask swooped her feathered wings as Catherine pushed Leo in the stroller. He reached for Olivia with every swoop. They fell asleep in the car on the way home and after Catherine lay them down for their naps, she picked up where she had left off with her mother. Whenever she could, in the five years since finding Mary, she squeezed these moments into the tiny spaces of her day. With the address book entries all transcribed, she had started making calls. Sometimes she got through. Elodie Arquette. *Mary cared for me like an older sister would.* Sometimes she didn't get through. Alan Bing, Truro, Massachusetts. *The number you have dialed has been disconnected.* But underneath Alan Bing was another entry. Joseph Bing, Kansas City, Missouri. Mary's letter had said...*The wind rises and falls in the last grip of winter as you drive into spring. Kansas City.* Was Joseph a brother, a father? She dialed. "I'm Catherine Lind, the daughter of Mary Zadora." She explained how Mary had placed a child for adoption before moving to Provincetown, and that she was that child. That Mary and Alan had known each other in Provincetown. That because Mary had died before Catherine found her, she hoped to talk with Alan to learn more about her mother.

Joseph seemed receptive to her story. "Alan is in New York City," he said. "He's at home caring for his six-month-old daughter. Give him a call. He'll be happy to talk with you."

She dialed Alan. "Mary, wow," he said. His voice was expressive, a storyteller's voice, with a hint of a southern accent. "Yes, yes, I think she told me about you, a soul born of her soul."

"Going through her things I came upon a photograph of a man who I think might be you, and a letter she wrote to you after you'd left Provincetown."

"Provincetown..." There was silence like a rush of memories flooding in. "We had some special times together, at the Shrine, the space of all creations, my place in Truro, jamming, sharing music, the music of life. She was a good soul. Special times." He spoke as if he were in a dream. She heard a baby's cry in the background. "That's Henny. Henny's awake," he said. "My little girl! I've got to go, but give me your email address."

*

The woman in the mirror sported a short bob, almost boyish. She shut her eyes. In any one battle of words she could outmaneuver him — the professional arguer, the attorney. Her practical logic was her defense. But over the years, as she tried to make it all work out, had she given in and given up more than she realized? She opened her eyes reluctantly. How much of herself had she let him trim away?

*

Catherine opened her laptop on the kitchen island. An email from Alan. *Mary was a friend and a lover who possessed a fierce inner spirit and a huge appetite for life. May she be up there with her kin, free of pain, laughing, loving, and meditating. Warm regards, Alan.*

With his words still making paths through her mind, she picked up the *City Pages.* Her horoscope, Sagittarius.

Your soul's epic journey is in the midst of a plot twist that's so complicated and beautiful. Among the many opportunities you now have, these are the most spectacular: 1. The possibility of making your existing problems more interesting than they've ever been; 2. The possibility of attracting fresh challenges more stimulating and useful than your same old predictable dilemmas.

*

Fragments of life, a drawing, raw emotion scrawled sideways in a sketchbook, a memory shared by a stranger at the other end of the phone line. A picture was forming, swirling in her head. She dashed it out on a writing pad on the kitchen island.

She was an artist, in tune and offbeat.
She was the life of the party, outrageous, intense, reckless.
She had it all.
She was Gypsy, nomad, tracker.
She was lost, had lost, and was found, a little too late.
Sexy, lover, loved, she was a battered mistress.
A true friend, kind, soulful, willful, she was a child.
But whose?
She might have been your child or your sister.
She was my mother.

*

White cumulous clouds tinged pink floated lazily across a deep blue sky. Arms stretched, Olivia pushed Leo in the stroller, holding onto the rim of the lower compartment, zig-zagging along the sidewalk. Catherine laughed as she guided the stroller away from the hedges — "A little more this way Sweetpea" — and she tucked the locks of dark curls behind Olivia's ears. The leaves of the elms and oaks conversed in the summer breeze and Catherine heard Leo giggling and she could see, as plain as the clouds above, her mother trotting, skipping, almost dancing beside the stroller, her smile embracing the wild little driver and giggling passenger, her gaze rising to Catherine's waiting eyes. As long as they kept walking she could hold onto the vision. She wished the park were a lifetime away.

*

Double adoption. The severing of child from mother, two generations in a row. Erasure. Stroke by stroke. She called Helen at Catholic Services in Saint Paul. "I want to find my mother's birth parents, or any living relative. How can I do that?"

Helen explained that just as Catherine's birth mother was named in Catherine's adoption record, so too Mary's mother — and maybe father though it was unlikely — would be named in Mary's record. Catholic Services in Sandusky would have that record. That was where to start.

But it was a false start. "I'm not sure what's wrong, Helen, but Catholic Services says they don't keep those records. They're sending me to Ohio Vital Statistics."

"Catholic Services Sandusky keeps the adoption records, just like we do. I'm sorry Catherine. I wish they weren't taking that stance, but I'm not shocked. There's a lot of that kind of thinking — lock the records and throw away the key."

*

"Fairy is swimming in the lake," Olivia's hand inside the fish puppet dove into the sequin fabric lake on the family room carpet where her smallest stuffed animals, the *Littlests*, floated. Leo gummed the pink and white stuffed fish as he watched in fascination. Catherine punched the number into the phone.

"Vital Statistics," a woman's voice answered.

"Yes, hello. This is Catherine Lind, and I would like to request a copy of my mother's original birth certificate."

"Usually it's the adopted person asking for their own records."

Catherine explained that Mary was deceased, and that she was Mary's daughter. "Her adoption records are open. She was born in 1948."

"Do you have some identification that shows you share the same name, a birth certificate, or driver's license?"

Catherine hesitated. "But we don't have the same last name."

"If you're married, your birth certificate will still show your maiden name."

'I can't, well it doesn't, because I'm adopted too."

"Well then, that's different." The clerk fumbled over her words "I'm not sure...we've ever encountered this situation before." A pause. "Without a document showing your linkage to her, you cannot have access to her records."

"I have been advised that deceased people do not have privacy rights."

"But you have no linkage to her."

"No linkage?" Catherine's chest flushed hot. "I have her pocket book with her Social Security card and driver's license in the den. Her paintings are hanging on the walls in my living room. Do you understand? She is my mother."

*

Catherine pulled the car into the alley behind the house on Edmund Boulevard, gave the gas an extra punch to surge over the alley's ice ridges and into the garage. Olivia whooped with delight, "Do it again Mom!" Leo smiled ear to ear. Olivia scrambled out to the yard and Leo followed as Catherine brought in the first load of groceries and set them on the family room floor. She hurried back outside. "Olivia?" There was no answer. Leo, struggling to hoist himself to the swing, echoed, "Livia?" Catherine called again, "Olivia, say yes Mom."

"Yes Mom," Olivia's voice called out from behind the big elm tree.

On the kitchen wall the answering machine was flashing.

As she listened to the message she could hardly comprehend the words she was hearing. The warm voice of an older woman. *Hi Sarah, it's Mary, I've got the coffee on, whenever you want to come over.* She played the message again. Sarah. It was what Mary called her.

*

Catherine opened an email from Alan.

Sad news. My wife Susanna has left New York for Charleston, South Carolina. She took our daughter, Henny, with her. We are separated. Our marriage has been rocky for a while, but the loss of my daughter to such distance is something I can hardly bear and hardly believe. I will visit her whenever I can. With a sad heart, I remain in New York alone and continue the quest to get my books published. — Alan

Dear Alan, Even as your life changes, remember that a daughter loves her dad, always. — Catherine

*

At Rainbow Chinese Restaurant on Nicollet Avenue in Minneapolis, Catherine opened her fortune:

Many people fail because they quit too soon.

*

January 2006

"Hiya," Lulu answered Catherine's call.

"I'm going to search for my birth father."

"But he wasn't named right? How can you find him? You've already been on a wild ride finding your mother. Are you sure you can handle all this so quickly?"

"I've been waiting thirty-six years." Outside the kitchen window a flurry of snow gusted from the roof. "I'm not afraid of my own story."

"Gumption, like I said the first day we met. Well if you do find him, you've gotta write a book. Nobody could make this up."

*

Her mother and father. She was beginning to understand that they weren't in a relationship. It was the free-love 1960s, the era Catherine's eighth grade Social Studies teacher Mr. Callahan must have harkened back to every time he sat on the edge of his desk in his gray plaid slacks and yellow polo shirt and scolded the class as they sat bewildered: *All you kids like these days is sex, and drugs, and rock and roll* — with an emphasis on the three evils, his wiry salt and pepper curls jiggling. Surely it was the same scolding his own generation had endured, though his scolding always ended with the hint of a grin. It was Mary's generation, everyone was in the groove and on the make. But ultimately she was one of the unlucky ones who got pregnant. Catherine understood the devastation, what a fix Mary would have been in. Abortion was illegal. She had to tell her parents. And Catherine knew that if she were in that fix herself, telling her parents would feel impossible, with impossible consequences.

*

Under the covers, her journal propped on her knees, the pages scratched with notes. Lulu was right. How could she find him without a name? She had searched Mary's sketchbooks and found nothing. She had asked everyone who knew Mary. She had even searched the 1969 Dayton University yearbook and contacted Mary's dorm mates. No one knew. There were no leads, except that her father likely crossed paths with Mary at Dayton. She tried to imagine another way to go about it, some way that might provide a clue.

She was sleepy. The kids were in bed. Alistair was still in his office down the hall. She set the journal on the nightstand and turned off the bedside lamp. She pulled the covers up to her chin to seal out the cold. So tired, her eyelids could no longer resist the weight, she drifted into sleep and dream.

Mary knelt at her bedside, brushed Catherine's forehead with a kiss. In a tender voice she said, "Your father died. He's not here anymore." Mary placed a photograph in Catherine's hands. "You can see what he looked like."

He was in a chair, bending down, concentrating on something, unaware of the camera, his image frozen in that moment. He was slim but muscular. His hair was a lighter brown and straighter than her own but parted on the same side. She and her father shared the same broad nose and dark eyes. She and her father....

She drew a breath. Eyes open, she sat up on the edge of the bed, awake, breathing. She looked at her hands, just her empty hands. *Something she and her father shared. Imagine another way to go about it.*

*

New York City, March 2006

The staff survived another Universe Society Annual Dinner at the Ritz-Carlton. Today, Sunday, was the Annual Meeting and Report to the Board of Directors. James took his turn at the podium, the directors and some hundred or so Society members waiting jovially for the next recitation of statistics and successes.

But there was no denying it. The vibe was different this year. Connor's term as president was coming to an end and a new president would be elected by the end of the day. The committee chairs could feel the sand shifting under their feet. They were anxious to show they were high performers worthy to continue their duties under a new regime. The unease trickled down. James could feel it. Surely everything would fall into place after the succession was complete.

*

Minneapolis, June 2006

Catherine, Our divorce is now in progress. We will share joint custody. But what does that mean when Henny's so far away? I thank the gods for several really tight friends I can lean on here in the City. I am within months of finishing a novel years in the works. Have you started your book about Mary? — Alan

Alan, Separation from a child is beyond words. I know you'll find a way to stay connected with Henny. My book? Standing in the way is my horticulture final project. I'll be finished this time next year. Beyond that, I'm not really sure how to begin! — Catherine

Catherine, Read a handful of memoirs to get your bearing. But your story is all your own. I always write my best stuff by hand. I once drove to Saint Louis just to see Beckett's notebooks. How to start a book? You start by writing a sentence. One fucking sentence. The first draft should be wild and completely uncensored. Later you edit. Tone down what you might be embarrassed about — or not. But every sentence must be careful and precise. That's how a good book is made. — Alan

*

Seven-thirty and time to rise because it was Saturday. Every Saturday all summer long Catherine visited the Minnesota Landscape Arboretum, taking photographs of plants for the final project of her master's degree.

Alistair stood at the door, Leo on his hip, Olivia's arm wrapped around his leg. A clean diaper sprouted from his shirt pocket. "No more than four hours and back by one o'clock" — he said — "including the drive."

River Road, its iron-red pavement winding through oak savanna along the steep wooded bank that plummets to the currents of the ancient Mississippi. She recalled the cold spring mornings four years ago, right after Olivia was born, when Peter Ganz marched the *Woody Landscape Plants* class at a swift pace around the arboretum, identifying trees and shrubs in every nook and cranny. *Look at the bark. Learn the patterns. Ash trees have diamond-shaped bark and hackberry is warty.* He taught them to stand at a distance, *Look at the form. Is it a vase-shaped elm or pyramidal poplar?* It seemed forever ago that Olivia, just three months old, looked up from her blanket on the family room floor, while Catherine gently tapped her feet together in rhythm, singing a song of Latin tree names. *Gleditsia tricanthus inermus, Juglans nigra, Eleagnus angustifolia!*

Eight-fifteen on the dashboard clock as she turned into the arboretum gates and flashed her student ID. Up the little hill past the lilacs, the narrow paved road wound around the tulips and tall grasses, rock gardens and edibles. No visitors in sight, only an occasional gardener watering. A gentle incline to the sprawling swamp white oak tree standing at the peak of the hill, its great long branches resting on the ground, surely a contender for national champion. And finally down the hill to the parking lot by the woodlands.

The wood-chipped path under her feet led her into the forested garden of the woodlands, the air cool and damp. The cottonwood trees with their deeply grooved bark towered above. *King of the Forest,* Ganz called them. Beneath the branching canopy, she scanned the forest floor for dainty maidenhair fern. "There" — she whispered —"Adiantum capillus-veneris." She kneeled and took the shot.

A jolt of fear. *Has Leo wandered away somewhere? Was Olivia eating something she shouldn't?* She sighed, they're home with Alistair. Her motherly instincts. You can't just turn it off. Above green leaves covered the sky, hints of blue peeking through.

The narrow dirt paths weaved through the woodlands among asters, euphorbia, and cup plant, her favorite. Tall as Catherine they stood in crowds in the sunlight where the forest canopy opened to sky, topped with clusters of sunflowers, like yellow top hats. Their giant leaves in opposite pairs met at the stem forming a cup where rainwater collected and birds and insects drank. Well designed. She leaned close, very still, and photographed the water pooled in the cup.

The morning sun had warmed the car and she drove Three Mile Drive, elbow resting on the opened window, winding along the narrow road past the shrub walk, the larch trees, the azalea trial gardens to the Nut Grove.

Golf-ball sized nuts turned her ankles as she climbed the shady hill beneath butternut, buckeye, and horse chestnut up to the crest where she emerged to sunlight and windswept grasses. Across the valley on a distant hill stood a farm with red barn and out buildings. Someday she would paint it, acrylic on canvas, but that wasn't part of the life she lived now. The sun was high. She had to get back.

The clock on the dashboard read twelve-thirty. She put in a CD, The Jayhawks, *Waiting for the Sun.* Mark Olson's harmonica and Gary Louris' lyrical voice filled the car and flowed out the open windows, her seatbelt flapping in the wind as she cruised the highway. She turned it up and sang.

*

On the way to Montessori school that morning Catherine and Olivia drove passed a lawn sprinkler, water glistening in the morning light. *Mom, a rainbow!* Olivia's voice exclaimed from the back seat, *I see the beauty you don't have time to see!*

Catherine walked Olivia to the main door and watched her skip down the hall to her classroom in her favorite dress, denim with seven pockets. She pulled the car onto River Road. September. The river bank was just taking on fall color. No she wasn't going home just yet. Alistair had the baby monitor on his desk. He would hear if Leo woke up. She pulled into the lot across from Olivia's school. At the edge of the high bank above the Mississippi River, Catherine grasped the railing and peered through the trees, deep into the woods where pale yellow leaves mingled among great curving trunks leaning for sunlight. Her own stillness revealed the woods' never-ending motion. Leaves fluttered like the roll of maracas. And with a subtlety only things of nature possess, the exfoliating bark of the birch trees peeled back from the trunks in curls, too slow for the human eye to see. Slight variations caught her eye. A brightly lit yellow leaf, almost transparent in the sunlight, while others in deep shadow blended together in muted color. Brush strokes and composition formed in her mind.

*

"The stroke isn't something you're doing, it's about the subject telling you what it needs — feather-light there, heavy there, heavier, give me more!" Cal loved to talk about painting when Catherine brought the kids over for a playdate. While Alistair and Cheri were following the rule of law at work, she and Cal talked about art, how there were no rules, you had limitless freedom to do whatever you needed to do to express your subject.

The last time she had painted was thirteen years ago. On the floor in her one-bedroom apartment upstairs from Alistair, she had painted a watercolor scene from a page of her 1993 calendar, a red barn and winter foliage covered in snow. A Christmas gift for Mom and Dad.

*

Bohemian Flats, the grassy lowland along River Road on the West Bank of the Mississippi. Leo strained against the straps of his car seat, eyes steady on his target, and when Catherine opened the car door wide and released him, he ran wild, arms outstretched, to the flock of Canadian geese. The geese waddled, honked, and spread their wings. Head tilted back, blonde waves almost to his shoulders, mouth open, he watched as they took to the sky.

*

With an eight by ten inch canvas before her, acrylic paint, a pencil, a cardboard palette, and brushes, she sat on the bed and began. Paint on the bed. She knew it was a bad idea and was glad Alistair wasn't there. Leo was napping, Olivia was in her bedroom watching Rubber Dubbers. All was quiet. She penciled the scene, the wooded riverbank across from Olivia's school. She squeezed raw umber onto the palette, then crimson, cadmium yellow, white, and touched the brush to the paint, working umber into crimson. Then brush to canvas, she made her mark.

*

New York City, August 2006

I'm not sure what's going to happen at the Society, James wrote to Kelly. *The new management is talking about increasing efficiency. Everyone is wondering if layoffs are coming. Nice forty-fourth birthday present, huh? I think my job is needed, but I guess everybody thinks that until they get the pink slip. A friend of mine, a Society member, suggested I volunteer my web skills for an international school here in the City where he serves on the board. It could be a stepping stone to a new job, if I need it.*

*

James nodded to Andy, steadied himself with a hand on the bar as he stepped toward the restroom door, opened it. There was Eddie, doing a deal. His customer looked up, caught in the act. "It's okay," Eddie said. "It's just James."

*

Minneapolis, September 2006

"He says I'm forgetting my obligations, as if it's some kind of contract, but life isn't a court case, it isn't that straight forward." Catherine held the receiver to her ear at the kitchen island. "I just don't know how to help him understand. It feels like we're only getting farther apart."

"Now slow it down," Lulu said. "Tell me what's going on."

"When I found Mary, I finally found myself. But the more I embrace who I am, the more conflict I'm having with Alistair."

"Catherine, there are some big things changing in your life, and probably in his too. Maybe you just need some help finding your way through this. What would you think of trying marriage counseling?"

"It sounds like the perfect court room for Alistair to argue his case."

"I understand your fears. But I just have to say, counseling really helped me and Derrick. Why not give it a chance?"

*

Catherine gazed up to the waiting room ceiling three stories high. She and Alistair had been in marriage counseling for a month now. She wished she could tell Mom and Dad, but she didn't want to make them worry.

She opened her notebook to the homework assignment from the last session:

What are your household cleaning standards, as if you were on your own?

1. I am okay with clothes on the chair.

2.

3.

She couldn't bring herself to finish the assignment. Counseling was for both of them, but when Alistair brought up the housecleaning, she knew exactly what he was doing, turning the focus from himself to Catherine. She would be the one who had to change her behavior.

The glass door to the waiting room swung open. It was Alistair. They had driven separately, he from a client, she from dropping the kids off at Cal's. She watched now as he walked to a chair on the opposite side of the room and sat down, crossing one leg over the other. He didn't look at her. He rarely did anymore. Maybe he didn't recognize her since she'd started growing her hair out. He stared into his cell phone, tapping, tapping. And when it rang, he stood and walked right past her, eyes steady on the door, and stepped out to the foyer.

Upstairs Catherine sat on the love seat. The therapist kept the conversation neutral — "Fall is in the air today!" — until Alistair appeared with a knock on the door. "So sorry, I was on a work call." He sat in the chair across the room.

The therapist rolled toward them in her swivel chair, "How have things been going? Did you complete your assignment from last session?"

Catherine focused, determined to make herself understood. "Maybe we have different ideas about cleaning but this really isn't about the cleaning, it's bigger than that. It's about giving each other space to be who we are. I'd like to talk about that."

The therapist swiveled to Alistair, "What do you think, does that sound like a good idea?"

He straightened himself in his chair. "Well, I think keeping house is a significant issue," he said with a sense of concern. "But I'm willing to talk about both."

After a lengthly discussion about the housecleaning, Catherine brought the conversation back to her concerns. "Finding my birth mother has led me in new directions. I've come to realize that something was missing from my life, making art. It fulfills me."

Alistair looked to the therapist and shook his head, his mop of hair falling across his furrowed eyebrows. The therapist intervened, "Could you give Alistair a sense of what you're asking him to do?"

"I'd like you to give me the freedom to make art, and to be supportive, not just tolerate it."

Alistair shot a glance at the therapist, who looked to Catherine and said, "I think it would be difficult to find someone who would be comfortable with that lifestyle."

Catherine was incensed. Where was the impartial approach? The therapist was verbalizing for Alistair. All he had to do was dramatically whip his head in her direction and she was stating his case.

The therapist rolled her chair toward Catherine. "For your next homework assignment, I want you to define your idea of freedom, but choose a different word."

*

Catherine crossed the liquor store parking lot, a six-pack of Newcastle in her hand. She hopped in the driver's seat and pulled onto Lake Street toward the setting sun. A straight shot to Cal's. The bright gold of the boulevard hackberries echoed the setting sun. Fiery red hearts topped the maples. Color took flight in the wind. She crossed Blaisdell, just a few blocks from her first apartment where she made the garden. Lyndale, where she and Alistair bought their first duplex, on into Uptown where she'd worked at Applause Records, and over the lagoon between Lake of the Isles and Lake Calhoun.

Why don't you come over some night, I'd love your thoughts on some of my paintings, he had said on the last playdate.

She pulled into the driveway of the 1930's cottage. Evening was near, there was a chill, and heavy dark clouds loomed in the west behind the house. Cal appeared on the stoop, his long arm holding the door open wide, his sandy-blond hair pleasantly mussed. She passed beneath his arm and into the living room. Inside they embraced with the usual peck on the lips. The living room, which normally looked like a page from *Architectural Digest Magazine,* was cleared of furniture, the coordinating upholstered pieces shoved against the wall. "Sure looks different in here."

"Better for viewing the paintings from a distance," he said.

She presented the six pack.

"Just what I needed," he said and opened a pair of bottles.

"Where's Cheri and the kids?"

"At the cabin for the weekend." He took a swig.

Not what she expected, an evening alone with Cal. What would Cheri think? And what if Alistair found out?

She settled onto the kid-size stool and examined the paintings. "This one of Lake Harriet with the trees, it's a little hard to tell the foreground from the background. Maybe if you darkened the trees in the lower left, it would bring them forward a bit."

He sat on the floor beside her and contemplated. "I think you're right. I'll give that a try."

"In the painting of the rose gardens, the brush strokes give you the sense the leaves and petals are flipping in the wind. That's a nice technique."

He smiled, "You make good observations, as an artist would." He leaned back on his elbows. "Being an artist comes with a lifestyle, but some people try to live the lifestyle without actually being an artist. They dress exotic and walk around acting like they have something special going on, but really, there's nothing happening. But you" — he looked at Catherine — "you're a real artist."

"My mother Mary was too. She was a painter."

"I bet you're a lot like her." His eyes lingered a moment. "Should we move to the screened porch? I'll make us some tea."

She followed, pausing in front of his waterlily canvas in the dining room, three by four feet, reminiscent of Monet but rendered in Cal's signature impasto brush strokes.

"You want a little honey?" he asked, peeking his head around the kitchen doorway.

She flushed a moment, then sorted out his words. "Please." She stepped down the single step into the little screened porch and settled into the wicker chair by the window. The porch had always been just the way to the backyard, the kids stampeding through, she a step behind and Cal a step ahead, turning on the sprinkler, playing, chasing among scattered toys and beach balls. But tonight it was different, a space all its own. She opened the window a crack and leaned close to peer through the screen into the black night. Closing her eyes, she listened to the soft fall of raindrops. A mist laden breeze washed across her and with it a memory. The gentle rumble of thunder that drew her from her childhood bed. On top of her desk at the double windows, arms wrapped around her knees, she listened to the rain fall, how it grew louder when the wind picked up and rushed along the curb beneath the streetlamp, lightning tracing a jagged line behind a distant stand of trees.

Cal handed her a steaming black tea and took a seat across the coffee table in the dim light. She wrapped her hands around the warm cup.

"One more thing," he said and hopped from his chair. He returned with a candle and bent to his knee. She watched him strike the match, its hiss and burst of flame tapering to a steady flicker as he cupped his hand and touched it to the wick, the flame composing a scene of moving shadows around them. "Your eyes are beautiful in the candlelight."

She avoided his eyes, green like the sea. "Are you still playing with your band?"

"Now and then we get together and jam, but we're not writing new songs any more."

"We've been listening in the car to the cassette you gave me. Leo likes it. He says, 'Turn Cal on, turn Cal on!'"

He chuckled. "That's cute."

"There's this one song where you know you're not following your dreams," she said.

"Yeah," He shifted in his chair. "It was back when Cheri and I were dating. There was a lot of conflict and after a while, well, you know how she is, so I took off in my car and started driving. I didn't even care where I was going. I just needed to get away."

"I know you two have been through this before. So where do things stand, are you following your dreams?"

"Well, with this new series of paintings I've done at the lake, I made a lot of sales the first summer and Cheri seemed supportive, but then things slowed down and just last weekend she moved everything in my studio out to the garage. She said she has plans for the room and doesn't want me painting in there anymore."

"The nerve."

"Hey, do you want to go downstairs and listen to some music?"

"Sure."

Downstairs he took out some paper and a bud, "Do you want a hit?"

"Why not!"

He lit the joint. Smoke swirled around his head and his cheeks pulled tight as he took a hit then passed it to her. The cherry still burning brightly, she took a little hit, held it and exhaled. With a wrinkle of his eyes and a curl at his lips, he took another, moved closer. As he slowly exhaled, the smoke streamed gently toward her. She leaned in, taking the smoke into her mouth. They burst into smokey, choking laughter.

"Come on, let's put on some music," he said.

He strummed along with The Beatles on his guitar. Sitting side by side on the floor, backs against the couch, they sang, he *Hello,* she *Goodbye.* She watched him strum. He grinned, buckling over his guitar in laughter. *Hello. Goodbye.*

The night flowed so innocently from one thing to the next. He wrapped his arms around her and, like children playing, they fell to the floor rolling and laughing. His body pressed against her. He was hard and a zing of electricity ran through her. There had always been comfort and ease to their friendship, and she always suspected there was more. The evening of art and music and laughter could continue into daylight. She looked at the clock — two in the morning! *How will I ever explain this to Alistair?*

Buckled into the driver's seat, she waved to Cal in the open doorway, pushed the key into the ignition, and breathed in deeply, trying to ground herself. With a last glance to Cal, she backed out of the driveway and sped down the road.

The electricity. She felt alive again. All of her senses peaked, like there was possibility around every corner. She had never meant to settle for a marriage without it. But somehow it had happened. Tonight the idea of settling went up in flames. She needed real love, real understanding. And real sex. She wasn't the kind of person to have two lives going at the same time, a boyfriend alongside a husband. Though that's exactly what this would look like to Alistair. She hoped he would be asleep, that he wouldn't know, and that she wouldn't have to explain.

*

New York City, October 2006

James walked through the lobby and waved good morning to Raymond at reception. "James, James. You'd better check your email. Or better yet, stop into Saanvi's office. She'll give you the news."

James stepped back. "What are you talking about?"

"You know she'd have kept you on if she could."

*

Kelly was quiet on the other end of the line.

"It's not like I'm the only one," James said.

"This happens everywhere," she said. "Workplaces change. The real question is, so what now? Will you try to find something else there in New York, or...?"

"Oh, yeah," he said. "There are plenty of possibilities. I'm still volunteering at the international school. And I know the editor at *Audubon* and the copy chief at *Scientific American*. They know I'm looking for work." He paused. "Though they're coming up with zip so far."

*

"James..." Almost out the door, he set his hand on the back of a Black Betty dinner chair to steady himself, and turned. Andy, the big ring of keys in his hand, was staring straight at him. "Watch your back. Okay?"

James nodded, he knew to be careful, nice of Andy all the same. He stepped out into the lamplit dark of a city night long gone. Morning not yet in sight. Empty streets. He walked Metropolitan to Bushwick Avenue, passed Maujer Street, the four-story brick apartments. Passed Scholes and Meserole. Onto Johnson Avenue, close to Morgan now. A sound of plodding footfalls, unseen behind him, faster, his shoulder gripped hard, "Don't move!" the whispered shout, blunt metal pressed against his neck, "Gimme the bag, gimme the bag," James fumbled to unhitch his briefcase strap, suddenly shaken sober, and it was ripped away, "Get on the ground. Face down!" *Is getting down dying?* Metal against his neck. *Or is making a move to run dying?* He got on the ground. "Stay down, don't get up!" Receding footfalls. He glanced up. Mind awake, racing. His bag was on the sidewalk, emptied and flung away. Where he lay he watched the male figure in the distance look back before rounding the corner. James stayed completely still. *Had the figure seen him watching?* He leapt up, grabbed his bag, ran away, down Johnson Avenue, field of vision shaking up and down the three long blocks to Morgan.

*

Minneapolis, October 2006

Alan, We're in marriage counseling and so far it's only making matters worse. You asked for a picture of me. It's attached, and one of Mary too. — Catherine

Catherine, Step by step, I know you'll find your way. Seeing the pictures, Lord Almighty, I'm blown away at the similarities. Mother and daughter. You're on one hell of a journey. Few things in life lend themselves to seamlessness. Your mom lived very spur of the moment. And maybe the narrative of your book will be a bit like that. Later tonight there is a Jewish singles charity event at a hip club. Oh my fucking god. Maybe I'm not over the hill yet. — Alan

*

"I want you to support me in renting an art studio."

The look on Alistair's face, eyes wide, mouth dropped opened. "And I suppose you're going to tell me it's in Cal's building?"

"My own studio," Catherine interrupted. "You agreed to it in therapy, to allow space for my art since it's hard to find space at home."

"You're drifting further and further away. You can't deny it! I keep trying to reel you in, but you won't have it."

"Alistair, I'm not a fish and you can't put me in your tank."

"Blimey, is this the new Catherine?"

"It's the old Catherine, the one who lived in the apartment upstairs from you."

*

New York City, December 2006

As Salvation Army bell ringers claimed their lawful sections of frigid Manhattan sidewalk and panhandlers found refuge in heated subway cars, a job offer. Short-term, but real work all the same. Copyediting Alan's novel.

Friday night, James wrote. *I'll meet you to pick up the manuscript at five o'clock at Solas, on Ninth Street between Second and Third Avenues. It's an Irish bar with a wide selection of whiskeys. I will do my best to make your one-week turnaround.*

Friday is good, Alan answered. *I cut out an engagement tonight to wrap up the last three pages — a dense Kabbalah thing. Solas, five o'clock. Scotch mandatory.*

Everything about it was right. He was working with Alan who had been his first important contact in New York. Alan, who so often seemed to be in the clouds, did pretty good work as a guardian angel. And there was more. James never would have imagined himself copyediting fiction, but the fact was, he had read as many novels in the last year as in his entire lifetime before — Paul Auster's *Book of Illusions,* Michael Ondaatje's *Coming through Slaughter,* Chinua Achebe's *Anthills of the Savannah....* Embodied within every novel was the proposition that, whether or not these things actually happened, this is how the world works. It was as though he had to ground himself in reality for the first forty-four years of life before he could hope to find the reality in fiction.

Five days in, the one-week turnaround looked questionable. James had divided the manuscript's total pages by seven days and sat at his tiny fold-down kitchen table every day all day and into the night. There was no such place as Black Betty. Her siren call inaudible above the crazed dialogues of Alan's improbable characters. It was thrilling to be working like this. But the daily page count seemed impossible.

Hey Alan. I am now aiming for Sunday, December 17. It is a big chunk of writing, so I won't rule out the possibility of going longer. My marks are blue, and there are plenty of them. Mostly little punctuation or spelling matters. The big formless dress, for example, is correctly called a muumuu. Who would have thought?

*

Minneapolis, December 8, 2006

For forty-five minutes last night — Catherine wrote Alan— *l sat at Blue Moon Coffee on East Lake Street and wrote the first page of the book. It came easily. Whether it ends up in the book or not, who knows? It's about starting. Happy birthday Mary!*

Starting is the hardest part, Alan answered. *And the other hardest part is finishing. Now that it's begun, chomp down onto it like a ferocious starving wild fucking beast that's found it's prey. It will nourish you. You're beginning the ascent up the mighty mountain and while there will be pitfalls and false starts, there will be exaltations beyond what you have ever imagined. Your life will never be the same. I've always had the day job for stability, though I'm looking to jettison that if and when things swing my way. Boy am I ready to swing.*

And from my apartment in New York I join in the toast — *Happy birthday Mary! She was an artist, complicated, troubled; and just as easily light-hearted, funny, wicked, sexy, difficult, brash, and a hell of a lot of fun.*

*

December 12

Catherine, M7 is finished and with the copy editor. Then I send out my queries, and the rest is up to the gods, if there are any.

I was only able to be in Charleston for an overnight, so leaving Henny and seeing the look of confusion on her face was devastating. Though we had such fun at the park on the see-saw — her little face, her little face — my god her little laughing face. I cried most of the flight back to NYC. As I kept my hand over my face, wiping my tears with those silly napkins, a young Japanese woman next to me, who could barely speak English, took my hand for a little while. It was perhaps the most tender thing that ever happened to me. Hand in yours. — Alan

*

New York City, December 15

It took all of James' energy to stay focused, hour after hour, at the little kitchen table. And of course there were snags. Some of the secondary characters were too spare, especially the female ones. There was work to be done. He would allow himself to go three more days beyond deadline, but no more. *Hi Alan. I'm on page 223 of 309 and pressing toward completion. Let's meet Wednesday at five, Astor Place.*

*

A smattering of young professionals just starting their night, settled onto stools around the big wooden bar at Solas. Alan slid the manuscript into his satchel, ordered a round of scotches, and discreetly handed James an envelope. "Four hundred dollars. I wish I could pay you more. Here's to possibilities!"

"To M7 and a month's groceries paid!" James added, and he downed the shot of Glenfiddich. Alan savored it in sips.

*

"What is it you do again?" Penny Wu asked as James strolled beside her through Bryant Park on a cloudy Saturday afternoon. The glass towers along Forty-Second Street seemed to lean over the park to listen. James zipped his leather coat a little higher against the chill. Penny had known him almost a year now, but she could never remember what he did. It was one of the ways she wasn't a match. He knew she had considered him at the very beginning. But he didn't act fast enough. He was still kicking himself. Silky black hair, dark eyes, a sort of Hong Kong sassiness about her. *A one-night stand can* happen right when you first meet, but then the moment is lost and you can't go back. She had very clear cut ideas about how these things work.

"I design and manage websites. That's what I did at the Universe Society," he tried not to look annoyed.

"There's a webmaster opening where I work. Is that something you can do?"

Always that backhanded twist to her language. "Yes, that's exactly what I do."

"Dawson Hughes Global, it's public relations. You should apply. I'll put in a word for you with Nancy in HR, but only if it's really something you can do."

*

A week into the New Year, James walked into the Midtown Manhattan office on Third Avenue for the interview. From the fifteen-employee, six-story townhouse that was the Universe Society to the how-many-thousand-employee high rise that was Dawson Hughes. Penny's words echoed in his head. *If it's really something you can do.*

Nancy from HR was openly enthusiastic as she led him to the glass-paneled conference room. "You write music! We used to get a lot of developers who were musicians." Then the three managers from Communications entered the room. The online manager smiled and launched his killer question, "Are you comfortable writing CSS? We have six thousand lines of style code."

James felt a pang of fear. He had spent the past ten days teaching himself the first beginner basics of CSS, just enough to complete a pre-interview test. But from another place in his mind came a simple *you've got to be kidding.* Developers are minimalists. They brag about getting the job done with as little code as possible. "That's a lot of code you're trying to maintain," James answered. "It reflects what I see on the website — too many styles. A site is easier for visitors when there are fewer styles and each has a clear purpose."

The manager's eyes went fiery while the same smile remained sculpted on his lips.

Penny called two days later. "James, they were down to two candidates. The other was a friend of our online manager. You came really close, but I guess that doesn't help."

*

Minneapolis, December 21, 2007

Congratulations on completing M7, Catherine wrote. *What an amazing accomplishment! Since you asked, Alistair and I are drifting farther apart. I have a feeling this is going to be a long process. I want to get things a little more in order for myself before any big change. I'm applying for a job at Olivia's Montessori school as an assistant teacher. It would provide me with some flexibility and half-priced tuition for the kids. Leo starts there this fall.*

Life is a wild, uncertain ride. Alan wrote. *Times like this are hard, but know that however it works out, in the end, you will find your way.*

*

New York City, January 11, 2007

James rolled over and looked at his cell phone beside the mattress: three-thirty in the morning. All night he had rolled back and forth, no sleep. A new malady starting at the New Year, insomnia. He had never had insomnia before. What was this a sign of? He didn't believe in signs. Neither did Paul Auster, but Auster wrote incessantly about impossible coincidences, in pregnant detail, assuring all the while that it was just a coincidence.

When he awoke at eleven-thirty in the morning, he poured a juice, thought about breakfast cereal, looked at the bananas. Out the door, he would lunch at Kelloggs.

By the end of the day, there was really only one thing to look forward to. He tipped back the pint glass, a good gulp of Guinness, nodded to Andy, and felt like somehow everything was going to be okay. He would find a job one of these days, some kind of job. And he would find a woman. He never assumed that there was necessarily one right woman for every man and one right man for every woman. That would entail nearly impossible odds — a one in six billion chance. He just wanted his mate to be the best match possible. He had always imagined that when he met a woman who was a really good match, they would simply get along, and they would know — *This is good, we're good together.* But it wasn't going that way. He kept thinking how

Czeslaw Milosz wrote about the raw brutishness of relationships in Warsaw during the Second World War, how a man who had cigarettes had all that was necessary to get a woman into bed. James had already seen that kind of love-as-provisioning over and over again in New York City. A romantic partner is someone who has housing, money, controlled substances, plenty of anything you don't have. And, dressed up fancy or plain to see, maybe this was how matches were made.

*

Black Betty. Reverend Vince Anderson and His Love Choir, unitarian anarchist rock gospel blues, and Sofia at the bar, and the whole room held hands, and then and there no one was alone.

*

James opened an email message from Colleen. *Wow, James, you sounded rather plastered on that voicemail Saturday morning at quarter to eight. Were you still out from Friday night?*

Oh boy. That was the morning he had come home and seen the arepa food cart, the guy who sold to day workers as they bicycled down Morgan Avenue at sunrise. He had phoned Colleen to tell her how good the arepa was and that he was pretty sure it was the first time he'd eaten one since Cumaná. He had no idea really what time of day or night it was, or which was which, when he had brought her number up on his cell phone.

Her message prodded, *Uh, I don't mean to harp on the subject, but I think you need to ask yourself some questions about what this lifestyle is doing to your life.*

Good grief. He hadn't had a drop of alcohol since then — not Saturday, Sunday, or Monday. His system had cleared out. He'd probably have a drink tonight. Her email enumerated her concerns. His insomnia? That didn't correspond at all to his drinking. His memory? That was lame. He even remembered the arepa when he was trashed. His reputation? How would you even know? How would you know what people are saying about you?

*

Stewart walked into Black Betty. "How are you, Mr. Crossland?" he asked in his formal way. James always observed Stewart very carefully. He lived in an apartment above the bar and was a regular there and at Atlas Cafe and on the neighborhood's park benches and door stoops, where he chatted the afternoons away with Williamsburg's young hipster transplants. He once had been a young transplant himself, surely, but now he was mid-forties, just a few years older than James. It was clear they both savored their drinking. But where James was blatant about it, spending the night on the bar stool easily half the week, every week, Stewart seemed to have developed strategies. That's what you would have to call them. Carefully learned, carefully applied strategies.

1. He dropped into Black Betty nightly and had one drink and left. But later the same night, as James walked over to Bedford Avenue for dinner, he saw Stewart in the windows of other bars.

2. He had committed a year — he told James this story — committed a year to reading literary classics — *Moby Dick, Catcher in the Rye, War and Peace*. These were not books Stewart had an interest in. He read them to train himself as a fascinating conversationalist. James couldn't imagine reading something he didn't care about.

3. He was friends with bartenders like James was. But Stewart also was friends with bar owners and landlords who were always willing to give him a break.

And there were facts:

1. Stewart never had a steady job. His life seemed stitched together by odd jobs and favors.

2. His handshake was limp, day or night. James had noticed this in other "one drink" regulars. James' own hand wasn't limp. So he imagined it was a sign that their blood alcohol level never, ever dropped.

He had told Kelly over the phone, he knew he was drinking too much, and he wanted to drink less. But he hadn't figured out how.

*

James focused on Andy. Andy behind the bar. James sat up straight on his stool. Nights like this, there comes a point when you look up from the bar and notice they're gone, the hipsters, the partiers, the band if there was one. They're all gone. But somebody's still here. The people who work the night, the dealers and the people who work for them.

On that particular night, James looked up and saw Billy, a guy who worked with Eddie sometimes, on the bar stool next to him. And at a table were Eddie and his brother Ben. And another man. A man? A rock? A latino man bald and round like Eddie and Ben, but not at all like them. Eddie and Ben could look like a pair of big teddy bears. But this man was like a pile of rock, hard and cold.

James zeroed in on that big pile of rock and thought to himself, *I haven't seen him before. But I guess he's part of this whole circle of Eddie and Billy and all.*

James did what came naturally. He introduced himself, stepping down from the stool and extending his hand. "I'm James, glad to meet you."

The pile of rock turned his head to the side and eyed his people with a bemused look. He turned to James and extended his hand for a half-hearted shake.

"I see these guys all the time," James said. "I'm a regular here."

He reclaimed his pint of Guinness and the bar emptied. As Andy was closing up, he leaned toward James. "There are rules. Don't ever touch him. Ever. He could kill you."

James nodded, walked out the door, watched Andy close it behind him. The morning sun was shining. At Atlas coffee shop, two blocks down Havemeyer, he realized what had happened. It was about respect, the law of social order in New York City. Especially at night. If the pile of rock had felt embarrassed and offended in front of his people, he would have had no choice but to make an example, show that no one ought to be so bold as to touch him. "Take care of him, you know what I'm saying." A moment of decision. The pile of rock had decided differently. *I've got this. I'm going to let this roll.*

James paid for his coffee and looked for an open table, there were plenty at six in the morning as the groggy commuters streamed through for carry-out. And there was Stewart — either out all night or on a manic start-your-day-right correction after a binge. James sat down and told him the story. "I don't think I can go back to Black Betty," he said. "I'm freaked. I can't believe the kind of people you can run into, just having a night out."

"Yeah, when it's all night," Stewart said.

*

James keyed in Kelly's number. "I don't know if maybe you can help me with rent this month?"

*

Minneapolis, January 3, 2007

The full moon shone brightly through the tall windows of the art studio. Cal had helped her pick just the right space. It was her space for creativity. And even though she didn't plan it, it also offered her an escape from the tension with Alistair. She sat cross-legged on the oval rug, surrounded by brushes and paint tubes and pencils and sketchbooks, her creative mind bubbling with possibility. But she was not at peace. Crowded in front of every aesthetic vision was the clutter of Alistair's expectations. What to do, when to be home. Who to be. That person she had been, the girl who stood at the railing over Nine Mile Creek and marveled at fish mouths opening at the surface, the young woman who gazed across fields of scarlet poppies from the train window, who grew corn on the unpaved strip behind her apartment building, was trapped beneath a veneer of expectations.

She locked the studio door behind her and began the drive home along the river. Partway there, she pulled the car into the parking lot at Bohemian Flats. In her journal she drew the Mississippi River cruise boat docked at the water's edge. She drew, erased, and drew again, squinting to see the detail in the darkness. Finally, there was nothing to do but drive home. The moonlight glistened on the snow banks along River Road.

At the back door, the motion sensor blinded her. She pushed the key around until it found its way into the lock. Inside was quiet and dark. He must be in bed, she wouldn't be confronted, but then she heard something. Music, very faint. It was The Beatles. Cal's favorite.

*

Outside the kitchen window the stars shone brightly in the new moon sky. Catherine opened her computer. A message from Alan. The subject line read, *Fast car, cool shades, shocking offer...*

Cosmic

Minneapolis, March 2007

"**P**ut Puffy in the water, Leo!" Olivia demanded. Catherine rushed down the stairs and dropped her suitcase beside the dining room table. Olivia and Leo sat on the shores of the sequined fabric lake laid out on the living room rug. Olivia sailed the *Littlests* across the sparkling blue. Leo examined the pink and white stuffed fish as Olivia insisted with growing urgency, "Put Puffy in the water!" Leo opened his palm beside his cheek, and offered a new idea. "I think...I think...it's a monkey!"

The doorbell rang. Olivia raced through the kitchen to the family room and opened the back door, "Lulu!" Leo scrambled behind.

"Oh my god Lulu, your outfit is amazing!" Catherine said.

"I know, right? Reece Witherspoon wore this color at the Golden Globes and everyone noticed!" She walked the runway across the family room carpet. A canary yellow mini dress, cinched at the waist. And if that wasn't amazing enough, a matching beret pinned with a red star.

"Have you got your coat? Even in New York City it's only in the forties."

"I didn't hear *in the forties,* I only heard *in New York City!*"

Alistair peered through the kitchen doorway talking into his phone headset. Olivia tugged at his leg, "Daddy, let's play!" He shot a glance at Catherine and disappeared into the dining room.

"I've got to go now!" Her words followed just behind him and dropped away, a ball not caught, as he shut the door to the den. She swept her hair from her shoulders and gathered Olivia and Leo into the family room and held them close. "You'll have a fun weekend with Daddy, and I'll be with Lulu in New York." The phrase struck her in the belly, *You'll be here, I'll be in New York.* They had never been apart longer than the school day. "Can I see your eyes, Sweetpea?" She took Olivia's little fingers into hers and Olivia leaned into her arms and looked up with big green eyes. "I love you Sweetpea." Catherine scooped Leo up into her lap. He looked at her adoringly. "My big boy, I love you Leo!" Her lips touched his forehead, and she held him there a while longer before setting him down.

"Catherine!" Alistair burst from the den. "Did you think to pen the address of your accommodation?"

"You can always call," she held up her cell phone, then turned from his steady glare.

"We've gotta fly!" Lulu said.

Backpack over her shoulder, suitcase in hand, she slipped out the back door with Lulu.

*

Catherine clasped Lulu's hand as the plane gained speed down the runway and lifted, the bump of weightlessness, leaving behind the heavy snows of Minnesota. Out the window a stretch of white cumulus clouds was outlined in brilliant sunlight. *Fast car, cool shades, shocking offer.* Alan was leaving New York to be with his daughter. He cashed out his 401K, bought a new car. *Come to New York. A last spin. In three weeks I'll be on the road for Charleston.* For her it was an invitation to a daring escape. Flying one thousand two hundred miles away from the tension, the arguments, and the growing uncertainties ahead — all of it stripped away, if only for the weekend. The person for whom Alan's offer would be shocking was Alistair.

There's no way Alistair will go for this — Lulu had said — *you going to New York to meet some guy your birth mom knew. I'm your cover. Tell him I invited you. It's a girls' trip. That's what I told Derrick, and it's true!* Even so, Catherine had known she couldn't ask to go. She'd have to say, *I'm going,* and let the chips fall. Which way she hoped they'd fall, she didn't know.

She stretched her legs beneath the seat in front of her. Should she stay in the marriage and ride out her life as it is? Divorce would be the hard road. He was a lawyer. And he had resources. She had wanted it to work, hoped to build a life together. And before she found Mary, she didn't quite know what she needed, didn't quite know who she was. Was it her fault? She had done the best she could steering through life blindfolded. She didn't mean for them to drift apart.

Now as the plane rose to 32,000 feet, she took a deep breath. Slow and steady, she let it flow from her body. Mary was taking her on an adventure. New York City.

The flight attendants moved the beverage cart down the aisle, "Something to drink?"

Lulu straightened in her seat, "A Singapore sling please."

"We don't have that."

"Okay then, a caipirinha?

"A what?"

"French martini?"

"No."

"Woo Woo?"

"Excuse me?"

"Never mind, I'll just have a gin and tonic."

"And for you?"

"Sparkling water." Catherine popped the can open and poured it bubbling over the ice. She sipped slowly until she felt the burn. Bubbles misted her nose, then fell like little stars to her black silk blouse.

What would it be like meeting Alan face to face? She poked an ice cube with her finger, watched it sink and bob up again. She had learned of another man in Mary's life, another entry in the address book — Robert. But he was elusive. He lived in a boat docked at the marina and had no phone, just a post office box. She wrote him a letter, he called her from a friend's house — *I hope she knew I loved her* — and she never heard from him again. Meanwhile, Alan's messages frothed almost daily with insights and conversation. And Mary had kept a photograph of Alan, no one else. And there was the letter, really a love letter. Alan, like no other, had to be a living window into Mary's life.

Lulu set her cocktail on the tray table. "This Alan fellow has a thing for you, you know that, right?"

"What?" Catherine dabbed her finger dry on the little paper napkin. She leaned back, now second-guessing herself.

"A man doesn't invite a woman halfway across the country just to have coffee."

"He invited a friend of his to come along."

"A double date?"

Catherine couldn't imagine it.

"We'll be touching down in...about twenty minutes in New York City's La Guardia Airport," the captain's voice announced. "We appreciate you flying

Northwest Airlines. The weather in New York City...51 degrees and light rain."

*

They squeezed through the crowds gathered for the outgoing flight and rolled their suitcases into the busy concourse. The escalator carried them down a floor, baggage claim coming into view from below. "I think that's him." She saw him from the back, a big man dressed in black, sitting at the end of a long line of empty black vinyl chairs facing the baggage carousel. He sat perfectly still, as if he had been that way a long while and could be a long while more, sat watching the carousel already raided for all its bags but one, one bag that went round and round. Finally he turned and she knew him from his photograph, the gentle face, the head of salt and pepper curls. He heaved himself to his feet and extended a hand, "Wow, you look so much like Mary, it's wild." She was used to it after Provincetown. But when he went on to say, "It's great to see you," she wondered for a split-second if he was talking to her or Mary.

They walked out the automatic double doors into the mild damp air. The rain had stopped and little beads of water hung from the door frame, dropping softly on Catherine's head as she passed beneath. A line of travelers wound back and forth along metal railings. The line of cabs began from a little shack that looked like a Minnesota ice-fishing house and trailed along the curb as far as you could see. It was the job of one lone man to insert all these people, one by one or group by group, into cabs. He demanded of each party — "How many? Where to?" — opened the passenger door, motioned them in, and whipped the door shut as he spun to greet the next in line. As one cab sped away, another pulled up in its place, and the process repeated until...maybe forever, maybe the line never emptied, and there were always more people and more cabs. Finally it was their turn.

Alan leaned toward the front seat, "The Commodore Hotel."

"Manhattan?"

"Manhattan, Upper West Side."

The Commodore's elevator whirred as it tugged toward the fourth floor, clanking and knocking its way up the dark shaft. "I live over on the East Side" — Alan began, from out of nowhere — "so I figured we could all just share the room together for the weekend. There are two queen beds. I hope that sounds okay."

Lulu's eyes opened wide and she turned toward Catherine, hand over her lips stifling a laugh.

"I think that's fine," Catherine said.

"This should be interesting," Lulu whispered to the ceiling.

Alan opened the door to the room, set his satchel on the floor by the window, and let out a loud sigh — "Lord Almighty" — as he sat on the bed. "We can go to the bar, Jake's Dilemma, in just a bit." He pulled a joint from his breast pocket. "A smoke, do you want a smoke?"

Catherine shook her head, "There's no way I'd stay awake if I did."

Lulu looked at Catherine, "I really shouldn't, but light it up Alan! What happens in New York, stays in New York!" Lulu met Alan at the window and took a generous hit. She coughed, "Santa María madre de Dios, perdóname!" choking it out all the way into the bathroom.

Catherine watched Alan at the window now, looking down onto the streets of Manhattan as he took a toke, exhaled slowly, took another. She stood beside him. Yellow cabs, a yellow bus with white roof, black coats, a red coat, colors and shapes merging and passing. Did he love Mary like Mary loved him?

Lulu emerged from the bathroom, "Who's ready for a cocktail?"

They hit Amsterdam Avenue surrounded by a steady hum of traffic, sirens, and voices. Pedestrians skirted briskly around them as they strolled the sidewalk, Alan staring at his feet, hands in his coat pockets, while overhead the sun broke through the clouds.

"So tell me about your time with my mom."

"Oh, wow, it was so long ago." He breathed in the chill March air and exhaled a memory. "She would come over to my place, the Shrine, a cottage near the Atlantic Motor Inn, just outside Provincetown. I'd play guitar and she'd sing. Sometimes she'd play the keyboard."

"What kind of music?"

"Covers. Yeah we played a lot of covers." He raised his face in a smile, "And Mary would write songs. Or we'd improvise."

They ducked in below a pale yellow awning and Alan opened the door to the dark of Jake's Dilemma. He led them past a long bar, backed with mirror and lined with what seemed like endless bottles of liquor. They followed him through a floor-to-ceiling red velvet curtain into the back. Heavy lounge furniture anchored an expansive dimly lit room. Alan ushered them to an L-shaped red velour couch.

A server greeted them, "What would you like to drink?"

Lulu whispered to Catherine, "I'm almost afraid to ask."

"A Scotch, Scotch for me," Alan said.

"A Newcastle please."

"Can I have a Singapore sling?"

"Certainly."

Lulu took Catherine's arm, "Heaven, I'm in heaven!"

"So Alan, how long were you and my mom together?" Catherine asked.

He cocked his head to the side. "It was off and on. We weren't an exclusive thing. I was just one of several guys. Mary went out and danced and partied a lot. I was quieter."

"Alan, let me ask you something," Lulu said. "Have you ever written for the stage? A play or..."

A buzz sounded from Alan's pocket. "Hello." His face lightened. "Okay man, that's cool...we're at the bar, Jake's Dilemma, in the back, behind the curtain, we're in the back...okay, we'll see you in just a bit." He slipped the phone back into his pocket. "That was James, my friend. He's running late."

The server brought a tray of drinks, "Would you like to start a tab?"

"Do you make caipirinhas?" Lulu asked.

"Of course."

"We are totally starting a tab!" She raised her glass to the others and all chimed together.

Catherine's eyes settled on the big man beside her. There was a gentleness about him, her confidante and companion in email. She could see Mary standing at the keyboard, looking to him as he lays down rhythmic chords on his guitar, her melodies dancing above. "Was it love, between you and Mary?"

"Love? Well, maybe. There's a vastness beyond vastness." Lifting his eyes to the ceiling, he opened his mouth and chuckled. "We used to go round and round! In my Chevy. The circle at Provincetown Inn! Good times. We were like kids together." He sipped his Scotch, looking like he wasn't sure what to say next. "I wonder where James is." He held up his phone. "I'm not getting any bars in here now." The curtain closed behind him.

Catherine turned to Lulu, "He's more prolific in writing for sure."

Alan re-emerged from the curtain, "I got ahold of James. He'll be here in ten minutes."

*

James rose from bed about two in the afternoon, put the coffee kettle on the stove, poured corn flakes with milk, and slowly spooned the soaked flakes into his mouth as a wave of nausea passed over him. And, oh yeah, it was coming back to him, the dinner and drinks tonight with Alan and the girls from Minnesota. Alan knew women everywhere, an old flame in California, one in Missouri, and there was the lesbian woman from Kansas who married a man in Canada but still fooled around with Alan — it was something like that, James couldn't even follow.

Alan's invitation was also a call for help. "Two women at once... ahh... how do I...how do I entertain them? If you could come, you could talk to her friend so I can focus on Catherine. Kind of a double date." Alan had been his guardian angel, and he didn't mind returning the favor in this small measure. "We'll get a drink at Jake's Dilemma," Alan went on. "It's dark, very film noir, but, jeez, do you know a place for dinner?" James had thought a moment. "I don't really hang out on the Upper West Side. But Penny took me to a Malaysian restaurant over there. I'll take care of it."

So there it was. Except for Black Betty. Last night, all night. One of those nights when no one in particular showed up — no Polish beauties, no drinking buddies, no band. But that didn't change the fact that James didn't get home until five in the morning. He didn't feel like he could handle another night of drinking now, and if he went out, he knew he would drink. Colleen would know what to do. He phoned her and lifted the cup of steaming Cafe Bustelo to his lips.

"Well you've gotten yourself into a bit of a pickle haven't you?" she said.

"What do you mean?"

"You promised your friend you'd go and now you drank too much and you're thinking maybe you just won't go."

"I know. No, you're right. But it's not just that. I mean, why would I go meet two girls from Minnesota? If I like one of them, what are we going to do? I'm not moving to Minnesota."

James dedicated every night, without saying it, to meeting a girl. It didn't happen, hardly ever happened. He longed in antiseptic purity for every unrequited love, knight of the round table hunched over a Guinness, while she perched beautiful on her bar stool, chestnut hair flowing, laughing with every other guy. He was crazy with the sight of her form, the scent of her femininity. Brunette, blonde, red, silken black, he had moved on and longed for another and another and maybe two or three nights a year actually got laid. Like some kind of freak, two or three nights a year in a city of five million women. And it wasn't even about the one night. The fact was, he always hoped the one night would plant the seed of a lifetime together. How naive. And this, the two weekend visitors from the Midwest, hardly seemed like the chance he'd been waiting for. He was from the Midwest and he knew who was out there. He had left and never gone back. By now he had lived in the Northwest, the Northeast, Africa, and South America, not to mention the visit to his parents in Malaysia. No where had felt as real, as intense, as open to possibilities as New York City. His future was here. And if there was a girl for him, chances were, she was here too. And precisely, not to get too pedantic about it, but precisely because he wasn't only looking for a one-night stand, it just didn't make sense to go meet these girls. "Colleen, if I like one of them, how would that even work? It just doesn't make sense."

"Doesn't make sense?" Oh god, he knew she couldn't believe it and wasn't going to leave it alone. "Why wouldn't you go for dinner?" she said. "You can just go and talk and have fun. You should go." Colleen had always said the best way to live the nightlife in New York was to say yes. Be in charge and take it just as far as you want, but take it for a ride and see where it goes.

He pulled himself together for another night out, as he had done many times before. By the time he was ready, he was going to be a half hour late. He called Alan to let him know, then locked the door behind him and headed down the steps to the Morgan Avenue L train. The subways took him under the East River and up Manhattan's Upper West Side to the Museum station. His cell phone rang as he emerged to the street. A check-in from Alan. "I'm ten minutes away," he assured and pressed ahead on West Eighty-First Street, footfalls leaning left or right around other pedestrians and boulevard trees and absent-minded figures in coats. He pressed toward sunset. And because it was sunset, the lighted interiors drew his eyes to windows just above and just below street level, to indoor people whose affairs he knew were not part of his day and none of his business.

Propped in seats at a long table, banquet-style, in a lower-level restaurant, girls age five to seven wore birthday hats. They chewed and gestured and their lips moved in silent speech behind the glass. What a delicate balance between happiness and sadness, what an evening of risk and looming disaster — a child's birthday party. The disaster is a childhood disaster — of hurt feelings, of a moment irretrievably lost when a scoop of ice cream falls to the floor and no other scoop can replace it because it is not the same scoop and it is not the same moment. He noted it in passing, not stopping or slowing, and more than anything else that traversed his mind as he pressed on to meet his buddy and go through the paces of a double date, more than anything else he wanted the birthday girl to know that everything would be okay.

He crossed Amsterdam Avenue and turned south. Just a few doors down he saw the pale yellow awning, *Jake's Dilemma* in black capital letters, styled as if scratched on a bar napkin. Past the long bar he saw the red curtain drawn.

"Mr. James!"

"Hey Alan," James leaned in, patting him on the back.

Alan introduced his guests and James shook hands. Her eyes were so serious, Catherine's eyes. A server paused, "Can I get you anything?" "I'd love a drink, but we have a dinner reservation." He glanced to Alan and the two women.

"We're good," Alan said, looking relieved, as if James' being here was something better than Scotch.

Penang Malaysian Restaurant was just down the street. Winter shouldered out spring as the sun set, and the chill night swirled around their ankles until they stepped into Penang's warm vestibule.

"Four for Bing," James said. The host led them to the upper level. Alan paused as if the top of the stairs were the edge of the world, paused at the bluster of crackling conversation, the bright lights, the tables massed with gesturing diners.

"Or do you prefer the lower level?" The host led them back down the stairs to a rustic dimly lit room, brick walls, a ceiling of old wooden beams. The tables waited, dressed in white linens topped with folded napkins and wine glasses. A flick of the light switch and the room took on a comfortable glow.

"Oh yeah, fantastic, this is fantastic," Alan said. "A bottle of red and a bottle of white."

"Certainly. Any table you'd like."

They slid into a booth and lifted the menus, each at their own tilt and distance. "Let's see... Well... Hmm..." Alan chuckled and laid his menu flat. "I don't have a clue what any of this means!"

"It's written in Bahasa Malaysia," James said. "I was there for a summer with my parents. Usually people order a few dishes to share."

Lulu nestled the wine glass in her hands as she leaned to Alan across the table. "Catherine said you work at the museum?"

"Oh yeah, the American Museum of Natural History, photo and film archive." Alan settled back into the booth and crossed an ankle over his knee. "Photographs, hundreds of thousands, in large file cabinets. T-Rex digs from the 1800s, extinct animals, spectacular insects, gems and minerals, even shamans in Mongolia!" His eyes widened. "Up the special elevator to cold storage, rare glass plate images, very rare. I license them for books and films. It's freezing in there. I always wear a coat. There's even a locked steel section for rare books and manuscripts."

"So you're the keeper of these rare treasures. That is gasp-worthy!" Lulu lifted her glass for a long sip, eyes steady on Alan.

"The physical collections are stored in folders" -- his mouth opened before the words emerged -- "and the folders within boxes, and the boxes within compartments!" He laughed with wonder.

"Alan is on a roll," Catherine said. It was funny to hear her talk about him like an old friend. Opposite spokes on the wheel of Alan's friendships. James never knew she existed until now.

"Alan's on a roll," he agreed. "And it looks like Lulu's going along for the ride."

"So what about you?" Alan asked Lulu. "What do you...what do you do?"

"I'm a social worker at Alliance for Community Involvement in Minneapolis."

"I would love to be involved in your community."

Lulu covered her mouth and turned to Catherine, who snorted and choked and laughed, "O god, I'm gonna have wine coming out my nose. Lulu, what in the world are you two talking about!"

"I thought I was telling him about my job but it's going a whole other direction!"

"Chicken satay" — the server laid out the dishes in the center of the table — "cendawan goreng, mee goreng, and nasi kerabu."

Catherine drew a deep breath. "This all looks wonderful. Look at this blue rice, Lulu, it's like a painting!" She angled her slender legs to the side of the table and turned to James. "So what brought you to Malaysia?"

"I was visiting my parents, my summer break from college. My dad was teaching mathematics there. We lived in Ghana in West Africa when I was nine and Venezuela when I was a teen. My family moves around a lot." He opened his hands in surrender, he couldn't really explain it. But something in her dark eyes made him want to. "After my dad got that first overseas job in Ghana, it was like, I don't know, an escape for him. To be someplace where he could redefine himself."

"What was he escaping from?" She twirled noodles around her chopsticks.

James put his fingertips to his chin. "I don't actually know. He never said. It was just this exciting opportunity. And maybe that's all it was." James drew a bite of satay off the skewer with his teeth. "Venezuela, Malaysia, and then Qatar — I always wondered what he was looking for."

Laughter erupted from the other end of the table as Lulu and Alan leaned back in their chairs, then leaned close again.

"Would you like more wine?" James reached for one bottle and then the other — both drained dry. In the time they had finished their first glass, Alan and Lulu had finished the bottles.

"No wonder they're getting on so well," Catherine laughed. 'So tell me," — she cupped her hands around her wine glass — "what was it like in Malaysia?"

"It's a mix of old and new, ancient Buddhist temples right in the heart of the capital, Kuala Lumpur. Holy incense drifting among skyscrapers."

She gathered her hair to one side, then leaned in toward James. "I can imagine what your dad may have been looking for. Sometimes it's not about redefining yourself but finding yourself. When I was twenty-two I went to

Europe for the first time. I saw another way of life that was different from everything I had known. It should have been unfamiliar and strange. But instead it felt more familiar than the place I grew up. I returned to Europe as often as I could."

James nodded and thought for a moment. "For me it wasn't so much that it felt familiar, it was more like these places became a part of me, added to who I am."

"And what has New York added for you?" She spoke louder now over Lulu and Alan's banter at the other end of the table.

"You ask serious questions. I like that. New York taught me to chill out, to get along with all kinds of people. And just like you said about Europe, I feel like I belong here."

"I picked up the check while you weren't looking! What's next on the itinerary?" Lulu looked to Catherine, then back to Alan who looked to James.

James lifted his leather coat from the back of the chair. "There's a cool Irish bar, Solas, down in the East Village."

"But first" — Catherine said — "the restroom!"

Catherine sudsed her hands at the sink while Lulu puckered in the mirror and pulled two tubes of lipstick from her purse. "I'm telling you, these boys think they're on a double date!"

"If it's supposed to be a double date, they seem to have forgotten who's with who."

Lulu held the tubes up to her outfit, "Which one, Purple Passion or Race Car Red? Or maybe Forbidden Fuchsia." She reached for her purse. "Which says *I'm ready for adventure?*"

"Lulu, it's not a double date!"

"Let's have a little fun, a little play acting. Nothing naughty, just fun."

"Race Car Red," Catherine laughed. "But you three are the ones on the double date, not me."

*

Alan leaned against the cool stone of the hallway outside the restrooms. James stood beside him. He had to say something after spending the entire dinner talking with Alan's date. It was delicate business. "It looks like you're getting along with Lulu."

"Yeah," Alan said hesitantly.

"How are you feeling about Catherine so far?"

Alan squinted and inhaled through his teeth. "Well, I don't know. It's a trip. I just keep seeing Mary."

"And that makes you...more interested? Not so interested?"

"I don't know."

In a way it wasn't delicate, because the facts were clear. It was right there in front of them. "Do you want to switch?" James asked.

"Yeah, sure, I guess."

*

Double date, double dip, second scoop, second chance. Something was happening that night, and I felt it twice. I met my friend and his friends, and met her eyes. I wanted to rescue a little girl who needed to know that everything would be all right. And I wanted her to help me know. And that's how I met a girl that night.

*

The four gathered under a streetlight on the corner of Columbus Avenue and West Seventy-Second Street, and James hailed a cab.

"Where to?"

"Solas Bar," he said. "Ninth Street between Second and Third."

The cab cut across the Central Park Transverse, down Fifth Avenue to East Fifty-Sixth Street, then zoomed down Second Avenue hitting all the greens, lofting gently over every intersection. "Right on Ninth Street," he said, "This is it on the left."

Solas was awash with whiskey, alive with laughter, amiss with spills. Bartenders poised eye and ear to the order, hands swift to the pour. Customers shoulder to shoulder happy. The four took the only seats in the house: stools wrapped around the corner of the big wooden bar.

Lulu leaned to Catherine and waved to James and Alan on the other side. "I thought we were traveling to New York, but did you hear the bartender's accent?" Lulu drank up the whole room, the New York-tilted Irish lilt of it all. But Catherine's eyes strayed to James' long black curls and bright blue eyes. She cupped her hand and called across the corner, "So you didn't mention yet, what do you do?"

"I write. Anthropology. Or maybe its philosophy. For work I managed the website at the Universe Society, a private club for adventurers. They

319

were restructuring, laying everybody off. I'm still looking for a new job. What about you?"

"My two kids are my full-time job, but I'm also an artist. I've done a bit of everything. Photography, painting, so many things inspire me. I've just started a book." His eyes were a kaleidoscope of emotions. She didn't know if Alan had told him anything about her. He glanced to Alan, then smiled quietly at her, tasted the Guinness, set the pint glass down with a measured firmness. She wanted to sneak away to a quiet booth together, her shoulder against his, and talk into the night, but..."I'm not sure what we're doing here, Lulu." Catherine's eyes darted to James.

"Chiquita, you're thinking too much, I can see it. We're here for you to learn more about your mother, and do you want to know the truth? We're also here to have a good time. You don't need to get crazy" — now Lulu glanced to James — "but you do need to relax a little. Let the night take you for a ride. Bartender, can I see a cocktail list?"

"There's no list, love. You want it, you ask for it."

Lulu squealed, "See what I mean?"

Drinks all around, Alan raised his Scotch, raised his eyes into a distance far beyond the high ceiling. "Wind, sandpits, craters. Dunes of the Provincelands. Mary and I. Where are the roads? I asked. *There are none,* she said. Where are the trees? She pointed to the shrubs at her knee. Does anyone really live here? *Everyone does,* she said. And she stood at the edge of a crater, spread her arms like wings, and ran down into the depths and up the other side, slipping, sand sliding, struggling to the surface again. *Come* she said. I shook my head, I don't think I can. *Everyone can,* she said. Here's to Mary..."

They raised their glasses and Catherine watched James' eyes misting up. Her thoughts were spinning. The evening was spinning. Circles and circles at Provincetown Inn. If anyone was in the driver's seat now, it was Mary, the one who wasn't there. She was the play and they the players, she was the fire and they the embers. *My spirit is fiery, above us it glows.*

"James, Lulu was saying she wanted to drive up Broadway," Alan said. "Where do we...Do you...do you want to join us in the cab?"

Eyes full of light, he gave a cool nod. The four filed out to the street. They pulled collars tight, buttoned top buttons. "We can catch an uptown cab at Third Avenue," James said. A taxi van pulled over and James motioned to Alan who slid into the front seat.

"Where to?" the cabby asked.

Alan paused and James leaned inside, "Broadway and Forty-Second Street. We want to see the lights. And then — where is it Alan?"

"The Commodore Hotel," Alan said. "Ninety-Fourth Street, Upper West Side."

James slid into the bench seat. Catherine slid beside him, slipped her hand in his. He clasped her palm tight. Cruising under the glare and sparkling light. The Lion King, Mama Mia, Rent. They didn't let go until the Upper West Side.

*

At the Commodore, Alan plopped onto the bed by the window. "Lord almighty!"

"Don't you go falling asleep mister!" Lulu sat beside him and strenuously patted his shoulder. "You told me you would do a dramatic reading. You were very impressive at the bar!"

"Yes, very impressive while I'm downing Scotch. Now it's catching up with me. But yes, I'm sure I've got something I can read."

"Do you have *M7*?" James sat on the edge of the other bed and Catherine settled beside him.

Alan rummaged in his satchel and pulled out a thick sheaf of paper. Adjusting his eyeglasses, he opened the manuscript with care and began reading somewhere in the middle. His voice rose and fell with the turn of events, delighted, almost laughing, as the M7 character navigated his odd surroundings. Catherine tried to make sense of it. James listened and laughed and Lulu rounded out the reading with vigorous applause.

"Thank you, thank you! Can I please just close my eyes now!" Alan laughed and sank into the mattress.

"Looks like we're losing Alan." James stood from the bed. "I'd better catch a train before it gets much later."

"Not yet," Catherine said. "I have something to read too." From her backpack she pulled a single handwritten page. "This is the letter my mother wrote to you," — Alan stirred, eyes opening — "the day you left Provincetown for Kansas City."

He sat up in bed as she read aloud:

7 May 1988, 7:20 A.M. Saturday
For Alan
I sit in the Chevy at Herring Cove. I have just taken an hour to quietly
cruise through Provincetown, taking in the places you have been and seen
for the past years that you have been a part of this town. The water is a
cold greenish gray, the sky a mournful blue. The wind rises and falls in the
last grip of winter as you drive into spring. Kansas City. Back into the perils
that created the special person that you are. Deep and seeking, mild and
caring, yet still hurt, still alone. My spirit goes with you. The Witches of Hell
Town already feel your absence. And the loss of such a beautiful presence
as yours. I miss you already... yet I wish the best for our futures... to endure
the trials and make beauty from adversity, love out of hate. We are not
alone. We are not separated at all. I love you.
— Mary

Alan heaved himself to his feet. A light rain streaked the window as he peered into the Manhattan night. Stories of random lighted windows. Catherine stood beside him. "Do you remember this letter? Did she ever send it to you?"

Lulu motioned to James. "You and Alan can sleep in that bed. Catherine and I will sleep over here. It's too late for anyone to be running around catching trains. But no funny business!"

Alan squinted and shook his head, "I don't recall ever receiving a letter like that from Mary. He gazed into the distance. "There was a love between us, a vast love, not a possessive love."

"I'm just trying to understand who you were to her, Alan. Your place in her life." Her eyes clung to him.

"It's possible" — he said quietly — "that you already understand as much as I do." He took her hand. "The thing you're really searching for, is the one thing I can't give, a moment to stroll the beach beside her at sunset, feel the soft breath of her words, hear her laughter shimmer in the wind."

Catherine's eyes filled with tears.

"I think you know Mary more fully, more deeply than any of us ever did. You carry her spirit. She lives within you."

Outside the window the wet streets reflected the red and white lights of yellow cabs.

Lulu puffed the pillows at the head of the girls' bed. "This has been one doozy of a night!"

Alan lay down next to James. They dimmed the lights and the room was quiet. Catherine turned on her side, pulled the covers close, then turned to her back, breathed in a big breath and sighed.

"Catherine, whatever you're thinking, go to sleep, Chiquita."

Catherine climbed out of bed with a creak and gingerly sat on the edge of the other bed. "Are you asleep, James?" she whispered.

"Not really, no."

"I'm not sure I caught what Alan's reading was about," she said.

James sat up against the head of the bed. "Yeah, he probably should have started at the beginning. It's a wild but somehow innocent story." He turned to her, alive with what he wanted to say. Alan snorted and rolled to his side. James lowered his voice. "M7 is this young guy who works in a library, but the library contains all of human knowledge. It's a world of its own, and there is no way he can ever comprehend it or his own place within it. I edited the manuscript for Alan last December."

"That was you? He mentioned a copyeditor."

"Yeah, Alan had read M7 at his writers group down in the East Village the month before. We huddled in our winter coats in the glow of a solitary shop light, like campers around a fire, in this abandoned storefront. Alan's words began weaving sense and nonsense in our ears — library attendants standing guard in velvet suits, unnavigable corridors of glowing light, kooky sexual innuendoes. M7 was trying to do what he thought he was supposed to do, and be who he thought he was supposed to be, and all the while the absurdities were piling on top of him. And that's just how life is. Life dresses you, bit by bit, in a ridiculous coat of expectations. And when you see yourself in the mirror, you just have to laugh. I was dizzy by the end of it."

Alan stirred — "I'm going to take a bath" — and lumbered into the bathroom.

Lulu bolted upright in her bed. "If nobody else is sleeping, then neither am I!" And she followed Alan.

Catherine and James listened in the dark to the muffled roar of the tap resonating through the closed door. The water stopped.

"Do you hear singing?" James asked.

"She always sings like that when something's awkward."

"Maybe the bath is reviving Alan."

Water sloshed. Lulu's voice admonished, "This is really a tub for one!"

They crumpled, suppressing their laughter. Moments later the bathroom door flung open and two indistinct figures stumbled to the other bed. There were noises and movements in the dark. Lulu's voice, "I don't want you to get the wrong idea!" Alan, "Oh baby!" Lulu, "Oh baby yourself, mister!"

Finally the long night tapered. Catherine and James slipped under the covers into each other's arms. Catherine looked into James' eyes. "Have you ever been married?"

He propped himself up on his elbow. "I've always wanted to. I remember a dream when I was seven years old, I was marrying a girl with long black hair." He smiled, "Was that you?"

She wished she could start over, do it all differently this time. "I'm married, you know."

"Yeah, I guess you mentioned your children."

They lay quietly for a few minutes. She could feel the warmth of his cheek beside hers.

"I'm really drawn to you," his voice was soothing, yet vulnerable. "Women I've met don't care about the things I care about. They talk about jobs and TV shows, and they glaze over when I talk about sonata form and social theory. I feel like I could talk with you about everything."

"I like to talk about things that are real, real life," she said. "I've been thinking all night that I want to talk more, learn more about you." She hesitated. "I need to know. Why are you okay lying here with me when I'm married?"

He grew serious, contemplating. Then he said very simply, "You don't seem like someone who is in love with someone else."

She was stunned. It was a revelation of her own truth, what she had known all along but couldn't say to anyone, not even herself. She lay silent and still. Mary was leading her.

"Love finds us," he said. "We don't choose it. It chooses us." He brushed a hair from her eyes, her fingers followed the contour of his shoulder. Their lips touched.

*

Early morning light flowing between the hotel curtains. He awoke, not to a Midtown high-rise, not to an East Village basement. He awoke to her.

As Alan and Lulu slept, James and Catherine walked West Ninety-Fourth toward Broadway. A cold silence swept the streets. Only an occasional taxi or delivery van. "This is the one time of day when the City sleeps," he said. It was something he had noticed before, a peculiarity of New York, that although the city never sleeps, there is a space between the hours, between night and day, when the people who were awake all night are just arrived home, and the people who slept all night are dressing for the day, while the streets wait empty. "There's got to be someplace to eat," he said. Scraps of trash raced over the sidewalk to the inside corner of a building, jogging in place like runners at a red light until a gust swirled them into the air. He zipped his leather coat. "Aren't you cold?"

"My sweater is warmer than it looks. It's twelve skeins of Alpaca, I knitted it myself."

On Broadway they stepped into the steamy warmth of Manhattan Diner, noisy conversations, clanking silverware, the aroma of coffee.

"Good morning, how many?"

"Just the two of us," he said.

They followed the hostess down a narrow aisle to a table by the storefront window, the only open table in the house. "Coffee?"

Catherine nodded absolutely. "Two coffees," he said. He looked to the street through the steamed windows. "I can't believe how cold it is out there."

"In Minnesota the wind doesn't gust like this without a storm."

"You know my dad grew up in New Ulm."

"So I come to New York and meet someone with family from Minnesota?"

"Yeah, this is all pretty wild. In fact..." He looked down at the table, trying to see into a new world created overnight. "We still have a lot to learn about each other" — her eyes in his gaze, he took her hands in his — "but I feel like we're really good together. If we keep feeling this way, then I'd like to be together."

Her eyes grew serious. "So, how would we do this? Would you move to Minnesota?"

"Well, I don't know. Maybe you would decide to move here."

"I can't move here!" She drew back in disbelief. "I have two kids. Leo's a toddler. When I divorce, it's joint custody. I can't go anywhere."

"So we'd have to live in Minnesota?"

"Yes. I can't go anywhere until they're off to college."

He stared at the table. "Wow, Minnesota," he said, half to himself.

*

They walked together past groves of oak and sycamore.

Catherine glanced at a sign. "The Ramble?"

"They have names for all the different areas of Central Park."

The path took them beneath a great green slope called Cedar Hill. "Olivia and Leo would love to run down a hill like this!"

"Is it hard being away?"

"It is. I talked with them on the phone yesterday, and today, but it's not the same."

His hand reached for hers and she held on as the City — stone, brick, and glass — reappeared through the branching limbs of the canopy. "Fifth Avenue," he said. "We can walk down to Sixty-Eighth Street and catch the Six Train at Lexington. That's where I used to take the subway home from work."

She could see something in his eyes. As if his life in the City was at half turn, passing into what used to be, even if he didn't know it quite yet. They descended the subway stairs to the token machines. As they stood in the subterranean chill on the broken concrete of the subway platform, she wondered how many times he had stood there at the end of a workday while a thousand miles away she ran laundry up from the basement and made dinner for the kids and Alistair. Wind streamed from the tunnel, metallic screeches and creaks as the train braked to a stop. The doors opened and people, and more people, rushed out. James took her hand and waited. He seemed to know exactly when he wanted to board, waiting until the outrush dwindled and then quickly inside to find a place as others poured in behind. She gripped the floor-to-ceiling pole, while six other hands gripped above and below — a May Day pole wrapped with fingers and outstretched arms. The train jerked into motion down the track.

At Union Square they ascended the steps to the pedestrian tunnels. They crisscrossed the streaming underground crowd and descended the stairs to the L train platform. Under the East River they rode, then stepped up into the sun at Bedford Avenue in Williamsburg.

The cityscape was shorter now. Quaint little streets lined with old brick buildings two to four stories tall, like the Main Streets of Red Wing or Hastings or a hundred other small towns in Minnesota. Except that the streets were filled with crowds. A mix of young and old. "Those two guys in black-brimmed hats with curly sideburns, are they Amish?"

"Oh, they're Jewish, Hassidic. They do look a bit Amish."

They walked Bedford. Past S and B Restaurant — "The pierogi is really good." To the mini-mall that had no name but the one left over from another era — *Real Form Girdle Company* — letters cut in steel above the double glass door, the door frame plastered with rock band and anarchy stickers. And inside the mini-mall, the Tibetan store, Pema, steeped in incense, where she browsed the colorful silk scarves, shawls, and dresses. And finally Spoonbill and Sugartown, where she watched him weave around the tables of books. As the silvery sheen of Tibetan fabrics had drawn her eyes, now book covers drew his. Was it the design? The title? She didn't know. But at the point where she had closed her eyes and opened the fabrics to her fingers alone, following the stiff strands of silk thickening to a nub and thinning again, he combed the tables with eyes alone. Eyes feeling for something to touch his mind. And when it did he lifted the book in his hands and opened the first pages. The big title page. The pages of tiny print nobody wants to read. Searching for something. And when he turned to the first page of the first chapter, within seconds he scrunched up his face like a city bus had just blasted him with exhaust and slapped the book down on the table. Until finally with a flash of recognition he lifted a paperback with a simple black-and-white cover. "I read a collection of essays by W.G. Sebald this past summer," he said, as if that explained everything, and then he followed his routine, and nodded cautiously after the first page and held it close all the way to the cash register.

Down the Bedford subway steps again, a train was just arriving at the platform. An announcement rang in an almost musical lilt. "What did that say?" She smiled, mouth open in surprise.

"This is a Brooklyn-bound L train."

She laughed. "It sounded like, *This is a broken-down L train!*"

At Morgan Avenue they stepped up to the street alongside a corrugated metal wall covered in advertisements and graffiti. Ahead the street was lined with small, scrappy boulevard trees and old three-story apartment buildings. More modest than she had expected.

"We go the other way," he said. She turned to a burnt-out brick building. He shook his head, "That place burned four years ago. It's been boarded up ever since."

She pointed down his street. "So the first thing you see when you're coming home is a Do Not Enter sign! Did you ever notice that?"

"Yeah, Morgan is one-way up to here," he answered, very matter-of-fact.

Continuing down Morgan there was a huge brick warehouse, Qmart Import-Export-Wholesale, and across from Qmart, a graffitied concrete wall topped with a little sign, All American Transit Mix.

Bits of gravel spit from the load of an eighteen-wheel dump truck as it rumbled toward them and around the corner onto Harrison. She blinked and waved the dust from her face. It was a world that, as a matter of fact, was summed up perfectly in that very ordinary road sign. *Do Not Enter.* His ponytail flowed in dark curls. A man of books and gravel and burnt-out buildings. She felt a surge of electricity along her spine as she realized now seeing his brow heavy with thought, his eyes gazing into the distance, that it all came together inside his head. There, not the gravel under his feet, was where he lived and where they walked now.

*

They met Alan and Lulu at a Cuban restaurant on Amsterdam Avenue in Manhattan. Floor-to-ceiling windows trimmed canary yellow, royal blue awnings — Cafe con Leche. Lulu was ecstatic as they all sipped pineapple margaritas, "Alan and I toured famous film sites around the City...The New York Public Library, Grand Central Station. But Catherine, the best moment was standing in front of Tiffany's! You know that scene where Audrey Hepburn peers through the windows in her black evening gown and pearls?"

After lunch they walked together the fifteen blocks to the American Museum of Natural History, ascended the granite steps, and passed through the iron entrance beneath a massive inscription, *Truth, Knowledge, Vision.*

"I can get free passes. Be back in a few, back in a few." Alan walked down a dark hallway, somewhere deep inside the museum. M7 disappearing into the Library of All Human Knowledge. In the quiet echoes of the marble lobby, James waited with Catherine and Lulu.

"So Alan knew your birthmother. What have you learned about her so far?" James said.

"I've learned that I'm a lot like her. When I read her obituary, I couldn't believe it, it was like reading about myself. She loved painting, photography, knitting. All the things I do, yet we were never together beyond the day I was born. It's incredible how strong the genes are!"

James crossed his arms. "Of course culture plays a big part."

"I think genes might play a bigger part."

He pulled back, his chill New York vibe unraveling. He could never explain himself with a simple phrase because nobody but him and a dozen dying professors saw the world through the lens of classical anthropology. So one explanation always required another, and each step took him further from the popular truths anyone was likely to understand. "Anthropologists like Clifford Geertz have written that human behavior is very generalized." He saw Catherine's eyebrows furrow, but he stood firm to make his argument. "We're not hard-wired for specific behaviors the way most animals are. I mean photography and knitting are cultural — not something humans are genetically programmed to do. What's your basis for saying its mostly genes?"

"What's got in to him!" Lulu muttered.

Catherine's eyes got big then focused hard. "In college when I was studying psychology, I was taught nature and nurture were fifty-fifty. But in my experience since then, I've realized that it's more like this is nature" — and she held her hand upright like a stiff hello — "and this is what culture can do" — and she loosened her hand, waving like sea kelp in a gentle current. "But culture can't do this" — she marked a place and swept her hand to mark another. He stood staring, speechless, waiting for a scholarly citation that would never come. Somehow his whole career of anthropological studies, in school and in the decades beyond, seemed threatened by this self-assured woman with her special hand gestures.

"I've got the passes." Alan, out of breath, innocently entered the scene.

"Look, over there is an exhibit on human evolution," Catherine looked to James.

He nodded, still feeling unanchored, wanting to get beyond it. "Yeah, let's see it."

They stood before the first installation, a model of Sahelanthropus tchadensis, a hominin who lived in North Central Africa seven million years ago. James leaned toward the caption on the wall, not sure whether she would stop and read, not sure how long she would want to linger. She lingered, she leaned into the same caption. He understood he could read softly aloud for both of them: "Walked upright but retained an opposable toe that could grasp tree limbs, this meant it could live in diverse habitats." She read the next.

"Alan and I are checking out the Hall of Mexico and Central America" Lulu whispered. "Hasta pronto!"

"We'll catch up," Alan added. "Catch up with you guys in a bit."

They were alone now among the whispering crowds of strangers. Her hand brushed his, and his fingers laced between hers. Strangers to each other until yesterday. Whatever had happened between them just before, whatever it meant for their possibility together, she was holding his hand again.

"Orrorin tugenensis lived in East Africa six million years ago," she read softly. Every installation a skull, a thigh bone, a fragment. And from it a life reconstructed in an ink portrait, a silicone cast, a paragraph of text.

"Multiple hominin species evolved simultaneously," he read. "Sometimes their ranges overlapped. They may have met."

They stood before the central installation of the exhibit. A model of an Australopithecus afarensis couple holding hands as they walked the sands of an East African shore three million years ago. Catherine read, "The fossil footprints show they were male and female walking in step together, the way people do when holding hands." She gazed intently. "Walking on the sand" — she whispered — "they probably felt they could walk that shore forever."

Everything in him sank. "It must be getting late," he said.

They found Alan and Lulu in the marble entrance lobby. "Our flight's at seven," Catherine said. "We should probably be heading out."

Lulu crossed her arms, "We have to see the butterflies before we go."

They entered the humid warmth of the brightly-lit vivarium. Bits of color flitted around them, yellow, orange, purple, pink, blue. "The whole world should be like this!" Lulu opened her palms.

"Look, a swallowtail!" And even as Catherine said it, a memory emerged. The tiny spirit she once tried to save, the black, yellow, and white caterpillar she had rescued from a winter frost, had nourished indoors with parsley until it formed a chrysalis and transformed, in the middle of a Minnesota winter, into a beautiful swallowtail butterfly. She hatched a clandestine plan to deliver it into the steamy safety of the botanical conservatory at Como Zoo. She rode two-year-old Olivia in the stroller through the greenhouse rooms until she found the orchid display, waited until no one was near, then let the swallowtail free. It fluttered among the blossoms.

*

Luggage gathered from the hotel, one more time Catherine watched James hail a cab. She kissed him goodbye, hugged Alan, and slid into the backseat beside Lulu. The cab pulled away and raced into the flow of traffic. Out the back window she watched his figure become smaller and smaller, motionless on the sidewalk, unable to step away. She felt a sinking feeling in her chest. The fact was, she couldn't be sure she would ever see him again. Her new life, just arrived, faded into the distance.

DNA

Falling in love happens drop by drop, and another drop falls for no particular reason when you aren't even expecting it and warmly splashes your eyes.

*

Manhattan, June 2009

"**C**ome on Leo, to the swing! To the swing!" Olivia, seven years old, dark locks of rich auburn down her dainty shoulders, raced across the wood chips of the East Ninety-Sixth Street Playground in Central Park. James gave her a gentle first push, her toes pointed to the sky. Leo scrambled after. "Mom, I want a push too!" Catherine hoisted him up — "Ready Poot-Poot?"

"How does it feel being back in the City?" She glanced to James. He looked so natural against the backdrop of yellow cabs streaming beneath Fifth Avenue's stately brick apartment buildings. "Do you miss it?"

"It's good for a visit, but Minnesota feels like home now."

It was a relief to hear him say it, in his old surroundings, the day before their wedding. This was exactly the moment a character in a movie might run, merge back into his familiar old life, into whatever it was that drew people to this over-busy, overstimulated city. But life doesn't imitate art. He gazed at her with eyes that said everything about the pain and stress and hope of their past two years together in Minnesota, settling in, looking for work, building a new life with an old life in tow. Tomorrow this beautiful, naive, maddening, wonderful man would marry her, and her children, and her ex-husband who had been, what could she say, a complete asshole through it all. An asshole lawyer — Dad was annoyed when she called Alistair that, but it was exactly why she had to move fast, a chip shot over Alistair's head. He was angry, felt like everything he had built was being stripped away. He could easily have outmaneuvered her if she hadn't stayed one step ahead. She hardly knew how she had moved so fast. A month after that weekend in New York, she held a signed divorce agreement in her hand, and in July she walked out of the Hennepin County court house with the decree.

She reached for James hand. "It hasn't been easy."

He looked down, closed his eyes, shook his head with a smile.

Olivia jumped from the swing mid-air down to the wood chips and danced in circles, "Windy, windy!"

Dark clouds rose above the tree canopy and Catherine looked to the sky. "Is this our weather for the wedding?"

He laughed. "Doesn't matter. No storm is too big. It's you and me...and Olivia and Leo..."

"And Alistair," she added.

He shook his head. "We'd better get back to the B and B. It looks like a nor'easter."

"Come kids, let's go. See the clouds? There's a storm coming."

"Storm, storm, storm!"

Catherine took Leo's hand. "Storm, storm!" He echoed.

Big drops plunked down on their heads, and they dashed across Fifth Avenue as the clouds unleashed windswept torrents.

*

Catherine rubbed her eyes with one hand while Leo tugged on the other. "Momma, I wanna go on the swing." James was just blinking awake in the B and B apartment, a third-floor walk-up on Ninety-Sixth Street. "Here's your dress Mom!" White chiffon with ruffles draped over Olivia's arm. "That's your dress honey," Catherine said. She had found it in an antique store on a visit to James' parents and had altered it to fit Olivia. "Mine is draped over the chair...but I've got to re-sew that one gusset on yours. It looked too tight yesterday. James!"

"Yeah, what should I do?"

"I've got my hands full. The kids need breakfast, there's cereal on the counter."

Lulu walked in with two big bouquets and a to-go tray of lidded coffees. "Rise and shine, you're getting married! And the sun's come out!"

*

Eleven in the morning they stood in a sheltered circle of lawn in Central Park's Shakespeare Garden, the air still cool, impatiens blossomed along the split-rail fence glistening with droplets from the night's storm. Behind the fence pink rose shrubs and a stand of young white pine gave refuge from the crowds touring the park's walkways. Within the circle she and James and Olivia and Leo and thirteen family and friends.

She watched Alan as he spoke the opening phrases he had specially written. He got ordained online, just for this moment, for them. The part suited him so naturally.

James' eyes were clear and blue as the sky above. So dignified in his four-button charcoal blazer, exotic in his Ghanaian ebony and ivory necklace and medallion, no boring necktie. She wondered if he knew he was pursing his lips. He must be stressed. It was a lot. His first time. And her first time feeling absolutely right.

Olivia beside her, her long dark curls crowned with a tiara of white rose blossoms. The chiffon ruffles over her shoulders so winglike it seemed as though she might take flight and flutter above the gathering. And Leo, wavering between pride and timid discomfort in his blue blazer. His golden hair mussed by the breeze.

James was reading his poem. "You are the sun. Shine. I am the oak. Thrive, in fertile ground. Drawing your sugars down, to drink them up again. You raise the day..."

"Just a moment," Catherine said. "I'm sorry. Leo, are you hungry? He won't make it through if he's hungry. James, the crackers are in that bag, the blue bag over there. Sorry, thanks everybody. Here Leo, you can sit comfy right here and have your crackers."

James lifted the page again. "You raise the day. Glow. You set down the night. Shadow. I can be alone that long only because I know, you're rounding the world and coming home."

As the June sun found noon they shed blazers and shawls, sat crosslegged on picnic blankets, swigged waters, and relished sandwiches.

"It took us a while to find you all," Colleen said.

James looked to L.J. "You're the trekker, you probably got here first!"

"I think first place goes to your friend Alan."

"Thank the gods it's only five minutes walk from the cab on Seventy-Ninth," Alan said, otherworldly in his pin stripes and round purple spectacles, his hair more salt than pepper.

L.J.'s younger brother Royce waved his hands in the air. "Whoa, wait a minute, Mister Bing. What about your people's forty days and forty nights? What happened to that?"

It seemed like a good point. Everyone turned to Alan.

"Lost to the sands of time. But I'd like to make a toast, everyone." Alan stood and dabbed his lips with a napkin. "We don't know what life will bring us along the way. Who would have thought yesterday that today the sun would beam its thousand rays? Mary has brought us through the storm, to that oneness she always wanted for you, Catherine. Safety and love." He raised his bottled water. "To James and Catherine, and Mary!"

*

Edmund Boulevard, Minneapolis, December

James looked up from the snowy sidewalk — shoveled behind, unshoveled ahead — and gazed across the River Road to the tall tress on the high banks of the Mississippi River, trees that withstood in stillness this bitter cold before sunrise, before twilight, before any light but streetlight. He waited with the trees. His breathing slowed and his brow cooled as he felt the place where he stood, the frozen ground. This was a world of seasons. His breath rose into the dark air. He moved now, head down, shoveling hard to keep ahead of the looming chill. Round the corner, up the front steps, he finished quickly, clearing just what was necessary. Then stamped his boots inside the door, pulled the gloves from his stiff fingers and there was Catherine in the kitchen, a steaming kettle on the stove.

She smiled. "I saw your note, and thank you for shoveling."

It was one of the things he had learned during the first two years after moving from New York, after the divorce was final. She had an unusual need to know where he was at all times.

"It's weird," he had told Kelly on the phone. "Like if I go to the bathroom, she's calling my name, and when I explain I was in the bathroom she says, *I didn't know where you were, you just disappeared!* Do I need to report everything I do? Isn't that controlling?"

"Well, you are part of a family now. But it does seem a bit extreme. I wonder what it's about for her. Does she control other things you do? Does she tell you what to wear or what to say?"

"No." He had thought a moment. "But she's very demanding about how I spend my time, that I need to be job searching more, and doing more to help around the house."

Kelly hadn't seemed impressed with his examples. "But I do think the bathroom thing is a little odd. When you're in a relationship, it's easy to worry that you're out of sync with each other, and that worry can become a problem all its own, when really everything is okay. Does that make sense?"

*

In Minnesota everyone was nice. They smiled when they passed on the sidewalk, mouth closed, lips pressed together in a stiff straight line. There were very few of them on the sidewalks. Or on the roads. Or anywhere. *Where are all the people?* he asked Catherine. There were many, many flying things. Beetles, house flies, fruit flies, fireflies, damselflies, gnats, bees, wasps, mosquitoes. Too much nature.

They parked their cars in ramps, which was okay because ramps were parking garages. They budged in line instead of butting in line. After complaining all winter about the cold, when summer finally came, they went Up North, where it was colder.

They were orderly. Bicyclists used all the official hand signals no-one else in America knew how to use, and none of the unofficial hand signals everyone else in America used.

On James' arrival, he was amazed that you could see, even from the airplane window, that the Twin Cities was shockingly clean. They were highly educated. They were highly skilled. Even the office professionals knew carpentry, hunting, fishing, metalworking, weaving. There was something special about this place and the people rooted here, and he felt instantly at home. But he wasn't sure they were ready to accept him.

They wouldn't hire him. Of course it wasn't just them. It was the Great Recession. He had managed to relocate, for the second time in a decade, in the middle of an international economic crisis. He finally landed a temp job. Reception desk at a hospital's corporate offices in Saint Paul. Five weeks at twelve dollars an hour. What followed was a sequence of sporadic temporary assignments, some as high as fifteen dollars an hour, some as low as ten. His first year in Minnesota, his second year, even after the wedding as his third year began, it still hadn't gotten any better. At least he was contributing something, a small addition to Catherine's modest income at the Montessori school.

She got the Edmund Boulevard home and Alistair got the rental properties. James gazed at the house around him — living room, family room, dining room, kitchen, den, and bathroom, and a whole other floor up above. It was a mansion by any standards he or Luke had known in New York City. And modest though it was as a Minnesota home, it cost more than their modest income to maintain.

Days with the kids, he brewed the morning coffee and prodded Olivia and Leo to dress and comb their hair and pack their backpacks for school while Catherine made breakfast and got them the rest of the way dressed and combed the hair they forgot to comb and ran everywhere finding the things that were supposed to be in their backpacks but weren't. He helped herd them into the car after they ran to the backyard to play on the swing. Tried to collect himself in the front seat before Catherine let him off at his latest temp job. Nine hours later, he was relieved to see her waiting at the curb, kids in the backseat, after his fluorescent day of answering phone calls, making photocopies, and learning which files had red stickers and which blue. And when the kids were with Alistair, there was still work but the world opened a little wider, the bigger world of art and thought and exploration.

They drove Up North to Mille Lacs, to Dassler's place. His booth at the Shoreview art fair last summer was the one where they lingered, captivated by assemblages of wood and stone and mechanical parts. *These are so organic* — James had said — *They feel natural, like they rose up out of the earth!* Dassler had smiled a faraway smile. *I've never quite been satisfied with the universe around me* — he had said — *So I decided to make my own.*

They coursed up U.S. 169. Snow everywhere. Red and gold grasses poked through. Evergreens and birch bent under the weight. On the county road, they crossed the Rum River, spotted his address on a steel stake, pulled into a drive that lead them around an open field, past a frozen pond with snow-dusted cattails, and around the bend where poplar woods sprouted from three feet of glistening snow. From an out-building appeared Dassler, who motioned them into his pickup. They climbed in the front passenger seat and shoulder-to-shoulder they bounced along to buy a bale of hay for his two horses. The farmer loaded the bale into the pickup bed, examined the bills, nodded. James wasn't sure whether even a single word was exchanged.

"One more stop," Dassler said. "Kingbird's place. I owe him a book." They parked at the end of a long drive, and trudged through snow ten minutes until a log cabin appeared amid the poplar, smoke curling from the chimney.

"I had to take a while with this one." Dassler handed the book to his friend.

"Cézanne's Composition, I was wondering where it was. When did I lend it to you?"

"A while ago. You're gonna see it in the next house I build. I'm seeing planes in a new light."

They warmed themselves around the wood stove and Kingbird threw in a freshly-chopped log while expounding on Dutch masters and Impressionists.

Tiny snowflakes lofted in the wind as Dassler drove down the two lane road lined with white pine and bare poplar, trunks gray against the white snow. As they climbed from the pickup a flock of Canadian geese flew honking over Dassler's open field. Along the edge of the woods a long row of assorted structures stood desultory. There were two livable houses, a wood-fired boiler house that heated them, two not-so-livable-looking houses, and an old RV. Dassler made everything out of everything. He collected salvage — furniture, eighty-year-old farm tractors, refrigerators, electric ovens. He built his houses from salvaged lumber and stone and brick. And to store his salvage he collected other salvage. The RV became a shed piled with furniture. And then there were the two not-so-livable houses. One looked as though it might have been someone's living room, the double sliding-glass doors opening not to a patio or deck but to the grasses of the field. Inside the glass doors were bicycles and farm implements. The other was the second-floor of a house that he brought in with a crane, planted on the ground, and filled with appliances — *got a good deal on that one* — and when he found a roof he couldn't pass up, he propped it on top of the other roof, a little off-kilter, but he liked the asymmetry. As James walked with Catherine back to the car, he turned for a final look. The brilliant gold of the evening winter sky filtered through the trees, a gray-blue ascending to deep magenta to light pink to lightest gray. Every built surface tinted pink. "It's a town," James said. "Dassler has made his own town."

"Dasslertown!" Catherine said. He kissed her cheek and marveled. It was all too beautiful to understand.

*

"I love your homemade potato soup!" Lulu spooned another mouthful. James cupped the bowl in his hands and inhaled the aroma. Catherine smiled, "It's good on a winter night. Tomorrow we're back to hotdogs with the kids!"

"Everything you make is delicious. Do you know what I mean? I used to eat out all the time in New York. Nowhere had meals as good as yours." James reached for the wine bottle.

"James." Catherine's voice warned. "You've had two glasses. Two is enough."

She breathed relief when he set the bottle down, unpoured. It had taken them two years to get this far, where he wouldn't argue or make excuses to pour a third or fourth glass every night. Or the horrible December evening, their first year together. James went out with colleagues after work for happy hour and when it was getting late she called him and he didn't answer, didn't answer. And when he finally answered he was slurring like an idiot. It was awful. How did he think he could be part of a family, two small children to care for, and act like that? *You can't do this anymore. You have to limit your drinking, or stop altogether.*

*

"The coffee is ready!" James' voice from the kitchen was still a miracle. Of safety, understanding, companionship. Even though he was still learning — how many years would it take — how to be a family. Even though he too often seemed hard to reach, floating away up into the clouds of his own thoughts when she wanted him to focus on their life together. She frowned. Coffee in hand he was headed for the studio and the company of his desktop computer.

*

A tiny heart in the sky, propelled from a larger heart in swirls of water. Catherine studied the pencil drawing in Mary's sketchbook.

Leo's voice called, "Mom."

"I'm here Leo. Mom's coming."

*

The kids rushed in the door and through the family room. "First one to the top of the stairs wins the race!" Leo exclaimed.

"It's Alistair's day and he knows it." James tossed off his coat and unbuttoned his work shirt, all a bit too dramatically. He was incensed. "What the hell is he doing scheduling consultations end of the school day? As long as he knows you'll hop to it whenever he drops the ball, then he'll keep doing it."

"What do you want me to do? Do you want an eight-year-old and six-year-old left sitting alone at school after hours? You've got it all worked out in principle, what's right, what ought to happen. I'm dealing with what's actually happening."

"And this is how our life get's jerked around?"

"For as long as I'm their mother, and that's forever."

*

March 2010

The backyard had reappeared. The same pale, dormant grass, the same fallen leaves last seen in November. Broad swaths of snow still blanketed the shaded ground beneath the evergreens and along the north side of the house. But before long that snow too would stream tinkling across sidewalks to join the gathering rush of ice-melt coursing the streets.

Between household tasks, Catherine wove art-making into the fabric of her everyday life. In a house she owned, a city she knew, with a family she made, this was one of the few gifts he could give her — the freedom to be herself. She sorted stone beads into sets of symbiotic shape and color for necklaces and bracelets. She coiled fine silver wire around a wooden dowel, clipped it into open rings, interlacing, fused the circles closed with a butane torch into a delicate silver bracelet.

He watched her work and worked his thoughts into penned strokes in his paper journal. "Ugh, what's the word? I'm a writer and I'm always

340

forgetting words. You know, a word that means to make something, create, manipulate..."

"Wait." Catherine plunked the glowing silver hissing into a bowl of water, then stood beside him. "How about fabricate."

"No that's not what I meant. But." Motionless he stared at the sentence in his journal.

"Why did you even ask? You always do this. You say the best work comes from collaboration, but when I share an idea..."

"No, you're right, you're right. I do want to collaborate." He always got caught like this. Yes, wanting to collaborate, but how could she possibly understand where he's going with an idea, understand what's in his head? But actually. "Fabricate is concrete, real, it's just right."

"See? We can help each other." She dried the silver bracelet with an old burp cloth and laid it onto the little steel bench block and let loose with her forged ball-peen hammer. She glanced to his quizzical eyes. "It strengthens the rings!" she said above the peel of hammer strokes. "Realigns the electrons!"

*

She taught him the names of the trees. The form and bark and leaf of the white oak and burr oak and pin oak. Norway maple and sugar maple. Cottonwood, poplar, birch. Walnut, sycamore, Russian olive. He had only ever known oak and palm. And pine, which to him meant evergreen. "This is jack pine, see the short needles and tiny waxed cones? That one is red pine, there's a red hue to the bark. And see the one there, towering above the others? That's white pine. Their mature limbs break under heavy snow loads, giving them a wild form."

"What kind of pine is that one?"

"It's juniper, it's not pine at all. And that's cedar."

"So they are all evergreen?"

"Except for the larch. I'll show you one sometime. Larch are bare in winter, like deciduous trees. You can call all of them conifers."

He scanned the woods. There were names for the many shapes he saw, if only he could remember them.

What would Cape Coast have been beyond brush if he had known the names? What would Cumaná have been beyond palms? Mom and Dad had taught him some things so intricately. But other swaths of the world had been blind wastes that held no interest for them. Catherine taught him to know the names of rocks by color and pattern. Taught him the kinds of cow by color of coat — black-and-white Holstein are raised for dairy, red or black Angus cows for meat. And suddenly he knew from the color of cows what the local economy was based on and where their politics might lean.

He looked at her silently. Suddenly desperate. What if she weren't there? How could he hold onto all these names without her? How much of his world would disappear?

*

She walked into the den. "James, did you see the email I forwarded from LoLa Art Crawl? They're asking me for an artist statement."

He looked up from his desktop screen. "Could you say that again?"

"Did you see the email from LoLa Art Crawl?"

"Yeah, a statement about why you make art. What are you going to say?"

"I don't know, I guess I never really thought about why I make art, I just do it."

He turned his chair toward her. "Well, for example, I wrote music because there was something I wanted to hear, and the only way to hear it, was to write it."

She looked at her hands, imagined herself working the pliers to twist fine silver wire, mixing paint with a brush, pushing the knitting needle through a loop of yarn. That was it. "James, I think I have this primal urge to work with my hands."

"That's concrete and to the point. I wish I could make my theory so down-to-earth."

"I can help you with that, anytime." She walked through the dining room into the kitchen, took three carrots from the fridge and the peeler from the drawer and leaned over the trash, peels flicking like orange confetti.

*

She couldn't wait to tell him. "James, I'm back!"

"How did it go?" He kissed her.

"I had trouble finding the College of Biological Sciences but Dr. Kaddouri was nice about me being a little late. I wish you could have come along. He did a study on identical twins separated at birth and reunited decades later. He showed me photos, how they had the same posture and gestures, with their hands straight out, or arms folded, with the same expression on their faces." She could see him preparing his counter-argument.

"You know, it could be culture too. People in every society around the world..."

She planted her hands on her hips while he continued.

"...have shared ways of expressing emotions. Europeans raise their hands to say I don't know. South Asians swoosh their head in a kind of yes-no."

"But it makes sense, James, doesn't it? If their bodies have the same build, then they would move the same way and feel comfortable in the same position."

"That's true. That does make sense when their bodies are built the same way."

She could see his mind engaging, the ideas starting to come together. "You know" — she said — "my mom and her sister bought the same dishes without even knowing it. Maybe if your brains are wired the same, you have the same personality, the same preferences."

"Well at that point you would have to say that everything is controlled by the genes."

*

He carried the two Willem Gebben mugs, white polka dots on charcoal black, into the dining room and there through the living room archway was Catherine. With a damp paper towel she deftly wiped each dark glossy leaf of the zig-zag plant.

"Shall we have our coffee together in the dining room?" he asked.

She gave a final wipe and pulled three sketchbooks from the living room bookshelf and laid them on the dining room table. "I can't remember which of these you've seen."

He watched as she opened a hard-bound sketchbook. Outside the window the crabapple tree held onto its last fiery orange leaves. "Look at this one," she said. "Hands reaching for the baby, the very moment she's giving birth. There are more like this scattered throughout her sketchbooks." She leafed through the next booklet. Baby faces. Hands reaching. A woman naked with a black hole in her abdomen. Catherine's fingers traced her mother's figure. "Can you imagine what it was like for her? And in some of the paintings there's a ball of light." She left the room, returned with a portfolio case. "Here, this one." In watercolor, a young girl, her face illuminated by a glowing ball cradled in her hands. Behind her a stairway ascended into darkness.

"Is the glowing ball some kind of life force? Are you the ball of light?" James stood beside her.

"I think maybe it's her. I'm the child. I'm not sure."

*

"Crossland residence."

"Oh, hi Dad, it's James! How are you and Mom doing?"

"Hi James. Let me put Mom on."

James mouth, poised to speak, closed and he waited. This was how it usually went, Dad serving as the operator, connecting the call.

"Hi James!" Mom's voice was delighted, expectant.

"Hi Mom!" He relaxed into her stories. "We had the floor tile people over today" she said. "You wouldn't believe the mud tracks they made down the hallway carpet on their way to the kitchen!"

*

"You see we're in San Francisco..."

"Yes, I know, that was the plan," Catherine said.

"And tomorrow we're off for a scenic tour of Mount Shasta. I'd like another few days."

"Another few days?" It had already been a week, and that was hard enough.

"We're on holiday. The West Coast. Mount Shasta is an opportunity I simply don't want the children to miss."

"I suppose. Can I talk to them?"

Olivia's voice. Leo echoed. Redwoods, seals, Golden Gate. The words streamed by. She heard her voice tremble, *I love you,* watched herself hang up the phone.

*

James saw what it did to her. And what it did to them as a couple. When the kids were with Alistair, she had a hard time with the separation. She was preoccupied and there was less room for anything else in their lives. He was patient, helpful, annoyed, fucking annoyed. It was her house, her kids, her ex, her crises. And on top of that, his own crises. He still didn't have a real job, and they were an inch away from qualifying for poverty benefits. It was nothing like what he thought love would be. He found her, found love, and all this other shit dragging along with it.

*

Summer 2011

She focused on Lulu. "Without names I can't find anyone!"

"Look at everything you've already accomplished. You found Mary, her paintings, her journals. You know all her friends. I'm just saying, you can be proud of what you've done."

"It's just so maddening," Catherine said. "I have a right to know where I came from, but Catholic Services won't give me a single name!"

"Why don't you try one of those DNA sites, you know, like 23andMe, that matches you to relatives. You might find your mom's parents. You might even find your father."

Lulu always knew what to do.

*

"I don't see how we can." James, bath towel around his waist, pulled open the dresser drawer. "We don't have the money. We don't have the time."

"A week after we met you were telling all your friends, *I'm going to get married and have a baby,*" Catherine pulled the comb through her hair.

"I know, I know. I'm still looking for a real job. We can hardly provide for Olivia and Leo. It's already too much. The bus is in ten minutes, I have to get dressed."

In the evening while she sliced avocado in the kitchen, he sat by the family room window, a glass of red wine on the side table and a notebook on his lap. His eyes traced the limbs skyward, the massive tree across the street. *Cottonwood, king of the forest,* she always said. He sketched a phrase. Another. Crossed it out. Wrote again, kept writing.

There is a zebra-striped tree, taller than many. Bark deeply grooved. Massive limbs rise. Leaves glossy one side, matte on the other, flip in the wind one side to the other. Each moves alone. And the multitude shimmer. That's the word, shimmer. Ten thousand wheels turning. Ten thousand flags waving. Ten thousand prayers for sun sustaining this old seed through its trajectory from earth to sky, monument to recurring life. Cottonwood by my river home. Fly your seed. Let it be my progeny as good as any. Multiply for me.

*

Catherine sealed the envelope and wrote the address, Ohio Vital Statistics. A request for Mary's original birth certificate, another piece of the puzzle. Vital Statistics who had told Catherine, *you have no linkage to her.* That was part of the whole Catholic Services dead end in 2005. The engagement to James in 2008 had given her an idea. She wanted to take his last name, Crossland, so why not take Mary's as a middle name? New York doesn't let you change your middle name on marriage, so before the wedding she appeared before a Hennepin County judge to add both as legal names. She became Catherine Tomczak Lind Crossland, and if there had been nothing else going on in her life she might have contacted Ohio Vital Statistics the next day. But there was the wedding and honeymoon and job and kids. And maybe it wasn't such a bad thing that another few years had gone by, more time between her rejected attempt and this new attempt. Even now it felt like a long shot.

*

Your DNA results are in. It was an email from 23andMe. "James come see this!" She plunked herself onto the family room sofa with her laptop computer and he sat beside her. This was what she loved, sharing discoveries together. "Ancestry Composition, ninety-nine percent European — Northwestern, Southern, Eastern. And one percent Unassigned."

"No wonder you kept going back to Europe in your twenties. You were trying to get home!"

"You're laughing" — she said — "but there's probably something to it. And look, here are the DNA matches: Second cousin once removed, Third cousin. They're all pretty remote relations."

"But they are blood relatives."

"That's true. Do you talk to your cousins?"

"No."

She scrolled further down the list. Fourth to Distant Cousin.

*

Sometimes you just need another way to find what you're looking for. There was a thud on the floor beneath the mail slot. A credit card bill, Minneapolis Public Schools, and a thick envelope with *DOH501420* stamped in bold black ink in the bottom right corner and *State of Ohio Department of Health* printed in the top left.

She sat at the dining room table and opened the envelope, stared at a page of densely typed text, flipped to the next page. Certificate of Live Birth. "Oh my god. I can't think straight. James!"

He emerged from the den. She handed the papers to him and watched as he read. "Full name of child, Iris Kaminska. Mother of child, Irene Kaminska. Father of child, Unnamed." He looked up at her. "In anthropology I could never follow when they got into lineages, so this is whose child?"

"It's my mother. My mother's birth name is Iris Kaminska. That's Mary! And her birth mother, my grandmother, is Irene Kaminska... That name, I know I've seen that name." She jumped from her chair and pulled one of Mary's sketchbooks from the bookshelves. "This must be it" — she opened to the marked page — "Mary Casey, Mary Oliveira, Mary Kaminska. James, she knew! Mary knew her birth mother's name."

"Do you think they met?"

"Not necessarily. I haven't seen anything in her sketchbooks about a reunion. And none of her friends mentioned anything. It doesn't always work out. What else does the birth certificate say?"

He read: "Birthmother age twenty-two at time of birth. Single. Tall, slim, curly red-hair, very attractive. Left high school after eleventh grade. Previously employed in a factory. Background Slovakian."

"Slovakian! James, I've been there, well, near there. It was called Czechoslovakia when I crossed the Vltava River looking for Jesus — the figurine for Mom. People always asked me, Are you Irish? Are you Native American? Everybody had their ideas about where I was from, but I had no idea." She held a lock of her hair between her fingers. Red highlights under incandescent light. "I'm Slovakian. What else does it say?"

"Birthfather: Age twenty-two at the time of birth. Single. A lake man. — Wait a minute. If they can list his age and marital status, why not his name?"

"That was the law back then, Helen Quinn told me. If the couple weren't married, they weren't allowed to name the father."

"After that it says — Baby was six pounds, eleven and a half ounces at birth. Born December 8, 1948. Placed in the home of Mr. and Mrs. Tomczak on April 9, 1949 in Sandusky, Ohio."

"That's where they placed Mary," she said. "She grew up in the same town where her birth mother still lived! How could they even do that? They would have run into each other! And their names start with the same letter, Irene and Iris. Just like Mary gave me the name Michelle." She jumped up and ran to her computer on the kitchen island. "Irene Kaminska. There seem to be hits on this site, Ancestry.com, but I have to do a free trial to sign in."

"Sure, go ahead."

As soon as she was registered, the record popped up and she read aloud — "Irene Kaminska born 16 March 1928 in Huron, Ohio, died 2 October 2007." She looked at James.

"Okay, she's passed away" he said. "She's a generation further back, so in a way we'd be really lucky if she were still living."

She had already turned back to the laptop. There were family trees attached to the record. "Marin Family Tree. There she is, Irene Kaminska Marin. The tree's owner is Richard Marin." She opened his profile page and saw a button. "I can message him." She gaped at James. She wrote her message and clicked send.

James held her close. "Someone living is out there. Someone is going to answer." And two days later, someone did.

Hi Catherine. This is unexpected. I am Rick Marin, Irene's son. I'm not aware of my mother having another child, so pardon me if I'm a little skeptical. There are a lot of scams out there. Can you provide some kind of proof of your relationship?

People need a little help and a little time to process. All the cold calls to Mary's friends had taught her that. She messaged back: *If you would like to share your email address with me, I will send you my mother's original birth certificate naming your mother Irene Kaminska as her mother. I'll also send my original birth certificate connecting me to my mother. I'm adopted too.*

*

Hello Catherine, Well what do you know — it looks like I'm your Uncle Rick. I can say it is surprising, but still not all that surprising. Mom was a wonderful woman, so beautiful and caring but also very independent. She made her own decisions.

When Mom died, I found a large sketch book. All the sketches are dated December of 1948 and January of 1949. I always wondered why she never shared it with us and why there weren't any other sketches. I wonder now if it was to distract her from the impending adoption? Going through her things I also found multitudes of started projects that she never finished, crochet and various crafts. I take after her in that respect. I have a tendency to jump from thing to thing because there is always so much I want to do. It's exciting to know you and to know I had a sister Iris, or Mary. I only wish I could have met her. Though I have to tell you, I'm a little concerned about how this will go down with my dad.

*

Uncle Rick. Birth family, living birth family. She could see James was thrilled for her. And she wished she could share it with Mom and Dad too. But for them, there would always be that seed of fear that the newfound family might replace them. It wasn't rational. Mothers-in-law don't replace mothers. Step-fathers don't replace fathers. And birth family don't replace adoptive family. But she could see it in their eyes whenever she talked about birth family, and so more and more she didn't.

She emailed back and forth with Uncle Rick. Then phoned back and forth, she and Rick finishing each other's sentences, laughing or groaning at the same moments, as he tried to figure out how he was going to break the news to his aunt and uncle and cousins. She listened to his voice on the kitchen island answering machine. "Well, all hell broke loose here with the family. Give me a call when you can."

Uncle Rick said his dad, Mack, had always been somewhat of a loose cannon. Everyone said it was the war. He fought in the South Pacific. He was erratic, sometimes calm as the lake on a windless day, other times he lashed out at Rick's mom or at the refrigerator on the fritz, anyone or anything that crossed his path. He was a time bomb none of the family wanted to go near. When Uncle Rick told his wife and kids about Catherine, that's when the fuse was lit and burned sparking and smoking and the kids told their cousins, who told their mom Emma, who told her brother Sam, who told their mom Alice, who told Sam not to let anybody tell Uncle Mack, and that should have been that, but the fuse just kept burning until somebody — nobody was sure who — told Mack. So anyway all hell broke loose but now it was done. The gale swept through, then they put it all back in order. After all, Mack declared Mom was a saint, period. They were all sensible people, more interested in facts than fuss. Catherine's family. But one fact was still to be settled, the identity of Mary's father.

Hi Catherine, I drove up to my sister's in Sandusky on the weekend and went through my mom's boxes again. I found two photos I wanted to send you right away. My mom loved taking pictures. They're from a couple of years before your mom was born. One is a man standing with my Aunt Alice, taken on the family farm. I showed Aunt Alice the photo and she said she doesn't remember his name but he was the man my mom was living with when she became pregnant with your mother. The other photo is dated the same year — two sailors at a restaurant, both looking at the camera. I don't think Danny is the same man in the photo with Aunt Alice, but he looks to have a nose similar to your mom's. There's your mystery. — Your Uncle Rick

Catherine held the first photo, turned it in her hand. "It just says 1946. No names on the back." Shot in black-and-white. A man and woman in their twenties, long slacks and sweaters, posing in front of a clapboard house. Maybe early spring. A tree cast its shadow of leafless branching limbs across the clapboards, cast it from the side so that remarkably the house bore its projection but the man and woman did not. They stood in full sun, a shadow tree behind them.

James looked on over her shoulder. "So your Uncle Rick said it was your mom's mom Irene taking the shot, and the woman is her sister Alice. She look's like she's putting up with the guy next to her, doesn't she?"

"Doing it for her sister I guess," Catherine said. "And we know he's my mom's dad, but we don't know his name." She picked up the second photo, another black-and-white. "And there are these two sailors in uniform in the restaurant booth."

"Look at the insignias on their sleeves. It's straight out of some World War Two movie. And your mom's mom shot this photo too right?"

"Yeah. And under this sailor she penned, *Danny Greenfield looks blue.* Funny, but he does look a little depressed. And under the other, *His buddy Billy Canada.* That's quite a name!"

"Do you think it's a nickname?"

"I don't know. But it's dated the same year as the other photo."

"Is it possible one of the sailors is your mom's father, not the guy in the other photo?"

"But Alice confirmed that the guy in the other photo on the farm is my mom's dad. And look how he's standing with his hand on his hip, one leg crossed over the other. It's just like Mary in the newspaper photo with the governor of Massachusetts. And Olivia in the photo at the lake, hand on her hip, one leg crossed in front of the other. I stand that way too." James looked unconvinced.

"Remember Dr. Kaddouri from the U of M, identical twins separated at birth? Same posture, same hand gestures, same facial expressions. Do you ever stand with your leg crossed and hand on your hip?"

"No, I don't."

"See, you have to be built that way." She studied the sailors in the other photo. "Danny Greenfield and Billy Canada. There's something so familiar about the look in his eyes."

"Which one?"

"This one, Billy Canada." More than anything it was the feeling behind the look. A feeling Catherine recognized. It was how she felt as a child, waking every morning hopeful and excited for the day's possibilities. Looking into that sailor's face, she was looking at herself. "And he has a little space between his front teeth like I do, and the peak in his hairline..." Catherine ran to the mirror in the bathroom and pulled her hair back from her forehead, tracing a line down to her eyebrow, then raced back to the dining room. "Look James, we both have a peak in our hairlines in the same place, off-center to the right."

"Your Uncle Rick thought Danny Greenfield has your mom's nose."

"But look at the way Greenfield ties his sash. It's a mess!"

"I think it's a neckerchief. A sash would be..."

"Mary was good with her hands and meticulous about detail. Billy Canada's sash is flawless."

James picked up the photo and scrutinized the uniforms. He exhaled like a deflating balloon. "It can't be your sailor because your Aunt Alice remembers it was the guy in the farm photo!" He cast the photo onto the table, the photo spinning one direction while he spun the other. She frowned. And laughed. But now she saw an idea taking hold in him.

He laid the photos side by side. "What are the things you always say to look at? Details like the shape of the nose, the eyebrows, the chin. And the personality, right?" He studied the photos. "Catherine, these two are the same guy! The neatly dressed sailor and the guy at the family farm. Look at the features of his face. And the confidence. Greenfield looks depressed. But Billy Canada is self-assured. This sailor is the guy at the farm. He's your mom's dad. And how about that name!"

The name was a problem. Internet searches brought up people with the first name William who live in Canada, people with the last name Williams who live in Canada, a company called Williams Industrial Service Group, in Canada. She did what she always did, she kept searching. There was no family tree on Ancestry, but she found a death record for a William Canada in Fayetteville, North Carolina and a more recent city directory listing for a William Canada in the same city. Maybe he was the son, Billy junior. She called the phone number in the directory and Billy junior's wife answered. *Call Sally, Billy's sister, she'd be happy to talk to you.* And she was. And it wasn't a nickname. And they weren't Canadian. And when Catherine emailed the photos to her, she said, "That's him. I don't think I've ever seen a photo of him when he was in the Navy." The family came over from Wales to North Carolina two hundred-fifty years ago. Someone's version of an old Welsh name, Aunt Sally said. "My dad, your grandfather, he loved people, and he loved to work with his hands." Catherine thought of her LoLa artist statement. "If you want to learn more" — Sally had continued — "there's a book *The Record and History of the Canada Family in America.* Check it out. We've all got a copy."

*

James slid into the front seat. "I am so glad the day is over. Isn't that an awful thing to say?"

"I'm sorry you have to work at that awful place. I'd rather not be working at the Montessori school either, but I guess this is life."

"I know, I know." Her earnest assessment was as right as it was depressing.

"But go ahead and tell me about your day."

"It was stupid. The photocopier jammed. Just stupid."

"Now there's something I want to share with you" — she said — "so I hope you're not going to be cranky. You'll never guess what I found. I was reading *The Record and History of the Canada Family in America.* And the description on the first page says, *The Canada family are honest, sober, and always busy."*

"That sounds like you!"

"Doesn't it? Down through the centuries they were weavers, engravers, mechanics, engineers. The first Canada who came over was a weaver, and here I am with my sewing and knitting and jewelry, and Mary with her sewing and painting, always making something with her hands!"

He wanted to support her. He held his tongue. She was staring at him with those penetrating dark eyes. And here came the questions.

"Do you think my need to work with my hands could be hereditary?"

"Those are skills we learn through trial and error and by observing others and that's culture."

"How can this same trait keep appearing generation after generation?"

"The behaviors you're talking about — weaving, sewing — are passed on through learning."

"But no one taught me how to do it."

"Well..." He had to get himself on track, follow what was in his mind. "If everything we did was genetically programmed, we'd be robots. And that line of argument, genetic determinism, leaves no room for social change..."

"I have an innate need to work with my hands."

He stared at his docile hands. "I can sit for hours reading and thinking. My hands are motionless all the while. I don't doodle, I don't whittle, I don't feel any urge..."

"Exactly."

"So maybe people can be born with a lesser or greater capacity for fine motor skills. Variations in a fundamental capacity that, yes, is genetically determined. And then what someone does with that capacity..."

"Yes."

"...that's where culture comes in. What handiwork the handy people will do depends on what handiwork is available in the society and era they live in."

"Do you remember what I showed you with my hands, when we first met?"

"The special hand gestures." It was the phrase they both used to bring a little humor to the recurring argument. But this time was different. Now he needed those gestures to hold onto a new understanding. He held his right hand upright. "These are your genes." He wiggled his hand like kelp in the current. "Culture can do this. But it can't do this." He positioned his hand stiffly to mark a place, then swept his arm to mark a new place. He wiggled his hand again and looked at her. "This wiggle is enough room for culture. Your model gives me a place for genes and culture."

*

She added James to the Ancestry family tree. Once you add someone, it's only natural to branch back to their parents, and their parents' parents. It was so ridiculously easy to do for James because he knew what most people know — his parents' and grandparents' names, and at least some of the great grandparents. Catherine laid the pizza dish on the dining room table. "We're looking for James' family now."

Olivia raised her brows and smooshed her lips to one side. "Mom, James wasn't adopted. You should know that."

"We're tracing his family back into the past."

Olivia's raised shoulders were question marks. "I can see Olivia is very impressed," James teased. "What do you think, Leo?" Leo shrugged, his mouth full.

"Now," Catherine said — "Was your father's father named Kirk? And was your father's mother, Grace?"

"Yep."

"Was your father's father's father, Challys and your father's father's mother, Caria?" She could see he was already lost, but he blurted suddenly, "Challys, yes Challys is right. But I don't know about Caria."

She knew how to investigate. It was all about the intersection of time, place, and people. Ancestry gives you leads to other family trees and historical documents that might relate to your someone. But those leads are only useful if you're sure that it's really your someone they relate to. Did the creator of the other family tree rely on family lore, sometimes accurate, sometimes not? Or did they rely on independent, primary sources like marriage and death records, census listings, and city directories?

In the U.S. Census, find a person. Examine names and ages of family members. Adjacent listings in the census sometimes reveal family members living next door or nearby. What are their names and ages? What's consistent and makes sense?

She took it back to Challys's parents, William Crossland and Martha Trimble. "I remember my grandpa mentioning that name, Martha," he said. "She was the side of the family that went back to the Calverts who founded Maryland. George Calvert, First Baron Baltimore. I don't know why I never heard about William. It's like some parts of the story get handed down but not others. You begin to wonder how much else you don't know."

Generations

2011

Morning sun filtered through the limbs of the trees, blinding her for a moment as she pulled into the Montessori school parking lot. Autumn. Oak and maple leaves tumbled over her feet, skidded dry and hollow across the asphalt. Between the slats of the wooden fence Catherine caught sight of the swing set. A memory of little Olivia, her pointed toes reaching for the red and yellow maple leaf as big as her beaming face. Now Olivia was at the performing arts school, fifth grade, and it was just Leo at the Montessori school, third grade. And Catherine was no longer a teacher, just one of the crowd of parents walking their children to the door. Last spring term she had gotten the notice. Budget cuts, contract not renewed. She was still looking for another job. Leo dragged his feet up the walkway but livened when he spied his friends inside.

"Good morning Leo!" The staffer at the door extended her hand, but he rushed past to join his friends, no handshake today.

"Hi Catherine!" Another parent, Jacqueline, was coming up the walkway with her little daughter Daisy. "It won't be quite the same in Daisy's classroom without you!"

"I'll miss being her teacher, but look, I'll still get to say good morning whenever we meet at drop-off! How are you this morning, Daisy?"

The little girl smiled and jiggled her body, "I'm ecstatic!"

"Oh, that's a good word! And is that what ecstatic looks like?"

"Yep! And I'm going to be a big sister!"

"Congratulations Daisy. How exciting. So Jacqueline, when are you due?"

By sunset the feelings inside her had come full bloom. James was cracking open a can of Guinness in the kitchen. He could raise any objection he wanted, because that would be his knee-jerk reaction, but she knew somehow that it didn't matter.

"How was your day?" he asked as he filled his pint glass.

"I had an inspiration this morning at drop-off."

"Are you thinking they might hire you back?"

"Oh, no," she shook her head absolutely. "I saw Daisy's mom and she's expecting."

He swallowed wrong and choked.

"James, I think it's time. We should have a baby."

"We hardly made enough money to get by when we were both working. Now we only have my temp job. I don't see how this is the right time."

She laughed in disbelief. "But James, that's just it. To have a baby you need time, and time is exactly what we have right now."

He stared silently, his mind churning.

*

Rocking, rocking, tumbling. Her voice, rumbling through the water.

*

Rice Lake, Wisconsin, November 2012

"Honestly Catherine, I'm a little worried," Mom said. "You look as though you might have that baby before dinner!"

Catherine lowered her knitting to her belly, mending the gold, green, and rust colored scarf she had knitted for Dad so long ago. "I've still got a couple of days. But if today's the day, I guess we just drive home." Outside the window snowflakes wafted among the pines along the lakeshore. "It's just flurries so far," Catherine insisted.

When snow flurries turned snow shower and regular contractions began, James was helping her into the passenger seat under the flood light of the cabin driveway. There was no pink, no violet in the November evening sky. It was gray to darkening gray and James held the steering wheel tight as flakes hurled toward them like little snowballs bright white in the headlights. "I'd say our visibility is less than a quarter mile," he said. "I'm slowing to fifty."

"Turn on the windshield wipers. And you're pursing." Another contraction reminded her: slow deep breaths.

"It's coming down harder. At least the car tracks are still showing here in the right lane."

"I can drive James. I'm more accustomed to driving in snow."

357

"You can't drive. I mean not now. Just help me watch the road. It snowed like this in the Palouse country. It's just a matter of taking in all the information available."

She listened to his voice, kept breathing.

"Wow, our lane is totally covered now. I'm slowing to thirty. But see there? Even though we can't see the road, there are still smudgy tire tracks in the snow. And ahead you can see a slight curve left."

She kept breathing. Not here, not the baby here. Turned to him to distract herself. "Let me know if you need me to do anything."

The two-hour drive became three hours. Finally, the lights of the Metro. Home on Edmund Boulevard at ten thirty, she eased onto the family room sofa and asked James to call the hospital. He paced, cell phone to his ear. "They want to know how far apart your contractions are."

"Six minutes. With Olivia, they made me wait, and by the time I got to the hospital I practically had the baby in the waiting room."

"Six minutes." He listened to the phone. "They say to wait."

"Tell them..." Catherine gasped. "Tell them this always happens. I need to come in."

James made his plea, maybe she should have gotten on the phone. "They said to call back when your contractions are five minutes apart. What else can we do?"

So they went to bed. Catherine turned uncomfortably while James slept beside her. Her mind was a blur of exhaustion, until she felt wetness. She rolled and stood beside the bed, a puddle at her feet.

"James, wake up!" He roused. "We have to go to the hospital, my water broke."

"You mean right now?"

"Right now. I'm going to have the baby."

*

Midnight. One o'clock. Two o'clock. Three o'clock. They paced the halls, slowly, round and round, learned every landmark: the hazardous waste closet, the antique infant gown framed in gold on the wall, the nurses station where the shifts had changed. Catherine's elegant fingers wrapped around his. Elegant, long, sinewy, her fingertips calloused by handiwork. She was a rose in the prairie. He looked at her profile: exhausted, lovely. "We're almost to Hazardous Waste," he announced. "There goes Hazardous Waste." That got a little laugh out of her. And around again. They returned to the delivery room. Rested. Waited. "They come when they're ready," the nurse said. "But let's see if we can give a little encouragement." Catherine settled into the delivery room tub, a warm bath to speed the contractions. She looked at him. "Tell me something. Anything."

He cast his glance around the room, looking for words, something to spark his mind. Until he realized the only thing he could think about was her, her and the tiny person they had created who was still deciding when was the right time to enter the world. He held up his left hand bearing the braided eighteen carat gold ring, handmade by a metal smith in Mille Lacs. "When I first put this wedding ring on my finger, I felt like I belonged in the world in a way I never had before. I'm not sure what I'm trying to say." He felt a little lost, but there in her waiting eyes he found his way. "I guess I'm saying, I wouldn't have that if it weren't for you."

"Oh, honey." She winced. "I'm exhausted and the contractions are still the same. I might need help. Pitocin. I needed it for Olivia, and for Leo. I'm forty-something. If I forget — tell the nurse I need Pitocin."

"Pitocin?"

"Pitocin."

The night passed. Sun shone through the hospital windows. Afternoon. She lay on the delivery bed, an IV tube in her arm. He watched the slow drip from the solution bag.

The nurse walked in. "You still here? Let's take a look. You're dilated."

"I'm so exhausted." Catherine seemed to be speaking to the air above her. "I can't. I just can't."

"I don't think that's going to be an option. Now I'm going to share some important information with you. Are you listening to me, honey?" the nurse said. James touched Catherine's arm. "You were the first last night, and the crowd that followed you have all had their babies. It's three ten in the afternoon now, and there's a new crowd coming in, and we've got precisely one delivery doctor on the floor." James watched the nurse's gaze glide to him and back to Catherine. "If you don't have that little baby of yours in the next twenty minutes, you're going to have to move to the back of the line."

Catherine arched her head up. "I'm ready."

"I'll get the doctor right now."

It was a flurry, a blur of...

Now push.

He's crowning.

Another big one, now push.

Nuchal cord, the baby's not getting oxygen.

Follow through, follow through.

Their baby. There he was. The doctor was holding an implement toward James. "Would you like to cut the cord?" How could he possibly do that? He took the scissors in his hand. He did it. They washed the tiny baby, face blotched red and purple all over. Catherine held him, peered into his dark eyes blinking open. "Our little Calvert," she said. James' eyes welled as he gazed speechless, a love he had never known before.

*

She has light. He's with the light. She's with everything.

*

Within the first few days at home, baby Calvert's eyes fixed on the little white lights that James and Catherine had strung along the moulding of the family room ceiling. James wasn't sure at first that it was possible. He carried Calvert away from the lights and the tiny infant's eyes held on as long as they could, then relinquished the light to wander across the ambient aura of the room. And when he carried Calvert toward the lights again, the tiny face again was transfixed. "He likes the lights, Catherine, Catherine!"

*

James at his desk in the den opened his notebook and wrote. *My whole life to 2002, Mary Zadora Kaminska was unknown to me. She became, in 2003, a woman my friend Alan had known in Provincetown long ago. And in 2009 she became my late mother-in-law. In 2012 something entirely new happened. She became my son's late grandmother, our lineages entwined, our blood combined. Mary's blood, the blood of my kin.*

*

Calvert was a traveler. Like Mom and Dad Crossland, like James and Catherine. James lifted the back of the all-terrain stroller, Catherine the front, and they carried him across the three-foot bank of snow the plows had thrown up from the street, a wall against their trek down the icy sidewalks. A family walk to Blue Moon coffee shop one week after Calvert's birth. Olivia whirled ahead of the stroller, leaned to the snowbanks and lifted her hands from the prints. "Does Calvert want to make hand prints?"

"He's too little, but he likes watching you do it!" Catherine assured and Olivia printed another. Leo ran ahead, scooped the fresh snow, ran back to the stroller. "Here," he said. "Calvert can touch it."

And a month after his birth, a Christmas Eve flight to Chattanooga, Tennessee. Mom Crossland was overwhelmed. She had always hoped he would find someone, make a family of his own, hoped without any real expectation as her black hair grayed to silver-white while his lonely years in Boston and New York dragged on. In her eyes now a bewildered joy at the real infant in her arms. And Dad Crossland. James watched for any reaction in the one who never seemed to react to anything outside those fully alive years in Cape Coast and Cumaná. But there was a reaction, decipherable under James' intent observation. His brow raised and his eyes grew serious. Dad Crossland, Grandpa Crossland, was quietly amazed.

"I wrote a poem for Calvert," Mom said. She snuggled a soft light gray and white stuffed dog no bigger than her palm into Calvert's tiny grasping hands and read.

> *Little doggie says woof, woof!*
> *He means he wants to eat.*
> *Give little doggie a treat.*
> *Little doggie says woof, woof!*
> *Looking out the window.*
> *He wants to feel the wind, oh!*
> *Let's all go out, but stay together.*
> *Little ones don't walk alone.*
> *Mommy and Daddy, Calvert, Leo and Olivia — and doggie!*

*

"Look at you, another baby! To tell you the truth, I'm surprised you waited this long. Can I hold him?" Lulu leaned back on the family room sofa to receive the tiny bundle. "Isn't he beautiful, that tuft of black hair!"

Catherine settled beside her. "My body is still a baby-making machine! Almost forty-three when he was born."

"There will come a time, Catherine, when you'll look back and say, thank God I did it while I still could!"

"We almost didn't." Catherine leaned against the armrest pillow, stocking feet toward Lulu, and peered out the window at the tall cottonwood across the street.

"What is your mama dreaming up, little Calvert?"

Catherine's gaze turned to Lulu. "It's more about what you dreamed up. What about your dreams?"

"Are you talking about Broadway? Seriously, Catherine?"

"In Minnesota it's called community theater. And yes, I'm serious. You're a performer."

"Oh, Catherine." Lulu's voice was pregnant with possibility. "Dios mío. You know how to get me thinking." She smiled at Calvert — "Oh baby!"

*

April 2013

"James, I finally got past him."

"Who?"

"James Crossland."

"Me?"

"You know I'm not talking about you." Catherine clicked a record on Ancestry. "James Crossland, born in 1733 in Prince George County, Virginia, was your sixth great grandfather. He died after 1774 in North Carolina. Did you know your name, James, recurs every few generations? His parents were a bit of a mystery, but I finally found them in another family tree and the supporting records checked out and..."

"How do you find all these people?"

"...then I traced your line all the way back to another James Crossland who arrived in Virginia on a ship called the Treasurer in 1613."

"What the fuck! That's before the Mayflower. When was the Mayflower?"

"Wikipedia says 1620."

"In Boston I remember some guy bragging about how his family came over on the Mayflower. I've got him beat by seven years!"

"I'm not sure it matters. Are you...proud about that?"

"Fuck yeah. This is amazing. Is there more information about him?"

"Apparently there was a 1624 census record that said he sailed on the Treasurer with Captain Samuel Argall. Family histories say he was a soldier."

"A census, way back then? That doesn't seem right." He reached for her computer.

"Don't grab my computer. You're so impulsive sometimes!"

He raised his hands in surrender. "Okay, let's find out what was going on. Search *Jamestown history*. There, look at this, after the Powhatan uprising in 1622, the Crown took control of the colony from the Virginia Company of London. That explains why they would want a census. See if you can find the census online."

Catherine passed the laptop to James.

"Virtual Jamestown, Virginia Muster 1624/25. This must be it. There's James Crossland and everything he owned in 1624." He read aloud —

Name: James Crosslande
Household Status: head
Location: Charles Cittie, Jordans Jorney
Ship: Treasuror
Date of Arrival: February 1613
House: 1
Powder: 2 pound
Shot: 20
Piece: 3
Armor: 1
Coat of Steel: 1
Corn: 30 bushel
Dry Fish: 100 fish
Neat Cattle: 2
Swine: 1
Poultry: 10.

"So he's a fisher and farmer. And any of the settlers might have had firearms and shot. But armor and a coat of steel? He was a soldier. Let's look up Argall. Encyclopedia Brittanica says the Treasurer brought soldiers and supplies to Jamestown in late 1612."

"But that doesn't match the census."

"Brittanica says the ship carried out a number of missions along the coast. Maybe 1613 is when he finally settled." James set down the laptop and stood in awe. "Mayflower beat by eight years, not seven!" He knew it was silly and he loved watching Catherine laugh and shake her head. And in a way it wasn't silly. It was the Crossland family never being quite what anyone expected.

*

Catherine carried Calvert into the den where James sat at his computer. "Anything?" Calvert reached for James, "Gung, gung, gung."

"Nothing, It seems like just a few companies post all the jobs. I've applied again and again. Look at this description: *Join a fast-paced team of self-starters, expanding our brand.* Fucking bullshit. But I did get an email from Alan. Nothing huge, he didn't find a publisher, but he got a job editing the correspondence of a scientist who was a pioneer of the psychedelic movement, so he's thrilled which is cool. He deserves a break."

"Maybe you need a break like that too. Never mind the job listings. What do you really want to be doing?"

"That's the problem. I want to be writing my theory."

"Okay, well we have to be a little bit realistic, something someone will hire you for, something they're doing that you'd genuinely like to be part of."

He relaxed back in his swivel chair, gazed about the room looking for clues. His bookshelves spoke volumes. *How Institutions Think, Stone Age Economics, The Wheels of Commerce, Marx and Keynes on Economic Recessions.* "I guess economic decision-making has been percolating in my head ever since I worked at the Universe Society, how all institutions are forums for economic bargaining and how that shapes culture — something nobody else cares about. But how about a place that works on economic policy?"

"Then let's find all the places in the Twin Cities where you could work on that."

For the next month he bookmarked the online contact pages of nonprofits devoted to researching or influencing economic policy. One by one he emailed or phoned the highest-level person he could reach and asked to meet over coffee. Some responses were polite but perplexed. Some said they would love to, but simply were not available right now. And a few said yes.

Peering into her placid blue eyes under close-cut gray hair, James listened, evaluated phrases, word choices, expressive gestures, the clues to an institution's place within society's debates. He probed the economic issues over the first cup of coffee, heard the stall in the director's flight of oration, saw her glance to the coffee shop door. He purchased spare minutes — "a coffee to go?" And in those minutes the director offered a consolation. "You should talk to Minnesota Next Economy, they're over in Saint Paul. Your questions sound like the work they're doing."

The following week he sat across a round table from Salvador Bollwerk. The sweeping brush of white hair could have crowned a sugar maple in a snowstorm, while the curling flare of gray eyebrows drew James' gaze to the warm, burnt-umber eyes.

"When you grow up on a farm, you know there's the way things ought to work and the way things actually work. We all have to follow the fads to recruit funders — this doesn't come for free." Salvador swept his hand across the suite of offices that were spokes around the axle of the conference room. "But we can still think a little, damn it." And with a plunk of his fist on the polished tabletop, he stood and walked to the bookshelves. "I saw you eyeing these." He peeled off his glasses, rubbed his eyes with a fatigue that seemed emotional more than physical, plunked them on his face again. "I can tell you ninety-nine out of hundred people who sit down in this room never notice anything but the wallpaper."

James stood and lifted a hefty book from the shelves. "Braudel, *Wheels of Commerce.* I'm not quite halfway through this one. Life gets busy. I'll eventually come back to it." He returned it to the shelf and ran his finger along the spine of another. "Lewis, *Common as Air,* that's an amazing book, the same historic breadth as Braudel. Marx! I read volume one in the mid-nineteen-nineties."

"Not one of these books has the answer in it." Salvador waited for James to lift his eyes from the page. "But each has a piece of it."

The deal was that if James could help them secure a three-year grant, he was hired. He grasped what was fundamentally innovative about their project and rewrote their proposal to spotlight it. Two letters of congratulation: Next Economy got the grant, he got the job, Policy Associate. They wanted him to boost their media presence with published articles, policy analysis that would connect Next Economy's vision to current political debates. They wanted him to write.

*

Catherine set the grocery bag next to the refrigerator, put the milk in the fridge, corndogs in the freezer. Olivia and Leo would be home tomorrow, from London. A trip with Alistair to see his parents. It was the first time they'd been abroad. She was glad Alistair could give them this, something that was still out of reach for her and James, even with his new job. Europe opened her world, and she knew it would open theirs too. But it was so hard when they were away. Tomorrow. She would hear all their stories, hold them on her lap even as big as they were.

She startled at the ring of the phone. "Alistair! Are you at the airport already? You're what? Another week?" She felt an ache in her chest. "What did you say, about your mother? Oh I'm sorry, yes of course. You need to be there for her. Can I talk to Olivia and Leo? Oh, they're with her right now?" Still grasping the phone receiver, she felt her head lower to the kitchen island. Her shoulders shook in silence. A hand at her waist. A voice, "Catherine?" The ache burned.

Darkness chased the sun below the wooded canopy of Longfellow, below the bungalow rooftops, below the edge of the world. James swore and waved his hands at the dinner table — *He needs to know what this does to you, the effect he's having!* — then glimpsed Calvert's wicker sailing ship in which he voyaged room to room. James quieted and raised a glass of red wine to his lips.

"It's not his fault. It's just how things are," she said.

He set down the glass, and she felt his touch even before his hand cupped hers. "They'll be home soon."

*

He often brought work home on weekends, especially if he was on a deadline. Catherine peeked in the den, "A new article?"

"No, I'm still good for a while. I just got that Pioneer Press op-ed published last week, the one on employment incentives."

"Are you working on your theory?"

"Well, kind of." He scooted his chair back from the desk. "I'm emailing Gar Alperovitz at the University of Maryland. He wrote a book called *America*

Beyond Capitalism. It's funny, he's a political economist, but I feel like he's not fully grasping the raw power of ownership on politics and the economy. So many of these authors I read start off so promising, target the social research problem they're going to solve, but they never quite find their mark. They don't complete the analysis."

"So they're not finishing what they started."

"I mean, they finish writing the book, obviously. And they've got half of it right, but without the other half, they can't solve anything. I'm pointing them toward the other half."

She waited. Waited to hear how this had anything to do with writing his own theory. "So you're writing, what's his name, Gar, to tell him what he's doing is wrong."

He exhaled. Always the deflating balloon when she tried to help him sort out his life. And whether he liked it or not, it needed sorting. "James, you're always trying to correct other people's work. Isn't that what you did, emailing Mary Douglas about her grid-and-group charts that you didn't like? I'm just trying to figure out whether it's displacement or maybe a sort of avoidance, focusing on these other authors' work instead of your own."

He stiffened in his chair. "I'm writing articles. Sure, the articles don't lay out my whole theory, but I'm already writing parts of it. If I'm going to get my ideas out there, I need to be part of the conversation these scholars are having, that's why I'm contacting them, it's about sharing ideas."

"And telling them their ideas are incomplete. But your theory isn't completed either. Maybe nothing is ever final. But they've completed enough to publish a book."

"But I...I..."

"It's a club, James. Researchers who have a book out. They only want to talk to people in the club, and you aren't in the club until you get your book out." She hesitated, laid her hand gently on his shoulder. "What was that dream you had as a child? Something about blocks and building a city?" She felt bad, he almost winced as he turned to her.

"Yeah, I just remember saying to my mom, *I can't, it's too big.*"

"Is it possible you're still afraid?"

*

They came back. Of course they would.

"Mom! Calvert!" Olivia and Leo ran to them.

"I missed you," Catherine said holding them tight, little Calvert squished in the middle. "What was it like being so far away?"

Olivia threw her hands in the air and danced around the family room, her dark curls swirling. "London! I love London!"

"Me too!" Leo echoed. "Maybe next time you can come with us!"

*

Alan, I'm finding it difficult to flesh out Mary's story. There are so many gaps. I'm not sure I have enough information. — Catherine

Catherine, You can only piece Mary's life together from fragments. She was a conundrum. Let her lead you and meander, don't judge anything with the first draft, let it rip. Things really begin to coalesce later. — Alan

*

You have a message from Edward Radcliffe. Usually it was generic automatic alerts: *You have new DNA relatives.* But this was a direct message from another 23andMe member. She logged in.

Hello Catherine, my name is Edward Radcliffe. We were matched as first to second cousins. I don't think we are related through my mother. For years I've wondered who my father is. I'm hoping our connection might shed light on his identity.

First to second cousins. Mostly her DNA matches were distant cousins, third, fourth, dozens of them, but this was the closest match yet. According to 23andMe, a first to second cousin can mean first cousin, half first cousin, first cousin once removed, second cousin, great grandparent, great uncle, or half uncle. She clicked on his username. Birth year 1953, so he was a generation older. That filtered out some of the possibilities. He wasn't a first cousin and probably wasn't a great grandfather or great uncle. Location Ohio, that was the right place. His profile photo was a young boy in a cowboy hat holding a cork gun. Probably him as a child. She didn't really see a resemblance. Her lips puckered in a twist. She clicked on Radcliff's DNA details: Maternal haplogroup V. Hers was H. So they couldn't be related through their mothers. Like he said, *For years I've wondered who my father is.* Neither of them knew anything about their fathers. How could they possibly be of any help to each other?

*

Mary's documents and sketchbooks, Mary's dorm mates at Dayton, the university yearbooks. All offered clues, but none of them could point the way to Catherine's father. She was still finding more leads on her mother's line. Mary's mother's mother, Veronika Lukáčová Kaminska, emigrated from Slovakia to Ohio with Mary's mother's father Andrej Kaminska in the 1920s. One scrap of documentation led to another and another. But there was nothing, not a single scrap of name or place on Catherine's paternal line. Her father might have been a student, a professor, a visiting professor from who-knows-where, a man from town, even a man Mary encountered on a weekend visit back home in Sandusky. Do you see how there was really nothing to grab onto?

She had plenty to be thankful for, living maternal family and a growing crowd of maternal ancestors. Her great-grandparents Veronica and Andrej were farmers who knew the ways of plants and animals, made a life for themselves in a new land. Her grandmother Irene, loved photography, used the earnings from her factory job to buy a camera at a time when few people even knew how to operate one. The Canada family were weavers and machinists working their craft. And Mary. Mother, artist, lover, nomad. Their lives pulsed through Catherine's veins from the day she was conceived, entirely unknown to her. Until now.

*

Catherine watched him seeing. James seeing Calvert's attention to the plaid blanket of his wicker basket, so much like James' mom's love of pattern in the fabrics from Cape Coast. James seeing how the restless journeying with his dad and mom echoed Crossland family migrations from England to Virginia to North Carolina and Tennessee, to Arkansas and Iowa, to Minnesota — generations, even centuries before. When she showed him Virginia Colony court records detailing the ancient Crossland family selling land, selling off piece by piece the security of property that the first James Crossland had worked so hard to build, she saw the flash of insight and indignation as he grasped that those same opposing currents swirled within the family he knew, in his own grandfather Kirk who had built a small wealth in New Ulm and yet had nothing to pass on when he died. In Dad Crossland who worked ceaselessly at mathematics but scoffed at saving for the future. James, her James, was wrestling with the history of his forbearers and she knew why. For the first time he understood that their story was his.

*

She laid the cubed tofu onto the cookie sheet, poured tamari and sesame oil over it, closed the oven. And there stood James, in another world.

"Are you going to say anything to me?"

He put his hand to his chin.

"What is it?"

"I was thinking about those clients at your old social services job, how you said some of them suffered from PTSD. I wonder. When the kids are away with Alistair, or how you felt as a child when you were alone in the gift shop..."

She carried the shell-patterned stoneware plates to the dinner table. "Wonder what?" James followed her into the dining room and was staring into mid air. She wished he would just spit it out and help set the table.

"So your clients would have a...what seems like an extreme reaction to something happening right now that takes them back to something that happened in the past."

"Right. It's like a veteran having a fight-or-flight reaction to a car backfiring as if it was gunfire on the battlefield. They're reliving that initial trauma."

"Right. And I wonder if your strong reactions, when you have them, which isn't all the time, if it might go back to something deeper."

"I think it's only reasonable that if the kids are climbing Mount Shasta or in London on the other side of the ocean I would worry. What if something happens to them? How can I protect them?"

"True, true. But do you know why I always announce to you when I'm going to go to the bathroom?"

"Do you do that? Why?"

"Because during our first year in Minnesota, whenever I left the room, you were upset. *I didn't know where you were,* you said."

"I don't even remember that. We can talk about this sometime, James, but right now it's time to get dinner on the table."

*

—

He couldn't imagine. Never to have known your mother beyond the day of your birth when you're an infant who doesn't know anything. His own mom had always been there. In the oxygen tent with him when he had pneumonia at age three. In the kitchen at White Oak making consommé soup when he was, who knows, five? Tending him through all his grade school illnesses. Wishing him goodnight as he settled into his canvas cot in Cumaná, his *Beethoven's Symphonies* cassette playing softly as she smiled, *You're going to be happy here.* How much was wrapped into that one sentence. Hope he would find what he needed in life, and promise. A promise to care for him forever. She did. But forever doesn't last. How could she be gone? How is it possible for a person to be there, everything that a person is, and then not be there.

Suitcases propped open in the bedroom in Chattanooga, the summer after Calvert's birth. They had filed down the stairs, James in front, Catherine behind with Calvert in her arms. "We finally woke up!" James announced. Kelly's tense smile. Dad's somber face, his announcement. "Mom's not doing too well this morning." The summer visit devolved into kitchen table meetings about doctor's appointments, test results. All her vitals look good, the doctor explained. But she wasn't okay. Pain, fatigue, her quick mind perishing in confusion, days warped by fear, defiled by delusion. From her innermost depths to the outermost membrane of her mortal skin. Lesions. A fabric wrenched apart that could not be sewn together again. Cell phone calls at odd hours back home in Minneapolis, Kelly's voice or Margaret's — *We have to decide what to do.* A final visit. James sat at her bedside, a home care hospital bed in the piano room. He knew enough now, five decades into life, to say everything, anything at all he might later wish he had said. *Thank you for taking care of me, for always supporting me in whatever I wanted to do. I still remember you holding me, Mom. I'll always remember.*

*

Years ago James had attended a lecture at the New England Conservatory, a cognitive scientist who had theorized that our earliest memories of sound in the womb can shape our response to sound in adulthood. What does an infant know? Calvert had been entranced by the string of white lights, later by the plaid blanket of his wicker basket, all within weeks of his birth. Before birth, in the dark warmth, he would have heard their voices, Catherine's and his, recognized their voices, remembered.

*

March 2014

"Crossland residence."

"Hi Dad."

"Oh, hi James." Dad's voice, right there, not going anywhere. The students in freshman math, the neighbor's tree that fell down the day before the big storm, yes, fell the day before, it must have known what was coming, Kelly's news when she called the other day.

"I was thinking about Mom this morning," James said. "How she used to set me and Luke up in our high-chairs with watercolor paint and paper on our trays. It comes out of nowhere, the feelings, not just the memories."

The long space before the words. "Some days are harder than others."

"I love you Dad."

"I love you too."

*

They settled into bed, tiny Calvert snuggled between them as always, everyone exhausted as always. Catherine had told him, before he even moved to Minnesota, that his life was about to speed up. He had chuckled back then, "Hey, I live in New York City!" He hadn't understood that it wasn't about the city you lived in. It was about the two children he would inherit the day he moved in and the third they would have together.

Calvert was restless tonight. He wanted his pillow, then wanted nigh-nigh, his name for breastfeeding, which couldn't happen when he was on his pillow. Then he wanted his pillow again, and then his cozy blanket so that he and Ma and Da could all go inside like a big tent. *Under my house,* he called it. Maybe this last adventure of the day would satisfy him. But no. He crawled out of *his house* and sat up in bed. "Vacuum p-obably in closet," the tiny voice intoned.

James smiled, lay back as Catherine had already done, closed his eyes, and answered softly. "Yes, it's probably in the closet downstairs."

"Da, no talk to me."

"Oh, okay." The turns of a two-year-old mind. He couldn't have imagined what would come next.

"Sing anunner song," Calvert announced into the darkness and then intoned in a sing-song with no discernible melody, "Vacuum p-obably in closet, or maybe in Da's den." And, "Sing anunner song — Vacuum p-obably in closet. Sing anunner song — Vacuum p-obably in closet, or maybe in Da's den. Sing anunner song..." So he continued in the dark, for ten minutes until he tipped over onto his pillow and fell asleep.

*

Da's hat on head. Da's gloves on hands. Goggles on head, looking through.

Mom's voice, "Do you like your swimming goggles?"

Mom likes goggles. Vacuum in closet. Ugh, pull, pull. Plug in. Turn on. Big vacuum sound. I like vacuum! Me. Calvert. Big sound! Feeling whoosh in vacuum. Clink. Rumble. Clink. Funny, funny, funny!

*

Calvert wore his favorite pastel blue and yellow duck fleece pajamas. She had bought them at Goodwill for Olivia whose stuffed animals conversed with the fleece duck, then passed them on to Leo who quacked and flapped his arms all around the dining table, now on to Calvert who had pulled the vacuum from the closet. The wand, grasped in his little hands, was longer than he was tall. He delighted in the soft hum of the engine, and more than that, in the sound of something sucked through. Clink. It always made him laugh. He was a little James, a carbon copy — his long face, dark curls, smile upturned in the corners, his fascination with the world around him. And his favorite word, *no*, was James first response to almost everything. Every time she told Calvert, *You have Da's hair,* he said, "No, Da has Da's hair."

But there was no questioning it, he had her love of texture. He explored the world with his finger tips. And he had her big brown eyes. "Calverdalver, it's time to meet Da at Nina's Cafe. He's probably already walking over there from work!" She bundled him in his winter clothes, like she used to bundle Olivia and Leo. Olivia would be a teen next year. Amazing. She had her dad's eyes, but she had Mary's spirit. And baby Leo would be eleven, not a baby any more. His face a carbon copy of Catherine's.

Calvert bundled, they were out the door. Olivia's rope swing on the elm in the backyard swayed empty in the winter breeze. They would come on the weekend. She would make it special.

*

"Well, when I was five years old, alone in the gift shop, I thought my mom had left me," Catherine said standing at the dining room window. "Of course she was only in the shop next door, but I was afraid pacing the aisles looking for her. That's probably why I got upset when you disappeared to the bathroom." She had promised he could bring it up again.

"Your mom leaving you alone in the store was scary — I remember feeling scared when I was seven and I lost sight of my parents in a crowd at the Fourth of July fireworks. But is it a trauma? Would it cause PTSD?"

She had imagined explaining herself, laying out her defense, but she didn't. Because what happened in the store those many years ago actually didn't fit her own definition of trauma. "So you're saying that the experience in the gift shop was a trigger? For a different trauma?"

"That's what I'm thinking. I would expect sadness when the kids are away. And for sure disappointment and concern when they're away longer than we expected. But you were out of your head, out of your body. And obviously your reaction to me disappearing to the bathroom was out of proportion to what was happening..."

Her thoughts were aloft.

"All I'm saying is that there's something deeper going on, deeper than any of those things."

She backed up to the dining room table and plunked down onto the chair, looked out at the crabapple tree under the blue Minnesota sky. A chickadee flitted down, perched perilously on a delicate twig, its beak opened in a silent call beyond the glass, its head nervously scanning the landscape. And in an instant, it was gone.

"My mother. Mary. It's Mary" — she turned to him — "I knew her voice. I became a person hearing her voice. When I opened my eyes to the world, I opened them to her. And she was gone."

*

There was a continuing flow of DNA matches on 23andMe. Third Cousin, Fourth to Distant Cousin. Every one was family. And that meant that in the chain of her origins, every one of them was a witness to some link before — *My aunt was so-and-so from such-a-place. My great uncle once told me. There was this family story.* Like witnesses come forward in a cold case. Where a hunt for answers persists beyond any reasonable hope. But when was hope ever a thing of reason? She quietly carried on her investigation, contacted DNA matches, combed through family trees on Ancestry for any connection, any clue. The cold case of her birth father.

A member post on 23andMe recommended triangulation. It was a complicated word, as complicated as the process it represented, isolating DNA matches who share DNA on specific segments of the same chromosome to identify a common ancestor. It felt overwhelming. But if it was the only way to find him, she would figure it out.

*

"You imagine Mary beside you every day, I think." James was puzzling over something.

"As far back as I can remember. Somehow I've always known she loved me."

"But it's not quite the same with your birth father, is it? I know you want to find him, but it all feels a little more removed. I don't quite understand why there shouldn't be that same primal connection to him."

"You have to think in concrete terms. It's not about should or shouldn't, it's a practical fact. My mom carried me, we were bonded. I didn't have that same bond with my father. You see, Mary didn't tell him about her pregnancy, so he wasn't there. He had no idea there was a child he should be looking for."

"If you were never bonded, then why do you even need to find your father?"

"I still only know half of who I am. He's my other half." He nodded, gazing into the air. She knew the look, an idea finding its place in his mind.

*

Rice Lake, Wisconsin, July 2014

"Catherine, would you put these rolls on the table? And tell those two, ten minutes." Catherine peeked into the living room where Calvert was playing with old Tonka trucks on the carpet, then set the rolls and butter on the table and poked her head out the sliding door to the screened porch. "Mom says ten minutes until dinner. Isn't the glare from the sun bothering you? I'll lower the blinds."

"Thank you, Catherine. It does glare off the water by this hour," Dad said and turned his attention back to James. "I remember in the 1980s there was a similar policy in the news. It seemed especially popular with the smaller businesses looking to expand."

"Exactly, the small businesses that Greater Minnesota relies on." James caught her eye as she lowered the last blind. "Thanks honey, I was starting to squint, but it's so gradual you almost don't realize it."

So gradual. She passed through the sliding door and glanced at Dad's white head and James' graying head, both nodding and tilting into the conversation. Mom and Dad had taken a long time to warm up to him. Hard to replace the rising attorney their son-in-law Alistair had been with the low-wage office clerk James was until last year. But his surprising shift into the new position and new salary had made him the kind of man they expected for their daughter. It wasn't how she saw the world. She loved him for who he was. She looked in at Calvert. Who had Mom and Dad expected her to be? Maybe someone like them. That would be natural enough.

"The hot dish is coming out of the oven! Get those two in here, will you Catherine?"

James passed through the sliding door. "It's not hot dish if we let it get cold, right?"

Mom laughed. "I've been trying to tell Paul that for years!"

Catherine lifted Calvert into his high-chair. His dark eyes peered into hers. It wasn't in her nature to be like them. But she loved them, and she knew they loved her too. "You still need your Coke, Mom. I'll get it from the fridge."

*

"How is your book going?" James asked. She set her coffee mug down on the patio table. The back yard was alive with activity, birds at the suet feeder and squirrels racing around the trunk of the big elm tree. "I'm taking a few liberties with some of the people in Mary's story, combining them. I've seen it in some memoirs, and Alan thought it would help to focus the story." She wanted to ask — *Have you started yours?* But maybe, better to give him some time.

*

You could hear the geese honking before you could see anything, before they finally emerged over the tree canopy a mere hundred feet above the backyard at Edmund Boulevard, flapping slowly south ahead of the coming evening chill.

The flame-tipped maple leaves licked the cold winds, a dazzling taste of change to come, until the day they lost their grip, leapt into the wild current of yellow elm and ash and cottonwood leaves.

And when only the oaks leaves held on, copper brown against the pink violet blue of evening, then the sky densed white. Not an empty overcast, but a weighty solid white that broke from the sky in cross-currents of crystals over the Cities and their shopping center suburbs and scattered farms. Bare trees leafed out in black crows fluttering, taking flight to maraud the neighborhood. Sound amplified by snow as if echoing off every flake.

Winter. Hot soups and baking and sewing. Reading, art-making. Searching. Still a cold case.

Until the skies thundered and ice-melt flowed, streamed across sidewalks and coursed the street gutters to the drains, and the honking apparitions flapped north above the glowing green lace canopy.

*

Summer 2015

While James wiped errant coffee grounds from the kitchen counter, Catherine carried her steaming cup to the family room sofa. Calvert, almost three years old, climbed into the Ghanaian reed basket, its colors faded, the same basket Ignatius filled with rice and kontomire from Cape Coast market when James was a boy. Calvert held onto the handle then rolled to his side and the basket tipped him to the floor. "Opey-goodness!" he exclaimed.

"Opey-goodness!" Catherine smiled and his little face smiled back. "Let's see what's new at 23andMe!" He giggled as she opened her laptop and logged in. "James, look at this. My Northwestern European is now German and French and a little Scandinavian."

"I guess the estimates become more defined as more people from more places submit DNA. Where do they list sample sizes?"

"I have no idea." She handed the laptop to him and joined Calvert on the carpet. "Here, I'll hold the basket while you climb in again!"

James navigated the site. "It must be here somewhere. Here it is. German and French combined is one thousand and twenty-four persons. That's not very many. I wonder how many people are in the whole database?"

She looked up at him.

"Just over six hundred and fifty thousand." he said.

Her eyes grew wide. "That's it?"

"That's it, worldwide."

The years of searching flashed by. The slim leads, the Dayton contacts, DNA matching, still nothing.

He looked at her, concentration in his eyes. "What's the other thing you mentioned, the other method?"

"Triangulation. But it seems like everyone you're looking at in the triangle has to be a DNA match, and they have to have a family tree like on Ancestry."

James sat down to the laptop. "Let's see. Your birth father could be from anywhere, right? World population is 7.2 billion."

"Not all of them could be my father, they're not all men."

"True, but the same is true of the database and there's no point cutting both world population and the database in half because the proportion would stay the same."

"What about age? Everybody on 23andMe is an adult."

"So super rough, we divide the 23andMe total database, assuming all are adults, by half the world's population." James keyed it into the calculator.

"And? So what are the odds?" she asked. He was just standing there.

"You have a point zero one eight percent chance, a less than one fiftieth of one percent chance. It's basically like winning the lottery."

*

Across the river, in the Highland Park neighborhood of Saint Paul, they dined with the Linds at the Cleveland Wok. "What did you get in your fortune, Leo?" Mom Lind asked.

"I didn't read it, I just ate the cookie!"

The murmur of crinkling plastic and cracking cookies swept around the table. Catherine opened hers, the tiny paper slip unfurled between her fingertips.

Success is going from failure to failure without a loss of enthusiasm.

*

A week had passed since she had cracked open that fortune cookie, and despite the odds, she pressed ahead with the search for her birth father, combing through every clue. James poured the kettle water steaming over the coffee grounds, a tinkling as it filtered into the stoneware pot. The rising sun glowed hot orange over the oaks and cottonwoods of the river bank. "Might be a day for air-conditioning," he said, but she scarcely heard him as she clicked open the notification, *You have a new message.* "Oh my god, James."

"What is it?" He leaned over her shoulder. "Shit!"

Hi, Catherine. You were listed as my half sister on 23andMe. It was only that, only a snippet of the full message. Her mind raced through the possibilities. She was Mary's only child. This had to be her birth father's family. Her fingers fumbled across the keyboard to log in and read the full message.

"Here's your coffee. Or maybe I should pour you a glass of wine!"

"Let me concentrate, I need to read this."

Catherine, You were matched as my half sister on 23andMe. I am sure this is just a miscalculation. I wonder if you are a cousin I am not aware of. I assume you know your birth father? How old are you? I am thirty-nine and have two sisters, ages twenty-nine and twenty-five, all from the same parents. Would love to hear from you! — Kat

Her username was Katherine Anastase. She messaged back.

Kat, I'm very happy to hear from you. I am forty-five years old. I have been searching for my birth father for nine years. My birth mother placed me for adoption in Saint Paul, Minnesota, December 8, 1969. She attended Dayton University in Ohio in 1968 and 1969. Does any of this history help? — Catherine

She and Calvert got James off to work. No other stops, she had to get back to her laptop. And when she did get back, there was more.

Catherine, Your message was very powerful and surprising to read! I would like to explore this further. Here is some information for you:

Both my mother and father attended the University of Dayton but my mom only in late 69 to 71 I think, for her junior and senior years. My father went to UD for all four years, from around 67 to 71. I think my father would have been a freshman or sophomore in the same timeframe that your birth mother attended.

Did you know your birth mother? Did she ever share information with you about your birth father? My dad was born in September of 49 in Akron, Ohio. My mom and dad met at UD and married in 71.

I suppose it's possible that my father and your birthmother had a relationship early in college although I have never heard anything about it, but why would I necessarily, especially if they decided to take an honorable and loving route through adoption?

I am keeping this information private until I know more. I hope to hear from you soon. :-) — Kat

Katherine Anastase, sister of Catherine Crossland, or Lind or Kaminska or Anastase. She knew why Mary tried out names in her sketchbooks. Anyone might have been her parents. Any name might have been her own. Catherine searched the Whitepages online for "Anastase" and "Ohio." Okay, 1949 she thought, so he would be sixty-four years old. This must be him. Ronald Anastase, age sixty-four, Columbus, Ohio. She browsed relatives in the listing, and there was Kat. All the details fit, it had to be him, her father. She was bursting. She looked at the time on the computer. Quarter to noon. "We have to meet Da for lunch, Calver-dalver! And we'll tell him the news!"

She scored the loft table at Nina's — the lone table on the little indoor balcony at the top of the flight of stairs. One of the many charms and quirks of the writers cafe nestled in the Cathedral Hill neighborhood of Saint Paul. She held Calvert on her lap and watched for James.

"We get the scenic view to today!" he said, a little out of breath as he reached the top step.

"My father is Ronald Anastase!" He seemed unable to process the sentence, so she tried another. "I found him, through my sister!"

That got through. He sat down in a wonder. "This is big. I can't believe it. Are we going to meet him? It's probably too soon, right? Wow."

"I can hardly eat," she said. "I still have to email Kat back."

*

She set Calvert on the family room floor with his blanket and Emmy, his favorite stuffed dog, and opened her laptop. She wanted to write — *There's no question! We're sisters! He's my father!* — but she knew from experience to give

Kat more space, more time to understand what was unfolding. She was painfully gentle.

Kat, It is sounding like we should explore the idea that we are half sisters. My mom was born December 1948 and died before I found her. My father wasn't named in the records. My mom didn't tell him she was pregnant. Her parents urged her to leave school and place me for adoption. It's what families did in those days. My mom was a sophomore at the time.

I assume that your dad was not aware of me and that his relationship with my mother may have been very brief. My mother was Mary Louise Tomczak from Sandusky, Ohio. He may or may not remember her. I would enjoy talking more! — Catherine

She hit send and waited. Waited. Realized she had no way of knowing if Kat was even still online. So she did what she did every day. Busied herself with laundry and cleaning the kitchen and checking on Calvert and 23andMe in between, and dinner, what could she possibly make for dinner? She wrote up a grocery list but there was no way she was going out. She checked again on Calvert and her inbox. Message.

Catherine, I think you are right...we might be half sisters. It is scary and thrilling all at the same time! My dad's name was Ronny. I am sorry to tell you he passed away suddenly in 1991 of a brain aneurysm. He was forty-two. Two weeks before he died, he taught my mom how to balance the checkbook. It was like he knew. I miss him every day still.

Catherine kept reading without comprehension, nothing but momentum.

He was a wonderful father. He has two brothers living. He had a sister who passed away a few years before him. Both of his parents, my grandparents, are passed on. On my dad's side we are German and Romanian.

I am not sure I totally understand how the 23andMe DNA matches work, so I still need to get to my uncles in Youngstown and get either one of them to test.

By the way, my dad's job took him different places and we lived in Indianapolis, Indiana and Lexington, Kentucky before we settled in Columbus where he was a law enforcement instructor at the Ohio Peace Officer Training Council. He loved to teach.

I'm hoping to talk with you more! — Kat

Her eyes welled with tears. She hadn't even realized. All these years since learning of her mother's death, she had been leaning on her father's shoulder, relying on the comfort of his embrace still to come. In an instant it fell away. Everything falling, darkness, somewhere deep inside herself. No, not this time. Her fingers grasped the sofa. Trembling, she held on. Calvert was crying, a reaction to her reaction. "It's okay, Mommy's okay Calvert." She wrapped her arms around him and thought back to the night in the hotel in New York City, to what Alan had said, *You carry her spirit. She lives within you.* Her birth mother, and father. A love within that could never be taken away.

She was quiet during dinner, during cleanup, during an evening's never-ending work. Later as Calvert sat on Da's lap in the family room, she stepped out the back door into the night, the last warmth of day already gone, and stared up into the sky at the far away flicker of stars, too far away to reach. But the light. The light reached her eyes. She looked down to her hands and opened them to the sky. See it or not, she held the light in her hands.

*

Mary's life reached into hers at unexpected moments. A letter in the mailbox. A phone call from a friend. A package from Bette on an autumn afternoon.

"What do you think Bette sent us?" she asked Calvert. He raised his toddler hands and laughed, "I donnow!"

She unwrapped the tissue paper and lifted an eight by ten inch painting from the cardboard box. Oil on canvas in a simple handmade wooden frame. Calvert sat on her lap and gazed at the painting of a large red heart floating like an island in blue waters, a swirl of shore, a tower rising from it, and blue-pink skies above. On the back was penciled, *Harbor Heart, Mary Zadora, Valentine's Day 1986, Provincetown Ma.*

Still inside the box was a folded sheet of stationery.

Dear Catherine, I'm delighted to send you this painting your mother made. I visited my friend Nan at the Warren Tavern a month ago and was reminiscing about what a shame it was that the painting had disappeared off the wall a decade ago. Mary entrusted it to me some twenty years ago. "I want this message out there" — she said — "in case we're meant to cross paths." I had asked Nan to keep it on display where people passing through would see it, but then it disappeared. And in just the way things always happen that have anything to do with Mary, Nan called me last week and said the painting reappeared sitting on the back lid of the toilet. That's not where she displayed it! But that's where she found it now. I can't quite figure it out.

The dramatist in me imagines that one of the regulars had a moral lapse one night and nabbed it off the wall, and then heard me tell the story last month and wanted to make things right. Well, almost right. They didn't come clean, but they returned the stolen goods. I don't know, but I'm thrilled to put this message-in-a-bottle into you're hands. It's a big heart, and she painted it on Valentine's Day, so I guess the message is clear. — With love, Bette

She picked James up from work end of the day. "I want to show you something that came in the mail."

While Calvert ran for the vacuum cleaner, the start of his busy evening of clink-clink, James poured his cup of red wine and settled beside her on the sofa. "So Bette said it was Mary's message for you?"

"Yeah, and I keep thinking there's something more. You know how Mary hid faces inside of faces in her drawings, little hidden surprises in her paintings. The patterns in the water, in the reflection of the towering monument...I feel like there's something there." She turned the canvas upside down, scrutinized it, turned it sideways. "What are you smiling about?"

"It's fun." He took a healthy sip. "It's like we're settling into a mystery."

She snuggled closer. "It is a mystery! And one with sound effects!" Calvert had turned on the vacuum again for another round of clink-clink.

James pulled up a map of Provincetown on the laptop. "The only building in the painting is the Pilgrim Monument. I'm assuming this sweep of shore at the golden mean is the harbor shore of the town?"

"James, I see something. Oh my god. The dark squiggles in the water, it's not the monument's reflection, it's writing. Look at the cursive swoop of a big letter M, and a small O, and it's separated a bit, but see this? It's a small m!" She stared at James. "The monument marks the spot. Mom is there."

"Wow, I think you're right." He reached for the canvas, tilted it. "Look at the hook of land right here. This little hook left of the monument must be Long Point. The heart isn't in the harbor."

"It's called Harbor Heart!"

"I know but look. This tiny oval under the monument is Provincetown Harbor. The big heart is in Cape Cod Bay. She gave you the whole picture, from the shore of Massachusetts Bay, to the shore of Cape Cod Bay, to the hook inside the tip of the Cape, and the monument right there like a peg, I can't fucking believe it. It's a map! A map to your mother!"

She traced the curving edges and felt with the flesh of her fingertips the impasto ridges of the three painted letters.

*

"We're almost to Grandma and Grandpa's, Calvert! We'll have some pizza..." Her cell phone was ringing, somewhere in her coat pocket. An Ohio number. She pulled into the Bloomington Civic Plaza parking lot.

"Hello?"

"Catherine? Welcome to the family, honey! This is your Uncle Donny. Your dad's brother!"

"Oh my god! Hi Uncle Donny!"

"When your Uncle Johnny called to tell me the news, he said, *Get a grip, 'cus you ain't gonna fucking believe this shit.* I said, *Let it fly.* And man, he let it fly, I could hardly believe it. Ronny, the golden child of the family."

Uncle Donny was a storyteller, Catherine could already hear it, the way he settled into his monologue.

"I did some investigating and found your photo online, at a website where you, I guess, sell your jewelry?"

"I hardly even use that website anymore, but yes, you found me!"

"Well honey, when I saw your picture I said to Johnny, *Damn, she"s beautiful,* and he said, *Yeah, well whadya expect? The girls were always crawling all over Ronny.* They were. But more than that, looking at your picture, it's like we've got a little piece of Ronny back again!"

"That's wonderful to hear. Thank you Uncle Donny."

"You're part of the family, DNA doesn't lie! We're so blessed to have found you. We love you, honey. You've got my number now. Let's talk again soon."

That voice, that rich growly voice. Kat had sent a short video of their dad, Ronny, spoofing an advertisement for sunglasses. Uncle Donny had his voice.

She pulled the car into mom and dad's driveway. "Let's have pizza with Grandma and Grandpa!"

"Gramma and Grampa!" Calvert echoed from his carseat, hands raised in the air.

*

Catherine gave Calvert a push on the swing. A yellow leaf sailed down from the great elm tree above. "The tree is snowing leaves!" Calvert's face beamed with his new idea.

"How about we make some hot chocolate?" She helped him down from the swing and he ran for the door. Inside she heard James' voice. She peered into the living room.

"Dad, I think you've hit on exactly what I was struggling with." He was on the phone, gesturing like he did when he was excited about something. "Yes, yes. It's this old split between social philosophy arguing what should be and natural philosophy explaining what is. Social philosophy is what I do at my job now, advocating for policies, and I use elements of my natural philosophy theory, so I feel like I'm writing about my theory but really... Yes, exactly. It's just fragments, and it's just to make a case for policy... Right, that's right. I need to write the theory, a book laying out this theory I've been working on my whole life... Yes. No, not just an article. A book." His eyes met hers.

*

Duluth, Minnesota, January 2021

Lake Superior shone blue in the distance from East Hillside the day last June when they signed on the house. Today the lake was a hazy mass of blowing whiteness. "Now there's a new variant." Catherine's laptop computer was open on the kitchen counter. Snow gusted outside the big picture window like the scene where Santa cancels Christmas in *Rudolph the Red-Nosed Reindeer*. COVID canceled Christmas, at least the annual trip to see Dad Crossland in Chattanooga, and there was a gathering sense that something was happening that nobody thought could happen any more, not now, not here, not to us.

"Half a million people dead in the U.S. alone. Can you believe it? The CDC is reporting that a more transmissible COVID-19 B.1.1.7 Alpha variant has emerged in more than thirty countries. So no end to the masking and vaccination, not for a while. I'm so thankful to Salvador, letting you work from here."

James joined her in the kitchen while Calvert's voice resounded from behind his closed bedroom door — "Do you want to know my new strat? I've been grinding on it for, like ten or forty minutes. It is so O.P."

"What's O.P.?" Catherine asked.

"Who is he online with?" James asked.

"Ah, ah, of course now it would fail! Ah!" Calvert's voice trumpeted — partly big eight-year-old, partly the same little boy he had always been.

James gazed out the picture window onto the great slope that is Duluth. Snow-covered spruce in pairs and rows towering over the rooftops that cascade down the hill to Canal Park and the lake. Even in a blizzard the white squall above the lake was different, brighter than the heavy gray above the hill. James set his coffee mug on the kitchen table. "It seems like you're making some real progress on your book."

"I can write here," Catherine said. She joined him at the window. "Driving up Interstate Thirty-Five from Mom and Dad's, when we pass the exit for Askov-Finlayson and the landscape changes to hills of spruce and birch, little blue lakes in the valleys, it's like we're in a new world. I just miss Olivia and Leo. I'm glad they're coming up this weekend."

*

"Yes! Yes!" He combo-ed. Had never combo-ed like that. Broke the bed, legit broke the bed. "Ma! Da! I won!" Calvert burst out his bedroom door. Ma and Da at the kitchen window looked over, they were listening. If he took too long explaining they might say they're in the middle of something. He pulled his thoughts together carefully but quickly. "Ma, Da, this is amazing!"

Infinidad

El Caribe, September 2045

As the flight attendant continued down the aisle, Calvert peered five thousand feet down across the cobalt blue sea, across the great green mountains and peaks above peaks in a sea of blossoming clouds. Morning sun poured across a continent. America del Sur.

He leaned back. Mind starting to race. Watch for the driver from the universidad at baggage claim, van to Cumaná, meet the department head, don't expect to dive into the project right away — Da prepped him — slow down, it's possible no one will be in their offices, find a hotel room on your own if you have to, eventually you'll connect with everyone.

For him Venezuela would be mind-opening stochastic training data for his own thinking. For Telligenz, an inroad to new collaborations and new markets. If that's what they needed him for, fine. But that wasn't his story. His story was more than that, went deeper than that, because it wasn't his story alone.

He wanted to reach for Mom's hand right now. *Trust your instincts, think your choices through to the end, step by step, you know how.* He'd call her, call them soon.

*

Estado Sucre, Venezuela, March 2046

Massive cumulus clouds sailed the blue sky, forged where the winds of Pacific and Atlantic converge over Amazon and Andes. Calvert sat beside her in the scrub grass under the golden blossoms of the araguaney tree on the banks of the river, el Rio Manzanares.

"I remember they told me the story. And I said something like, *So now I know everything.*"

"Tu crees que saves todo." She smirked and puckered her lips. The ruffles of her cobalt bikini top fluttered in the wind. Her bronze skin radiant.

"Mentira! I know I don't know everything."

"See, you even know that."

He crumpled into laughter, eyeing her between laughs. "So anyway." He tossed a pebble into the sparkling currents. "Then they said, *Actually, we could never tell you everything. There are all the things we don't know, things we couldn't possibly remember, and others we could never imagine.*"

"You with your conquistador ancestor, James Crossland."

"And what about you? Conquistador and Indio all in one!" His strong hand caressed the silken black hair from her forehead.

"I'm glad the Indios Powhatan didn't kill your tatara tatara tatara..."

He picked up the thread, laughing — "Yes, great great great..."

"...abuelo." She capped it off. "Because you would not be here."

"And if the conquistadores had killed your Indio tatara tatara tatara..."

"Caramba, here we go! Great great great..." Her words devolved into giggles.

"Then only half of you would be here, but which half?"

"I will not answer a stupid question!"

A warm breeze swept through the palms that sheltered her parents' cabana. Small private plots of land on the riverbank, simple huts open to the air, the shallow river a sparkling stream, families came here to get away. A short drive up the dirt road to Villarroel o Quebrada Seca, they were forty minutes into the lush green wilderness, away from the bustle of Cumaná.

"This is something people need." He scanned the canopied hills around them and breathed the mild air laden with the sweet scent of araguaney blossoms. "Humans spent two million years looking at green flora and brown earth and blue sky. You can't just take that away. It's two million years of biological machine learning. People get how artificial intelligence works, but they don't get that we bio-organisms work the same way."

"So why do you do your AI engineering? You should write about people."

"De acuerdo. But the Universidad de Oriente can't get a grant to pay me for that. And I wouldn't have my job in New York, and that job is the whole reason I can bring my research here. But yes. I'd rather be writing about people."

"You told me your papa, your da, wrote a book? And your mama too?"

My da completed his theory but never got published. My mom's book is published. It's probably still available online. Let me check. There, I sent it to your mobile."

She laughed.

"You don't have it on you, do you?"

"No me conoces? I don't like the machines! I ask you about your mama and papa and you only talk about what is on your mobile. And your mama still talks to her sisters, yes?"

"Yes, with my aunts, Kat and Amanda and Natasha. She's different from them in a lot of ways, but there's a bond there, this unbreakable bond. It's the same way with my brother and sister."

"Leo and Olivia. Their names are like nombres Venezolanos, do you think so?"

"Pero nadie tiene nombre tan bello cómo Luisa!" He jumped to his feet, tore off his t-shirt, and leapt onto the leaning trunk of a palm, his muscular six feet and three inches grappling toward the fronds, sun releasing the red flare of his shoulder-length auburn hair.

"You will not get away from me, you know this. I will climb up and get you!" She ran to the foot of the tree, her whole soul peering up at him.

"Beautiful," he whispered and tossed a coconut to the ground. "Will you open it, amor?"

"Claro. But why? You know how."

"I'm a sweat with butter knives. Big blades are your thing!"

"Tonto!" She didn't move, watched the whole while as he descended to Earth. She kissed him with a whispered — "El tonto que tanto amo!" — fetched a machete from the shed and deftly sliced the top, losing only a little of the clear milk. She licked the edge and handed it to him and he drank as he sat on the river's edge.

"Do you know how amazing this is?" he said, watching her as she hung the machete, laughing like she did every time he extolled the wonders of fresh coconut milk. "It's like water cubed, water with extra dimensions!"

"Seguro," she said. "Se multiplica infinitamente. Inside each one is nourishment for another."

The casual poetry of her words, the infinite poetry of her dark eyes. 'Mi dama sabia," he whispered. There was a world within her.

She sat beside him. The sun warmed their bare shoulders. Her eyes swept him silently, her lips parted. He looked to her expectantly, uncertainly, leaned in as she whispered. The corner of his mouth curled, then his eyes grew serious, and he gazed across the lush green hills. It was exactly what he dreamed she might say, but in a way he never could have imagined. Their eyes met for an instant. His face lifted to the infinite cerulean blue above and a smile burst from his lips. His hand clasped hers and the wind blew warm across the Rio Manzanares as massive white clouds sailed above.

Acknowledgments

Coconut is a novel, a work of fiction. But like every novel, it also is the true story of the authors' understanding of the world we live in, an understanding evolved over a lifetime of experience. As co-authors, we almost feel we should thank everyone we ever met or whose life's work, recent or long past, touched us along the way. We have room here to thank, at least, a few.

Our deepest love and gratitude to our parents, Elaine and Bob, and Winnie and Bob, for your love and support — you've made our paths easier. And to our children, Ellie, Jack, and River, for their patience all the endless nights and weekends when we said, "We're working on the book."

Thank you to family far and wide, especially Kristin, Paul, and Trish, Matt and Chris, Bethy, Claire, and Lauren, Aunt Bets, Aunt Sue, Dan and LeAnn, Aunt Eleanor and family, and Uncle Jim and family.

Our labors to create this book are a small expression of our immense gratitude to Mary Majka Boyle for treasures left to find, for your poetry, letters, and reflections embroidered and reimagined here, and for the painting on the cover. Your art and words reflect the beauty you see in people and the world around you.

Mark Katzman, your friendship brings us endless joy. We are indebted to you for your innocent requests that yield astronomic bequests. Serendipity follows in your cosmic wake. And thanks for allowing us to use your real book title *M7* fictitiously here.

A special thanks to Victoria Redel for the writing crystals, for coffees in Provincetown and Manhattan, for inspiring us through your own written word, and for your critical early guidance on our manuscript.

To our publisher Nate Ragolia at Spaceboy Books, deepest thanks for your support of our work, your expert guidance, and your collegiality as a fellow writer and creator.

Heartfelt thanks to Rod Argent for the inspired day when you wrote the 1960s classic, "She's Not There." To all the Zombies for bringing the song to life. To Chris Tuthill and Cindy Da Silva of The Rocks Management and Will Adams at Wise Music for guiding us through the permissions maze, and to

Verulam Music Co. Ltd. and Marquis Songs USA for permission to reprint an excerpt of the lyrics.

A galactic hug and thank you to Rob Brezsny of Free Will Astrology for generous permission to quote your Sagittarius horoscope of April 2006.

We gratefully acknowledge the late Jackson Lambert, writer of the "Jackson's Hole" column in the *Provincetown Banner*, as author of the unpublished poem, "The Empty Barstool," a copy of which he graciously gave to Elizabeth Clay twenty years ago. We made every reasonable effort to identify a living copyright holder but were unable to do so. We welcome outreach from a copyright holder with supporting documentation, if one exists.

Many thanks to our expert printer Tim Kretzmann for meticulous digital reproduction of Mary Majka's painting for the book cover. Stand five feet from any of Tim's reproductions and you will be convinced you are staring at the original painting, brush strokes and all.

Thank you to our beta readers who gave valuable feedback: Beth Oancea, Jen Comstock Zettel, Kim Guedes, Molly O'Reilly, and Denise Smit. And thank you to the Ramsey Hill Association in St. Paul for beta public readings where the positive audience response reassured us that we had started a novel worth finishing.

Our sincere thanks to Stephan Peter, Leanne Schild, Joe McEllistrem, Maureen Murray, Elizabeth Pizzulli, Debbie Wong, Willem Gebben and Hjordis Olsen, and Gary Crawford and Bonnie Janda for your friendship and support.

Thank you to Mike Smith and Gina Rodriguez for insights into the magic of New York's night scene. To Steve Williams, Paul Frazier, Rev. Vince Anderson, Jonah Smith, Brian J, Earl the Pearl, Chauncey Yearwood, Marcus Farrar, Chris Merkley, Greg Caz and Sean Marquand for music after midnight. To Kenneth Moore, James Bellis, Br. George Klawitter, Rev. Patrick Gaffney, Irwin Press, Mary Douglas, Robert Ceely, David Sanford, Alonso Guedes, and Kevin Ristau for intellectual stimulation. Warm thanks to J.R. Harris of the Explorers Club and Lloyd Harris for your friendship and for insights into the world of global trekkers and researchers.

Thank you to the many friends of Elizabeth's birth mother who accepted us so graciously. Elizabeth holds her mother more fully in her heart because of you. A special thanks to Diana Cleaveland for your loving thoughtfulness, your insights through poetry, and for the knocking on the wall. Countless thanks to guardian angels Elizabeth McBride and Marley Greiner for your support and unmatched expertise in adoption search and policy.

For a deeper understanding of the birthmother's perspective in the adoption triad, we relied on the extensively researched and heart-rending book, *The Girls Who Went Away,* by Ann Fessler.

In addition to our visits to Provincetown, we relied on these works to better understand the land across the bay from America: *Cape Cod* by Henry David Thoreau, *Time and the Town: A Provincetown Chronicle* by Mary Heaton Vorse, *Building Provincetown* by David Dunlap, and *Provincetown: Stories from Land's End* by Kathy Shorr.

We browsed Wikipedia, Google Maps, and Merriam Webster Dictionary and Thesaurus almost every time we sat down to write. Two sources were crucial to our understanding of genealogy and DNA relative matching: 23andMe and Ancestry.com. For seasons and climates we used weather.gov, timeanddate.com, and dnr.state.mn.us, as well as the pamphlet "Climate of the Great Plains Region of the United States," by Norman J. Rosenberg.

We found useful information about the Catholic Catechism at stmaryofthesevendolors.com/prayers-2/list-of-mortal-sins-every-catholic-should-know/. Thank you to John's uncle, the late Rev. John Clay, for insights into the spiritual gifts and challenges of the Catholic faith.

Thank you to Darla Gebhard at Brown County Historical Society for valuable insights into historical New Ulm, Minnesota, to Minnesota Lawyers for the Arts and Springboard for the Arts for legal guidance, to John Wareham at the Star Tribune for tracking down copyright information, and to Debra Orenstein for expert guidance.

Finally, we wish to thank our foremothers and forefathers, and Earth, the Cosmos, and the Big Bang, without any of which wonders this book would have been impossible.

JOHN & ELIZABETH CLAY

Book Club Guide

Mark Katzman in Conversation with John and Elizabeth Clay

Mark: *What led you to write this book?*

Elizabeth: Writing a book is something I always thought I might do. After sharing the story of my search for my birth parents, friends would often ask me if I was writing a book. I think that helped me make the leap, to begin writing the story. Another event that changed everything was when I met John and learned he was a writer, and I asked him if he would like to write the book with me. Having another person help with what seemed like an impossible endeavor made it easier to begin.

John: As child I had always wanted to write. And in fact I have spent my adult life writing. Poetry, journaling, correspondence, publishing in online and print media. But the book had to wait for the two of us to join forces. I had never tackled anything of this length before. Elizabeth's determination to write a book, a whole book, inspired me to believe that, yes, this is actually possible.

Mark: *How do two people write a book together?*

Elizabeth: Writing a book with another person can be really rewarding. Putting your ideas together, all of that creativity makes for some amazing stories. Having another person to share ideas with, work through challenges with, and edit with, and edit some more is truly invaluable. Being open to each other's ideas and being able to set your own ideas aside sometimes so that the other person's ideas can blossom is really important to allowing the work to reach its potential. Working with another person year after year and then finally coming out the other side with a completed quality piece of work is a true accomplishment, one that brings you closer together.

John: On one hand, it was easier because we split the workload. While one of us was crafting rough drafts into finished narrative, the other was rough-drafting new material. And when we edited, one of us would catch issues that the other missed, and if one of us was struggling to come up with a fix, usually the other had an idea. On the other hand, it was harder because we had two drivers at the wheel. Sometimes we sorted out differences quickly, other times it was a long and painful negotiation. The fact is, this book is better because we created it together.

Mark: The novel has an impressive scope. How did you decide on the structure of the book?

Elizabeth: I've always had a real gut sense about what this book had to accomplish, both with the overall structure and with the way in which the story would unfold. Once John became co-author, the book became so much more. He's so imaginative and when we put our ideas together, the story would evolve in such interesting ways. As our ideas blossomed, relying on that gut sense helped to keep us on course.

John: At a high level, the book is structured as a family tree. We go from grandparents to parents to child. On a smaller level, we do what every writer does, we assemble scenes that represent a life lived. You can't tell every story of a life, but you can tell the whole life story by assembling the right moments.

Mark: Adoption figures strongly in the stories of Mary and Catherine. Can you talk a little about that?

Elizabeth: Catherine and Mary are both adopted and as they move through life, they each struggle with their identity. They both have this sense of being uprooted, not knowing who or where they came from, and they each deal with it in different ways. Mary creates her identity as she moves through life. Catherine has to go back before she can move forward. The story shows that the path to finding their place in the world can be a winding one.

John: A big part of the novel is the struggle of the characters to live true to themselves. It's a struggle we all face as we venture out into the world hoping to find a career, like-minded friends, lovers. I've learned that knowing where we came from, something most of us know and take for granted, really helps us understand our true selves. It grounds us in ways we're hardly aware of, ways that matter.

Mark: Has writing this book changed you, made you think differently about life?

Elizabeth: Writing this book has realized my life as an artist in a new way. It was, aside from becoming a mother, the longest project I have ever taken on, even longer than the fourteen-year quest to find my birth family. Writing is all-consuming. All other creative endeavors fell to the wayside. I've come to know the art process at a deeper level, that no matter the medium, the process reveals itself along the way, takes on a life of its own, becomes a partner to interact with.

John: Something important about writing this book is that in trying to understand the characters and what motivates them to do what they do, I've had to look deeper into my own life and what motives me. It's like method acting, finding the feeling in myself so that I could then give it to a character. I think it has helped me to understand myself better.

Suggested Topics for Discussion

◆ Coconut highlights the experiences that were formative in the characters' lives. What struck you most about how the characters lives evolved over the course of the story?

◆ What are some of the key moments in your life that have shaped your direction?

◆ What traits of character seemed to persist throughout the lives of the each of the characters? What traits seemed to carry across generations?

◆ What traits do you feel have remained a part of you over the years? Do you see any of these same traits in your parents and ancestors?

◆ What do you know about your family history? Have discoveries about your ancestors changed or deepened your understanding of yourself?

◆ What early memories of your own childhood came to mind as you read the childhood scenes in Coconut?

◆ What are some of the scenes from Coconut where you noticed different characters who crossed paths without even knowing it?

◆ How has adoption affected Catherine? How has adoption affected Paul and Heidi?

◆ How does adoption change Mary and Catherine's lives, making them different from Henry and James' lives?

◆ Are there adopted persons in your family or among your friends? How does Coconut affect the way you think about their experience?

◆ Why is genealogy important to Catherine?

◆ James participates in Catherine's genealogical research. What does it mean to him?

◆ If you could choose a scene in the novel to magically drop into and become part of, which scene would it be?

About the Authors

Photo by River Clay

John and Elizabeth Clay are writers and artists living in Stillwater and Duluth, Minnesota — sometimes with their three mostly-grown children. John spent formative years of his childhood in Africa and South America, and Elizabeth traveled extensively in Europe. They have been writing, editing, and making art together since 2007. They produced a commissioned public artwork titled "Strong as Steel" on display in St. Ingbert, Germany since 2019. John's non-fiction writing has been published online or in print in Minnesota, Georgia, New York, and California USA, and Saarland Germany. He holds a bachelor's degree in anthropology and a master's degree in music composition. Elizabeth was adopted into a loving family in the Twin Cities and, through exhaustive research, has found many of her birth relatives. She holds a bachelor's degree in psychology and a master's degree in horticulture.

About the Publishers

Nate Ragolia is a lifelong lover of science fiction and its power to imagine worlds more hopeful and inclusive than the real one. His first book, *There You Feel Free*, was published by 1888's Black Hill Press in 2015. Spaceboy Books reissued it in 2021. He's also the author of *The Retroactivist* (2017). His most recent book, *One Person Can't Make a Difference* (2022), was featured on Tor.com's Can't Miss Indie Press Speculative Fiction list, and was translated into Italian for Ringworld Sci-Fi in 2023. He founded and edited *BONED*, a literary magazine, and also created two webcomics. Nate is also a husband and a dog dad.

Shaunn Grulkowski has been compared to Warren Ellis and Phillip K. Dick and was once described as what a baby conceived by Kurt Vonnegut and Margaret Atwood would turn out to be. He's at least the fifth best Slavic-Latino-American sci-fi writer in the Baltimore metro area. He's the author *Retcontinuum*, and the editor of *A Stalled Ox* and *The Goldfish* for 1888/Black Hill Press.

www.ingramcontent.com/pod-product-compliance
Lightning Source LLC
Chambersburg PA
CBHW021227190726
48289CB00005B/1209